First Glimpse

When I stepped out of the forest into a small clearing, I heard laughter and a screen door slamming shut. Moments later, two young people came racing out of the house just across the lake. One was a girl, and the other . . .

The breath went out of me as sharply as if someone had punched me in the stomach. The sight of him walking barefoot with his towel wrapped around him stunned me. They both walked out on the dock and stood looking out at the lake. I was terrified he would see me spying.

Suddenly, the girl turned on him and pushed him from behind. He screamed, his towel fell off, and, naked, he fell off the dock and into the water.

He came up, spouting water like a whale, and shook his fist playfully at her. She laughed. Then she dropped her towel and dived, naked, into the lake.

I brought my hands to the base of my throat and nervously watched them swim around each other and then tread water at the dock while they talked softly. He was facing in my direction. I didn't move. Did he see me?

I stepped back, hoping to be covered more heavily in the shadows, but instead, I fell over a thick dead tree limb. I didn't cry out.

But I heard him laugh anyway.

He had seen me.

V.C. ANDREWS®
The Unwelcomed Child

THE UNWELCOMED CHILD

Virginia ANDREWS

**SIMON &
SCHUSTER**

London · New York · Sydney · Toronto · New Delhi

A CBS COMPANY

First published in the US by Pocket Books, 2014
A division of Simon & Schuster, Inc.
First published in Great Britain by Simon & Schuster UK Ltd, 2014
A CBS COMPANY

ble
from the British Library

Hardback ISBN: 978-1-47113-378-7
Paperback ISBN: 978-1-47113-379-4
Ebook ISBN: 978-1-47113-380-0

This book is a work of fiction. Names, characters, places
and incidents are either a product of the author's imagination or
are used fictitiously. Any resemblance to actual people living
or dead, events or locales is entirely coincidental.

Printed and bound by CPI Group (UK) Ltd, Croydon, CR0 4YY

For Bill Andrews,
whose wonderful sense of humor and enthusiasm
for the written word was and remains an inspiration.

Prologue

Religious icons in gold with dark red backgrounds or in silver and pewter hung on almost every wall in my grandparents' modest two-story Queen Anne home just outside the hamlet of Lake Hurley, New York. They were especially prominent in my small bedroom at the rear of the house. Almost every year, my grandmother added another one on my walls, pounding the small nails to hang them on as if she thought she was pounding them into my very soul.

I wouldn't have complained, even if I could. Almost anything dressed up the room, especially anything with any color. It had dull gray-brown walls in desperate need of a new paint job or wallpaper, a saucer-shaped ceiling light fixture with a weak bulb to save on electricity, and a standing lamp on a brass pole with an anemic, yellowing white shade that I had to use for my desk lamp. The floor was charcoal-painted cement with a six-by-eight, well-worn olive-green area rug vacuumed to the point where the floor showed through in some places. The rug had been in the living room when my grandparents first bought the house, now close to thirty-five years ago.

It was easy to see that my room was not meant to be a bedroom. There was no window. The only fresh air came from a vent near the ceiling and the open doorway. The door had been removed fifteen years ago so that my grandmother could look in to see what I was doing anytime she wanted. The room was originally designed to be a storage room. The holes in the walls where the shelves were once attached were still there. The room confirmed the view I had of myself. I always felt as if I had been placed in storage in this house.

However, regardless of what it was and what it had been, the room had to be kept as immaculate as any other. My grandmother was fully convinced that cleanliness was next to godliness and was fond of chanting it at me whenever she ordered me to polish or wash anything. She had that as one of her needle-work sayings framed and hung on the hallway wall just outside my room. When I was much younger and we walked past it together, she would frequently pause in front of it, touch it, and recite it, getting me to repeat it. It was also all right for me to touch the religious icons, as long as when I touched them, I did so with reverence and said a silent prayer for my own troubled soul. If I left even the smallest smudge, I was sent to my room without dinner. From an early age, I realized that the dirt I left was somehow dirtier than any my grandparents left.

As soon as I was able to handle a mop and a rag, mix soap and water properly, and put some muscle behind scrubbing, I was made to clean my own room first thing every morning. I never cleaned it well enough for my grandmother's liking and still don't even now. She had eagle eyes when it came to a spot of dirt or a new stain, and pounced on them with as much glee as a hawk has when it pounces on a baby squirrel. She made me feel I was deliberately missing the spot, as if being dirty was part of my very nature.

I'm sure there were few, if any, six-year-old girls in our community forced to do this kind of housecleaning and to wash and dry their own clothes, too. I also had to iron, and I consequently burned myself a few times because the iron was heavy in my small hands. The first time, I wasn't given anything to ease the pain, no matter how hard I cried.

"Pain," my grandmother told me, "is the guardian of good. It keeps you from violating a commandment, a rule, or a law. Suffering is the only really effective teacher. Cut yourself playing with something you shouldn't, and you won't play with it again. That's why people are in constant agony in hell."

Despite all of this religious fury blowing through our house with tornado intensity at times, my grandparents weren't avid churchgoers. If anything, they saw the clergymen they knew as hypocrites. They actually railed against organized religion, complaining about corruption, both financial and moral, and never contributed to any religious charity run by the church. They believed a well-kept religious home was church enough if the people living within it followed the commandments and were pure at heart, whatever that meant. Sometimes I imagined my grandmother taking her heart out and scrubbing it in the sink with the harsh side of a sponge.

I can't remember the actual moment when my light blue infant eyes were able to focus and my developing nervous system was able to interpret shapes and colors. No one could remember that, but I'm confident that the first face I really saw clearly was the face of the infant Jesus. For my first few years in that back room of the first floor, the room that was hastily set up as my nursery and stayed my room, this framed print of the infant Jesus was all that was on the wall I faced daily. I woke up with it and fell asleep with it. It's still there today among the other biblical prints and plaques.

When I was old enough to do so, I was ordered to recite my prayers to the picture of the baby Jesus before I went to sleep and the moment I awoke. My grandmother designed the prayer so that the first line, which didn't make sense to me since I had little chance to sin while I was sleeping, was "Forgive me, Jesus, for I have sinned."

When I was a little girl, I feared that my grandmother could see the moment my eyes opened and would know if I didn't recite the prayer. The punishment, when she either saw me not pray or believed I didn't, was no breakfast and some added task such as scrubbing the kitchen floor, with the aromas of eggs and bacon swirling around me, making my stomach growl and bringing fresh tears to my eyes.

For almost anyone else, I'm sure these biblical scenes, depictions of saints and prophets, and framed needlework prayers and sayings would provide a sense of security, a holy wall keeping out what Grandmother Myra called the "nasties out there." She had me believing that they came right up to our front door at night and would have come in to devour us if we didn't have the icons and blessings in clear view. Nevertheless, despite all her warnings and assurances that the obedient are protected, from the day I could conceive of escaping, I was beguiled by the thought of living out there, free from any commandments except the ones I declared for myself.

It seemed to me that I was always sitting by a window, looking out like some lost and lonely young woman waiting for her Cinderella prince to come riding up on a magnificent white stallion. He would beckon to me, and I would rush out to take his hand, and he would gently pull me up to sit behind him. I could see us galloping off, leaving all of this behind and forgotten like some terribly unpleasant dream.

That's what my life in this prison-home quickly had become and still was, a nightmare. Just to go outside like any other child and explore the wonders of nature, the wildflowers, the insects, and the different birds, even just to lie on the grass and watch the clouds being sculpted by the wind, was like a short break granted to a convict in his otherwise heavily regimented day in a cold and dismal place. Whenever I was permitted outside, I would take deep breaths of fresh air as if I had to store it in my lungs for weeks until my next release.

If I tried to bring something back in with me,

something as innocent as a dead bee because I was intrigued with its shape and features, I was in for a paddling, with the same paddle my grandfather's father had used on him, and then sent to my room without supper. I learned that the paddle had been retrieved from some box in the attic shortly after I was able to walk.

Everything I did, no matter how small, was watched, studied, and judged. From what I clearly understood, this scrutinizing of my every breath, every move, and every sound began in the cradle, as if something a baby did, the way she looked at them, the way she cried or even burped, could be interpreted as either something good or something that smelled of evil.

Instead of common baby toys such as animals that made sounds, or toys that made music, or toys I could take apart and put together, I was given crucifixes and crosses to touch and study. One had the figure of Jesus with his crown of thorns attached. I would trace the body of Jesus with my tiny fingers, intrigued, and even, when I was older and had more control of my arms and hands, try to take it off the cross, which frightened my grandmother. From what she would tell me later, that was one of the first clear indications that I was polluted the way a lake or a pond could be polluted, and it was her and my grandfather's task to do what they could to cleanse my soul. It was her way of explaining why everything harsh they did to me was necessary.

I was born in this house and in that back-room nursery on a dark, foggy night when the air was full of cold rain not yet ready to become drops. The weather on my birthday was very important to my grandparents. The fact that it was their home that would welcome me into the world terrified them enough as it was, but the ugly weather that night only reinforced their fears. That's what my mother would tell me when I finally met her and we talked. While she was describing my birth and the howling of the wind, I kept thinking of the witches in *Macbeth* saying, "Fair is foul and foul is fair: Hover through the fog and filthy air."

"The fog, the wet darkness, and the cold air that seemed to seep into the house through every crack and cranny confirmed all their darkest thoughts that night, Elle," my mother said. "I'll never forget the look on their faces when you came out looking normal, with two legs and two arms. I think they, at least my mother, expected you to have a tail and horns."

My grandmother more or less had confirmed all that. Maybe she didn't believe I really would have horns and a tail, but in her mind, it was as if I did.

"There was no joy at the sound of your first cry," my grandmother admitted to me when she thought I was old enough to understand and appreciate her efforts to purify me. She described how she and my grandfather crossed themselves and held my hands: "Your grandfather on one side and me on the other, reciting the Lord's Prayer. You squirmed as if hearing those words was painful."

She made me clearly understand how much fear they had in their hearts at the sight of me. But she didn't tell me all this and more in greater detail until nearly twelve years later, when I began to wonder constantly about why I was so restricted and questioned the heavy rules under which I lived. Every time I saw a young girl or boy go by our house or saw images of children in books and on the little television I was permitted to watch, I longed to understand why I wasn't permitted to play with any, much less speak to any.

It was shocking to learn that I was born secretly and not given a name immediately. Sometimes I think that if they could have, they would have kept me anonymous forever, but they couldn't go on denying my existence. Finally, they decided to name me Elle because it could mean God's promise and that there was some hope. Otherwise, I'm sure they thought, why bother? I used to wonder if my grandmother was capable back then of drowning me the way I'd seen her drown baby mice. I was told that before they named me, they simply called me "the child" or referred to me as "it." "It's not eating." "It's not sleeping." "It's crying too much."

Right from the start, I was more like a creature than a human child in their eyes. Of course, I often wondered what my mother and father could have been like for my grandparents to harbor such thoughts. For years after I was old enough to begin to think about my birth, I would ask about my parents and only be more frustrated with the answers.

"Where is my father? Where is my mother? Why don't I ever see them?"

"You will never see your father," my grandmother told me finally. "He dropped his sperm into your mother as casually as someone drops a letter into a mailbox and didn't wait to see it delivered. You might see your mother someday, although I doubt it."

My grandfather nodded after these answers, but he didn't look happy about it, and I didn't know what sperm was yet. It sounded like some sort of letter with our address on it. My grandfather added, "Don't worry. Someday you'll understand it all, and you won't hate us." He didn't make it sound like a threat. He smiled when he said it.

Instinctively, even at a young age, I knew that if I were ever to see any softness, any kindness, it would come from my grandfather. At times, after I had been punished or slapped for something I had said or done, something I had no idea was wrong, he would wince as if it were he who had been punished. On occasion, he would tell my grandmother to ease up. "She's got the point."

She would glare back at him, and he would look away.

Nevertheless, I couldn't stop wondering about the man and the woman who had created me. Why didn't they ever want to see me? Why had they no interest in me? From reading, I knew that fathers more than mothers abandoned their children. There were many biblical lessons my grandmother taught me about such things, but I always wondered how my mother could give birth to me and then just leave and never return. No matter how many times I asked, sometimes being slapped for doing so too often or told to go to my room and read a passage from the Bible, I continued to inquire. Many times, I saw my grandfather on the verge of telling me, but he never did.

What my grandmother was willing to tell me was that no matter what my mother might tell me, she fled from me because she couldn't abide the evil she had seen in her own child.

"She had looked into the face of evil many times, so she knew what it was," my grandmother said.

Whenever she said something like this, I felt the tears come into my eyes. How could I be so evil? What had I done after I was born? What could I have done before I was born? It made no sense, and I think my grandfather especially realized that I knew it didn't make sense for them to continue telling me this.

Finally, one night, when she thought I was old enough to understand the truth, she sat me down in the kitchen and told me everything, laying it all out like one of her biblical stories that had a bad ending to illustrate some sin.

She ended with "And it came to pass that you were born without the grace of God."

That made it sound as if I was born without a soul, and when I asked her if that was true, she said, "We'll see. We'll see what you become."

What a horrible childhood I had endured, and what a hard life I still had. To this day, I would like to blame my mother for everything, especially leaving me to live with them, but under the circumstances that were finally revealed to me, that was impossible. I never believed she fled from me because she saw evil in me. She never looked at me long enough. She never wanted to, but how could I blame her? If anything, the truth left me feeling just as sorry for her, if not sorrier.

How do you blame a young woman for being raped and forced to have the child who was created, a child no one wanted, and who my grandparents feared would bring the wrath of God down on their heads?

1

Until now, I never had a birthday celebration, and the presents I received on Christmas would not even bring a smile to the face of any other child. They were always only something I needed, such as new pairs of socks or underthings, a toothbrush, a hairbrush, even a few bars of soap, pure soap, never soap with any delicious scent.

Sometimes they gave me biblical storybooks, but I wasn't permitted to read much else until I was deemed old enough by Grandmother Myra to begin my homeschooling. The requirements for that forced her to give me reading she would have otherwise forbidden, such as most of the novels and plays being read in public school, especially when I reached junior and then senior high school age. However, if she didn't want the state education department on her back to have me brought to a public school, she had to obey and follow the prescribed curriculum. Of course, she did it begrudgingly, complaining about how loose the standards had become in public schools.

She had been a grade-school teacher in a parochial

school for five years, but she was never very fond of formal classroom teaching, always criticizing the way parents were bringing up their children. I read between the lines whenever she talked about her short teaching career and imagined that she was unpopular not only with her students but also with their parents, because she wasn't shy about giving them a piece of her mind. Perhaps she didn't quit teaching. Maybe she was not so gently nudged to leave. After that, she went to work for an accounting firm, where she met my grandfather, who was one of their clients.

Because my grandmother homeschooled me, I never had a close friend or any real friends, or even acquaintances. I was never invited to someone else's birthday party or to any party, for that matter. All I knew about the wonderful things other girls my age had and enjoyed is what I learned from reading books and plays and, when permitted, watching what my grandparents called decent television, usually never for more than two hours at a time.

I had no television or radio in my room. I'd never been to a movie. Even if I had some music CD, I had nothing on which to play it, and I was never given a computer or any of the modern-day devices I saw advertised, such as an iPod. They had none of this technology, either. My grandmother said that the Internet was Satan's new playground. The little music I knew came in bits and pieces from the short television viewing I was permitted or when I was outside and heard a car go by with the windows open and music spilling out. I would cling to the sounds the way someone dying of thirst might follow the final drops of a glass of water.

Of course, Grandmother Myra and Grandfather Prescott had their hymns and made me sing along with them on Sundays, but they didn't listen to or play anything else themselves. My grandmother claimed her favorite song was "Amazing Grace." I often wondered if there had ever been anything remotely romantic about them. They never spoke of a honeymoon, and when their anniversary arrived, they usually had a very simple dinner and talked about how different things were now from the day they were married, how much more things cost, and how the village had changed but not for the better.

If I believed what they said, or at least what my grandmother said, most of the time, nothing had gotten better with time. Progress seemed to undermine the important and especially the moral things in our lives. One of her favorite expressions was "I wish I could turn back time." Sometimes I thought she prayed for it. Her refrain at the end of grace was always "and spare us from the new horrors outside our door."

The way she said that made me think that monsters were camped on our front lawn, especially when I was younger. I was so frightened that I repeated her refrain almost as loudly as she did. I accepted the power and the hope that prayer provided. What else did I have?

There we were on Sundays, the three of us, holding our Bibles in the living room in front of a large crucifix, singing. Grandfather Prescott would read a passage, and we would then do a silent prayer. We would have something special to eat for lunch that day and maybe a homemade pie with an infinitesimal amount of sugar. It was the only highlight of the week.

How dreary their lives were, I thought when I was old enough to understand it all and could look back with clearer eyes. I even found myself pitying them, as much as or more than I pitied myself. In many ways, they were just as caged up as I was, except that they had crawled in of their own volition and then willingly locked the door behind themselves.

Before my grandfather had retired, he at least had his successful mattress-manufacturing business in Lake Hurley. That gave him more contact with the world, with other people, and therefore, I thought, more pleasure. Any real socializing they had done came out of his business connections and associates. From what he told me, at the high point of his enterprise, he was employing fifty people, including salesmen who sold his product in three different upstate counties.

Despite how well he did, he and my grandmother never lived more than modest lives. They still drove the same car they had bought ten years ago. They never went on any vacation, nor did they buy anything anyone would call luxurious for their home. My grandmother didn't buy new clothing for herself until something had been washed so much it was close to falling apart in her hands. Whenever my grandfather mentioned that he might buy a new pair of shoes or some clothing, she told him he didn't need it or simply asked, "What for?" Usually, that was enough to stomp his urge to death the way she would stomp on an ant that had begun a foray in our kitchen.

After they were married, my grandmother had worked for the mattress company, overseeing all the finances. She had left teaching but was so good at math she had been hired as an assistant to the accountant my grandfather had been using. During one of the infrequent times he talked to me about their courting and marriage, he told me that the first time he met my grandmother, she made some very sensible financial suggestions to him.

"I knew I had a blessing in disguise when I met her," he told me.

I wasn't too young to think that he must have been blind. Was that really a reason to marry someone, her skill at seeing a wasteful expenditure? However, when I did get the opportunity to look at some old photographs, I was surprised to see how naturally pretty Grandmother Myra was. She was much thinner now, and her facial features were sharper, her skin spotted with age and her hair a dull gray with just a touch of her once dark brown shade in places. She kept it so tightly knotted behind her head it pulled her forehead and thin cheeks as firmly as a drum skin. She was about my grandfather's height, with surprising strength in her long, thin arms.

My grandfather still had a very handsome face, with a strong, straight mouth, bright blue eyes, and a full head of still thick light brown hair. Grandmother Myra was always after him to go to the barber, but he avoided it for as long as he could, until she would threaten to cut it herself while he was sleeping. I had no doubt she would, and neither did he. She always cut my auburn hair to the length she thought proper. It was years before I even knew what a beauty parlor was, and only then because she ranted on and on about how wasteful an expenditure that was, especially "women having their toenails cut and painted."

When I was twelve, my grandparents began to take me on occasional shopping trips. Many times, they made me stay in the car while they went into stores, and when they did bring me into a store to buy some clothes I needed, my grandmother hovered over me, forcing me to concentrate only on what I had to buy and not look around, never attract any boy's attention, especially, and never, ever speak to anyone except the saleslady, and that was just to say, "Thank you."

"You never talk to strangers," she warned, and since I knew practically no one, everyone was a stranger. How would I ever have a conversation with anyone?

When we drove, my grandmother would periodically look back at me and say, "Don't gape out the window. You look like a fool."

Of course, that was exactly how I felt, like a fool. There were things out there that were so obvious to other girls and boys my age, but to me, they were like things discovered in outer space. I was fascinated by signs and posters, especially those advertising concerts and films, the style of the clothing girls my age were wearing, the jewelry I saw on them, and, of course, the makeup. I had yet to hold a tube of lipstick in my hand, much less use one. Grandmother Myra never used any makeup, so I couldn't even try something she had.

When we walked through a mall and I was drawn to the covers of magazines to look at the beautiful women and girls, my grandmother would seize my head and force me to look straight, nearly tearing my neck. I moaned in pain.

"Don't look at trash," she would say. "It will spoil your eyes, missy."

I didn't have to ask if she was serious. There was never any question that evil was seen as a disease, something I could catch like a cold. My grandparents believed that because of what had happened to my mother and because I was the unwelcome result of it, I had a poorer immune system when it came to evil. I would catch it faster, and it would be far more serious for me. They also believed that was true for actual diseases and illnesses. Even though seemingly good people had terrible health problems, my grandmother believed there was something in their past or their parents' past that caused it. It was one of her favorite biblical quotes: "You shall not bow down to them or serve them; for I the Lord your God am a jealous God, visiting the iniquity of the fathers on the children."

Even though I was very healthy and didn't have to see a doctor much at all, the possibility of something horrendous happening to me always loomed out there. She had me expecting to be struck down by some debilitating disease. However, when they took me to a dentist twice a year, he would always remark about how perfect my teeth were.

"She doesn't eat horrible sweets or chew gum," my grandmother would tell him.

That wasn't a lie. Except for the pie on Sunday, the sweetest thing I was permitted was a tablespoon of honey in a cup of tea. I had no cookies, soda, candy, or cake and had never tasted ice cream. My grandmother told me that the longer she kept me from indulging in the lust for overly sweet foods, the better chance I had to be pure of blood.

When I was younger, I never understood what all the talk about my blood meant, but my grandparents made it sound as if there was something rotten or spoiled in my blood, and the whole purpose of how they were bringing me up was to purify it and destroy the strains of evil that flowed through my veins. In fact, whenever I cut myself, I studied the blood that came out, looking for something dark or ugly. When I asked her why it wasn't there, she told me to stop being stupid.

Gradually, I realized that in their minds, evil was something inherited, or, at least, the tendency to commit it was. This wasn't so different from what I understood to be original sin. Everyone, they told me, even they, had that stain on his or her soul, but I had more of it, and deeper, so I didn't have just what everyone else had. I had something extra. It did no good in my earlier years to ask what it was or why. I was told that it was there, and that was that.

It was my grandparents' burden in life to work at driving it out of me. If I listened and was obedient, it could happen, and then I would be able to be free. That goal they had set for me kept me at least a little hopeful.

From the comments they dropped here and there like grass seed, I gathered that my mother was far from the perfect child in their eyes and that the man who had raped her was obviously pure evil, if not the devil himself. But if she were a better person, he wouldn't have been so drawn to her. This was why I had inherited a tendency toward evil itself. Not only was I fathered by a rapist, but I also had a mother who was more evil than most girls her age. As long as I was with them, I had no choice but to accept their view of me. I could look at myself in a mirror for hours and not see any good in my eyes, which had tiny black dots swimming in the blue, according to Grandmother Myra, another sign of something dark inside me. I tried to look at myself as much as I could to see if there was something inside me I could see. I couldn't, of course, and looking at yourself in mirrors for longer than a few seconds to check something on your face was forbidden anyway. It led to narcissism, she said, which was the main fault of Lucifer in heaven.

I had no mirror in my room, and when I asked for one, she said, "It's enough to look at yourself in the bathroom to see if you're clean. Why else would you look at yourself?"

Did I ever dare say or even think, to see if I was pretty?

Seeing what was available out there when I went on the shopping excursions inevitably made me ask for more and complain about how little I had. My grandmother's reaction was to shake her head and tell my grandfather, "We have given her a taste of the apple. It can lead to no good."

What apple? Where was the snake urging me to defy God? Was it living inside me? Why was wanting nicer clothes and pretty things going to lead me to no good? It was all so confusing, so frustrating. If I complained too much, the periods between shopping trips would grow longer. I had to learn to keep my thoughts all bundled up inside and never look at anything with any special desire or admiration. In many ways, I was my own jailer, slapping down my hands if they reached out for something new, shutting curtains if I looked at something exciting.

Sometimes I would study a fly caught in a spider's web. I watched how desperately and futilely it struggled. I imagined the spider was sitting off to the side somewhere, enjoying the sight. Usually, I would destroy the web and set the fly free, because I was like that fly.

Someday, I thought, *someone will tear apart the web I'm in, and I will be just like everyone else.* That thought gave me hope, but it was easy for a young girl like me to lose her optimism. There were many times when I thought about running away, of course. I dreamed of finding my mother and hearing her say, "Oh, I'm so sorry I was selfish and left you with them. Forgive me. Now we'll be a real mother-daughter team, our own family, and I'll buy you nice things and get you into a school where you can meet other girls and go to dances and have a boyfriend and not feel guilty about it.

"I'll show you how to wear makeup, get you a decent hairstyle, and buy you fashionable clothes. I'll drive the horrid memories you have of your terrible childhood out of your mind so that it will be impossible for you to recall anything. It will be as if I was able to get into your head and wash your brain."

And then she would hug me, and we would go to a fun place to eat and laugh, and she would tell me things I longed to know, not just about her but also about the world out there, things like how to find a boyfriend and what to do when he began to hold and kiss you and touch you in places you were afraid to touch yourself. At least, I was afraid, thanks to my grandmother's warnings, which would all have something to do with how I came into this world.

My mother wouldn't tell me about the rape right away. I would understand how painful it was for her to remember it, and I would think that wasn't so important now anyway. Eventually, though, I would, as I did often now, wonder about my biological father. Did he just come out of the night, a dark shadow raging with lust, and overwhelm her? Did she get to see his face or hear his voice? When she looked at me now, did she see him in me? Were my grandparents right after all? Was there something sinful embedded in me?

Did I have to be extra careful? Would she tell me the truth?

But in my dream scenario, even that would be pleasant. "No, no," she would say. "There is nothing significant of him in you. You're all me. Don't give it a second thought. I tell you what," she would add, laughing, "think of yourself as an immaculate conception. That's what my parents should have thought. If they trusted in their God so much, why didn't they trust in you, in the wonder of you?"

How wonderful she would make me feel. I could go to sleep, snuggled up comfortably with her nearby. I would hear music, see movies, read magazines, and eat sweets and fun foods like pizza. The invisible chains that I had felt wrapped around me would be gone. It would be as if the whole world had opened up to me. I had gone through a door, fallen through a magic hole, like Alice, and entered the wonderland I envisioned in my lonely, dark moments shut away by not only doors and windows and walls but also my grandmother's angry glare. It was like looking directly at the sun. I had to turn away and seek the cool darkness.

But all of that was over now that I was older and stronger.

They could take away my freedom for now, I thought, but they couldn't take away my dreams.

Could they?

They seemed to be able to take away so much, even from themselves. This fantasy I had about my mother was nothing more than just that and never would be, I thought. What I realized from reading between the lines of what they told me about my birth and my mother's horrible victimization was that she didn't want to give birth to me. If she didn't want me then, why would she want to see me now?

When she realized the rapist had impregnated her, she had come to her parents, expecting that they would arrange for an abortion, but they wouldn't hear of it. I gathered that once my mother passed a certain point in her pregnancy, she was unable to end it, especially since she was practically kept the way I'd been, a virtual prisoner in her own home.

"It was too late already when she came home," my grandmother told me. "It was just like her to ignore something wrong."

So I understood that they had forced her to go through with it. Later, my mother would tell me she assumed they were going to give me away, get me out of everyone's life, but they felt they had to do something else, too: they had to atone for the evil that my mother had invited into her life.

I learned bits and pieces of the story as I grew older and asked more questions. I hoped I would learn it all someday, but for now, that was all they would tell me.

It was only recently, in fact, that they even permitted me to see a picture of my mother. Right after I was born and my mother literally fled her home, they hid any pictures they had displayed of her. It took me years to learn that my mother's name was Deborah Ann Edwards. My grandmother was always angry at her, it seemed, especially when my mother began to permit people to call her Debbie instead of Deborah. If someone called and asked for Debbie, she would say there was no one there by that name and hang up. I would later learn from my mother that when she had a friend over and my grandmother overheard the friend call her Debbie, she would ask the friend to leave. She even bawled out one of her teachers who casually referred to her as Debbie.

Grandmother Myra had given birth to my mother late in her marriage to Grandfather Prescott. She was thirty-eight years old. Again trying to read between the lines, I understood that they had tried earlier, but she couldn't get pregnant and certainly wasn't going to take any medication or do any procedure that might heighten her chances for pregnancy. From the way Grandfather Prescott described it once when my grandmother wasn't nearby to hear him, it came as a total surprise to them when she had begun to develop the signs of pregnancy. Back then, before my mother had disappointed them, they believed an angel had come into the house and touched Grandmother Myra in her sleep.

They told me my mother was a beautiful, perfect-looking infant, so much so that the nurses in the maternity ward called her a cherub.

"I should have known she would turn out to be anything but," my grandmother said bitterly. "Right from the start, she cried too much, demanded too much, almost sucked my breasts dry."

The image of that widened my eyes. Rarely, if ever,

did my grandmother refer to her own body as anything but a vessel for her soul. But the feminine journey all girls travel made it impossible for her to keep me innocent and asexual. She didn't have to prepare me for my menarche because one of the science books I had to read included some basic human reproduction facts.

The day it happened, she made me stand in a hot shower, almost too hot to bear, and recite a prayer asking my guardian angel to keep me from succumbing to the temptations of the flesh. I babbled the words as quickly as I could, not understanding all of them. When it was over, she told me never to mention my monthlies to any man, even my grandfather. She told me to care for myself in silence and never complain about any cramps to anyone but her. Then she went into a long explanation of why women were punished with this biological event, tracing the blame back to Eve in the Garden of Eden.

Whenever she spoke of these things, she was the most animated. It was as if everything to do with sex was an affront to our spiritual well-being, at minimum a test God threw down upon us to help him choose those of us who deserved to be in heaven and those who deserved to be embraced by Satan and suffer in hell. Years later, when I told my mother about all this, she shook her head and told me she used to imagine my grandparents making love.

"Dad had to poke it through a hole in a sheet she had wrapped around her."

"Really?" I asked.

"I don't know. Maybe," she said, and then we both laughed.

How did they get to be that way? I wondered. Like me, my grandmother was an only child. Of course, I wondered why she was so reluctant to talk about her parents, her father especially. Finally, I learned that he was a serious alcoholic who died one night in an alleyway. Her mother and she had a very hard life because of that. She blamed her mother's early death on her father, claiming her tiny, fragile heart couldn't take the burden any longer.

Like her parents, Grandfather Prescott's parents were long gone. Never once did either of them take me to visit their parents' grave sites, but I did believe Grandfather Prescott visited his parents' graves on his own from time to time. They were in a cemetery close by.

Grandfather Prescott had a younger brother, Brett Edwards, a talented musician. He began playing the trumpet in junior high school and went on to win prizes. His parents wanted him to go to a business school, just as Grandfather Prescott had done, but he rebelled and ran away from home to join a band playing on cruise ships, the first being a remodeled steamship that went up and down the Mississippi from New Orleans. Grandmother Myra wasn't fond of my grandfather talking about his younger brother. As far as they knew, he was still unmarried, although she said on more than one occasion that she wouldn't guarantee that he wasn't a father.

"Men like him spread their seed all over, indifferent to what misery they cause some poor young woman. You mark my words, missy."

"We don't know anything like that to be true," Grandfather Prescott said. It was practically the only topic on which he held his ground. She usually retreated but not without a condemning grunt.

Nevertheless, I had the feeling my grandfather harbored love for his younger brother and a little envy, too. Maybe deep down inside, he longed for the freedom my great-uncle Brett enjoyed, especially now. When I looked at pictures of Brett, I saw a very handsome, much happier-looking man. I had never met him. My grandmother didn't welcome him to their home anymore. I understood that he had been there last a year or so before I was born and never since. For me, he was almost a fictional character. Years later, my mother would describe the terrible crush she had on her uncle when she was younger and how much she looked forward to seeing him whenever he was able to visit.

Grandmother Myra disapproved of her liking him so much.

"He's a philanderer," she told my mother. "A womanizer, selfish, venal, and, like all those musicians, into drugs, I'm sure."

My mother said they had terrible arguments about him. "It was one of the few times I can remember that my father came to my aid, but no matter, she was never hospitable to Uncle Brett. I'm sure that was why he saw us so infrequently. I know that was why he gave up visiting, even calling them."

She said she had always kept up a correspondence with him, and later, he came to her aid. He often sent her postcards from places where he played, and occasionally, he sent her some small gift, a doll, a trinket, inexpensive jewelry, even a watch. My grandmother told me she had thrown out whatever my mother had left in the house when she ran off, so I never saw any of it.

Sometimes I felt I was putting together my background, whatever family I would claim, like someone doing a big puzzle, finding a piece here and there. It was far from complete. There were deep gaps, but I had confidence that someday I would fill them. The real issue was, would I be happy I had?

With all this heaviness on my shoulders, I carried out the daily chores I was assigned, completed my homeschool reading and math, and sat gazing out windows, focusing on far horizons. I was like some Old World explorer just waiting for permission and financing to set out on his journey, his eyes focused on the future.

The possibility of his discoveries kept his heart beating, his body strong.

Maybe I would find nothing special, but I could never be disappointed, because the journey was what I craved. One day, I would simply open the door and take my first step forward. All the steps to follow were already out there, waiting for me to fill them.

In the end, I would plant my flag in the soil of my own identity, wouldn't I?

I would look into those forbidden mirrors, and I would see who I was.

"Hi," my reflected image would say. "I've been waiting for you for a long time."

2

My grandmother wasn't going to celebrate my fifteenth birthday at all differently from any of my previous birthdays. There were never any presents and never any cake and candles. For years, I didn't even know when my birthday was. Eventually, the day, June 25, was acknowledged reluctantly, almost as a passing thought. Until then, my grandmother simply announced that I was eight or nine, whatever, dropping the fact in the middle of some sentence such as, "You should know better for a six-year-old."

I never had any doubts that she viewed it as a day of infamy as bad as December 7 or September 11. My birthing was like a bomb dropped on their otherwise happy home, not that I could imagine it ever being a house of much happiness. All I knew during those years was that my mother regretted my birth and deserted both me and my grandparents, and they never really wanted me and the responsibility for me. I supposed I should be grateful that eventually they began to see me differently, differently enough by the time I reached my fifteenth birthday that my grandfather that morning after breakfast talked her into celebrating it.

"She's been a very good girl, Myra. It's good to make people aware of what awaits them when and if they favor Satan and sin, but there is also a time to reward," he said. "She is doing well with her schoolwork, she keeps her room as clean as she can, and she says her prayers regularly. All of this also means you've done a very good job with her. You can take a deep breath and rejoice."

My grandmother thought a moment and nodded. "We can take her to dinner," she said.

My eyes popped open. *Take me to dinner?* I knew my grandparents were frugal people. Having money never meant spending it. People who were not cautious and conservative when it came to that were usually "ripe fruit for the devil's picking," Grandmother Myra told me. One of the items topping her list of wasteful spending was going out to eat and paying five times the cost for the same food made at home. "And that doesn't include the tip!"

"Well, the Marxes are always talking about the good value at Chipper's," my grandfather said.

Sam Marx and his wife, Trudy, were my grandparents' closest friends, in that they were practically the only couple ever invited to dinner at our house and the only couple I knew who invited them. Sam had been my grandfather's factory manager. They had no children. Trudy dressed a little nicer than my grandmother, but as far as makeup went, she used nothing more than some lipstick. Whenever they came to our house, she looked as if she had barely brushed her lips with it. I had the sense that the Marxes were still treating my grandparents with the same deference and respect shown by employees. I never heard them disagree about anything.

When they were here for dinner and I was helping out, serving and cleaning up like some hired maid, I could feel Trudy's gaze on me. It was creepy; I sensed she was looking for some evidence to indicate that I would do something or be someone evil. I had no idea what my grandmother had told her about me over the years, but sometimes, when I glanced at her while she stared at me, I felt she was looking at me with delight. I felt confident that if I were her granddaughter, I'd be treated far better.

"Well, then, choose something clean to wear. Pin up your hair better, and make sure your nails are clean, missy," Grandmother Myra told me.

I nodded, trying not to look too excited about it. I sensed a long time ago that if I showed too much enthusiasm for something, she would become suspicious and then forbid it following another one of her credos, "Better safe than sorry."

I said nothing. I also knew that if I spent too much time thinking about what I would wear and too much time on my hair, she would reconsider. I went through the day as if it were no different from any other, completing my homework, reading what I had to read, washing clothes, polishing furniture, and, since it was Wednesday and the schedule she had set up required it, washing the kitchen floor.

Because I had something to look forward to, I wasn't as tired in the late afternoon as I usually was. I had picked out my newest dress. It did nothing for my figure, but I chose it because it was at least a brighter color than anything else I had, a sharp light blue. I had nothing like matching shoes and no jewelry, not even a wristwatch. She had permitted me to have some colorful ribbons to use to tie up my hair.

Whenever she relented and bought me something new to wear, she always seemed deliberately to choose a size too big. Any curves that had developed in my body were well hidden. I hated my shoes. They were so dull now, a worn black. She insisted on my having flats: "You're springing up too fast. People are quick to mistake height for age, and I don't need anyone who sees you thinking you're older than you are, especially men."

The very thought of a grown man being interested in me was so foreign to my thinking that it became intriguing after she had told me that. Whenever my mind drifted to thoughts about boys, and now men, it was always to draw them up as rescuers, handsome, strong men who could swoop in and take me away. Of course, Grandmother Myra equated physical beauty with some form of danger. Either the woman who possessed it would become too conceited and therefore vulnerable to sin, or she was in danger of attracting the wrong set of eyes.

I suppose it would be impossible for someone like me living in this house not to grow up with these fears embedded so deeply in her that she believed in them herself. I was very self-conscious about how long I looked at myself in the bathroom mirror. Whenever they took me anywhere, I did keep my eyes down and avoided looking at boys especially. Every sexual thought I had I immediately subdued. My grandmother had convinced me that I was more vulnerable than other girls. I was on constant guard, waiting for that evil seed inside me to start sprouting.

She inspected my hands immediately when I came into the living room. I had taken great care with my nails. It satisfied her. She looked at me in my oversize dress, fixed a strand of my hair that had escaped the knot, and then nodded approval.

"You look very nice," Grandfather Prescott told me. He looked at Grandmother Myra.

She reached for a box on the sofa side table beside her and handed it to me. She said nothing.

Grandfather Prescott said, "Happy birthday, Elle."

I was shocked. What could be in a box like that? Slowly, I opened it and saw the silver cross. It was a good six inches long and four inches wide, at least, and it was on a silver chain. How could I wear something so big around my neck? I plucked it out carefully, stunned.

"I'll put it on you," Grandmother Myra said. She took it from me and went behind me. I stood there while she fastened the chain. The cross fell over the crests of my breasts.

"Isn't it . . . too big?" I asked, trying not to sound ungrateful.

"It's so you'll never forget," she said. "You can put it inside your dress."

I did so quickly.

"Thank you," I said.

"Take your sweater," she told me. "There's a chill in the air tonight."

It was late June, but nights could be cool in Lake Hurley. It was why people from New York City bought and rented summer homes there. We didn't live on the lake, but we were only about a half mile from it if we went through the woods right behind the house. I had done that only once with my grandfather, who wanted me to see it at twilight. We didn't see much of it. It was as if we were gazing at something forbidden. He wasn't a fisherman and never suggested we go for a boat ride. The only way my grandmother acknowledged the lake's existence was to comment about a breeze that came off it. Many times, I was tempted to go there on my own when I was outside at the rear of the house, which was where my grandmother preferred me to be. But I was afraid of walking off our property without specific permission to do so. It was as if we had an invisible electric fence, and if I crossed the line, I would suffer a stinging shock.

"You stay in the backyard, missy. No need to be attracting the curious eyes of those city people who come up here and drive past our house," she told me. "A young girl just standing around or even sitting and reading will bring unwanted attention."

Maybe it was unwanted to her, I thought, but not to me. I craved any attention.

Nevertheless, I avoided the front of the house, afraid that she would further restrict my going out alone. Our house was on a good-size lot, but what made it private was the fact that the land to our right was in some family dispute for as long as I could remember, so no one could build on it, and the land to our left was owned by someone who was waiting forever, it seemed, for its value to go up. The nearest house to ours was a good half mile away on both sides. The sense of isolation was just fine for my grandmother, who wasn't the type who would walk over to a neighbor's house to borrow a cup of sugar anyway.

I loved this time of the year, because the trees were so full and, maybe because of the moisture coming off the lake, so richly green. No matter how bright the day, the inside of the woods looked dark and cool. From time to time, I would spot a buck or a doe and its fawn. Of course, there were too many rabbits and not enough foxes to control their population. No matter how hard my grandfather tried to protect whatever vegetable garden he had created, the rabbits had the best of it. All sorts of birds brought the woods to life with melodies. I could distinguish a robin from a blue jay just by the sounds they made. I knew there were wild ducks on the lake in the summer. I could see them fly in, but except for the one time my grandfather took me there, I never saw them floating on the water.

My grandfather kept a nice patch of grass in the rear of the house. Occasionally, he would permit me to cut the lawn, but only in the rear. Sometimes, when I sat in the backyard and thought about all this, I imagined I was truly some sort of nature child, so alien to

the world around me that I'd be considered as wild as
an aborigine or some girl in a lost African tribe. If my
grandmother stepped out to see what I was up to, she
almost always warned me about thinking too much.

"Idle hands are the devil's workshop," she would
say. "Find something useful to do instead of just sitting there thinking."

Why did that frighten her? I wondered. Should it
frighten me?

I imagined that despite my good deeds and my
obedience, my grandmother never stopped believing
that somehow, for some reason, I would let the devil
into their lives. It was as if he was just biding his time.
He knew where I lived. After all, he didn't create evil
progeny and just let them drift away, did he? When
the time was right, he would call on me. It got so I
began to watch for him myself. Maybe he would just
come walking out of the dark forest one day, smiling,
his arms out.

"You're ready," he would say, and the actions and
thoughts my grandmother always expected would
begin.

My grandfather slapped his hands together, shaking me out of my reverie. "Well, then," he said. "Let's
set out. I'm getting hungry."

I put on my sweater, and the three of us walked
out to their car in the driveway. The cross was cold
and heavy on my chest, but I said nothing. *I'll get used
to it,* I thought. I kept my head down and tried desperately not to look too excited, but this was going to be
my first time in a restaurant.

I got into the rear of the car and sat back with my hands folded on my lap. Grandmother Myra looked at me, and for a moment, I saw her face soften in a way I hadn't seen.

"She's getting to look more like Deborah," she said.

My grandfather turned to look back, as if he hadn't ever looked at me. "Yep," he said.

"Thank God for that," Grandmother Myra said.

I had to agree but not for the same reason she was thinking. I thought my mother was a very pretty woman in the pictures I had been permitted to see.

Because of the relaxed atmosphere, I thought I might risk asking a question or two about my mother.

"What college did my mother attend?"

"She went to the state university at Albany," my grandfather said before my grandmother could object to our talking about her. He started to back out, turning around to see, and added, "She could have gone to a few colleges. She had decent school grades, thanks to your grandmother making sure she did her work properly."

Grandmother Myra grunted. "That wasn't an easy task. If I didn't ride herd on that girl . . . besides, her grades weren't that good, Prescott. She was barely above average."

"She couldn't finish college, then?" I asked.

She spun on me this time. "Of course not! How could she even contemplate such a thing? All that was ruined. All the college tuition lost. Why do you think you're here?"

"I just wondered," I said.

"She might have gone back to school," my grand-father offered.

"Believe that, and I'll offer you a bridge in Brook-lyn for sale," Grandmother Myra muttered. "Where would she have gotten the money?"

Even then, without yet meeting her, I thought perhaps she got it from Uncle Brett, the mysterious, handsome, and adventurous Uncle Brett. My grand-father might have suspected that possibility, too, but wouldn't dare suggest it.

I wondered if I should push on with another ques-tion, but I was terrified that she would get enraged at my continued curiosity and make my grandfather turn back. Instead, I looked out the window and remained silent. Less than twenty minutes later, we pulled into the parking lot of Chipper's restaurant. I knew what an old-time diner was and thought that was what it looked like. It was certainly not what anyone would call an elegant or expensive restaurant. There were two large windows in the front, and the building was rectangular. It had a dark brown front and a flat roof. It was well lit inside. I thought it was too bright, but when we entered, I was surprised at how crowded it was. Almost every table and booth was taken.

"Mr. Edwards," my grandfather said to the hostess.

I could tell from the way my grandmother was smirking at her that she didn't approve of her short skirt and tight bodice, with just a little too much of her bosom revealed in the V-neck collar. Grandmother Myra looked at me and nodded as if to say, "See what happens when young girls are given too much free-dom, missy?"

The hostess led us to one of the booths. I sat across from my grandparents and could view most of the restaurant. I couldn't help but be fascinated with all of it, the activity of the waiters and waitresses, the vibrant conversations being held at the various tables, some of which seemed to be occupied by families. I saw a few young couples, one of whom appeared involved in a very serious, intimate discussion. For me, it was a bigger visual feast than the food I would enjoy.

The waiter brought us our menus and took orders for our drinks. My grandmother ordered mine, a lem-onade, before I could even look at the choices, which included sodas I had never tasted.

"These prices aren't that reasonable," my grand-mother told my grandfather.

"Compared with what is being charged in other places, they are."

"What do you know about it?"

"I remember going out to eat, Myra, and Sam tells me about places he and Trudy go."

"They were always careless with a dollar," she replied. "Just lucky you were paying him that good salary."

"He was worth it."

She grunted and looked at me. "You should have the chicken dish," she said. "You're not used to eating rich meats or these Italian foods. We'll get you a salad, of course. Twelve dollars for mixed greens and toma-toes," she added, shaking her head.

The waiter returned with our drinks and took our orders. My grandfather looked as if he wanted the steak, mumbling about it, but he chose the chicken dish instead. My grandmother did the same.

"I never enjoyed eating with all this noise around me," my grandmother told me. "Even when I was as young as you. It's not good for digestion. People eat too quickly in restaurants, because the waiters are told to rush them along so they can get someone else to sit at the table and the restaurant can make more money."

"Really?"

"Of course, really. Would I tell you something that was untrue?"

"Why do people put up with it?" I asked, looking at the other customers, none of whom seemed particularly unhappy being there.

"They're too stupid to realize it, that's why," she replied. She began to examine the silverware.

"I'm sure everything is clean, Myra," my grandfather said. "They have an A in the window for their inspection."

She pursed her lips and looked at the fake flowers in the vase disdainfully.

My attention was drawn to a couple coming in with two children, the older one a boy who was probably eighteen or nineteen. He had wavy, long light brown hair and reminded me of an illustration in one of the biblical storybooks my grandmother had given me. He looked like a young Judah Maccabee pictured in my book. Although I was intrigued with him, I was also very interested in his sister, who looked about the same age. She had the same light brown hair and features so similar that I wondered if they could be twins.

Although I was drawn to watch every move they made, I was very aware of the way my grandmother was studying me, probably trying to determine if what I saw and heard was influencing me badly. That was always her concern whenever I went anywhere with her and my grandfather. What effect would it have on me? It was as if she believed I could look at something for only a few moments or overhear some conversation and immediately turn into some evil creature.

So I shifted my gaze back to the fake flowers and then sipped my lemonade. My grandfather started to talk about some of the nicer restaurants he had gone to when he was a young man in business college. He described foods I'd never heard of, much less tasted. We never had lobster or clams or oysters. Grandmother Myra was always very careful about her food budget. I think the truth was that she didn't know how to prepare seafood.

The waiter brought us our salads, and we began to eat.

"How you could afford to go to a restaurant while you were attending college is a mystery to me," Grandmother Myra told him.

"It wasn't easy," he said, smiling. She looked at him with such disapproval he stopped smiling immediately and changed the subject to the new development he saw being done in the area.

"All this modernizing," Grandmother Myra said.

"For what? Things were good as they were. All it's doing is bringing in too many people."

"Have to improve and build your economy," Grandfather Prescott said. On this, he wasn't going to back down. Whenever she saw there was a topic he wouldn't avoid, she simply grew quiet or directed her attention elsewhere. Right now, she was criticizing the way some of the waiters and waitresses served food.

"I see how their fingers touch the potatoes or the pasta," she said.

I looked again at the family who had drawn my attention when they entered. They were waiting for a table, and the one they were brought to was only two tables from us. When they were seated, the young man was facing me. After their waiter took their drink orders, he looked at the menu, but then his gaze shifted toward me, and I quickly looked away.

Our food was brought to our table, and I tried to concentrate only on that while Grandmother Myra went through her litany of complaints about it all. Nothing was made the way it should be, the way she would have made it. She couldn't believe it was clean enough. There was dust under the table. Eating out never was worth the money.

"It's Elle's birthday celebration," my grandfather said softly.

"I could have made her a better dinner."

"Tomorrow night," he replied.

She pursed her lips the way she always did when her thoughts bounced around in her head and were shut down before getting to her tongue. I thought my food tasted better than what she would do with a chicken dish, but I kept that to myself and even tried not to look as if I was enjoying it so much. When I ventured to gaze toward the young man again, I saw he was still looking at me, with a small smile on his lips as if something about me amused him. Despite my attempts to avoid any response, I could feel my face heat up.

"What's wrong?" Grandmother Myra asked immediately. "You look flushed."

I shook my head. "I think there's something too spicy in mine," I offered.

"See?" she said, turning on my grandfather. "They're sloppy about how they prepare. They put in too much salt, for sure."

He didn't say anything. I kept my eyes locked on my food. Even though I was really enjoying it, my excuse for the blush that had come over me forced me to leave the remaining portion. There were tears in my eyes, but they weren't from any hot spice.

"Maybe we should order her something else," my grandfather said. He started to raise his hand to catch our waiter's attention, but she stopped him.

"She's eaten enough," she said.

"Elle?" he asked.

"I'm fine, Grandfather."

"Okay," he said. "We're going to get her a piece of cake with a candle anyway," he said. "I made sure of that."

"Oh, how ridiculous. One piece of cake and one candle for a girl this age."

"It's symbolic. I didn't want fifteen candles on it," he said, smiling.

She shook her head, but she didn't put up any resistance. When the waiter returned, my grandfather ordered a cup of coffee and told him it was my birthday. Grandmother Myra said she was fine with her water, even though it tasted as if it had come out of someone's pool. I sat back, actually trembling. They were going to bring me a piece of cake with a candle. For something like this to happen in a public place with so many people around us made me very nervous. I glanced at the young man.

He was talking to his father, who wore a light blue lightweight sports jacket with a dark blue shirt opened at the collar. They seemed to be in a very serious conversation. I thought the young man's good looks were even more highlighted when he was serious. His eyes, which I could see now were a bit lighter than sea blue, brightened with his intensity. I wished I could hear what they were saying. He looked so serious, so intelligent. It intrigued me. What did other people talk about? Certainly not hell and damnation, I thought.

When the young man and his family had entered, I hadn't looked very much at the parents, but I thought the young man's father was as good-looking as anyone I had seen on television. I didn't get a close enough look at the young man's mother, but now that she was seated next to her son, I could see she had the same shade of light brown hair, styled beautifully around her face. Her eyes were more of a gray-blue. She had soft, exquisitely small facial features, with lips that looked a little puffed. Her daughter's hair was as long as mine but brushed freely around her shoulders. I always wanted to wear my hair like that and couldn't wait to untie it before going to bed.

Not only our waiter but two others came with my piece of birthday cake, the candle lit. They stood by our table and sang "Happy Birthday" when I blew out the candle. I felt like crawling under the table. My grandmother didn't look as upset as I thought she would, however, and my grandfather was smiling brightly. After they finished singing, it seemed the whole restaurant applauded. I gazed at some of the other customers and saw them smiling and nodding at me. I didn't know how to react, so I just swallowed hard, forced a smile, and lifted my fork. The waiters clapped. One handed my grandfather his cup of coffee, and I gingerly put my fork into the cake. Would anyone here realize I had never had a piece of cake, only a practically sugarless piece of pie?

"Don't eat it too fast," my grandmother warned. "It will give you a bellyache."

I took the smallest piece I could. Anyone watching would think I was afraid the cake might be poison.

"Well?" Grandfather Prescott asked.

"It's delicious," I said.

"You make sure you brush your teeth well when we get home," Grandmother Myra told me. "Sugar will rot your teeth."

I nodded but cut a bigger piece. Then I looked at the young man again. His smile was wider and brighter. He nodded at me. *What do I do?* If I acknowledged him, my grandmother might see, but if I didn't, I would look snobby, I thought. I took a chance with a very small nod and a flash of a smile. Fortunately, my grandmother's attention was elsewhere. She was complaining about some woman wearing a dress that was so revealing she should be naked and get finished with it. My grandfather said nothing, but the moment I finished my cake, he signaled the waiter for the check.

"You don't leave more than fifteen percent," my grandmother told him, "and that's based on the net with the tax removed."

"I think I know how to leave a tip properly," he replied, which stunned me, because it was one of the first times I had heard him snap back at her so aggressively. "And if the service is very good, you should leave twenty percent."

"Ridiculous. There was nothing particularly good about the service anyway."

She pulled herself in and looked at the wall as if she couldn't stand looking at the bill when the waiter brought it to us. Grandfather Prescott studied it and put down the cash. Grandmother Myra was against having credit cards. She said it only encouraged reckless spending, and the interest rate, should you forget to pay on time, was downright legalized theft.

"Well, shall we go?"

"You'll have no argument from me," Grandmother Myra said.

"Thank you," I told them.

Grandmother Myra just sighed, but Grandfather

Prescott nodded and smiled. "You're very welcome, Elle."

I waited for them to get up. I thought that if they walked ahead of me, Grandmother Myra would not see me look at the young man. There was no way I could walk out and ignore him. As we passed their table, he leaned toward us and said, "Happy birthday."

I smiled at him but said nothing. Grandmother Myra hadn't heard it. When we reached the door, I looked back. He was talking with his father again. I was disappointed. I wanted one more smile.

My first thought as we walked out was, was that an evil thing to want? Was this the beginning?

3

Something significant had happened when I reached my fifteenth birthday, and I don't mean my grandparents breaking all their rules and taking me out to a restaurant for dinner. There was something more going on. I could feel it in the house, especially in the way my grandfather spoke to me and stood up for me at times. I knew from some of my reading that some Hispanic people celebrate the *quinceañera* to mark a girl's fifteenth birthday, but there was nothing remotely Hispanic about my grandparents. I think Grandfather Prescott just took a longer look at me right before my fifteenth birthday or right after it and concluded that they should loosen the bonds that chained me so tightly. My little-girl days had ended.

Finally, one night, I overheard a somewhat heated conversation about me going on in their bedroom. Their bedroom and what had been my mother's were upstairs, but the house wasn't insulated enough between rooms to keep all conversations and other sounds muted. At times, I could hear the murmur of their voices seemingly raining down on me through the ceiling, but if I was close to the stairway and their bedroom door was open, as I think it almost always was, I could hear their conversations more clearly, especially if one of them raised his or her voice.

"You should ease up on her," I heard my grandfather say with more volume and emphasis than he usually had when speaking to my grandmother. Immediately, I knew I was the "her" he referred to. I carefully took a few steps up on the stairway to listen better. The banister was just a little shaky, so I avoided putting any weight on it. So many places in this house creaked and moaned. If a house could get arthritis, this one would definitely qualify. Maybe it had been cleaned and scrubbed too much.

I wasn't formally forbidden to go upstairs. I was often sent up there to fetch something, and, of course, I was up there a number of times during the week to wash floors, windows, and bathroom fixtures. I polished furniture, made beds, changed the linen, and collected used towels and washcloths, returning with the ones washed and dried to stack them neatly in the bathroom closet. I also had to be sure the soap and toilet paper were replaced. I supposed if I had to go out and work for a living, I could easily get a job as a hotel chambermaid.

I never was permitted to go into what had been my mother's bedroom. That door was kept locked and the room never used. Maybe it was another one of their ways to keep the memory of her away. Even the windows in the room had their white curtains drawn tightly shut. I didn't even wonder why I wasn't eventually moved into it. That certainly wasn't because it had been turned into a shrine. It was simply forbidden territory, a place where something immoral or evil once dwelt and encouraged my mother's bad behavior. I didn't know too many incidences illustrating what my grandmother considered her bad behavior. She would mention something in general occasionally, as if she was slowly building a case for why my mother's fate was her own fault.

"Evil goes first where it's well received," she would say, and then tell me about my mother violating curfews, drinking alcohol with her friends, or getting in trouble at school. I imagined it was something like smoking in the bathroom or talking back to her teachers, but I was afraid to ask. It could show an innate interest in evil things.

The truth was, my grandparents had removed all traces of her, so it didn't surprise me at all that they would ignore the existence of her room. I wondered if my grandmother went into it at least to keep it clean, since cleanliness was so sacred. If she did, she did it without my knowing. Maybe she did it very late at night when I was fast asleep and when my grandfather was also asleep. I easily could imagine her mumbling in there, cursing at dust webs.

Whenever I was in their bedroom alone, I would timidly search for any sign of anything that had to do with my mother. Just like downstairs, there were no pictures of her displayed, but I always wondered if I might come across something in a dresser drawer,

maybe under some clothing, or in one of their closets. There were cartons all taped up on the floor of
Grandmother Myra's closet. I felt certain that any and
all of my mother's things that were once very visible
in this bedroom and downstairs were in them, but I
was afraid to pull away any of the tape to look. My
grandmother would surely discover it and punish me
for it.

My grandparents' bedroom wasn't much to look
at. They had the same queen-size bed that they had
when they had first moved into the house. The only
thing I knew that they changed regularly were the
mattresses, thanks to Grandfather Prescott's business.
Stacked in their garage were four new mattresses in
boxes that he had taken for them when he had sold
his business. Based on their own calculations from
when they operated their manufacturing plant, they
changed their own mattress once every five years. But
the cherry-wood headboard with posts and embossed
vines and leaves was never replaced. That and the footboard were polished and kept so well that anyone who
didn't know their vintage might think that they were
relatively recent acquisitions.

Listening hard on the stairway, I didn't hear my
grandmother react to my grandfather's comment, but
this time, it appeared he wasn't going to settle for her
silence.

"I mean, what has she done seriously to disappoint
you, Myra?" my grandfather persisted. I took another
step up to hear her answer this question as clearly
as I could. What would she say? She wasn't coming

after me these days because I asked or said something wrong. She was pleased with my schoolwork. She had even stopped criticizing my housework.

"It's not what she has done, it's what will she do? You never expected Deborah to be as loose with her morals as she was, did you?"

"Deborah was not as good a child as Elle is."

"Exactly. Because of the tight rein we've kept on her and keeping her away from bad influences."

They were both so quiet I thought that was that and was about to tiptoe back down the stairs. I turned, but my grandfather's next comment froze me.

"We should consider letting her attend a public school soon, Myra. She has to learn how to deal with other people, or she will be at a disadvantage, and that could lead to worse things."

"Public school," she countered, making it sound like some den of iniquity, a place where eggs laid by Satan himself hatched daily.

"Just think about it, will you? She's not a child anymore. She needs to grow in many ways. Don't forget, it was Adam's innocence that led him to sin. If you've never seen the devil, you won't recognize him when he comes. You've said that."

I heard her familiar grunt, which was not a yes and not a no. It wasn't even a maybe. It was simply acknowledging that someday she'd have an answer. How I hoped it would be yes.

"Just think about it," he repeated.

She said nothing.

I quickly tiptoed down the stairway and returned

to my room to finish my reading. For the first time in a long time, however, I found myself doing more fantasizing than thinking.

It had been nearly ten days since my birthday dinner at Chipper's, but a number of times, I had thought about the boy who was so handsome and had smiled so much at me. I replayed his "Happy birthday" in my mind and imagined him discovering who I was and where I lived. One day in my dream, he came over to see me. Naturally, in my fantasy, my grandmother would be appalled, but he would be so polite and deferential that she would have a very difficult time sending him off.

Grandfather Prescott particularly would enjoy his company and conversation. I envisioned all sorts of work his father did. Maybe he ran a factory, too, or managed another kind of enterprise, one that his son would take over when he was ready. I even thought of him as already being a college student, maybe studying business so that he and my grandfather would have an interesting discussion. My grandmother would sit and listen and reluctantly admit that he was a decent young man. Afterward, she would give permission for him to return, and days later, we would be more boyfriend and girlfriend than just acquaintances.

From there, I could see us holding hands, kissing, and maybe going a little further. I lay there pretending my hands were his and he was softly sliding them over my breasts and down my hips, over the small of my stomach, where my excitement began to build, my breath to quicken, and my heart to pound. When he touched me between my legs, I gasped. I put my hand on his wrist, but ever so gently, so that he didn't stop.

"What are you doing, missy?" I heard my grandmother cry from the hallway outside my room. I was on my bed. In the dim light, her silhouette looked larger. She was in her nightgown, with her hair down. I had no idea how long she had been watching me. She stepped closer. She didn't use makeup, but at night, she would put cold cream on her face, and when she moved from the shadows into brighter light, she looked as if she were wearing a Kabuki mask.

"Nothing," I said. "I think . . . I'm going to have a monthly. Cramps," I added.

She studied me for a moment. I held my breath. I grew up believing that if anyone could tell the difference between what was true and what wasn't, she could.

"I'll make you some raspberry tea," she said.

I breathed in relief. The tea was one of her home remedies, and to be honest, it did help when I had the cramps.

"Thank you," I said.

"It's the only thing good about getting old," she muttered. "That ends."

I lay there calming myself. She called me when my tea was ready and watched me drink it. I could practically feel her eyes studying every part of me, every movement in my face, and every breath I took. I had learned not to be intimidated by the way she concentrated her gaze on me, even though it was as if she had X-ray eyes and could see through my skin. I imagined that by now, I didn't have a gesture or an expression with which she wasn't quite familiar. She probably was always comparing me with my mother, looking for some sign that I had inherited the worst part of her. Or even worse than that, something from my evil biological father.

Apparently, I passed her inspection. She didn't look upset or critical. She looked surprisingly thoughtful. I knew something was coming. She wasn't one to keep her thoughts to herself.

"Your grandfather thinks you might be ready to attend public school next semester," she said. "How would you feel about that?"

I swallowed the remainder of my tea. *Be casual, almost indifferent,* I told myself. *If you show too much excitement, she'll think it's not right.*

"I think I could manage the work," I replied, shrugging.

"Of course you could manage the work," she snapped back at me. "You're most likely way ahead of other students your age. I'm not talking about the work. It's how you would deal with children your age, who are brought up in liberal homes, homes where their parents ignore what they do. The devil influences those he hopes to capture by speaking through their friends, instigating, tempting, and drawing them to the abyss."

"I'm not afraid of anyone's influence over me. I feel stronger than they are," I said. "Most of them probably don't know much at all about the Bible and probably rarely say prayers except on Sundays."

She seemed to like that response, but her smile evaporated quickly. "Beware of arrogance, missy. It leads to tragedy, moral and spiritual tragedy."

"I know, Grandmother. You've shown me so many examples in the Bible."

"Umm," she said. It was better than a grunt. It was her thoughtful leaning to say or do something I might like. "We'll see," she said. "We'll see. Get to bed early. It will help with your monthly."

"I will. Thank you, Grandmother," I said. I brought my cup to the sink, rinsed and washed and dried it, and put it back in the cupboard. She continued to watch me thoughtfully. "Good night," I said.

"Say your prayers louder and stronger than ever, Elle," she told me. She sounded a little softer, especially when she used my name and didn't just call me "missy." "The older a young girl gets, the closer she gets to temptation and damnation. This is not the time to forget them."

"I won't, Grandmother."

She watched me walk into my room and waited to see me go down on my knees. Out of the corner of my eye, I saw her leave and turn off the light, and then I rose.

I didn't feel like prayers. I felt like dreams.

What if the handsome boy I had seen was not as old as I thought? What if he was really my age or only a year older and the same was true for his sister? Most important, what if he and she attended the school I would enter?

I envisioned my first day. After I was registered, I started for my homeroom, and lo and behold, there he was, coming down the hallway toward me, with his friends around him listening to his every word and hoping for his approval, because there was no way to think of him as being anything else but the most popular boy in the school. The moment he saw me, he paused and smiled. He looked as if he had just had one of his wonderful fantasies come to life, too. He told his friends to go on without him. They all looked from him to me and nodded, looking sly. Maybe they kidded him with some silly words of encouragement. Maybe they were jealous.

"Hi," he said. "You're the birthday girl."

And it would begin.

I curled up on my bed, embracing my pillow as if I were embracing him. I caressed it softly with my lips the way I would caress his face and find his lips. We would kiss and hold each other so tightly, until he relaxed, the words flowing from his warm breath, words of love, words that magically touched my heart.

As I fantasized, I could feel waves of surprisingly new and stronger excitement building in my body. I pressed my comforter between my legs and kissed my pillow. The strong feeling undulated down from my breasts, over my stomach, to settle between my legs. I couldn't keep myself from moaning ever so slightly. The shock of how my feelings exploded again and again brought the blood up from my neck. I almost couldn't breathe. Terrified of myself, I froze for a few moments and then pushed the pillow and the comforter away. I turned over onto my back and looked up at the picture of the baby Jesus. I knew it was only my imagination, but he looked unhappy, even a little angry.

"Forgive me," I whispered, and closed my eyes.

When morning came, I welcomed how the brightness drove the memory of my passion down so deep in the caverns of my mind that it seemed to have been only a dream, a foolish young girl's dream. I wouldn't think about it. In fact, I worked harder on my chores, almost attacking the house as if it had become my enemy, every fleck of dust, every stain, and every spot something that had to be destroyed. My enthusiasm didn't go unnoticed. First, my grandfather remarked about it, and then my grandmother told me I should go at it easier.

"You'll exhaust yourself and get sick," she warned.

"Sometimes you're that exuberant about housework, Myra," my grandfather said quickly. He seemed to want to come to my defense.

"I know, and I have the aches and pains to prove it," she told him. "I taught her to wipe off the dust and wash away the dirt but not the furniture itself."

"Can't she have the day off, Myra? It's beautiful today," he told her. "There's nothing that can't wait."

"What would you do with a day off?" she asked me in a challenging tone. "And don't tell me you'd go out back and think, think, think."

"No. I would like to go for a walk, maybe to the lake and back," I said.

"She can't get into trouble doing that," my grandfather said.

"I saw some new fawns yesterday," I told him.

"Nature is spiritual," he said. My grandmother looked as if she was weakening. "She needs more fresh air. She's cooped up in here too much."

"She goes out with us."

"It's not enough," he insisted. I couldn't believe how determined he sounded, but I made sure to look down and not smile at him. I knew her well enough to know she might think we had conspired.

"To the lake and back," she said. "Nowhere else. Is that understood? We don't want to have to call the police to go looking for you."

"Oh, Myra."

"Well, if she strays too far, she could get lost," she said.

"She won't. She's not an idiot. You told me how bright she was when it comes to her schoolwork."

I looked at her, surprised. My grandmother had given me a compliment?

"Schoolwork is not the real world," she said. "And besides, you should make good use of every experience you have, even when you're just taking a walk."

"I've been doing some drawing," I confessed. I thought this might be as good a time as any to reveal it. I had been drawing for some time, but I was afraid of how she would view that, because it had nothing to do with my homeschool work and could in her opinion be wasteful.

"Really?" my grandfather said. "We have to see some of that."

"I've always wanted to draw some ducks on the lake."

"Deborah used to tinker a bit with art," my grandfather said.

"She tinkered a bit with everything and never got serious about anything," Grandmother Myra said.

"True, but if Elle has any interest or talent in that direction, she inherited it from her," he pointed out, so there would be no question about whether it was something I had inherited from the evil one. It seemed to satisfy my grandmother.

"Be back in an hour."

"She needs more than that if she's going to do some drawing, Myra. An artist has to contemplate her subject first, doesn't she?"

"Artist," she muttered. "All right, but don't be more than two hours," she said. "I want you to peel some potatoes and dice some carrots and chop some onions for dinner."

"How is she going to know the difference between an hour and two?" Grandfather Prescott asked. "She has no watch. You should give her one of those Deborah left behind. You have them in that carton in the closet."

I knew it, I thought.

She thought a moment and then shook her head. "None of them would work now. They all have dead batteries," she said, and looked relieved about it.

"Here," Grandfather Prescott said, rising and slipping his watch off his wrist. "For now, you can use my watch."

"Thank you, Grandfather," I said, and watched him slip it over my left hand. He made the band as tight as he could without it being too tight.

"Feel okay?"

"Yes."

"Don't break that watch, missy," Grandmother Myra said. "It's a very expensive one."

"She won't break it, and it's not that expensive, Myra."

"If she gets too close to the water, she could get it wet, and it's not waterproof."

"She won't go swimming in it, Myra."

"I'll be careful," I said.

As casually as I could, I went into my room, gathered my paper and pencils, and walked slowly toward the back door. I knew her eyes were on me.

"Have a good time," my grandfather called.

I looked back and smiled. He smiled, but my grandmother's face was as full of suspicion as ever. She didn't even nod.

I took a breath and stepped out as if I were someone fleeing, about to cross a border to safety, and then closed the door softly behind me. The sense of freedom seemed to cleanse my lungs. It was a most glorious day, with moderate temperatures and a soft, warm breeze just nudging the leaves on the trees. Small, puffy clouds looked as if they had been dabbed against the blue background. Maybe it was my wishful imagination, but as I stepped down and began to walk toward the forest, I thought the birds grew excited and called others to watch me enter their world.

"You've been waiting for me, haven't you?" I told them. "You've been waiting for me for a long time."

They chirped louder. A few moments later, I stepped into the cool, dark forest and felt as if I had entered another world and escaped from the one drifting away behind me. I didn't look back. I was so excited about being alone and far from my grandmother's scrutinizing eyes that my heart began to race. I walked faster, finding a natural path and pausing only to look at a narrow brook that seemed to erupt from under a pair of rocks and cut its path off to the right.

I heard branches cracking and turned sharply to my left just in time to see a doe pause to look at me and then calmly trot off in the opposite direction. I was tempted to follow it. *Where do deer go anyway?* I wondered. They were always moving in the woods, probably looking for food, but they had to have someplace they thought of as home. Instead, I continued in the direction of the lake. The time my grandfather had taken me through the woods was so long ago that I had forgotten where we'd come out. The woods were thicker now anyway. I could remember nothing. I didn't want to remember anything. I wanted this to be my first time.

I walked faster when the brush and the trees thinned out, and then I paused, because I was sure I heard human voices. Could it be someone in a boat on the lake? Curiosity overwhelmed me. I sped up, nearly scratching myself on some low-hanging branches, and then, through an opening ahead, I saw the lake.

It was narrower there. I had forgotten that some lucky people had homes close to or on the shores of the lake. When I stepped out of the forest into a small clearing, I saw that one of those houses was very close by. I heard laughter and then the sound of a screen door slamming shut. Moments later, two young people came around the corner of the house just across the water. There was a short dock with a rowboat attached. I pulled back as the two drew closer. One was a girl, and the other . . .

The breath went out of me as sharply as if someone had punched me in the stomach. The sight of him walking barefoot with his towel wrapped around him stunned me. There was no doubt. It was the young man from the restaurant, and the girl who followed him, playfully tossing grass at him, was his sister. They both walked out on the dock and stood looking out at the lake. I pulled myself farther back into the shadows when he turned in my direction. I was terrified he would see me spying.

Suddenly, his sister turned on him and pushed him from behind. He screamed, his towel fell off, and, naked, he fell off the dock and into the water.

Except for some vague drawings in the science textbook my grandmother reluctantly gave me, I had never seen what a naked male looked like. I knew their anatomy, just as well as I knew my own, but it was one thing to read some scientific information and a far different thing to see someone in the flesh, especially someone you had in your fantasy.

He came up, spouting water like a whale, and shook his fist playfully at her. She laughed. He turned away and started to swim.

Suddenly, she dropped her towel away and, also naked, dived into the lake.

I brought my hands to the base of my throat and nervously watched them swim around each other and splash each other, and then I saw him go under the water and come up behind her. She screamed when he put his hand on the top of her head and pushed her under. She came up quickly and went after him. He swam quickly away and then went under and came up to the side of her but far enough away so she couldn't get to him. They splashed each other playfully again, and then they both swam until they paused at one of the legs of the dock and treaded water while they talked softly. He was facing in my direction. I didn't move, but just to my right, another deer appeared, this time a buck with a good rack. The young man pointed in my direction. Did he see the buck, or did he see me?

She turned to look my way, too, and then she swam around to the other side of the dock and climbed up the short ladder. I thought she would wrap her towel around herself quickly, but instead, she sprawled out over it with her back facing the sun.

He remained in the water, looking in my direction. The buck trotted off deeper into the woods, but the boy didn't stop looking. I stepped back, hoping to be covered more heavily in the shadows, but I didn't watch where I was going, and I fell over a thick dead tree limb. I didn't cry out.

But I heard him laugh anyway. When I looked back, I saw that he was shouting something to his sister.

And I knew.

He had seen me.

4

I started to run for home and stopped when I realized I had been gone almost an hour and had nothing to show for it on my paper. I hadn't drawn a line. My grandmother was sure to question me about where I had been and what I had been doing instead, and I was afraid my face would reveal what I had seen. She was too good at reading me not to notice that something had affected me deeply. It put me into a small panic.

I walked in a circle through some brush and paused at a small clear area under a group of pine trees. There was a matted pine-needle floor over the forest's dark earth. The scents were very strong but refreshing. I looked back toward the lake, wondering if the boy had decided to swim in my direction. Surely he wouldn't step out of the lake naked to look for me, would he? What about his sister? Did he tell her he had seen me? Was that what he shouted back to her? Was she swimming in my direction, too?

I was so confused about what I had seen. It couldn't be common for brothers and sisters that age to swim naked with each other, could it? They looked as if they had been doing it for years. Many times, I wished I had a brother or a sister, younger or older, I didn't care. At least there would be someone else close to my age living in the house. We would help each other understand and prepare ourselves for what went on in the world outside my grandparents' restricted one. Sometimes I felt I was actually on another planet and spoke another language.

I felt so stupid for falling over that log and running away. I was sure I had looked comical to him. There was so much I didn't know about how people actually behaved, especially males and females my age when they were together. All I knew now was that the sight of them both totally naked and unconcerned about it excited and astounded me. I had no doubt what Grandmother Myra would do if she had any idea about what I had seen. She'd put me under lock and key. She might even throw away the key.

There was a large boulder just to my right. I went to it and sat. The sun was still high enough in the sky to pour strong rays through the tops of the trees and give my little natural art studio a magical look and feel. It helped me calm down. I opened my drawing pad and set it comfortably on my lap. Then I closed my eyes and tried to get a good image of the lake, but it was impossible to think of it without seeing the boy fly off the dock after his sister had pushed him. That image of him flailing in the air naked brought heat to my face.

Don't try to draw the lake right now, I thought. *Draw some trees, and imagine that doe you saw earlier standing in the midst of them.* Thinking of doing something else was the only way to get my mind off what I had seen. I started, but what I drew first looked childish, so I ripped off the page and started again, this time going much more slowly. When I had outlined the trees, I began to draw the doe, concentrating on its eyes. I got so involved in my picture that I was able to push the sight and sounds of the two I had seen far enough back in my mind to do what I thought was a decent preliminary sketch.

When the sunlight was more blocked out by the trees around me, I assumed too much time might have passed and anxiously checked Grandfather Prescott's watch. Claiming that I had been so involved in my drawing that I had lost track of time wouldn't work as a good excuse for my grandmother. She was always ready to pounce on any sign of daydreaming. She thought it was fantasizing, and fantasizing always opened the door to something evil.

Fortunately, I still had a good half hour, so I went back to my drawing, but suddenly, I was sure I heard the cracking of branches, and then I heard their voices. They couldn't be walking through the forest naked, but how else would they be if they did what I thought they might and swam to where I had been on the shore? I closed my pad and rose, listening.

"Hey!" I heard the boy call. "Hello?"

"Hello?" his sister called, and then laughed. "You imagined it, you idiot," she said.

"No, I didn't. I'm sure I saw her."

"The princess of the woods."

"I saw her," he insisted.

I couldn't move. I should run, I thought, but I would make too much noise. They would hear me and be more inclined to follow. The sound of the footsteps grew louder.

"Let's go back, Mason. This is ridiculous," I heard the girl say.

They were very close now. I turned slowly to my left and looked between a pair of large maple trees. I could see them, both with towels wrapped around their bodies. They hadn't swum. They must have decided to use their rowboat. I held my breath. The girl started to turn, and her brother put his hand on her right arm. She paused, and he nodded in my direction.

He had seen me. I felt the blood rise into my face. I wanted to run, but my feet felt cemented to the spot, and I was afraid that if I started, I would fall on my face and look even more ridiculous. He took a few steps toward me, and then he smiled.

"Hey," he said, pointing at me. "I know you. You're the birthday girl."

"What?" his sister asked, coming up alongside him. "Who is she?"

"She's the girl who had a birthday dinner in Chipper's when we were there with Mom and Dad."

"Oh," his sister said.

He continued to walk toward me. I hugged my notepad against my breasts and waited. Both he and his sister were barefoot.

"You live nearby?" he asked.

"Yes," I said. I nodded toward my grandparents' house. "Back that way."

"What's your name?"

"Elle," I said.

"Well?" he said, turning to his sister. "Meet my imagination. Are you satisfied now?"

"What are you doing spying on us?" she demanded, not happy about being wrong.

"She wasn't spying on us. Were you?" he asked. He smiled, liking the idea. "How many times have you done it?"

I shook my head. "Never."

His sister looked as if she didn't believe me. "Why haven't we ever seen you at the lake?" she asked.

"I haven't been at the lake for a long time."

"How long?"

"Years," I said.

"Why not, if you live so close?"

I didn't answer.

"You were spying on us, and you have been many times," she insisted.

"No, really. I'm not lying."

"You're not being very friendly, Claudine, cross-examining her like this. Please excuse my sister's behavior. She doesn't meet many people in the forest," he said, smiling.

I looked at her. Suddenly, she looked a little amused. Her smile started in her eyes and curled around her soft, full lips. I saw again how the resemblances between them were so clear.

"What are you holding so dearly?" she asked me.

"My drawing pad," I said, but I didn't show it to her.

"You're an artist. That's it," her brother said. "She came to the lake to be inspired, like Renoir's famous *Near the Lake* painting. My mother has a print of that in her bedroom back home."

"Back home?"

"We're from Manhattan. This is only our summer home," he said. "Our parents go back and forth. Dad's an attorney, and Mom has her own decorating business."

"Don't be so eager to tell her our life story, Mason."

He laughed.

"Were you drawing us?" the girl asked. "Is that why you were spying, hiding in the bushes, and why you're clinging so desperately to your pad?"

"No," I said, feeling the blush come into my face at the very thought.

"What if she was? This is terrific. We don't know anyone close to our age here. I'm Mason Spenser, by the way, and this is my impolite sister, Claudine."

"Yes, we're twins," Claudine said, like someone who was asked the same question all the time. "I'm older."

"By four minutes."

"*Vive la différence,*" she said.

"Ha, ha," Mason said.

"You know what that means, Elle?" she asked.

I shook my head.

"It's French for 'long live the difference.' People say it when they're happy or proud of the difference," she added, sounding a little like my grandmother when she was homeschooling me, but she turned her eyes on Mason. "I have more wisdom, being older."

"Ignore her, Elle. She likes to act superior."

"Only because I am," Claudine followed. "So what else do you do around here, besides spy on your neighbors once every ten years or so?"

"I wasn't spying," I insisted. "I went to the lake to draw ducks and heard you laughing and then saw you go swimming."

"Sounds plausible," Mason said.

"So what are you going to do now, run home and tell everyone you saw a naked boy and girl swimming?"

"No. I wouldn't do that. I can't do that," I added, but she didn't pick up on my point.

"You should come swimming with us," Mason said.

I must have looked quite shocked, because he immediately laughed.

"Don't worry. You can wear a bathing suit, and we'll put ours on if you come," he said.

"Speak for yourself," Claudine said.

"I always do."

"People think that because we're twins, what one of us believes the other does, too. Nothing could be further from the truth," she told me. "If anything, I tell him what to do and think. I have better grades in school. Half the time, I have to do his homework."

"She likes to blow her own horn," Mason said, and she punched him in the shoulder. He cried out and rocked as if the punch was strong enough to knock him over.

I noticed how her towel slipped a bit, revealing more of her breasts. She saw where I was looking and smiled but didn't pull up the towel. I looked down quickly.

"What birthday was it?" Claudine asked.

"My fifteenth," I said.

"Fifteen? I would have said seventeen," Mason said. "We're seventeen."

"I'm four minutes more than your seventeen," she told him.

"So you'll die four minutes before I do."

"If we die on the same day," she replied.

"We were born on the same day, weren't we?"

"Don't be stupid. You're making a bad impression on the forest nymph."

"I'm not a forest nymph," I said.

"I don't mean nymphomaniac," she said. "Unless, of course, you are one."

Mason slapped her a little bit harder than playfully, and she slapped him back.

"You're the one making the bad impression," he told her. He looked really upset.

She looked at me and reconsidered.

"Sorry. Actually, I meant I was sure you were a virgin. You have that virginal air about you."

"What?" I knew what it meant, but the only time I had ever heard the word spoken was in reference to the Virgin Mary. Was it proper to say the word in front of a male?

"Of course, maybe I'm wrong. Most of the girls who have lost their innocence in our school act in public like they haven't gone further than a peck on the cheek. Do you go to school here? I can't imagine it being much of a school."

"My sister's picture is next to the word *snob* in the dictionary," Mason said. "We attend a private school."

"No, I don't go to the school here. Yet," I added.

"Where do you go?" she asked, a slightly amused smile on her face. "You go to a private school, too?"

"No. I'm in homeschooling."

"Homeschooling?" She looked at Mason. He looked a little shocked. "Aren't you too old for that?"

"I'm probably going to the public school this year," I said.

They both stared at me as if they had trouble understanding or digesting my words.

"I keep forgetting where we are," she said. "Around here, I bet the iPhone means I'll call you."

"The what?"

"See?"

"Will you stop?" he said.

She stuck her tongue out at him and then turned back to me. "You didn't get that watch for your birthday, did you?" she asked, nodding at Grandfather Prescott's watch on my wrist.

"No. It's my grandfather's. I don't have a watch."

"You don't have a watch? Do you have electricity, indoor bathrooms?"

"Claudine! Stop picking on her," Mason said.

"I'm not picking on her. Who doesn't have a watch these days?"

"Plenty of people who need money for food. You know the percentage of people in poverty these days?"

"Oh, you're so pedantic. Don't let him start one of his speeches," she told me. "He'll wear down your ears."

"Those couldn't have been your parents with you at the restaurant the other night, right?" Mason asked.

"No. They're my grandparents."

"Why weren't your parents there?" Claudine asked.

I didn't reply.

"Do you live with your grandparents?" she asked me quickly, as if she had just discovered something very important.

"Yes," I said.

"Do your parents live there, too?" Mason asked.

I shook my head.

"I bet they're divorced. Is that it?" Claudine asked.

"No."

"Did one or both pass away?" Mason asked.

"I have to go," I said. I backed away.

"Hey, let's see what you drew," he said.

"It's nothing," I said. "I've got to go. I can't be late."

"Why not? Is it a very important date, Alice? I'm late. I'm late for a very important date. Alice!" Claudine shouted.

"My name is Elle," I said, and she laughed. "Don't call me Alice. I didn't fall down a hole."

I started walking quickly, still holding my pad tightly against my breasts.

"Come on back tomorrow," he called after me. "We'll pick you up in the rowboat."

I glanced back. They were both standing there looking after me. Claudine poked him, and he poked her back a little roughly.

"Just for that, you swim back!" she shouted at him. Then she ran into the woods.

He waved to me, and then he ran after her, shouting, "Like hell I will!"

I stood there listening to them disappear into the woods. Then I turned and walked slowly the rest of the way, my ears still ringing with the happy-go-lucky tone in their voices and their laughter but my body trembling as if all my bones were vibrating. Their innocent questions about my parents were a good prologue to what I was sure I would get when and if I entered a public school. It would be only natural for the other students to want to know more about me. How was I to answer? How was I to explain? Would I reveal that I had no father, no mother, or make up some story? Could I just come right out and tell them my mother had been raped, and as a result I had been born, and she had run off?

I was afraid to ask Grandmother Myra what I should say. She might interpret that to mean that I was afraid of going to school and then reject the idea. And yet I was confident that she knew those questions would come. Surely she would prepare me for them. Perhaps she had to prepare herself for them first. One thing was certain, she would never expect me to have confronted any girl or boy of my age during a seemingly innocent walk to the lake and have all these things come up.

When I entered through the back door, she looked up from the food she was setting out on the island in the center of the kitchen. She wiped her hands on a dish towel and gave me that studied look I was anticipating. Then she looked up at the clock and nodded.

"So?" she asked. "Where did you go? What did you draw?"

"There were no ducks on the lake when I got there, at least where I was, but I saw this doe standing not more than fifteen feet away and got a good look at its face."

I turned my pad and showed her my preliminary sketch.

She nodded. "Better than what your so-called mother could do," she said.

I guessed that as long as I was compared with my mother, I could find some appreciation in her words and looks. I was getting to the point where I was happy I had a mother, her daughter, with whom she found so much fault now. I couldn't lose if she continually compared me with her.

My grandfather walked into the kitchen.

"Did I hear we have a drawing?"

"Just a start, Grandfather," I said, and showed it to him. He took it from my hands and looked at it keenly, as if he were a professional art critic.

"Love how you've captured her eyes," he said.

"Good," my grandmother said. "Go wash your hands, and help me prepare dinner."

Grandfather Prescott handed my pad back.

"Can I go again tomorrow?" I asked.

"If the weather permits," my grandmother said. "After you do your chores and finish the assignments I've given you."

Although the twins made me very nervous, I was intrigued with the idea of seeing them again. I dared not think of going swimming with them, not only because I couldn't swim but because they'd surely have many more questions that were difficult for me to answer. Even if I wasn't able to do that, I thought I would stay up all night if I had to in order to finish the schoolwork and be able to go back into the woods and to the lake.

I headed first for my room and then into the bathroom. In between, I heard Grandfather Prescott say, "I told you she would be just fine, and she does have an artistic talent, Myra."

My grandmother gave her famous grunt.

Later, at dinner, after I described the place I had discovered under the pine trees, my grandfather casually suggested he might take a walk with me the next day. My heart sank, first because I was afraid that Mason and Claudine might come looking for me again and second because I wanted to be able to observe them again if they didn't, keeping myself a little less obvious.

"Don't worry," he added. "I won't hang around and look over your shoulder while you draw. I was

thinking, Myra, that we should get her some watercolors. We did that for Deborah."

"Wasted money."

"Won't be for Elle," Grandfather Prescott insisted.
"She'll need the brushes and, what do you call that
thing for holding the painting while you work on it?"

"An easel," I said.

"Yes, right. She'll need one of those, too."

"Don't go overboard, Prescott," Grandmother
Myra said. "You were always jumping to buy whatever Deborah fancied for the moment."

"Elle isn't as flippant," he said.

She looked at me. "Let's pray not," she muttered.

I cleared the table when we were finished and
washed and dried the dishes, while Grandmother
Myra put things away. Then I went right to my
schoolwork. A little more than an hour later, I looked
up to see her standing in my doorway.

"Your grandfather says you should come out
to watch a public television program on some artist
named Renoir," she said.

"Renoir?"

"That's what he says."

"Okay. Thank you," I said, putting my papers and
books away. Renoir was the artist Mason Spenser had
mentioned. I was eager to see that picture he had mentioned, too.

I followed her into the living room.

"It's just starting," Grandfather Prescott said, and
I sat on the sofa. All I could think was that if I happened to speak to Mason Spenser again, I would at

least have something sensible to say and not look like such a fool.

Later, when I went to bed, I thought about both of them. Mason had attracted me from the moment I had first set eyes on him at the restaurant, but there was something about Claudine that also fascinated me. I really didn't know the difference between what was a sophisticated person and what wasn't, but I imagined she would be thought of as sophisticated. She seemed so sure of herself. I envied her confidence and wondered if she laughed about me later, telling Mason I was a country bumpkin.

He seemed to like me. I could feel that in the way he looked and smiled at me and the way he tried to stop her from hurting my feelings. I was certain he really did want to see me again. Would he row over by himself if she didn't want to see me? From what he had said, I gathered that they didn't know anyone their age here. She had no girlfriends, and he had no buddies. When they were here, they spent all their time together. Maybe he was just bored with that. Maybe I was just a curiosity, and once he had spoken to me more, he would realize I was too different from the girls he knew, and that would be that.

I hadn't really looked at their summer home when I saw them on the dock, but from what little they had told me about themselves, I was sure they were rich. They went to a private school and had a summer home. She was only wearing a towel, but there was no question in my mind that she had very nice clothes, beautiful and expensive clothes. She probably ridiculed what I was wearing and everything else about me.

And yet I couldn't help but want to know her, to talk to her and learn things. I had little, really nothing and no one, to judge them against, but for now, they were the most interesting young people I had ever seen either in stores or on television. I began to fantasize about being with them, and this excited me more than I anticipated. What if I could swim and did go swimming naked with them? Could I be as casual about it as they were? The very thought of it kept me from falling asleep for the longest time. I had to finger my large cross to stop myself from all this forbidden fantasizing.

When I awoke in the morning and hurried out to the kitchen to have breakfast and start my chores as soon as I could, I felt my heart sink in a pool of disappointment. The sky was heavily overcast, and it looked as if it might start pouring any moment. It depressed my spirit. I didn't work with any enthusiasm. There was no question my grandmother wouldn't permit me to go into the woods. Grandfather Prescott was complaining about some aches and pains as soon as he was up, so there was no question that he wouldn't want to go for a walk in the woods.

"I can always tell when it's going to rain," he said. "My lower back lets me know."

Grandmother Myra didn't say very much. She went over the schoolwork I had done and told me I had done well. She wrote out some other reading assignments and some math assignments.

"Looks like you'll have most of the day now to do your schoolwork," she said.

It did rain but not anywhere as much as we thought or as heavily. A little after two o'clock, the sun sliced through some thinning clouds, and not twenty minutes later, more clear blue sky appeared. I had been checking on the weather all day before that. Before I had a chance to ask, however, she slammed down my hopes.

"It's too wet in the woods. You'll muddy your shoes and come down with something for sure."

"I can be careful," I said. "If it's too muddy, I'll come right back."

"They always say the rain clears the air, Myra," Grandfather Prescott piped up. "She's not made of paper."

"I finished the work you gave me," I told her.

"You ruin those shoes, and you'll have to walk around here barefoot to teach you a lesson, missy," she said.

"My goodness, Myra, the girl's only going out in nature to draw. She's not running off to meet some of her wild girlfriends or something," he said.

"I'm trying to decide whether or not she has good judgment, Prescott. I'm letting her make the decision. Well?"

She looked at me to see what I would say. Should I say she was right and not go out? I knew what she expected. She expected me to be like my mother when she was my age and whine or be stubborn.

"I can wait for a nicer day. Grandmother is right," I said.

She nodded.

"You wanted to go get some groceries, Myra," Grandfather Prescott said, rising. "You want Elle to go along?"

"I don't need her. We don't need that much," she said.

"Well, at least let her go onto the back porch," he told her. "A growing girl needs fresh air."

"If she wants," she said.

I didn't see what good that would do me, but I didn't want to seem ungrateful. The truth was, it would be more painful to step outside and not be able to go through the woods to the lake than it would be to shut myself up in the house. It would be like dangling a piece of bread in front of a starving person who could see it but not reach it.

Nevertheless, I got my pad and pencils, put on a light sweater, which was a hand-me-down from Grandmother Myra's wardrobe, and went out to sit on the small porch. It wasn't much more than six by twelve under a roof. There were two redwood chairs on it. There wasn't room for anything more. Grandmother Myra went out before me and wiped down one of the chairs. She gazed around the yard for a moment, as if she wanted to be sure there was nothing out there to corrupt me.

"We'll be back in about an hour," she said. "I'm planning on making a pot roast tonight."

I nodded and opened my pad. She stood there a few moments and went back inside. Not ten minutes later, I heard Grandfather Prescott start up the car.

I gazed at the yard. Stepping off the porch and onto the wet grass seemed as forbidden to me as eating the fruit was to Adam in the Garden of Eden. It was as if Grandmother Myra had drawn a line in the sand and said, "Cross this, and you'll go straight to hell."

Defiance flared up inside me. I rose from the chair, went down the short stairway, and reached out with my right leg from the bottom step just to touch the grass with the tip of my foot.

"Come on in. The water's warm," I heard, and leaped back, nearly falling over the steps.

There he was at the edge of the woods.

5

He wore a light blue sweater and jeans and was alone. He stood so still, with not a strand of his long light brown hair fluttering in the soft breeze. For a moment, I thought he might be an illusion, wishful thinking that had materialized. Then he started toward the house, and I debated rushing inside and closing the door or stepping off the porch and chasing him away. He paused, perhaps seeing the panic in my face.

"You all right?"

"Yes. You just shocked me," I said.

"I'm a shocking guy." He stood there smiling. "I thought the rain kept you from going into the woods and decided to look for you."

"Why?"

"Why? Maybe I need an artist. Maybe I just wanted to see you again. Maybe I'm a serial killer. Which one do you think?"

"Serial killer," I said, and he laughed.

"There, you do have a sense of humor. It's a little hidden but still there."

Did I? I wondered. Laughter was an infrequent

visitor to my grandparents' house. Whenever it did occur, I first questioned what I had heard. Had it happened? Was my grandmother actually laughing at something? When I saw her laughing, I saw how it changed her face, softened her eyes, relaxed her lips, and made her look younger. It was as if she could ride on the back of a laugh and return to happier days. There was magic in that, I thought, so yes, I wanted to have a sense of humor very much.

"It's not that wet, you know, and the day's turned out to be very nice," he said, holding his arms up as though he could catch the sun's rays in the palms of his hands. "Can you come out to play?"

"Play?"

"Ding. Joke," he said. "Remember that sense of humor." He shook his head at my dumb expression but kept the soft smile on his face. The sunlight highlighted the soft blue in his eyes. "Claudine said she thought you were too serious. She has all sorts of theories about it and is as interested in you as I am. Well, maybe not as much."

"She met me for only a few minutes and concluded I was too serious?" That sounded like a doctor looking at someone and saying, "You have pneumonia."

"Don't worry about it. A few hours with us, and you'll change completely," he said.

Would I? What if I did? Wouldn't that be dangerous? Wouldn't Grandmother Myra see that immediately, too, and question why?

"C'mon. Let's take a little walk, unless you want

to invite me to sit with you on your back porch and watch you draw. Maybe you'll draw me this time. I can sit very quietly if I have to."

"No," I said a little too quickly.

"I'm not that bad-looking."

"No, I mean I'll take a walk."

I looked back at the house fearfully, as if I thought it would report everything to my grandmother, and then I stepped off the porch and walked to him slowly, taking great care to avoid any puddles.

"I can stay out only a half hour," I said. "I have chores."

"Chores?"

"Things to do to help make dinner."

"Oh. You're a cook, too?"

"I can make things, but my grandmother mainly does the cooking."

He looked back at the house. "How long have your grandparents lived here?"

"Years and years."

"It looks like one of the much older houses. Are they still working?"

"No. He had a mattress factory and sold it to retire."

"Did you work there?"

"No," I said, laughing. "I wasn't old enough before he retired."

"So they're no spring chickens," he said, still looking at the house.

"No what?"

"Young. They're not young grandparents. My

grandparents are only in their sixties. My father's father still works in the law firm part-time."

"Oh."

"So what happened to your parents?" he asked.

"I don't like to talk about it," I said.

"Sorry." He looked down quickly.

"Where's Claudine?" I asked.

That brought a smile back to his face. "She is wrapped up in her karaoke."

"Her what?"

"Karaoke. We have one of those machines. You know," he said when I didn't show any recognition, "where you sing along? You have a microphone and act like you're really the main singer. You never did karaoke?"

I shook my head. I could just imagine his reaction if I told him I didn't even have a CD player or a radio.

"You'll have to come over to try it," he said. "Sure you can only stay out a half hour? It's early."

"I have other things to do in the house."

"You're not an indentured servant, are you?"

"What? Oh. How could I be?"

"Just kidding."

I looked down at my shoes. The wet grass had stained them a little. If I could get to dry ground, I might be all right, I thought. He saw my concern.

"We could go around front and walk on the road. It's dry. If you follow the street for another mile or so and turn right, you come to our summer home. I could show you the way."

"No, I don't have time for that," I said.

He shrugged and then nodded at my pad, again pressed against my breasts like a book of secrets. "Let's see some of your drawings."

"I only just started one," I said. "Yesterday."

"Of us in the raw? Was Claudine right?"

"No," I said quickly.

He laughed. "What, then?"

I slowly opened the pad and showed him the doe.

"This is pretty good. You going to paint it?"

"I think so. My grandfather wants to buy me watercolors, brushes, and an easel."

"You don't have any of that stuff yet?"

I shook my head. "They just found out that I like to draw."

He stared at me a moment, a small smile on his lips and brightness in his eyes. I had to look away. His gaze was doing all sorts of things inside me that made me blush.

"Just found out? What, were you doing it in secret or something?"

"Something."

He smiled. "You're really quite a surprise to me, too," he said.

"Isn't that good?"

He stared at me a moment and then laughed. "I think Claudine has underestimated you. She thinks that just because you're being homeschooled, you're not very smart, but I think she's wrong. How can you be homeschooled now? Who's homeschooling you?"

"My grandmother was a teacher," I said.

"Aha. I knew it. It's like continuous home tutoring,

not that I would want that. Don't you want to go to a school where you're with other kids your age? Being homeschooled makes it hard for you to have friends, doesn't it?"

"Yes."

"Why do they want you to be homeschooled so long?"

"They wanted to avoid any trouble," I said.

"From what?"

I stopped walking. Surprised, he stopped and looked at me.

"From everything," I said. How could I tell him that my grandmother once believed that if I was permitted to attend public school, I would corrupt other little girls and bring disdain and blame on them?

"Everything?" He thought a moment. "Something terrible happened to you or your parents, and that's made them cautious?"

I shook my head.

"Well, what are they, crazy paranoids?"

I knew that word from my vocabulary list and had thought that about them myself often, but it wasn't something I dared even suggest. "I've got to get back. Sorry," I added, and turned around.

"Hey."

I paused to look back at him.

"It's supposed to be really nice tomorrow. Come to where you were yesterday by the lake, and I'll pick you up and give you a rowboat ride, okay? Can you be there?"

"Maybe."

"When?"

"After lunch."

"When's that?"

"Two o'clock." I didn't want to explain about cleaning up before I could go out.

"Long lunch. I'll be there waiting for you," he said.

I didn't say anything. Better not promise him, I thought, even though the whole idea excited me. I walked back to the house carefully. My shoes were still stained by the wet grass. After I stepped up onto the back porch, I turned and saw that he was still there, smiling.

"Be there or be square!" he shouted, cupping his hands around his mouth.

I hurried inside, afraid that he would stay there too long and my grandparents would return and see him. Luckily, they weren't here when he came. My grandmother would have heard him for sure.

Once inside, I caught my breath and then pulled off my shoes quickly. Just wiping them wasn't going to be enough, so I threw them into the clothes dryer. It worked, and I slipped them on just minutes before I heard my grandfather turn into the driveway. I went out to help them carry in the groceries.

Grandmother Myra looked me over. I could see she was anticipating some evidence of my disobeying her and walking off the back porch. Finding none, she nodded her approval at me.

"Turning out to be a nice day," Grandfather Prescott said. "Looks good for tomorrow."

I smiled to myself as I carried in two bags and

helped my grandmother put everything away. While we worked, she went on and on about a girl they had seen at the supermarket.

"Not a day older than you, I imagine, and with a ring in her nose! Where are her parents? Do you see why I'm nervous about you attending a public school? It's like the end of the world out there."

"Did you add anything to your drawing?" my grandfather asked, coming into the kitchen to get her off the subject, I imagine.

"No. It's harder not being in the woods, where I saw her."

"Tomorrow, then," he said. "When you find something good to mine in yourself, something beautiful you feel, you go at it fully. Isn't that right, Myra?" he said, deliberately, to make her comment. She just grunted, but he smiled and nodded at me.

Whenever I could during dinner preparations, I glanced out the back windows to see if Mason had returned. I feared that he would think he could come knocking on our door to see me again so he could be sure I would show up tomorrow at the lake. I didn't know what to do. I didn't want to tell him he should never do that. It would either drive him away, because he would think I didn't want him to, or cause him to see me as so strange that he'd better stay away.

Later, after dinner and cleanup, my grandparents wanted me to sit with them in the living room. I knew this meant something serious was going to be discussed. It usually turned out to be one of my grandmother's lectures about the immoral behavior young people committed these days. I anticipated that, especially fresh off seeing the girl with the ring in her nose. The way she talked about what she witnessed "out there" when she did go shopping made it seem as if there was a time once, probably when she was my age, when the devil was close to going bankrupt. People were so much better behaved.

"While we drove to and from the supermarket, your grandfather and I talked more about your attending a public school now," my grandmother began. "I'm going to speak with the administrators first myself, and then, if I'm satisfied, we'll talk more seriously about it."

"Don't worry. She'll be satisfied," my grandfather assured me. "She'll get them to make promises in blood."

She gave him one of her sharp glares, but he just held his smile. Then she turned back to me. "Your grandfather insists you'll need some new clothes, so we'll do some shopping soon to buy you what's appropriate. After that, we'll talk about how you should conduct yourself. In the beginning, I don't want you getting involved in after-school activities. You'll attend, do your work, and come right home."

"It's like getting into a hot bath," my grandfather said, smiling.

"No, it's like navigating through a swamp of poisonous snakes," she corrected. "Anyway, for now, that's our decision."

"So you're sending me to public school?"

"That's what I've been saying, missy. You're not going to turn stupid on me all of a sudden."

"No, Grandmother. I was just . . . just wanted to be sure."

"The first weeks will be a test, of course. Do you understand?"

"Yes. I'll do the best I can, Grandmother."

"You'll do better than that," she insisted. "Your mother used to wail that she was doing the best she could. I'll decide if you're doing the best you can. You can't decide that for yourself."

"Your grandmother will see if there is an art class you can take," Grandfather Prescott said. "How would you like that?"

"Very much. Thank you."

Grandmother Myra shook her head. "You can go do your work. I want you to be so far above the others when you get there that there'll be no question you had good preparation at home. You should give your room a good going over, too. It's been a while," she said. "Vacuum under the bed."

"Yes, I will," I said, and rose. Before I left the room, I turned and said, "I won't disappoint you. I won't be my mother."

Neither replied, but for a moment, I thought they looked as if my words had added years to them instantly. Surprisingly, it made me sad.

Most of my young life, from when I was capable of giving it deep thought, I wondered if I had any affection for my grandparents. From what I had read and seen whenever I did watch television with them, I knew I should feel something more than the fear of disappointing them. The weight of what had happened to my mother and the added burden of caring for a baby, then a little girl, and now a teenager was probably heavy enough for people their age, but the fact that at least half of who I was came from someone brutally evil darkened all these days, months, and years.

Sometimes I hated them for their dreadful expectations. From the moment I took my first breath until now, they, especially my grandmother, were waiting for me to prove that something sinister was inside me. I was told so many times and in so many ways that Satan was just waiting for the right moment that I found myself looking for him, especially when I did gaze at myself in the bathroom mirror. I half-expected he would be standing right behind me, smiling, his long, thin red fingers on my shoulders, burning through my clothes and into my skin.

No matter how they had treated me and how unhappy I was most of the time, I fought hard to find some way to love them. They were all I had as family. I think I worked harder, tried harder, so that I could win their love, just so I could love them in return. Their decision to permit me to attend public school was almost a graduation itself. I had passed some great test in their minds.

The satisfaction and the excitement I felt at this moment seemed suddenly to be in terrible jeopardy. Just when they were showing me how much they trusted me, I was conniving to meet secretly with Mason Spenser, a boy I hardly knew, who wasn't ashamed about being seen naked. There was no doubt that they would rescind the decision to permit me to attend public school if they found out. Was it worth the risk?

As I left them in the living room, I was thinking it wasn't and that I would not go to the lake tomorrow. For the rest of the evening, I was in a wrestling match with myself, one part of me still very excited about seeing Mason and learning more about him and his sister and another part of me forbidding it. I worked on my room until I exhausted myself, practically scrubbing every inch of it. Grandmother Myra came to my doorway and watched me for a while and then said I had done enough.

"Go to sleep," she said. "As I told you, I'm going to visit the school tomorrow to speak with the principal. I want him to understand that you are special."

What does that mean? I wondered. Would she tell him how I came to be? How would she explain I was special?

"Special?"

"I'd like him to be sure he'll have your teachers look after you a little more than they do the other students, if they do at all. If everything looks good and proper, we'll take you shopping the day after. Don't forget your prayers," she added, and left.

I had been working so hard that my body was trembling. It didn't stop until I had prepared for bed and slipped under my blanket. I heard their voices, a low murmuring from the living room, and then I heard them go up to bed. The house fell into its own silence, imperfect because of the way some of it creaked.

All the washing, polishing, and dusting of this house couldn't wipe away the shouting, the cries, and the moans with the tears that fell within it, I thought. The walls were surely marked with all of it. To me, since it had been my world for so long, it was truly a living thing. It held all the secrets, but maybe those secrets were getting to be too stressful for it. Sometimes I felt the house spoke to me. I was embraced by it the moment I was born. What it wanted was for me to be able to throw open the windows and let the fresh air wash away its scars and wounds. I was its hope.

Despite the conflict raging inside me, when I awoke, dressed, and went out to breakfast, I saw how beautiful a day it was going to be. Grandfather Prescott talked about going to buy me paint and brushes again. He was taking Grandmother Myra to meet the school principal, and then they would stop at a department store that carried everything I needed. She didn't object.

"Why don't you make yourself a sandwich and have a picnic, too?" he suggested. "We'll be gone until the afternoon."

I looked at Grandmother Myra quickly, expecting some sort of objection, but she said nothing until they were preparing to leave.

"Don't be out there later than four," she said. "We're having the Marxes over tonight, and I'm doing a roasted chicken, and I want to have homemade potato salad."

"Okay, Grandmother," I said.

Ironically, they were the ones pushing me out now.

How could I go into the woods and not be drawn to the lake? I had told Mason I wouldn't be there until two, but since Grandfather Prescott had suggested I take a picnic lunch, I could be there much earlier. How would I let Mason know?

I made myself a peanut butter and jelly sandwich and took an apple and some milk. Then I gathered my pencils and pad and left just before they did. Grandmother Myra warned me once again to be back no later than four.

"Not that I know what you could do out there all that time," she added.

"Artists lose track of time," Grandfather Prescott reminded her. He gave me his watch again and leaned over to whisper, "I'm looking into getting you your own watch. Maybe today."

"What are you two whispering about?" Grandmother Myra asked. Nothing got past her. She seemed to have ears and eyes working for her everywhere in this house. From what I was able to understand about my mother, I was positive she couldn't wait to get out every day and escape the scrutiny.

"For us to know and you to ponder," he told her.

She grunted. "I remember enough of that between you and your daughter," she said.

Whenever she referred to my mother when talking to him, she never failed to call her my grandfather's daughter, as if she had nothing to do with her. A few times, I actually wondered if that could be possible, but then thought that she was certainly not anyone who would care for a child who had no blood relationship to her. She couldn't possibly forgive my grandfather for something like that anyway. It was stupid even to think about it.

He just winked at me, and they left.

I listened to the silence for a few moments, as if I expected the house to tell me what I should and shouldn't do. I heard nothing, of course. This was one question I had to answer for myself: risk being permitted to get into the world, mixing with girls and boys my own age, become unchained and able to explore everything, or stay away from the lake and Mason and Claudine?

I still wasn't sure what I would do when I stepped out of the house. My first thought was go to the clearing, draw, and have lunch, but when I came to that point in the forest where I could make a turn and head for the lake, I paused. My interest in Mason and Claudine was too strong to ignore now that I was out there. To my surprise, when I reached the place on the shore from which I had first seen them, I saw that they were both in the rowboat, but both looked asleep, the boat gently rocking. Were they asleep or getting a suntan? I waited and watched.

Suddenly, Mason opened his eyes and turned his head in my direction, as if I had called out to him. Maybe I had. Maybe I didn't realize it. He sat up quickly and nudged Claudine. They looked at me. I wasn't going to hide myself this time. Mason seized the oars and turned the boat in my direction. Claudine sat back, her arms folded over her breasts, looking like a queen being rowed about. At least they were both dressed, I thought.

"Spying on us again?" Claudine asked as they drew closer.

"No. I . . . Mason told me to come here. I just came earlier because I brought a picnic lunch."

"A picnic lunch?" She laughed. "Now, why didn't we think of having a picnic, Mason?"

"Not a bad idea."

He maneuvered the boat as close to the shore as he could.

"Get in," he said.

I hesitated.

"We won't bite you," Claudine said. "At least, I know I won't. Mason might have another idea."

"Stop it. You'll scare her. I told you . . ."

What did he tell her?

"Oh, just get in," she said. "I'm getting hungry, too. I'll make us some sandwiches, and we'll row out to the island."

"Island? What island?"

"It's not really an island," Mason said. "It's just a large clump of land with wild grass and some trees. It's just around the turn in the lake there. C'mon," he urged.

I stood and looked back at the woods. They could never understand how hard my grandparents' house pulled on me. It was like leaving some sort of safe haven and venturing out into a world full of dangers, despite the hard childhood I had been living in it all these years.

"I've got to be home by three," I said, figuring that if I said that, I would be sure to be home by four.

"Then get a move on," Claudine said. *"Allons!"*

I started to step onto the rocks.

"Maybe you should take off your shoes and socks," Mason suggested.

I looked up quickly, as if the suggestion was shocking.

"That's right. You'll begin your strip-down slowly," Claudine teased.

"Will you stop it?" he told her.

She laughed. "Okay, okay. He's right. Take off your shoes. The water is not really that cold."

I slipped off my shoes but hesitated to take off my socks.

Claudine shook her head. "Haven't you ever gone barefoot?"

Actually, no, I wanted to say, but I didn't. I took off my socks and held them and my shoes tightly as I went over the rocks. There was no way to keep completely dry, so it was good that I had done it. They wouldn't understand, but just the feel of the water on my naked feet excited me. Mason helped me into the rowboat. It rocked so hard I thought it would turn over, and I screamed.

"Relax. We're all right. Just sit down," Mason said, laughing.

I did. Claudine immediately slipped next to me, crowding me like someone who wanted to cuddle.

"Don't you wear toenail polish?"

"No."

"Your toes need it," she said.

"They do not," Mason said. "Don't listen to her. She wishes she had your feet."

She stuck her tongue out at him, and he laughed.

"What do you have for lunch?" she asked.

"Peanut butter and jelly, milk, and an apple," I told her.

"Peanut butter? I haven't had peanut butter since I was six or seven."

"I like peanut butter," Mason said.

"So why don't you ever eat it?"

"Never think of it. Doesn't Dad like peanut butter? I bet we have some. It's healthy."

"Oh, good. Let's be healthy," she said.

He dipped the oars in and pulled hard, turning the boat around in one fluid move. Then he rowed rapidly, as if he wanted to be sure to get me away from the shore before I could change my mind.

I looked back to where I had stepped forward barefoot and suddenly felt like an astronaut stepping out into space, free from anything that had once had a hold on me. I was, however, still tethered to the ship that had brought me here, held firmly in check by an invisible umbilical cord that kept me from being fully born.

Would that happen now?

6

"C'mon," Mason said after Claudine had stepped out and tied the rowboat to the dock. He kept a hold on it to steady it. Claudine held out her hand for mine. I hesitated.

"You're not going to wait out here while I make our picnic lunch, are you?" she asked.

I glanced at Mason. He nodded, and I stood up carefully and reached for her hand.

"You can leave your stuff in the boat," Mason said, taking it all gently from me.

I stepped up the short part of the ladder and stood on the dock, looking across the water at where we had started. Standing on the dock made me recall my seeing them both naked. The memory made *me* feel naked. I embraced myself and waited for Mason to step up, too.

"My parents won't be back until late tomorrow," Mason said as we started toward their house.

"Not that they would care about us bringing you here," Claudine added.

"No, no. They're always after us to make some friends up here. We've tried."

"Tried," she emphasized as we all walked toward the summerhouse. "We went to a mall and hung out, but neither of us saw anyone we would want to know, even for a few summer months."

"Even for a few summer hours," he added, and they laughed.

"You're the first interesting person we've met," Claudine said, and surprised me by reaching back for my hand. "You must trust us and tell us all about yourself, especially how you've grown up under lock and key."

"I didn't say that she was brought up under lock and key, exactly," Mason told her.

"He made it sound clearly like that."

I looked from one to the other. "I suppose he's right," I said, surprising both of them as much as I surprised myself. After all, it was the first time I had trusted anyone other than my grandparents with anything, especially the truth.

Claudine opened the rear screen door and stepped back for me to enter first. Their summerhouse was larger than our home. It was a three-bedroom house with a large eat-in kitchen and a living room about half again as large as ours, with very modern acorn-brown leather furniture, glass tables, and a fireplace with fieldstone up to the ceiling. Mason explained that they had a basement, too, with sliding patio doors that opened to another approach on the lake.

My attention was attracted to all the paintings on the walls. They were lake scenes and scenes of mountains and valleys, some with people and some with wild animals. I wondered if I could ever paint a picture that looked as good as those. I couldn't help looking for any religious icons or pictures. There was none in the rooms I was in.

"Ham and cheese or peanut butter?" Claudine asked him.

He glanced at me and said, "Peanut butter."

"Great. We'll all return to the sixth grade," she said.

"C'mon. I'll show you the basement," Mason told me. "We have a pool table down there."

"What?"

"Pool table." He took my hand and brought me to the door for the stairway. I had heard of pool tables and seen some on television but had never seen one firsthand. We descended.

The walls of the basement were paneled in a light oak, and there was wall-to-wall matching brown carpeting, a bar with stools, and another fireplace, with almost as much furniture as I had seen in the living room. Again, there were beautiful scenic paintings but no religious icons or pictures.

"You ever play pool?"

I shook my head. I knew you had to knock a ball into a hole, but that was it. How foolish I felt. Was this the way it was going to be for me when I attended public school, feeling dumb about things everyone else took for granted? After they knew me for a while, surely they would be asking when I had landed on planet earth. Yet Mason didn't seem startled. In fact, he seemed happy to have to explain things.

"We of the upper class," he began, imitating a

stuffy Englishman, "refer to it as billiards. We have a six-pocket table here and prefer to play eight ball."

He started to describe it and then had me try to hit a ball, coming behind me to show me how to hold the pool cue properly. Putting his hands over mine, he manipulated my fingers. His lips were so close to my neck I felt his warm breath caress my skin and his body pressing gently against mine. For a moment, I thought I couldn't breathe. Then he stepped back and said, "Go on. Try it."

I did, but I only brushed the ball to the side a few inches.

"You've got to hold your hands steady and concentrate on the center of the ball," he told me, and came up behind me again, his arms over mine, his hands over my hands, his lips touching my right earlobe this time as his voice softened, and he whispered, "A little tighter. Concentrate on the ball. Forget me," he added, which was impossible.

I had never been so close to anyone, even my grandmother, and certainly not a boy. I wondered if he could feel how my heart pounded or hear how my breath quickened. A pleasant warmth flowed up around my breasts and into my neck. I had the urge to lean back into him, to close my eyes and be cradled in his arms.

"You're moving fast," we heard, and he pulled back as Claudine stepped off the stairway. The warmth in my body quickly fell away.

"She never held a pool stick," he said, in what sounded like a weak defense.

Claudine laughed. "She almost got two."

"Shut up," he told her.

"Sandwiches are ready. I put in some chocolate milk," she said. "One for you, too, Elle. Or don't you drink chocolate milk?"

I shook my head. "But I will," I said quickly, and they both laughed.

"Never chocolate milk? The forest princess, not the forest nymph," Claudine said. "Shall we? You can go out the patio doors, Mason. I'll get a blanket for us and meet you on the dock."

"Check," Mason said, and saluted while clicking his heels together.

"You idiot," she said. She looked at me suspiciously. "Are you sure you knew nothing about pool?"

"What?"

"Just get the blanket," Mason said.

She hurried up the stairs, and Mason directed me to the patio doors and took my hand.

We stepped out onto a slate walkway that would take us around the house and toward the dock. There were views of the lake from every angle, it seemed. We paused to look.

"My parents fell in love with this view and the fact that the house is on an inlet, so we're not bothered by so many motorboats and such."

"It is very pretty."

"We get great views from all the bedrooms, too."

What would he think, I wondered, if I told him I had no window in my bedroom, and the only view I had was of religious icons and statues?

"How long has your family had this house?"

"About ten years. Before this, we spent summers on Long Island and sometimes went to southern France and Italy."

"That's fantastic," I said.

He shrugged. "I was too young really to appreciate it all. I'll just have to go back."

"Will you?"

"Of course. Don't you think you will go to Europe someday?"

"I don't know."

How could I tell him that I was surprised I'd be leaving the house to go to school, much less leaving the state or the country?

"C'mon," he said. "I'm starting to get hungry."

He took my hand and led me around toward the dock. Claudine was already at the boat.

"And what took you so long?" she asked.

"Long? What was it, two minutes?"

"It's all it takes," she said. She held up something. "Brought my iPod and a speaker," she said. "So we can have some music on the island."

"Great," Mason said. He helped me down the ladder and into the rowboat. Claudine followed, and then he untied it and got in. "We're off for an adventure," he declared.

"Steady as she goes, Captain," Claudine said. She snuggled up against me again.

Mason turned the rowboat and began to row with steady, strong moves.

"He's showing off," Claudine said. "I can always tell when he does."

"Like you don't half the time," he said.

"No. More than half the time," she replied, and they both laughed.

I didn't know whether I should laugh or not. Sometimes they sounded as if they were really critical of each other but a moment later laughed about it. I hoped I would soon be able to tell the difference between real anger between them and joking.

I wondered if being twins meant they could sense each other's moods and feelings faster than other people could. Sometimes the way they anticipated each other's actions and words made me think so. It was impossible for me not to be fascinated with them.

Mason continued his steady rowing rhythm. Claudine put her hand over the side and into the water. I did the same, and we laughed.

"Doesn't it feel great?"

"Yes," I said. I felt like a newborn baby discovering all sorts of new feelings, scents, and sights.

When we made the turn, the small parcel of land in the middle of the lake came into view. Now that the lake itself was wide open to view, I saw the other boats, most motorboats and a few sailboats. Grandfather Prescott and I never went far enough to view the main part of the lake like this. I was mesmerized. In some ways, it looked like a toy world, with the boats and people small in the distance, the sunlight glittering off the water, and the hum of the motors and thin sounds of laughter rolling toward us. I took a deep breath. How wonderful it was to be out and free.

"It is beautiful, isn't it?" Claudine asked me.

"Oh yes, very beautiful."

"I can't believe you've lived here all your life and haven't been out on the lake like this."

"Her grandparents aren't spring chickens," Mason said, and winked at me.

"It's not fair to her," she replied. "What do you do all day? Act like a nursemaid in an old-age home or something?"

"I have my schoolwork, but I do help with the housework."

"I bet you do most of it," she said.

"Probably," I admitted.

"Then what? You just watch television?"

"Not that much."

"Not that much? What do you do?"

"Stop asking her that, Claudine. She does what she does. Now she's doing this," Mason said sternly.

She cupped some water and threw it at him. He ducked, and she threw some again. He dropped the oars and leaned over to sweep some water at her, which also hit me. When she squealed, I did, too.

"Get him," she told me, and then we both started to splash him. We all went at it so hard and so long that we were all quite wet when we stopped.

"Don't worry about it," Claudine said. "You'll dry fast in this sun."

Mason picked up the oars again. "Try that again, and I'll use the oars on you," he threatened.

"He would," she told me. "You got your grandfather's watch wet," she added, nodding at it.

"What? Oh."

I quickly rubbed it off with my dress. She leaned over to look at it and said it was fine.

"Unless some water got in and gets to the mechanisms later," she added. "Just put it on a rock in the sun when we land and let it bake for a while."

"Okay," I said.

"They'd be angry if they knew you were at the lake in a rowboat with us, right?" she asked, her eyes narrowing with suspicion.

"Yes," I confessed.

"What, you're not allowed to meet people?"

"Not unless they know them first."

She looked at Mason, who shook his head.

"This is getting interesting," she told him, and he rowed harder, aiming the boat at a little bit of beach so that the boat hit it hard and stopped.

"We've arrived," he said. "Our own private island in the sun."

He stood up and helped me out first and then Claudine, who handed him the blanket and their bag of lunch. After that, he pulled the boat up a little more and sat back on the sand.

"I'm exhausted," he declared, and fell back completely on the sand. Claudine took the blanket from him and snapped it out and then over him.

"Hey!" he screamed, crawling out from under. "That's no way to treat your male slave."

"I just didn't want you to get a bad sunburn."

"Right."

He helped her straighten out the blanket. I took off my grandfather's watch and put it on a large rock to the left as she had told me. Claudine sat next to Mason and nodded at the space on the other side of him. He remained lying there between the two of us, his eyes closed, his face relaxed and full of contentment as the sun began to warm us all.

"I brought some of this," Claudine said, taking a tube of sunscreen out of their bag. She squeezed out some and then, instead of putting it on her face first, leaned over and began to smear it carefully over Mason's. He didn't open his eyes, but he smiled as she gently worked the cream over and into his skin with what I thought was loving care. Then she looked up at me.

"Get his other side, will you?"

"What?"

"The cream . . . smear it on the other side of his face."

She handed me the tube. I looked down at him. He hadn't changed expression. Carefully, I squeezed out some and began to apply it the way she had. He smiled even wider. *He is very handsome,* I thought, and his skin was so smooth, even where his beard and mustache would grow.

"She's more gentle," Mason said.

"She's more frightened," Claudine told him.

I was.

"Put some on yourself, or you'll get a good burn and have to explain it to Grandma and Grandpa Paranoia."

"Who?"

"Don't," Mason said.

"Just put it on. Trust me," Claudine said, and I did. Then she did the same to her face. She leaned over to fix some on mine around my nose. "Ten minutes of pure solar bliss first," she declared, and sprawled out beside Mason. I sat for a few moments, undecided. "Relax, Elle. No one can see us out here unless they come by in a boat, and the motorboats don't because the water is too low and there are too many rocks on this side."

"She's right," Mason said. "We know the lake like the back of our . . ."

"Rear ends," she finished, and they laughed.

I laughed, too, finding some relief in that, and then lay back as she did. The three of us were very quiet. Did I ever feel more content? I could fall asleep in a heartbeat, I thought. My arm grazed Mason's. He moved his hand closer to mine and then put his fingers over it. I felt myself tighten all over and then relax.

"So tell us how it is you're living with just your grandparents. Are they your mother's or father's parents? Or are they foster parents?" Claudine asked, her eyes closed. She had unbuttoned her blouse and lowered it to get the sun on her neck and the top of her chest, right to the crests of her breasts. I realized she wasn't wearing a bra. Her breasts were so firm it wasn't easy to tell.

"Mother's," I said.

"So? Tell us more about yourself. Why are you living with grandparents? We're not going to call a newspaper or anything. Friends can ask each other questions, you know. You're free to ask us anything."

"You can believe that. She loves talking about herself," Mason said, and she poked him.

"Mr. Modesty. My mother said he cried harder than I did when we were born because he wanted everyone to know he had arrived."

"She nearly smothered me in the womb."

"Did not. Don't believe him. So? What about you?"

I didn't know how to begin. The very thought of it was terrifying, but I also realized I was going to be put in this position often at school. I had to have a way of explaining.

"My mother wasn't married when she got pregnant," I began.

"Thought so," Claudine said. "Didn't I, Mason?"

"She thought so," he said, sounding as if he was giving her credit reluctantly.

"So?" she asked.

"She was very young and didn't want to care for a child."

"What happened to her?"

"She ran off."

"Ran off? Really? Wow. Where is she?"

"I don't know. My grandparents don't like talking about her now. They took down all the pictures of her and put them in boxes."

Neither of them spoke for a moment. Had I said too much? Would they want to stop being friends?

"What about your father?" Claudine asked.

"I never met him, nor do I know his name," I said.

"Wow. This is good," she said.

I looked at her. Good? How could she say it was good? She saw the expression on my face.

"I mean, a good story, not a good thing," she clarified. Then her eyes narrowed. "Your grandparents were left with you, but they weren't happy campers, right?"

"Campers?"

"They weren't happy about it, Elle. Jeez."

"Now, now," Mason said. "A little understanding goes a long way."

"Thanks, Dad," she told him, and punched his shoulder again. He just laughed.

"No, they weren't happy about it."

She thought a moment. "I don't know how I would feel if I were you. I mean, you're unwanted."

"Damn it, Claudine. Can you be a little more subtle?"

"She doesn't mind, do you, Elle? You don't seem to me to be someone who needs to be lied to or made to pretend things are not what they are."

"I don't like lies, no," I said.

"Well, neither Mason nor I will ever lie to you. We don't lie to each other, either, right, Mason?"

"Yes. I mean no. Wait, was that a lie?"

She punched him again.

"You see how she abuses me all the time?" he asked. "Usually, I just take it, but right now . . ."

Suddenly, he spun around on her and laid himself over her. She tried to push him off, but he grabbed her wrists and pinned them back on the blanket. She kicked and squirmed, and then he really shocked me by bending over her and licking her cheeks. She cried out.

"Help me, Elle! Please. We have to stick together!" she cried.

I wasn't sure what to do, but I rose and pushed him. He cried out, seized my wrist, and fell onto his back, pulling me over onto him at the same time. Claudine sat up instantly and joined me, pushing down on his right arm. Then she took a handful of sand and sprinkled it over his face and into his hair. He cried out for mercy and let go of me. The three of us fell back on the blanket.

"Ganging up," he said, shaking the sand out of his hair. "Just like women."

"Yeah, yeah," Claudine said. "We showed him," she told me.

I sat for a moment, stunned at what I had just done. I hardly knew them, and I was rolling around on a little beach with them. Was this a sign of a real friendship, or was it very odd? How do you know when you've gone too far with someone you've just met? They didn't seem to think so.

"Let's eat," he said. "I've worked up an appetite."

Claudine opened her bag and handed me a

chocolate milk. For a few minutes, we all just ate and looked out at the water. I was still feeling quite exhilarated. Everything happened so quickly, but it was all great fun.

"So, from what you're telling us, you're really insulated. I mean, you don't have any close friends, do you?"

"No, but I think that might all change soon."

"Oh. Why?" Mason asked before she could.

"My grandparents are thinking about sending me to the public school in the fall. They're visiting with the school principal today, and if all goes well, they'll take me for some new clothes tomorrow."

"That's good. I was going to ask you if that was one of your grandmother's old dresses."

"Claudine."

"What? Is it?" she asked.

"No, but I don't have anything that looks much better."

"I have to show you my closet," she said. "If there's time later. That way, you'll have an idea of what to look for, at least."

"Maybe she has different taste from you, Claudine."

"At this point, I don't think she has any. She hasn't been given a chance to develop any," she added quickly, before he could criticize her for saying so.

"You're right," I admitted. "I mean, I've seen clothing on television, and when I am shopping with my grandparents, I see what other girls are wearing, but—"

"Your grandparents don't approve? I can imagine," she added before I could respond. She stared at me a moment and then asked, "Are they very religious?"

"Yes," I said.

"Bible thumpers," she said, nodding. "I thought so."

"Bible thumpers?"

"Let's talk about something else," Mason said. "What's your favorite subject?"

"It's not boys," Claudine commented. "My mother accuses me of that."

"Justifiably so."

"Shut up. Look who's talking. He's like a spider dangling every girl he can on a thread of hope."

"Yeah, right."

"You had five of them thinking you were going to take them to the prom last year. He had some very nice girls to choose from and ended up taking Marsha Scrotum."

"That's not her name," he said quickly. "Her name's Marsha Scroman. She happens to be the probable class valedictorian."

"Why did you call her Marsha Scrotum?" I asked Claudine.

They both just looked at me.

"You didn't get a chance to answer my question," Mason said. "What is your favorite subject?"

"Art. I saw a television show on Renoir the other night, and I saw the painting you mentioned."

"Terrific."

"Would you like to paint me?" Claudine asked. "In the nude?"

"Claudine, jeez."

"Artists always paint nudes. It's very important to their development," she explained. "Anytime you want me to pose for you, just say. Even Mason would, right, Mason?"

He shrugged. "Anything to help the cause," he said.

"Speaking of the cause, I need a dip," Claudine said. She started to undress. "I wouldn't do this if you weren't an artist," she told me.

Mason and I watched her walk into the water.

"It's wonderful," she cried after fully submerging herself. "Come on in."

Mason looked at me. "You don't have to do it," he said. "She's just being Claudine."

"Since when are you so modest, Mason?" she asked.

"We have a guest," he said. "But I'll go down to my briefs." He rose and took off his shirt and pants. Then he ran into the water, dived, and came up beside her. "It's terrific."

"C'mon in," Claudine urged.

"I can't," I said.

"Mason will cover his eyes."

"That's not it," I said. "I can't swim."

They were both quiet.

"Of course she can't," he said. "She's never been in the lake."

"She could have gone into someone's pool."

"No," I said. "Never."

"Well, it's shallow here. You can stand and get cool," Claudine said. "We'll give you swimming lessons. I'm sure Mason will be glad to do it."

"You should know how to swim. It's important," he said.

"What about towels?" I called to them.

"We'll dry in the sun," Claudine said. "You don't have to strip all the way."

I thought for a moment. My heart was pounding so fast and hard I wasn't sure I could stand, but the excitement was wonderful. I undid the buttons of my dress and slipped out of it and was in my bra and panties. To keep my hair from getting totally wet, I retied the ribbon, bringing it up more tightly. I paused. Was I really going to do this?

"What is that around your neck?" Claudine shouted. I had forgotten about my birthday present.

"Just a cross," I said.

"A cross? That looks like part of a building. It'll weigh you down and drown you for sure."

"Shut up," Mason said. "C'mon," he called, and beckoned.

I walked slowly into the water. They both stared with the same expression on their faces. I didn't know whether they were surprised, happy, or laughing beneath it all. Then Mason smiled. He looked at Claudine.

"She's got a body as nice as yours," he told her.

She said nothing. She just nodded and kept bobbing in the water. I fully submerged myself, the water coming up to my chin.

The two of them cheered.

Someplace in the back of my mind, I heard a voice whisper, "This is the baptism that will have the most effect on you."

I had never heard her voice, but I suspected that it might be my mother's.

7

Mason moved closer.

"You can get your first lesson today," he said. "I'll hold you up by placing my hands on your stomach and you start to kick your feet first and just move your arms like this." He demonstrated. "Dog paddle. We'll stay in shallow water so you won't be afraid of drowning."

"Maybe that's not what she fears," Claudine said, moving closer, too.

"You're not being helpful," he told her, and turned back to me. "Trust me," he said. "I won't take advantage of you."

Claudine moaned. "That's what he told the last girl he taught how to swim."

"Shut up," he told her. "Don't listen to her. C'mon, Elle. Just lie forward."

I looked at Claudine. She was smiling and then shrugged. "We had a professional train us, but Mason is on the school swim team," she said.

"And?" he asked her.

"And he broke the school's freestyle record."

"Thank you," he said. "Elle?"

I did what he asked, and he put his hands under me.

"Go on, lift your feet off the bottom."

"Go, girl!" Claudine cheered.

I did it.

"Start kicking."

As I kicked, he moved me slowly through the water. He told me to start pulling with my arms.

"Take good breaths, too," he said. "That's it."

Not once while I went at it did I think about the fact that a nearly naked boy was holding me up. I was too determined to succeed. A few times, he let go of me, and I started to sink, but he cried out for me to kick harder and pull at the water. I stayed up for a few moments, and then he was under me again, supporting me. We did it repeatedly until my arms began to show fatigue.

"Okay. That's enough. Good first start," he said. "You'll be swimming by the end of the week if you come every day."

I stood up. Claudine had grown bored watching us and had swum some laps. She was walking out of the water. Because Mason was so indifferent to her nudity, I tried to be, but at the same time, I found it fascinating to see how casual she was about being naked. She had a beautiful body, for sure, so she wouldn't be ashamed from that perspective, but Grandmother Myra had made such a thing of exposing even the most innocent parts of ourselves. Even now, in the midst of summer, she wore her collars high and tight and rarely wore short sleeves. Her skirts were down to her ankles, as she insisted mine must be, and if a button on my blouse came undone, she was the first to notice. I hated even to think of how she would react if she knew I had seen a girl and a boy about my age undressed more than once and then practically got naked myself.

Claudine spread out on her stomach over the blanket. The sun made her skin glitter. For the first time, I wondered if I was as pretty as she was. Was this the first sign of the narcissism that Grandmother Myra predicted could trap me? Navigating in this world outside the one I had known all my life was like stepping gingerly over ice, where thin places could give way and drop me into the cold darkness.

"Just like Claudine, you'll dry off quickly," Mason promised, seeing how I was staring at her.

I sprawled out on the blanket just the way Claudine had. Moments later, he was between us but on his back. We all just lay there quietly. The sun was so warm that I could feel my panties and my body drying quickly, just as they had said. Claudine turned on her iPod and started playing music, music I had never heard.

"I'm crazy about these guys," she said. "Do you like them, Elle?"

"I never heard them," I said.

"What? They're the most popular group today."

I turned around and sat up. "I don't have one of those things. I don't have a radio or a CD player," I told her. "Before you ask, I don't have a computer, either."

"Why not? They're so cheap these days."

"My grandmother disapproves."

She sat up as if she were on springs. "Are you serious?"

"She wouldn't be saying it if she wasn't," Mason said, still lying on his back with his eyes closed.

"Isn't that against the law or something? I've got to ask Daddy. The girl's practically in solitary confinement. How's she expect her to learn anything?"

"Don't exaggerate. People learned before computers," Mason said.

"I'm not exaggerating. It puts her at an unfair disadvantage, nevertheless, and why? Daddy would agree. Maybe he'd even contact some government agency or something and have her grandparents investigated."

"Don't start trouble," Mason told her, opening one eye. He looked at me. "Really? No radio, CD player, or computer?"

I shook my head.

"I bet you've never heard of Beyoncé or Lady Gaga . . ." She continued to rattle off singers and singing groups. "Well?"

"I've heard of some of them," I said, "but not all of them."

"You do know what this is?" she asked, showing me her iPod.

"I know about it . . . a little, but I don't know how it works, how you get the songs in there," I admitted.

"Mason, are you listening to this?" she said.

"Relax. You'll frighten her."

"Frighten her? And when the other girls see that monster cross around her neck when they're in the locker room . . . She'll be crucified when she attends public school. They'll make so much fun of her for being so out of it."

"I am afraid of that," I admitted.

"We won't let that happen," he said.

"Oh, and how do you intend to stop it, o great one?" Claudine said.

"We'll bring her up-to-date," he said. He smiled at me. "By the time we're finished with you, you'll be more sophisticated than the most sophisticated girls here, which isn't saying much about them."

"Well, that's possible," Claudine said, calming some. "At least you won't be sent into the arena with girls and guys from a school like ours." She thought a moment and nodded, her face suddenly looking bright with excitement. "This could be fun. You'll be like Audrey Hepburn in *My Fair Lady*. We'll remake you. You'll have to spend some time alone with me," she said. "I'll teach you how to talk the talk, put on makeup, dress, and then walk."

"C'mon, she can talk, and you can't teach her how to walk like you, if that's your goal."

"Ha, says you. There's just so much Mason knows about the female sex, and besides, whatever he knows is distorted through male eyes," she added, glaring at him.

"Oh, come on," he moaned. Then he looked at me and smiled again. "Actually, she's right. There's no one

I know better to teach you how to handle yourself. You'll come see us every day?"

"I'll try," I said. "I have to go shopping tomorrow, I know. If everything is all right, that is."

"Maybe afterward. We'll always keep an eye out for you."

"Can't you use a phone, or is that a form of sin or something?" Claudine asked.

"I never have," I confessed.

They both just stared, and then Mason nodded. "Makes sense. She has no girlfriends, Claudine. Who is she going to call?"

"Relatives, maybe? You know how to use a phone, right?" Claudine asked.

"Come on," Mason said.

"Mason, I don't know what to think. We've never met anyone like her, have we? She like landed from another planet."

"No, but . . ."

"But nothing. Look, Elle, we can give you our telephone number here. It's 555-2020. You can sneak a call to us whenever you want to talk or when you can't escape the nunnery."

"Nunnery?"

"It sounds like you're in one. Just call, okay?"

I nodded, but the thought of even trying to do that brought a cold chill, even in the hot sun.

"What time is it?" I asked, and reached for my grandfather's watch. "Oh. I have to go back soon. They'll be back from the school and shopping."

Mason reached up to touch my breast before I

could pull away. I would wonder later if I even wanted to. I think I was just as interested in what his touching me would do to me as he was in touching me. It was as if the tips of his fingers could send a pleasant electrical shock through my body.

"Not quite dry," he said. "But if you're nervous about getting home in time, we'll wrap it up."

My answer came practically in a whisper. "I'd better."

He rose and put on his pants and started on his shoes and socks.

Claudine groaned. "It's the best part of the day."

"You can swim and sunbathe at the dock. If she gets into trouble, she definitely won't be able to return," he said.

She looked at me and nodded and then started to dress. I put on my dress, straightened it, and put on my shoes and socks, too. Then I helped fold up the blanket.

"You didn't get much of a chance to draw," Mason said, nodding at my pad.

"My grandfather's supposed to be buying me some paints and brushes. I'll wait for that," I told him. I didn't want to reveal that I still had time to do something after he had brought me back to the shore.

"I didn't see this drawing yet," Claudine said suddenly. She waited while I opened the pad to show her. She looked just like he had when he viewed the doe. "It's very good. Mason's right. You should pursue art. My offer still stands."

"Offer?"

"To pose for you, Renoir," she said, and smiled.

She and I got back into the boat while Mason pushed it off and then leaped in, getting his shoes wet.

"You should have waited to put them on," she scolded.

"Yes, Mom."

"No cookies for you later," she said as he began to row.

"I hope you had a good time," he said.

"Oh, I did, and thanks for helping me learn to swim."

"That's just the first lesson. We'll need at least twenty or thirty more."

Claudine laughed. "Watch him. He wants to teach you everything overnight."

"Everything?"

"Well, as Claudine said, we can't let you start school with any disadvantages," he said. "Right, Claudine?"

"*Exactement, mon père,*" she said.

"Isn't *père* French for father?" I asked. I remembered that from a story.

"Yes. Don't mind her. We've been calling each other Daddy and Mommy for as long as I can remember," he explained. "Private joke."

Claudine sat back in the rowboat so she could continue to sunbathe. I watched Mason row, and he smiled at me.

"I have a feeling I'm the first to tell you," he said, "but you're very pretty, Elle. You should never let anyone make you ashamed of what you look like or how nice a body you have, even though the clothes you wear do nothing for it. I hope they buy you more fashionable things tomorrow. You'll wear them well."

The casual way he gave me the compliments took my breath away for a moment. I looked at Claudine. She had a small smile, maybe more of a small smirk, on her face.

"Thank you," I said. I waited a moment and then confessed. "And yes, you are the first to tell me."

He smiled and said nothing more; he just gazed at me and rowed as if we were all alone. Claudine looked as if she had fallen asleep and woke with a start when we reached the dock.

"Why don't you get out and take our things?" he told her. "I'll row her back to the shore."

"Why didn't you do that first?"

"I forgot," he said.

"Conveniently," she said. "I hope you had a good time, Elle. Come back to see us." She surprised me by leaning down to kiss me on the cheek. I had my eyes open the whole time and saw her close hers, and then she smiled. As soon as she was out of the boat, Mason started to turn it and row for the place on the shore where he had come for me.

"I can't get the boat onto the shore as I did on the little island," he said, and he leaped out of the rowboat when we drew close. The water was shallow, but he was up to his calves and still in his shoes. "Come on," he urged, holding out his arms. "You don't want to get those shoes wet now."

"Look what you've done to yours."

"No worries. I'll get a new pair this weekend."

I moved to the edge, and he put his right arm around my shoulders and his left under my legs to lift me and carry me like a baby to the shore. Even there, he held on to me. Our faces were only inches apart.

"Mind if I kiss you good-bye?" he asked.

Before I could answer, he brought his lips to mine and just held them softly there. I had my eyes open in surprise. He opened his and then pressed his lips more firmly to mine and moved them gently but with such authority that I felt the blood rushing to my head. When he set me down, I was just a little dizzy. He held me, smiling.

"I'm pretty sure I never gave any girl her first kiss," he said. "Unfortunately, innocence is as rare in my high school as ice in the Sahara Desert. The girls in my school think virginity is a disease."

"Really?"

I wondered if it would be the same in the public school I would attend.

"Practically," he said. "What time do you think you'll be back from shopping tomorrow?"

"I don't know. I don't even know if I'm going for sure. It depends on what happened today when my grandmother visited with the school principal."

"You could call if you want me to do anything, be anywhere. You remember the number Claudine gave you?"

I nodded, but he could see I wasn't eager to use the phone.

"Okay. Forget phones. Let's be more romantic about it."

"Romantic?"

"Sure. We need a signal," he said.

"A signal?"

"Yes, something like a light in a window." He looked at the ribbon in my hair. "I have it. Tie this ribbon or any ribbon to the top of the banister on the back porch, and I'll know you can meet here. That way, I'll look for you. Okay?"

"I'll try," I said.

"Try hard," he told me.

I nodded and started away. He watched me walk deeper into the woods. I turned, and he was still there, so I smiled and waved and then hurried through the trees. I still had a good forty-five minutes and went directly to my forest studio. My purpose was to add something to my drawing of the doe, but I decided instead to sketch the lake with some sailboats on it and clouds in the sky.

Even though I was working faster than ever, my memory of that view was so vivid that the excitement didn't detract from what I was drawing. In fact, I loved how it was coming out. By the time I checked Grandfather Prescott's watch, I had a very full, detailed drawing. I was happy with it, because it reflected how wonderful I had felt out there on the lake. For that short time, at least, I was absorbed by not only the beauty but also the sense of freedom I had experienced. It was as if a door had been opened and someone had whispered, "This is what's waiting for you. Be hopeful, Elle."

I walked quickly back to the house. As I came out of the forest, I saw Grandmother Myra standing on the back porch. She looked as if she had been there for a while and was waiting impatiently for me. My heart began to pound. All my life, she seemed capable of knowing my every thought and anticipating my every move. I was raised without any privacy, no door on my bedroom, never permitted to close the bathroom door when I showered or bathed. Because my life had been so controlled, my every activity planned and scheduled, I rarely did anything spontaneous, and if I did, it was always followed by a cross-examination about why, where I got the idea, and what I wanted.

Had she discovered I had met Mason and Claudine and gone in the rowboat? Worse, did she know what we had done?

When I saw her, I walked faster.

"You are cutting it close," she said. She held up her wrist to show me her watch. "Five minutes to four?"

"I was very involved in my drawing, Grandmother. I found a nice view of the lake and decided to do that."

She gave me that half-grunt that sounded as if she was clearing her throat.

"You'd think you would be more interested in my meeting with the school principal."

"Oh, I am. Very much, Grandmother Myra," I said, stepping up onto the porch.

She studied me a moment. "What's this, missy? Your hair," she said, and touched it. "It's wet."

"Oh, yes. It got so hot out there that I dipped my hands in the water and patted my hair and face."

"I'm not sure that water is so clean."

"It looks very clean, very clear. I could actually see small fish swimming."

"Well, I'd like you to take a hot shower anyway before helping with dinner," she said, opening the door.

I walked in quickly.

"Go into the living room," she ordered.

I went through the kitchen. Grandfather Prescott was in the living room and brightened when he saw me. There in the center of the floor was an easel, and beside it were brushes, a packet of pencils, a large drawing pad, and a tin of paints.

"The man at the store told me this would be a good start for you," he said.

"Oh, thank you, Grandfather."

I approached it and looked at the paints and the easel, where he had placed the pad.

"That folds up easily and can be carried anywhere you want to work," he said, and he pulled a book out from between himself and the chair and held it up. "This is a basic art instruction book. It tells all about mixing colors, the differences between very hard and very soft pencils, how to make basic shapes, help with shading, and especially how to establish perspective.

It's just a start. A school art class will take you further along, but at least you won't walk in totally uninformed."

"Thank you very much."

"You're welcome. I expect to get my investment back a hundred times when you start to sell paintings."

"Don't fill her head with nonsense," Grandmother Myra snapped. "You did that to Deborah, and look where that got us."

He shook his head but put the book down. Then he reached into his pocket and brought out a watch. "We got this for you," he said, handing it to me.

It had a light blue leather band and was oval-shaped.

"It's beautiful," I said. "Thank you, Grandfather."

"You're welcome, Elle. The time's set right. Give me mine back and put yours on."

I did.

"Looks very nice on her wrist, doesn't it, Myra?"

"Yes. Sit," she said, and I sat across from them.

"I'm not terribly confident in this school. The principal actually was wearing a shirt opened at the collar and no tie, with a pair of jeans," she began, and my heart started to sink with anticipated disappointment.

"It is summer, Myra," Grandfather Prescott said softly. "They can relax their dress."

"Summer or not, a man in his position has to remember that he sets an example. I asked him about a student dress code, and the sheet of information he gave me is very vague. No shorts for either boys or girls, no halters for girls, but there's no measurement for skirts. T-shirts can't have any profanity or anything suggestive, but they permit them to wear T-shirts. Don't worry. You'll dress properly. We'll go shopping for your clothes tomorrow after breakfast."

"The fall fashions are out now," Grandfather Prescott interjected.

"I'm not worried about fashion for her. I'm worried about decent appearance. Also surprising to me is that there are no restrictions on makeup. From what I read, a girl could attend looking like a clown. I want it clearly understood that you are not to borrow anyone's lipstick or put it on while there and then wash it off before coming home. That was something your mother always did. Deceit began at an early age."

I nodded.

"I wasn't going to permit you to do anything after school," she continued, "but he asked if you had a good singing voice, and I told him you did because you sing hymns with us. He suggested that you be permitted to join the chorus. He assured me that the songs you would sing were standard, some classical, in fact. They have chorus practice every Tuesday and Thursday for an hour after school; otherwise, you're to come right home."

"You know, you can walk there and back," Grandfather Prescott said.

"Of course she can. It's just a little over a mile and a half. It should never take you more than twenty minutes."

"If it's raining, I'll pick you up," Grandfather Prescott said.

"Raining, not sprinkling," she corrected. "Now, they want you to take some tests before September to confirm your math and reading skills. I've scheduled that in three weeks' time. Until then, I want you to review what I've given you every day. I won't be embarrassed by poor results."

"She'll do fine, I'm sure," Grandfather Prescott said, smiling to reassure me.

She looked at him and shook her head, as if he was to be pitied. "Your grandfather has always been one to look at the world through rose-colored glasses. I've never been one."

"And thankful for that, I am," he said. "She's kept me on an even keel."

"I know that's the truth. Well, do you have any questions?"

"No, Grandmother. Thank you."

"Don't ever let me regret it," she warned.

"I won't."

"Good. Now go take that shower."

I rose and then paused in the doorway. My fear was that I would rile up the rattlesnakes of suspicion in her head, but I thought I had an opportunity to use the gifts Grandfather Prescott had bought me.

"Do you think it will be all right for me to take my new art materials into the woods tomorrow afternoon? I'll read the instruction book all night tonight," I added, more for him.

"I don't want you neglecting your preparation for

the tests," Grandmother Myra said. My heart started to sink. "But if you review what you've been taught vigorously, I guess you might as well make use of all this. Otherwise, it would be a dreadful waste of money."

"Thank you. I promise I won't neglect my studies."

"Please, don't make promises. You sound too much like your mother when you do that," she said. "Just do what you're supposed to do."

"I will, Grandmother."

I couldn't even begin to describe the new waves of excitement that were flowing through me. Was there ever a day when I was as happy as I was at this moment? I was going to attend a real school, meet girls and boys my age, even participate in a chorus, and I was going to be able to walk to school and back, see things I'd never seen, and hear things I'd never heard.

If I hadn't met Mason and Claudine, I'd be more terrified than happy right now, but they had promised to help prepare me. I would learn things I needed to know from them. I wouldn't feel like a fool. I couldn't wait to let them know.

Now I was going to get new clothes, too. And to top it off, Grandfather Prescott had bought me all the art equipment. I knew that for most girls my age, this would all be so simple they'd barely bat an eyelash of excitement, but I couldn't think of that. I thought only of what this meant to me. It was as if the doors were beginning to open. Maybe I didn't have a knight on a white horse coming to take me away, but I was coming out from behind that window and taking steps out into the world. It was as if I had just been born, and everything before was a dream I could forget.

At least, I hoped I could.

After I showered and just before I went into the kitchen to help with dinner preparations, I slipped out the back door and tied my ribbon on the banister.

8

As always, I knew that when I was too excited about something, Grandmother Myra focused her suspicious eyes on me, but the following morning, it was very difficult to contain myself and not show excitement. She had announced when the stores would be opened, and I was constantly glancing at the clock.

"I want to go over the math you had to do this week before we go anywhere," she said. "Don't worry. The stores won't close before we leave the house."

I had done well with the math, but I was so nervous now because I knew she was scrutinizing me with microscopic lenses, pouncing on the smallest errors, as if she was hoping for some reason to abort my attending a public school. After all, she was going to have to surrender much of her control of me, and although the last thing I wanted to do was feel sorry for her, it was nearly impossible for me not to see how frightened she was. I didn't have to be a trained psychologist to understand that she blamed herself for how my mother turned out. Maybe she blamed my grandfather more, but she couldn't escape

blaming herself, too. There was never any question
that she was determined not to make the same mistakes with me.

Despite how well I was doing in their eyes now,
I never sensed that they believed that whatever evil
I had inherited from my biological father was completely destroyed. If I let down my guard and took on
even a little of what they categorized as my mother's
disrespectful and immoral behavior, that inherited evil
would be nurtured and blossom like a black rose with
thorns inside me. I would prove to be fertile soil for
that.

My grandfather was less concerned, but he was
also sensitive to my grandmother's blaming him for
having that blind eye and, as she had said, burying
his head in the sand, especially when it came to my
mother's behavior. I didn't have to eavesdrop on their
conversations to know that she was constantly warning him that I could very well be different once I was
influenced by other girls and boys my age.

"And once that happens," I did hear her tell him,
"she could be an even bigger influence on them. I
don't want to be getting phone calls from parents
and teachers warning me that she is spoiling other
children."

"You don't have to worry about that. You've done
too well with her, Myra."

His reassurance did little to comfort her. "You
don't have to worry. I worry."

Today, because we were taking a serious step toward what I saw as my entrance into the world, where

I would be free to make my own decisions and suc-
cumb to temptations, she looked more concerned than
ever. I imagined she was constantly asking herself if
she was doing the right thing in permitting me to enter
school. Had she prepared me enough? Even though
I was sure nobody my age was as aware of her every
move, her every facial expression, and every word ut-
tered as I was, I was afraid that I would mess up when
we went shopping. If I looked at some boy the wrong
way or even looked with some admiration at a girl she
thought a floozy while we were shopping, it could all
be over in the snap of a finger.

She was happy with my math review and told me
to get ready to go shopping "for appropriate school
clothing." Little did I know how difficult it was going
to be. Once we entered a department store and began
to look at what was on sale for girls my age, she nearly
turned us around and marched us out. Skirts were too
short, and material for blouses was too thin. The new
bras were invitations in neon lights for promiscuity,
and "who would approve of her daughter wearing
thong panties?"

When I tried something on and stepped out, her
eyes rolled and her lips curled into her mouth. It took
hours to settle on two dresses, two skirts, and two
blouses. To get her to agree to some of it, I had to accept sizes a little too large. What didn't help was the
other girls shopping on their own, buying and giggling
over "sexually explicit" garments.

"And adults wonder why children have gone so
wrong these days," she told my grandfather.

He kept quiet most of the time, recognizing that if he offered an opinion, she might pounce on him and hurl memories at him, especially mistakes he had approved when it came to my mother. Ironically, the more she referred to her, the more fascinated I became with her. Someday, when I was older and more independent, I would seek her out, I thought. I was growing more determined about that.

We went to the shoe department, where she had an easier time approving two pairs and some running shoes for me to have for PE class. The principal had told her about the PE uniform. She told me that she had insisted on seeing one, and when he showed it to her, she wasn't totally happy with it and told him that it was too abbreviated. He reassured her that the board of education had approved it with input from the parent-teacher organization. She contained her criticism, but she didn't change her mind.

"We'll shop for your school supplies toward the end of the summer," she told me after we bought my new shoes. She sounded as if it was still undecided whether I would attend public school.

I didn't contradict a thing she said or argue for anything that didn't meet with her immediate approval. It was almost as if it didn't matter whether or not I was present to shop for what I needed. I saw pained looks on my grandfather's face but never attempted to get him to argue with her or disagree with her decisions.

Except for my blouses and dresses being a little too large, I didn't think my clothing would draw too much ridicule. For me, despite her attitude, it was like

Christmas. So much of what I possessed before was either hand-me-downs or bought at some thrift store where someone could find older fashions. As we were leaving the mall, Grandfather Prescott saw a French beret he thought would look cute on me. I loved the idea and held my breath as she considered.

"It's the proper hat for a budding new artist, Myra," he said softly.

She didn't offer any resistance, which was as close to an approval as we could get, and he was able to buy me the beret.

"I'd like to learn French," I said afterward. Claudine seemed to know so many French words and terms. I couldn't help wanting to be more like her.

I anticipated hearing that my mother had wanted to learn a language, too, maybe even French, and how that came to naught, but Grandmother Myra said nothing. It was my grandfather who approved and made the point that I was ambitious.

"When it comes to learning, that's very good," he said, and looked at my grandmother to add, "and it's all your doing, Myra. She's been very lucky having you as her homeschool teacher."

I wondered if my grandmother could sense whenever my grandfather contrived a compliment. Lately, it always sounded as if he was placating her the way an adult might placate a child. Whether or not she knew it, she usually looked pleased. It seemed to work this time, too, and I was grateful.

However, Grandfather Prescott almost ruined my morning by suggesting that they take me to lunch. She pounced on that, sneering at the garbage they called food served at high prices. When we arrived home and he helped carry in my boxes of clothes and shoes, he nearly spoiled things again. He looked at my small bedroom and said, "Maybe it's time we moved her upstairs, Myra."

It was as if he had lit a fire under her. Her eyes widened, and her mouth fell open for a moment. "What?"

"She doesn't have proper closets, and the lighting is so poor. It's a waste not utilizing that room."

"Next thing you'll be suggesting is we get her a telephone just for her."

"Maybe. She'll make friends, I hope, and it's only natural for them to want to talk to each other. You won't want our phone tied up, not that we get many calls." It sounded clearly like a complaint. She ignored it.

"Out of the question," she said, and practically fled.

Grandfather Prescott winked. "Give her a little time," he said.

Give her a little time? I'm fifteen, I thought. I doubted that any amount of time would ever matter, but I didn't say anything. I put my new things away as best I could and then went out to help make the chicken salad she had designated for our late lunch. Grandmother Myra's critique of the way teenagers dressed and behaved in the mall dominated the conversation at the table. I didn't think she had seen all that I had.

"Did you see how many girls have those rings in their noses and that girl who had her lips pierced?" she asked me.

Of course I had. I had been gaping at them a little too long, and they started glaring at me and talking about me, which sent a sharp electric fear through me. They looked so tough and mean, with their black lipstick and nail polish and short haircuts. I was afraid they might come over to complain and my grandmother would be enraged that I had given them any attention. Fortunately, they lost interest in me.

I shook my head. "No, Grandmother. I didn't see them."

"Good. That's a good way to determine whom you should speak to and whom you shouldn't when you're in school," she said. "Any girl who wears that disgusting makeup, has a tattoo, or wears rings in her face is poison, understand?"

I nodded. "The Bible forbids tattoos," I said.

She liked that. "Of course. God doesn't want us mutilating our bodies like savages and heathens."

I was still very excited about attending public school, but every moment, it seemed she was laying down another rule, something else that was forbidden, and then describing dangers I had to understand. It was more like traversing a minefield than attending a public school. Nevertheless, I filed it all as far back in my mind as I could and kept my excitement alive, my future hopeful. A real part of why I could do that was my new friends, Mason and Claudine. Not that I had any way of judging, but I thought they must be the most sophisticated and knowledgeable people my age I could ever hope to meet.

As soon as I finished cleaning up after our lunch, I gathered my new art materials and made for the back door.

"You're to be back here by four," Grandmother Myra called from the living room.

"It's almost two-thirty, Grandmother. Can't I have until five?"

I heard my grandfather mumbling, and then she said, "Okay, five, and don't get wet again."

"I won't," I said, and hurried out before she could issue another warning or change her mind. I hadn't taken the paints. I would do a sketch first and then begin mixing and painting tomorrow. There wasn't time to do much more.

The weather had held up nicely, with a nearly cloudless cobalt-blue sky. The small clouds looked like lost children who had broken off from their parents. It was the way I felt most of the time, drifting alone. As usual, the birds began to flutter and grow noisier, as if they had been waiting for my appearance. A soft breeze lifted leaves, making it seem they were greeting me as I tracked through what was now my personal pathway. The easel was light, and I had no trouble carrying it with my new large pad and pencils.

When I arrived at the place on the lake that offered the view of Mason and Claudine's home and dock, I put everything down and unfolded the easel. Mason appeared on the dock instantly. He had been waiting for any sign of me. I saw that he was in a bathing suit and barefoot. He waved, and I waved back, and then he got into his rowboat quickly and started toward me.

"Don't you look professional now," he said as he turned the boat in. "I love you in that beret. I guess this means your grandmother has approved of your attending public school."

"Yes," I said. "For now."

"I think you should set up your easel on our lawn, where we have that full view of the lake. I'll help you with it all," he said, stepping into the water.

"I can't get even a little wet today," I told him.

"Don't worry about it. You won't." He picked up my pad and pencils. "Okay?"

"I must be back home by five," I said.

"What, do they eat early-bird specials even at home?"

"I'm afraid so," I said.

"Okay, okay. I'll make sure you're back by five."

He put my things in the boat and then took the easel carefully and set it down over the middle bench seat. After that, I took off my shoes and socks. He put them in, and then, when I started into the water, he scooped me into his arms.

"No sense taking any chances," he said. He punctuated that with a kiss on the tip of my nose and gently set me in the boat.

Before we started out, I saw that Claudine had walked onto the dock, too. She was wearing a pair of very short shorts and a blue T-shirt with something written on it. When we were closer, I saw that it read, "Free love is too expensive."

"What does her shirt mean?"

"Don't ask me. She prints them herself. My father bought her a machine that does it."

We docked, and he began to hand up my art materials to her.

"We'll set her up just outside the basement patio doors," he told her. "She has to be back by five."

"Are you going to do me?" she asked.

"No, I thought . . . a lake scene." I showed her what I had drawn quickly yesterday. "I want to make it bigger on my new pad and then begin painting it tomorrow."

"Nice, but I'm more of a challenge," she said.

"Later, Claudine," he advised. "She's definitely going to public school."

"If my grandmother doesn't change her mind," I added.

"Why would she?"

"She won't," Mason insisted. "Stop worrying."

"What sort of clothes did she buy you?" Claudine asked.

I described everything as we walked to the house.

"Ugh," she said. "Tell you what. I'll give you some of my things. We're just about the same size. You can go to school in your Amish clothes and then go into the bathroom and change into what I give you."

"I can't do that."

"Of course you can. I do it all the time. My mother forbids me to wear something, and I stuff it into my book bag and change at school. Lots of girls do it."

"Lots of girls she knows, she means," Mason said.

"Other girls aren't worth knowing," she countered, and he laughed.

He set up my easel, and I put the pad on it and opened my small pad again. The two of them sat at my feet, folding their legs and looking up at me.

"We don't make you nervous, do we?" Mason asked.

"No. Well, maybe a little."

"Good," Claudine said. "You should always be a little nervous about anything you do. That way, you'll be more cautious, especially when it comes to boys. Always begin with the belief that they can't be trusted. That way, you won't be disappointed, and if they are trustworthy, you'll feel like you've struck gold."

"She's the cynical one in the family," Mason said.

"And therefore the happiest, because I'm never disappointed."

"Please, what about Willy Landers?"

"That was an anomaly. You know what that means, Elle?"

I nodded. If I was going to be truthful, I'd have to admit my grandmother had given me an education up to this point that was as good as, if not better than, the one girls and boys my age were getting at the public school. The intensity of my work and her high standards gave me the confidence.

"Something irregular, abnormal."

"Check," Mason said. "I told you, Claudine. You're underestimating her."

"Maybe with school subjects, but your life is about

to begin, Elle. You'll find yourself spending more of your attention and time on other things."

I nodded and kept drawing. Claudine put her head on Mason's lap and sprawled out.

"Our parents will be back tonight," she said.

"Right. I'll finally get some decent dinners."

"You eat everything I make and then some," Claudine told him.

He shrugged. "Beggars can't be choosers."

"Poor you. What about you, Elle? Can you cook?"

"I can make anything my grandmother makes. I've watched her prepare often enough. Nothing you would call gourmet, I'm sure," I added.

"Our mother fancies herself a gourmet cook. She takes expensive lessons from very well-known chefs and then experiments on us."

"No one complains," Mason said.

"You'll have to come to our house for dinner one night," Claudine said.

I stopped drawing. Didn't she understand that I was sneaking out to meet them?

I saw the expression change on her face.

"You still haven't told your grandparents about meeting us, have you?" she asked.

I shook my head.

"Why not?"

I didn't know what to say, how to put it. My grandmother would never approve of my knowing a girl who swam naked and especially not a boy who did.

"How are you going to make any friends when

you go to school? She expects you'll do that, right?"

I shrugged. She still didn't understand how new all of this was for me.

"As I told you, she'd have to know who they were first," I said.

"Inspect and examine them to be sure they were wholesome, huh?"

"Yes."

"Are we wholesome, Mason?"

"Not if you can help it," he said, and she laughed.

"Then we'd be forbidden," she concluded, but then she brightened. "We'll remain forbidden. I've never been considered forbidden. I think I like it."

"I don't think your mother would like it," Mason said.

"Then let's be sure not to say anything," she warned him. "Don't worry, Elle. We'll handle it all. Why don't you take five?"

"Take five?"

"A break. I want to see how some of my clothes fit you and get a little female talk in without you-know-who eavesdropping."

"I'll die of loneliness," Mason said.

"Don't worry. We'll figure out how to resurrect you," Claudine told him, and stood. "C'mon," she urged, taking the pencil out of my hand and putting it on the easel. Then she took my hand and practically dragged me into the house.

She led me up the stairs to her room and immediately began sifting through the clothes in her closet, tossing one skirt and blouse after another onto her

very comfortable-looking king-size bed. Even Grandmother Myra and Grandfather Prescott didn't have a
king-size bed. Theirs was a queen. I knew all about
mattresses, thanks to him. I pressed down on Claudine's to see how soft or hard it was.

"Try it," she said. "It's all right."

"Really?"

"Really."

I sprawled out on it and slowly laid my head back
on her oversize marshmallow pillows. The delicious
scent of lavender swirled around me.

"What sort of bed do you have?" she asked.

"Oh. It's a single bed with a very firm mattress."
More like a board, I wanted to say, but didn't.

"I have trouble sleeping on anything smaller when
we go on trips and vacations. I have the same bed at
home in New York. Do you have a nice room, at least?"

I couldn't lie about it. "No. My room's not very
nice, Claudine. It's about half the size of this."

"I'd suffocate."

Yes, you would, I thought. "Sometimes that is the
way I feel," I confessed.

She looked at me and nodded. "Start trying some
of this on," she said, indicating the clothing she had
chosen.

"Really, I don't know how I'm going to wear any
of these things."

"Stop worrying. Once you're in school a while
and you set your eyes on some boy, you'll want to
look more enticing, Elle. Once I'm finished with you,
they'll be fighting over you."

"It won't matter," I said, and she turned around, a mixture of frustration and anger twisting her mouth and igniting her eyes.

"Why not?" She paused a moment, thinking. "You don't think you're gay, do you?"

"No, it's not that. I won't be able to go out on a date," I said. "My grandmother won't approve."

The comment froze her. Then she nodded and sat on her bed. "Can you tell me why they treat you like this? Did you once do something? I mean, I'm no angel. I've been grounded lots of times, even for a month once, but they let me come up for air after I promised to behave, which I broke, of course. As Mason says," she added, smiling, "promises are like balloons, full of air and easily punctured. So?" She continued when I didn't say anything, "We'll do it like a game. I've done this with other girlfriends who were a little shy."

"What kind of game?"

"I'll tell you a secret, and you'll tell me one. Secrets are from one to ten, ten being the most secret. You want to start with number one or number ten or in between?"

"I don't have that many secrets," I said.

She looked at me askance with a half-smile, more of a smirk. "No young man has ever sneaked over to see you before Mason did, for example?"

"Oh, no. We don't have close-by neighbors, and where would I meet him anyway?"

She looked disappointed. "You have to have something wrong with you, Elle. I'm not a complete idiot.

Why have your grandparents kept you hooked to a ball and chain until now?"

"They're afraid for me," I said.

"You mean they really are just two nutty paranoids?"

"Yes, something like that."

She stared, her eyes narrowing with her suspicions. "Talk about your parents. How old was your mother when she became pregnant with you?"

"I'm not sure."

"What?"

"I mean, she was in college at the time, but I'm not sure if she was eighteen or nineteen."

"Well, when is her birthday?" she asked. I didn't answer. "You know your own mother's birthday, don't you?"

"I'm not . . ."

"Sure. I get it. So your grandparents were so angry at her that they threw her out and forbid any mention of her. Is that the truth?"

"Sorta."

"Sorta? I think I'm getting my dental degree here," she said.

"What?"

"It feels like I'm pulling teeth. You told us your mother gave birth to you and then deserted you. Did she desert you or run away from your grandparents or what?"

"No, she didn't want to be a mother."

"I can't blame her for that. I'm not crazy about the idea. Maybe later. Much later," she said.

I was hoping that would be the end of it and she would stop asking questions, but I could see she wasn't satisfied yet.

"Your mother must have told them who made her pregnant. Was it a local guy?"

I shook my head.

"But you really do know who your father is, right? Your grandparents must have known and mentioned it. C'mon, do you really know?"

"No."

"Bummer." She thought a moment. "I think I understand. Your grandparents made your mother have you because they're religious, right?"

"Yes."

"But now they think you'll be just like her or something?"

"It wasn't all her fault," I said.

"No, but you've got to memorize how to say no," Claudine said. "The thing parents and teachers don't get or don't want to get is that we have to be educated."

"What do you mean? That's why we go to school."

"There's education, and there's education. We have to know what can happen, and you can't just get that out of books and lectures. You have to be in battle to know what war's really like. Your grandparents are making a big mistake keeping you from experiencing things. Not everyone gets pregnant."

She stood up and began to pace, like someone giving a lecture, not looking directly at me.

"I'm not saying they have to buy you birth-control

pills or anything, but they're making a mistake putting you out there unaware of the traps. I saw thc way you reacted when Mason touched your breast yesterday. You didn't know what to do. I'm not saying it was bad for him to do it. Far from that, but someone else, someone not as thoughtful as Mason, could easily take advantage of you, and whose fault would that be? I'll tell you. Your uptight grandparents'. That's whose," she said angrily. Then she smiled again.

"What?"

"When you got undressed down to your bra and panties and went into the water, you looked like a little girl unaware of anything. I could see it in your face. You didn't see how you affected Mason. He was dying."

"Dying?"

"In actual pain. You couldn't see because he was standing up to his waist." She waited a moment. "You understand what I'm saying, don't you?" She waited a moment. "It's different when he looks at me. We were brought up practically in the same crib, took baths together, and got used to each other. There was never any mystery about what was different."

She waited, but I didn't know what to say or what she meant.

"I feel like I'm talking to some extraterrestrial!" she exclaimed. "Elle, the whole time Mason was teaching you to swim, he had an erection."

I felt my heart stop and start. Grandmother Myra didn't know how much about human reproduction I had learned from the science book I had to read, or if she did, she didn't want to mention it. She never questioned me about any of it to see whether I understood it all.

"We've got a lot to talk about," Claudine said after taking a deep breath. "Mason might teach you how to swim in the lake, but I'm going to teach you how to swim in the world. Try this on," she said, throwing one of her skirts at me. "And stop looking so worried. You won't end up like your mother.

"At least, not because of me."

9

I heard the pebbles hit the window.

I had tried on six skirts, three dresses, and four blouses. Everything I put on looked wonderful to me. I could only dream of wearing clothes like this, skirts this short, blouses this tight with deep V-neck collars, and dresses that clung to my hips and bosom with thin, soft material that Grandmother Myra would call "tissue-paper clothes."

"You look better, sexier, in some of these than I do," Claudine said.

Sexier? Being sexy was akin to being totally naked in Grandmother Myra's way of thinking. I recalled her lecture about it recently.

"Why does a woman want to be sexy-looking? How many men does she want lusting after her? How can it be harmless to stir up erotic desire in a man? And don't tell me these women are shocked to discover they're doing just that when something unexpected happens, missy. They know exactly what they're doing. I fault them as much as, if not more than, the men who cross the line of decency," she said, and I wondered how much of that applied to my mother.

"Don't the teachers and administrators get angry when you wear sexy things?" I asked Claudine.

"Of course not. You can't expose yourself or anything, but they can't punish you for looking beautiful. There's nothing I'm showing you that is forbidden in my school. Of course, if you attend one of those parochial schools, you might have to wear a uniform that makes it hard to tell if you're male or female," she said, "but you're going to attend a public school, right?"

"Yes. There are no parochial schools nearby, or that might be where they'd send me."

"Lucky you. Now, let's see."

Claudine decided which ones complemented my figure the best and even gave me a bracelet and a necklace to go with one outfit. How was I to tell her that this was the first jewelry I had ever tried on, let alone hoped to wear?

"How can you give me this?" I asked, turning my wrist every which way to catch the light on the bracelet.

"It's only costume jewelry. I have tons of it."

The pebbles hit the window again.

"What's that?"

She went to the window and looked. "Two guesses." She threw the window open. "What?" she called down.

"I'm getting bored."

"We're almost done. Hold your water!" she shouted. Then she smiled at me. "I don't think five minutes went by last night without him mentioning you."

"Me?"

"Yes, you, Miss Virginal Forest Nymph. Don't tell me you're surprised. I saw him kiss you yesterday and today when he picked you up. You didn't look exactly offended."

I felt the heat rise into my face.

"Don't tell me you didn't like it," she said.

I said nothing. It wasn't easy to tell someone, especially someone who was still somewhat of a stranger, what it was I felt and didn't feel. I had grown up tightly guarding my inner thoughts and feelings, often thinking that my face was turning into a stoic mask. Grandmother Myra was just too good at picking up on a movement of my eyes, a dip in the corners of my mouth, or even a quickened breath. She immediately pounced: "What are you thinking?" I was always terrified that she would see I was lying when I replied, "Nothing, Grandmother."

"It's all right to like it, Elle. Mason is a very good-looking guy. I can't tell you how many girls at school kiss up to me to get a better shot at him."

"Kiss up?"

"You know, try to make me feel good about them by giving me compliments, doing things for me, stuff like that. I let them do it, but I don't push anyone in front of Mason. First, he likes to make up his mind himself about any girl, and I'm not recommending someone and then getting blamed for it later. We kid each other, but we don't really interfere in each other's little romances. In your case, maybe, I'd make an exception. There's nothing dishonest about you. I like that."

She stared at me a moment and then smiled.

"You look terrified. Are you?"

"No," I said, but I was frightened. She was talking so fast and making me think about things that had always been so private and deep down inside me. Yes, Mason had kissed me. Both times, it had happened so quickly and seemed so casual, so easy, that I didn't want to make a big deal of it. Of course, his first kiss excited me, but I did all I could to avoid thinking about it, especially when I was in Grandmother Myra's presence. I had come to believe that she could sniff out sexual thoughts.

The truth was that Claudine didn't know how right she was. I was more than a little frightened. I was terrified that I was opening a forbidden door, and everything my grandmother feared and even predicted was going to happen. How do you grow up thinking that of all the people you should distrust, there was no one you should distrust more than yourself?

Claudine tilted her head and smiled again. "You're fifteen but really more like a ten-year-old, aren't you?"

"I don't know," I replied. I wasn't trying to avoid the truth. I sincerely didn't know how to measure myself against other girls.

"Sure you are." She sat on her bed again. "Tell me how you felt when you saw Mason naked that day. I'm really interested. Were you shocked? Did you cover your eyes because you were afraid you might burst into flames or something? What?"

"I was surprised," I said, hoping that would be enough of an answer for her. It wasn't.

"And? C'mon. Tell me what you really felt inside." She held her hand over her breast. "Did it thrill you, stir you up? What? I can keep secrets from him. I assure you of that. Not that there are many brothers and sisters like us. There's little we don't know about each other. I'll tell you more about that when I feel I can trust you more, Elle. To get me to trust you more, you have to be honest with me. Understand?"

I nodded, but I didn't add anything to my answer. I saw how that frustrated her.

"You're not telling me everything about your mother," she said sharply and quickly. She pointed at me. "You're not lying. You're just leaving things out. Am I right? Well? Am I?"

I was about to admit it when the pebbles hit the window again.

"Oh, jeez." She looked out again. "What is it, Mason?"

"She has only an hour more!" he yelled.

"All right. All right. We're coming down. Calm your gonads. Look," she said, turning back to me. "We'll have to spend some real girlie time without him looking over our shoulders. In the meantime, I'm going to pack up all the clothes that make you look good."

"I can't take them, Claudine. Thank you, but my grandmother . . ."

"Doesn't have to know. You'll figure a way to sneak them into your house. They'll buy you some sort of bag for your books or something and you'll hide what you want to wear in that, just like I do. If you keep acting like a lamb, she'll always be a wolf. Be a little adventurous. Take some chances, Elle."

"I want to," I said. "I'm taking a big chance coming here," I pointed out.

"Oh, jeez. She might catch you talking to a girl about your age. Pardon me if I don't go ga-ga. I'm talking about real chances. All right," she said, taking a deep breath. "Go on down. I'll pack it up," she insisted. "I'll be right down."

I started out.

"Elle."

I turned back to her.

"You didn't really tell me a number ten secret, but I'll tell you one just so you know you can trust me. I was with Mason when he had his first orgasm."

She laughed and turned back to the clothes. I hurried out and down the stairs, rummaging in my memory for all the scientific facts I knew about the word. I was sure I didn't know enough. I knew the word came from the Greek *orgasmos* and was described as a sudden discharge of built-up sexual tension, but as soon as I had read those words, I shut the dictionary as if I accidentally had looked at something forbidden. I remembered growing hot with fear and looking quickly at my opened doorway to see if my grandmother happened to be peering in at me. My heart was racing, not only because that worried me but also because I had already experienced what was described. I wanted to get on my knees in front of the picture of the baby Jesus and promise never to feel it again, but if my grandmother caught me kneeling in prayer, she would surely suspect I had a reason to ask for forgiveness, and the cross-examination would begin. I just looked at the picture and whispered a prayer and then went on to other vocabulary words.

Now Claudine had resurrected all that in a brief, almost offhanded way, suggesting that it wasn't anywhere as important or dangerous as I first thought. Nevertheless, I fled from her and out of the house.

Mason looked up, smiling. "Thank goodness. I was about to finish your picture myself," he joked. Then he looked at me and stopped smiling. "What's wrong? Did Claudine say something to upset you?"

"No, no," I said.

He looked up at the window. "I told her to go slowly," he said, raising his voice. He handed me my pencil. "You want to work on this some more, right? You still have time." He sounded as if he was afraid I was going to cut my visit short.

"Yes."

"Good. Get back to work."

I returned to the picture. I could feel his eyes on me more now. I wasn't as conscious of his gaze the other times, but after what Claudine had told me, I felt I should not be so indifferent or unaware. I didn't want to be a ten-year-old at fifteen. It made me angry to think that I was.

"So, did she find clothes for you?"

"Yes, but I don't know how I can take them, Mason. My grandparents would be very angry if they knew, and they would certainly forbid me to wear any of it. I can imagine my grandmother setting fire to it all in a garbage can."

"Really? It's that bad?"

I nodded.

"Well, just take them to make Claudine happy, and then bury them in the woods or something."

"I wouldn't do that. They're very pretty things. I'm sure they're expensive."

"Probably, but don't worry about it. She didn't give you anything she would miss or couldn't replace. You'll figure it out," he said.

He watched me for a while and then sat at my feet. "I like watching you work. You have such concentration. It's as if you can see just where you're going with your drawing. Can you?"

"I think so. Yes."

"That's important for an artist."

"I'm not an artist yet," I said.

"If it's in you to be one, you are one. Was your mother artistic?"

"I don't know. I mean, my grandparents said she dabbled in it."

"I'll bet either she or your father is. Stuff like that is often inherited."

Grandmother Myra talked only about one thing we inherit, sin, but I'd rather think the way Mason was thinking.

"So . . ." he said after another few quiet minutes,

"what did my kooky sister tell you? Did she tell you anything about me?"

"Stop cross-examining her, Mason," we heard as Claudine appeared, carrying a cloth bag in which she had put the clothes. "What I told her is none of your business. Girls are supposed to have secrets."

"I knew I'd be outnumbered quickly," he said, acting hurt. Then he laughed. "Okay. I'll keep my own secrets, many about you."

"Wow. I'm shaking with fear," Claudine said. She put her arm around my shoulders and then, out of nowhere, it seemed, kissed me on the cheek before setting the bag of clothes down at my feet. "Your bracelet, earrings, and necklace are in here, too. You'll knock them dead in these."

"She ought to know," Mason said, nodding at her. "The school corridors are lined with brokenhearted boys whom she tortured and teased to death."

"I don't want to do that," I said. "I don't think it's right to do something like that." I recalled Grandmother Myra's lecture about sexy clothing.

"Thanks," Claudine told him, her face reddening. "Thanks for making me out to be a hard-ass in front of Elle."

"If the rear end fits . . ."

"Excuse me. I'm famous for breaking hearts? Shall I remind you of a girl named Shelly Stone?"

"Shut up," he said sharply.

I stopped drawing. This time, he looked very angry.

"She was an idiot offing herself over a boy."

"Offing herself?" I asked.

Mason grew more crimson than Claudine had. "I said shut up, Claudine."

She turned away. "I think I'm going for a walk," she said. "Tomorrow I'll show you how to put on makeup," she told me. "And I'll give you other things you can hide and use only when you're at school." She glared angrily once more at Mason and walked around the corner of the house.

"I hope I didn't start an argument."

"You didn't. Don't pay any attention to her. She'll get over it. She can be very moody sometimes," he said, raising his voice and looking in the direction she had taken. I looked, too, to see if she would return, but she didn't. He looked at me and shook his head. "And you don't need any makeup, Elle. You're very pretty as you are." He looked after Claudine again and really raised his voice this time. "She's got a big mouth sometimes."

"I think I had better start back," I said.

"Okay. I'll help you with everything. You did a good job of transferring your picture to the bigger paper," he added. "You're a natural artist. It comes easy to you. Don't stop."

"Thank you," I said.

He picked up the bag of clothes and helped me carry everything back to the rowboat. I looked for Claudine to say good-bye, but she still hadn't come back. He started to row us away.

"Think you might get out here a little earlier to-morrow? My parents will be here, but don't worry about them. They're great when it comes to our bringing friends around."

"I don't know," I said. "It's the day we air out things like rugs and take down curtains to wash. My grandmother even gets my grandfather to put out the small sofa on the front porch. I have to help him with that."

"Air out a sofa?"

I nodded.

"What does she do, wear a surgical mask around everyone?"

"No," I said, laughing and imagining that. Then, as if it was just something triggered inside me, I recited, "Cleanliness is next to godliness."

"Well, thanks for telling me. If I ever meet her, I'd better be sure I wash behind my ears first."

I dared not think of him ever meeting my grandmother, even though I had dreamed of just that after I had seen him in the restaurant. Could that ever happen? Was there any way I could reveal that I knew him and eventually invite him to the house? And if I did, would they like him? Or would that end even talk of my attending public school in the fall?

"Don't worry," he said, seeing the look on my face. "I won't just pop over one day and say, here I am, your granddaughter's secret boyfriend."

Boyfriend? Did he think he was that? Did I dare hope it was true?

I didn't say anything. My silence said enough. He carried me to the shore when we arrived, and I sat and put on my shoes and socks while he brought everything else off the rowboat.

"Can I walk part of the way back with you?" he asked. "I won't get too close to your grandparents' house. I understand that might not go over too well just yet."

"Okay," I said. He took the easel and the bag of clothes. "I meant it back there, Mason. I can't take that into the house. Very little gets by my grandmother."

"She sounds like she has eyes in the back of her head."

"And the sides," I said. "You might as well leave it in the boat and take it all back."

"Claudine will drive me nuts if I do that and blame it on what I said back there. We'll have a bigger argument. We'll find a place to hide it for now," he told me, and we started walking.

"Who was Shelly Stone?" I asked, then quickly added, "You don't have to tell me if you don't want to."

He was silent so long that I thought he wasn't going to tell me, but then he paused, and I stopped walking, too. He looked down for a few moments, and when he raised his head, I saw how difficult it was for him to tell me. I wished I hadn't asked.

"She was a girl who had a ridiculously mad crush on me. I wasn't at all interested in her, but she didn't stop coming at me and eventually making up things about me."

"What sort of things?"

"Telling girls things I did with her, to her. She made them all up. It got so bad that I had to confront her at school in front of other students."

"Did that stop it?"

"No. She went into a deep depression and told some of the girls that I had turned her away because she wouldn't do . . . do some kinky things with me."

"Kinky?"

"Disgusting sexual things, Elle. Of course, I would never do them. I continued to ignore her. I had dates with other girls, and then, one morning, when Claudine and I had arrived at school, we saw there was something serious going on. There were kids in a crowd talking, and when they saw us, they stopped talking."

"What happened?"

"Shelly had sliced her wrists and gone into a bath so she would bleed to death. Her parents weren't exactly on the case, either. They weren't even home when she did it, and they didn't discover her until late that night, long after it was too late. She left a note saying she couldn't live without me . . . something dramatic like that."

"Oh, how terrible."

"Hell, we were only in the ninth grade!" he cried, holding his arms up. "How could anyone get so serious? Counselors were brought into the school to talk to the other students, and my parents sent me to a therapist to be sure I didn't carry too much guilt or something. I felt sorry for her, but it wasn't my fault. Honest. I didn't do anything to lead her to believe the things she believed about me. It was all in her crazy imagination. My therapist said that with a girl in her state of mind, if it wasn't me, it would have been some other guy."

I didn't say anything, but I was thinking about the power of imagination, the good and the bad of it. So much of my life was spent in the world of my imagination. Could I do something terrible to myself, too? Was I destined to be another Shelly Stone?

"That was really mean of Claudine to bring Shelly up. We haven't mentioned her name for almost two years. My sister can be cruel sometimes, especially if she's angry or annoyed. I was just teasing her. I hope you're not upset with me."

"No," I said. "But it's a sad story."

"It is, and despite what I just said, I do feel guilty sometimes. I often wonder if there was something I could have done, maybe reported her to someone who could have helped or something. But let's not talk about it anymore. You have your own problems, and I want us to continue to be friends, close friends."

"Okay," I said, smiling.

He leaned forward and gave me a soft but quick kiss on the lips.

"You're very special, Elle. I see that. Don't think you're not, no matter what your grandparents tell you. And believe me, they're not going to be able to hold you back. You'll be spectacular."

I smiled and started walking again.

"There," he said, stopping about five hundred yards from the end of the forest and the beginning of our backyard. "We can put this satchel under those flat rocks. See the small dip in the ground? We'll put some more around it to protect it. You can visit it whenever you think you can and take what you want, if you want."

I watched him move the rocks a little and then put the sack of clothes under them, move the rocks back, and add a half dozen more.

"Should be fine there," he said.

"I can't imagine ever taking anything with me to school and doing what Claudine said, Mason."

"You never know," he said. "Claudine's right about your wearing something better. Despite how angry I am at her, I won't deny she's pretty clever when it comes to fashion. She was on the cover of a teenage fashion magazine once."

"Really?"

"Yeah. She knows how to help you with all that. Of course, I'm not encouraging you to go out and find a boyfriend just yet. Not while I'm here," he said, taking my hand.

For a few moments, he just looked at me. I wanted him to kiss me now. I didn't want it to be a surprise. I wanted to welcome it with my own kiss back. He must have seen that in my face, because he moved slowly toward me, and then we kissed and held each other for a few moments before he released me a little, but then he kissed me on the neck. I felt myself weakening in his arms.

"I can't wait to see you again, Elle," he whispered. "Don't forget to tie the ribbon on the banister whenever you think I can."

He stepped back, smiling. I straightened out my clothes, picked up my easel and pads and pencils, and started away, moving in a daze for a few feet before turning to see if he was still there watching me walk away. He was. He blew me a kiss. I thought a moment, wondering if I'd look more like that ten-year-old Claudine accused me of being, but then I blew a kiss back at him, and he laughed.

When I stepped out of the woods, I was looking down and reliving those last moments and the sincere way he had spoken to me, revealing his true feelings about what had happened with Shelly Stone. That took great trust, I thought. He did see me as someone special. My heart felt so full. I don't think I was ever happier. What surprised me the most was the new sense of self-confidence I was experiencing. If both Mason and Claudine thought I could be successful in the world out there, then surely I could. From what they had told me, they were very popular and success-ful. If I listened to Claudine and to Mason, I would be prepared.

Of course, it would be impossible not to feel what any girl felt the day she was brought to school. For the first time, she would be without the security that she enjoyed at home. Despite my harder life and strict confinement, I was still so used to it that I depended on it. So many new experiences and feelings lay ahead. Someone else, many someone elses, would have con-trol and authority over me. There would be new rules to learn, not only rules the school put down but also the rules of socializing. How could I not worry that I would stand out and look so foolish that there would be no way I wouldn't fail?

Grandmother Myra would probably be happy if I did. She would be glad if I came running home

complaining about how the other students were treating me and how I was so unhappy, that my grades
were suffering.

"You don't need to be there. We don't need any
more ridicule or embarrassment in this family, missy,"
she might say, and take me out.

Her plan might then be to send me off to some
nunnery. Claudine had joked about it, suggesting that
I already lived in a nunnery, but that possibility for
my future loomed out there for sure. Grandmother
Myra had threatened it many times. What better
way was there to guarantee that the evil within me
and the tendencies to be immoral would be stopped?
What's more, if I was forced into becoming a nun, I
wouldn't be able to fall in love and marry someone.
There would be no chance for me to have children and
pass the evil seeds on to them. In my grandmother's
mind, she would have fulfilled her responsibility. My
grandfather never supported the idea of sending me to
a nunnery, but I had no confidence in him standing in
the way, not if my grandmother insisted.

When I stopped thinking about all this and raised
my head, I stopped walking, too.

Standing on the back porch was a woman in a pair
of jeans, a light blue blouse, and a pair of large sunglasses with frames that had some sort of jewelry built
into them, glittering in the late-afternoon sunlight. She
had short, brassy-looking blond hair, and even from
this distance, I could see she wore heavy makeup.
She was smoking a cigarette and standing with what
looked like a defiant, angry posture. She looked as if

she was waiting for someone she wanted to bawl out. The back door was open, but Grandmother Myra wasn't there.

Although the woman was staring right at me, she didn't move or do anything to indicate she had seen me. I continued walking very slowly, and as I drew closer, the realization of who she was settled into my thoughts like something floating down and spreading throughout my body. Despite the makeup and the large sunglasses, she was recognizable, and the resemblance was clear enough despite the time that had passed.

No one needed to tell me who she was.

I was looking at my mother.

10

"Hi," she said, as casually as she would if we had known each other ever since the day she gave birth to me. "Mom said you would be coming home about now. She says you're very prompt, unlike me, who never knew there were hands on a clock."

She laughed. It was a short laugh, the laugh of someone who really didn't mind the criticism rained down upon her. She would snap open her umbrella of indifference, making it seem she was proud of her faults and was mocking the criticism. She pounded her cigarette on the railing and then flipped it into the yard.

I just stood there looking at her, struggling to decide how I should react. The way she was smiling at me and holding herself in a relaxed posture, her arms loosely folded over her breasts, could indicate that she was thinking that the time that had passed since she had deserted me or her indifference to my growing up all these years was nothing important. That certainly didn't help me to feel good about finally meeting her. On the other hand, perhaps she was just trying to carve away the awkwardness as quickly as she could so we could get to know each other.

"I usually help with dinner," I said, pausing at the foot of the short stairway.

"I bet. Mom never let me have an idle moment. What's that saying she chants? 'The devil finds mischief for idle hands.' God, how all those sayings still haunt me."

I couldn't help staring at the makeup on her face. Her lipstick was a shade too brightly red, I thought. When I saw behind her sunglasses, I saw she had lavender eye shadow and black mascara. I didn't notice until I was closer, but when she turned her head a little to the left, I saw a tiny silver dot in her pierced nostril.

"I'm surprised she lets you go off by yourself to draw pictures in the woods and at the lake. I used to love being at that lake," she said, nodding in its direction. "I had many great nights there. Moonlit nights," she added, with a smile that obviously drew up some passionate memories.

She seemed to be waiting for my reaction, but I was still quite in shock. Seemingly, she had just popped out of a dream. Was I imagining her? She certainly didn't look the way I always envisioned her. Would she disappear as quickly as she had appeared?

"You're very pretty, prettier than I was at your age." A tone of surprise was in her voice.

"Thank you."

"My father told me they named you Elle. Where did that come from? Is it short for Eleanor or something?"

"No. Grandmother Myra said it meant God's promise, hope. She said she and Grandfather Prescott named me that to make it easier to raise me."

"She would say something like that. They broke the mold after they made my mother."

I continued up the stairs and stopped when we were inches apart.

"Let me help you with that," she said, reaching for the easel. "You know, I used to draw, too."

"Grandfather told me."

"My mother thought it was a waste of time. She called it doodling. I'm glad she's softened." She leaned toward me and whispered, "She's still almost catatonic about seeing me, but that doesn't compare to my surprise at knowing you were here and then seeing you. I never imagined that they would keep you and raise you."

She said it so casually that I didn't know how to react or what to say. It didn't make me feel good to learn that she was surprised my grandparents hadn't put me in some orphanage and completely disowned me.

She laughed that laugh again and put her free hand on my shoulder. "Don't look so surprised at my surprise. They weren't exactly happy to learn I was pregnant, especially after they learned how I became pregnant."

My first thought was, *Is she kidding?* Not happy to know she was pregnant and the circumstances? If there was any sentence that could be an understatement, hers was it. I wanted to say, *I have just spent fifteen years having that thought driven into me, into my very soul.*

Before I could think of a response, Grandmother Myra came to the doorway. I could see the rage in her face, which probably had come when my mother appeared and remained. It had brought the blood to the surface, reddening her cheeks and inflaming her eyes. Her shoulders were hoisted like those of someone who was anticipating a blow or had just had a terrible chill draping her spine in ice. Her rage seemed to have aged her by years in minutes.

"Why are you standing out there, Elle? Are you wet again?"

"No, Grandmother."

"Then come in. As you can see, we have unexpected guests."

"Guests?" I looked at my mother.

"My husband, Carlos, is with me," she said. "We're on our honeymoon, and I thought it would be a kick to stop by and see my parents. It was a kick, all right, a kick in my rear end. As I said, I didn't know you would be here, but my mother made sure that was the first thing she told me."

My grandmother grunted and stepped back so I would follow her command.

I moved quickly through the door, my mother following.

"Put those things in your room," Grandmother Myra ordered.

I took the easel from my mother and quickly went to my room. My heart was racing. I felt the air around me was full of electricity, with thin, short streaks of lightning snapping around my face, my neck, and my shoulders. My mother, my actual mother, was here? It wasn't a dream.

"You kept her in that room?" I heard my mother ask. She and my grandmother were standing in the hallway, watching me.

"Why would that or anything else about her concern you now?" Grandmother Myra replied, and walked away.

My mother looked at me, realizing, I imagined, that there was no door on my room. She shook her head and followed Grandmother Myra.

I put everything away neatly. I turned and hurried out when I heard a man's loud laugh. They were all in the living room now. I paused in the living-room doorway. Grandfather Prescott was in his usual chair. Grandmother Myra was standing beside him, her posture straight and as firm as a soldier's. My mother had sat on the sofa next to her husband, Carlos.

He had wavy ebony hair, a caramel complexion, and strikingly blue eyes. He didn't look much taller than my mother, if at all. He was slim, in a dark blue sports jacket, a white shirt opened at the collar, and a pair of jeans, with soft-looking blue loafers and no socks. I didn't think he was terribly handsome, despite his eyes. His nose looked a little too long, and his lips dipped on the right side in an unattractive way.

Now that she was seated beside him and her appearance was a little less shocking, I took a closer look at my mother, searching for resemblances between us. We had the same eyes, but I thought my lips were fuller and my nose more diminutive. She resembled my grandfather more than my grandmother. I had no idea what sort of life she had been leading, of course, but I thought she was still very young-looking. In fact, I could easily imagine anyone who didn't know us thinking that we were sisters rather than mother and daughter.

"She's really beautiful," Carlos suddenly said, gazing at me. "Just like you, Debbie." I saw my grandmother tense up.

"This is Carlos Fuentes, my husband," my mother said. "He's a drummer in the Eduardo Casanova band. They call themselves the Lovers." She laughed. Carlos widened his smile and pretended to tap on a drum. She laughed again. "He's always doing that after someone, especially me, says something significant."

"What was so significant about that?" Grandmother Myra asked.

"Casanova? Lovers?" She waited, but Grandmother Myra didn't smile. "It happens to be a very successful band, Mom. If you watched something besides the Discovery Channel or one of those religious networks, you'd have heard of them."

"We watch other things, Deborah," my grandfather said.

"Not that I remember," she retorted. "Anyway, we're booked into Melvyn's Night Club in Atlantic City all next month. You ought to take a vacation and come see us."

"We? Us? Are you in the band, too?" Grandfather Prescott asked.

"I sing a little," she said. "You might remember that, Dad."

"Oh, I remember. Elle's going to sing in the school chorus," he told her, and looked at me proudly.

"Really?" She looked up at me. "I'm glad I passed something good on to you."

"Little else," Grandmother Myra muttered.

"Oh, I don't know about that," my mother said, winking at me.

She couldn't have said anything more damaging, as far as I was concerned. Grandmother Myra turned to me, as if she could suddenly see something evil coming to the surface. I lowered my eyes.

"Let's not fight," my mother said. "Carlos and I would like to take you three to dinner. There has to be one good restaurant around here."

"I have dinner prepared," my grandmother said.

"Oh, can't you just put it in the freezer? We're not staying in Lake Hurley tonight. We're just passing through."

"That's good," Grandmother Myra said.

"I thought you would be pleased that I asked Carlos to stop."

Grandmother Myra stared at her. "'Pleased' doesn't quite cover it, Deborah. You've been gone more than fifteen years. I'd say 'stunned' was a more appropriate word."

"Staying away and out of touch wasn't my choice, as you very well know," my mother shot back. Then she smiled again. "Let's not get into that." She turned to me and widened her smile. "I didn't expect to see my daughter here, but now that I have, I'd like to spend some time talking to her alone."

"Why?"

"Why? She's my daughter. I'd like to get to know her."

"If you hadn't stopped, you'd never have known she was here."

"I didn't expect it. I told you that. Now I know it. So now I'd like to get to know her. Can't you let up for a few moments, if not hours?"

"Take it easy," Grandfather Prescott said. "I'm sure we have enough for two more plates, Myra. We'll eat here."

My mother smiled. "Thanks, Dad. By the way, I spoke to Uncle Brett the day before yesterday. He's going to drop by when we're in Atlantic City and jam with the Lovers one night."

Grandfather Prescott nodded, almost smiling.

"He's been doing just fine," my mother added. She looked at my grandmother. "Not that you care, I know."

The way my grandmother was staring back at her would turn me to stone. It was as if she could drill her rage from her eyes and into my mother's eyes. I saw the way my mother avoided her gaze. She looked at me.

"Can we go for a little walk and talk? As I said, I'd like to get to know you."

"What for?" my grandmother asked.

"I keep saying that I never expected to find her here, Mom," she said, her lips tight. "Figure it out."

"If you called or came back, you would have known. And don't blame that all on us."

"Well, I didn't. Now I'm here. Can I talk to my daughter?"

"It's all right, Myra," Grandfather Prescott said.

"Why is it all right?"

"I'm not going to poison her mind," my mother said.

"How could you help it?" Grandmother Myra said. "I warn you. We've devoted our lives to giving her a good, moral upbringing."

"I'm sure you have, but I couldn't ruin that with one conversation, could I?" my mother countered.

"Satan had only one conversation with Eve."

My mother laughed and nodded at me, then raised her arms and looked about the house. "I wouldn't say she's living in Eden."

Grandmother Myra looked as if her face would explode.

My grandfather reached for her hand. "Don't prolong this," he told her. "It won't do either of you any good."

She shook herself like a dog shaking off water or someone who had just suffered a chill. "I'm not going to waste time debating good and evil with you, Deborah. I lost that battle long ago. I've got to prepare dinner," she said. She looked at me. "You have to set the table before you do anything with her."

I nodded.

Carlos told Grandfather Prescott that he had a very special aperitif from Mexico that he'd like to share with him.

"I'll just get it from the car," he said.

"We don't drink alcoholic beverages," Grand-mother Myra said.

"Oh, you can just taste it. You don't drink much of it before dinner," Carlos said.

She looked at Grandfather Prescott, expecting him to agree, but he didn't. "Do what you want," she snapped at him. "I have work."

She glanced at me, and we went into the kitchen. I was actually trembling with the possibility of a private conversation with my mother. It was something I often had fantasized, and here it was about to happen. I was afraid I would drop a plate or silverware when I set the table. I did it quickly and then went out to the living room. My mother had been talking to my grandfather. Carlos had gone out to the car and was still there. They looked up at me.

"Where should we walk? In the woods or on the road?"

I looked at Grandfather Prescott.

"Better just walk a little on the road, Deborah," he said.

She stood up and held out her hand. "C'mon," she said.

I looked back toward the kitchen to see if Grand-mother Myra had changed her mind and would pop out to forbid it. She didn't, so I moved quickly to take my mother's hand. We went out and paused on the front porch as Carlos was hurrying back from the car.

"I forgot we buried it under all that luggage and stuff," he said.

"Get my mother to drink some, and I'll give you a

medal," she told him. "She could sure use something to loosen her up."

He laughed and went into the house. We started toward the road.

"Which direction do you prefer?" she asked.

I remembered what Mason had told me about walking to his house and said we should go right. For a few long moments, she didn't speak. She just walked beside me, her arms folded, her head down. I was afraid that might be all we would actually do, but she finally laughed. I paused.

"Sorry," she said, "but I'm having trouble believing they kept you. Never once during these years did I ever consider that a possibility," she said, and described how they had reacted to her being pregnant.

"They were always so concerned about their reputation in the community. Mom never let Dad go to work in his factory without wearing a jacket and tie, even in the very warm months. She scrutinized every employee they had with a magnifying glass. The CIA probably doesn't check its applicants as thoroughly as my mother checked theirs. By the time I was twelve and starting to look more like a girl than a boy, I couldn't appear at the factory unless I was . . ." She raised her hands and with two fingers of each hand drew quotes in the air. "'Properly dressed.' Heaven forbid I had a button on my blouse undone. I imagine it hasn't been much different for you. Probably, it's been worse. Am I right?"

I nodded. I didn't want her to stop telling me about herself and how my grandparents were as parents.

"I swear," she said, "half the things I did, I did just to annoy her. The more she said no to something, the more I wanted to do it. Is that the way you feel?"

I shook my head.

"Don't tell me she's done a better brainwashing job on you than she did on me. Actually, I'm sure she did. They were afraid of you," she added, and described the day I was born, how they had prayed and looked at me, expecting to see some sign of Satan.

"I'm not going to lie to you," she continued as we walked. "I wanted and expected that they would arrange for an abortion. I was betting on their concern for their precious pure reputation. How could they tolerate an unmarried daughter walking about pregnant in this small town, but they solved that."

"How?"

"They practically kept me prisoner in that house," she said. She looked at me. I nodded, and she saw that was something I understood. "That's how they've kept you," she said, concluding quickly. "Do you go to school?" she asked immediately, sounding like a detective reaching a conclusion.

"Not yet. This fall."

"So she . . . what do they call it? Homeschooled you?"

"Yes."

"She got away with that this long?"

"I take periodic exams. She was a teacher. I always do well."

"I know she was a teacher. She never let me forget it. Every poor grade I brought home was like another nail in my coffin. How could I, the daughter of a teacher, be such a bad student? Don't misunderstand me. I wasn't that bad, just bad in her terms. I was better than average, good enough to get into the state university. So what do you like? I know you like art, and you sing."

"I like reading. I don't mind math, and I really like science."

She nodded. "You're more like her than I am."

"No, I'm not," I said quickly. It made her smile.

"Maybe you aren't. She's kept you from knowing who you are, I'm sure. You probably have had no chance to have a boyfriend, even secretly."

I didn't say anything, but that just widened her eyes. "Do you?"

"No," I said. I was afraid she would mention Mason at dinner. "I dream," I told her, and she laughed and nodded.

"Yes, that's what you do in my mother's house, dream, dream of getting out. I think that urge drove me more than anything to flee. I would have ended up on my face if it weren't for my uncle Brett. He took me in and got me a job on a cruise ship he was booked on with his band. Later, he got me a job in one of the dance clubs he played in, and once in a while, I sang with his band. I was married for a while, a short while, to another musician before Carlos. He had wandering eyes. Carlos is more stable. I hope."

She paused.

"You're no child, but I'll bet you don't know any more about sex than the average ten-year-old."

I felt myself blush but not with shyness, more with anger. "I know more than a ten-year-old. I read. I . . ."

"My point is, she hasn't been much help in that area, I'm sure. I don't know what kind of sex my parents had." She told me the joke about the hole in the sheet. I tried not to look astonished that she would talk about her own parents that way. "Don't worry about it," she added as we continued walking. "I'm sure you'll figure it out when you have to. It comes natural."

I paused when Mason and Claudine's summerhouse came into view. I was afraid they would see me and come out.

"Maybe we should turn back," I said.

"Okay. If I knew you were here, I would have brought you something, something decent to wear, for sure, not that she would permit it. She might even cut it up at night or something. She did that to many of the things I bought on my own. We were constantly at each other. Dad tried to referee, but he was outgunned."

I nodded and smiled, picturing what it must have been like.

"There's something about you that tells me you're going to be all right. I think you have enough of me in you to survive."

Enough of you, I thought. What about what I had of my biological father?

"Can you tell me what happened? I mean . . ."

"How I got pregnant? I'm sure she told you I was raped. I was," she added quickly. "It wasn't one of those rapes where someone breaks in and attacks you or anything. I was drugged, the famous rape drug, at a party."

"Was he ever caught?"

"No. I mean, I knew who he was. I wasn't that out of it."

"How did it happen?"

"He was one of a group of local Albany boys, Sean Barrett. His father owned a bar and restaurant on Greene Street. My girlfriends and I hung out there with him and his friends. We could get whatever we wanted to drink. I mean, they weren't even college guys. College guys were too immature for us. These guys were dangerous, cruder, but hip, if you know what I mean."

I shook my head.

"Yeah, right. How would you know? Anyway, for us, it was like playing with fire. Maybe I got too close, but that didn't give him the right to do what he did. Smile or turn your shoulder flirtatiously at a boy, and he'll think he owns you. Take my word for it. Unless," she said, smiling, "you want him to think he owns you. Nothing wrong with that.

"Anyway, I didn't even see it coming. I should have realized how deep I was in. I wasn't about to get too involved with him or any of them. I still had high hopes, not for the life my mother had planned for me but a better life. You know, fall in love with someone rich as easily as you do with someone poor or average like Sean Barrett. I didn't have a chance to fall in love anyway.

"Afterward," she continued, "I was too embarrassed about it and didn't even tell some of my closer friends. I never thought I was pregnant, so that was an even bigger shock. I was so ashamed about it that I didn't tell anyone, especially my parents. I was in denial, you see. Months passed, and I knew I was pregnant, but I wouldn't face up to it. When I started to show, I got on a bus and came home from college."

She paused and looked toward our house.

"You know how when you're a little girl, and you cut yourself or something, and you run home to Mommy or Daddy, who you expect will fix it and make you feel better and comfort you? Well, that was how I was when I stepped off that bus and walked to that house. I was coming home so my parents would make me feel better and fix it, but not my mother. It was almost as if she was waiting for something like that to happen, just so she could drive home a lesson she had been teaching me all my life. She was determined to make me pay."

"But you were drugged and then raped."

"No difference to her. I'm sure she will be the same with you if something bad happens to you. It will be your fault somehow. You put yourself in that place. If I hadn't gone to that party, if I wasn't drinking and flirting with riff-raff, bad things wouldn't happen to me. See?"

"Yes."

She brushed my hair with her left hand. "When I look at you now, I'm very happy that she wanted me to suffer."

"Do I look like him?" I asked, and held my breath.

"I don't even remember what he looked like anymore," she replied. "I see only me in your face."

She sounded just the way I had imagined her in my dream, making me feel like I was some kind of immaculate conception.

"Well, I can't make these fifteen years up to you overnight, but I promise I will stay in contact with you now. Someday we'll spend some real quality time together. When you break out of the chains and you can be on your own, you'll come to me. Not that I have accumulated great wisdom," she said. "I've knocked around, and some of what I've learned might help you survive out there. Speaking of that, has Uncle Brett been here much? He doesn't like talking about them, so I don't ask. I haven't seen him in a few years now."

"No. I've never met him," I said. "I only heard about him a few times. I saw pictures of him, but they were taken when he was much younger. I don't recall him ever calling."

"Mom's probably his most disliked person. She wouldn't welcome him and let him know it whenever she could. As I said, he helped me survive when I ran off, gave me money, helped me find work. I told him what had happened to me and what they had done. He was very angry and promised he would never tell them where I was or what I was doing." She thought a moment. "It would be just like him to keep the fact that you were living here a secret from me. He thought that would be painful for me, I'm sure."

"I don't know what to tell you about him. As I said, I don't remember them talking about him except what he was like years ago."

She thought about it a moment and then smiled. "I bet he doesn't know you're here. It would be just like my mother to make sure my father never told him."

She laughed.

"Isn't he going to be surprised? I think he went on the road at an early age to escape his family as much as for any other reason. I guess it shouldn't surprise me. Many people I know have little to do with their relatives, but I promise," she added quickly, "I'll have more to do with you. If you want me to, of course, but I can't take you with me," she quickly added. "I couldn't weigh down my new marriage with the responsibility for a teenage girl just yet. Maybe later you can come to spend some time with us."

In fantasies, I saw myself finally living with my mother, but her coldly realistic view of it was like having ice-cold water thrown on me while dreaming.

"Yes," I said, with a neutral tone in my voice.

She smiled and hugged me. "Later, when my mother cross-examines you about our conversation, you should tell her that all I did was complain about how miserable my life really is. That way, she'll feel better."

"What?"

She held her smile, and then something happened that I never expected.

We both laughed simultaneously, as if we had been best friends for years and years and knew secrets we wouldn't share with anyone else in the world.

Despite the reality she had inserted into our conversation, it was as if one of my dreams really had come true. For a few moments, at least, we were like a mother and a daughter.

But I knew that dreams pop like bubbles in the morning, and stone reality beats them down so deeply sometimes that you lose them forever.

It's like watching something precious sink in deep water. You reach frantically but can only watch helplessly as it goes into the darkness and becomes as lost as an opportunity you had failed to grasp.

Maybe all of this was already drowned and gone.

11

To my pleasant surprise, Grandfather Prescott and Carlos were laughing when we returned. Grandfather Prescott was drinking some of the aperitif Carlos had brought. Carlos stood up immediately when we entered. I could see on his face that he was looking for some indication that everything had gone all right between my mother and me. She nodded and smiled.

"Short one?" he asked her.

"You bet," she said. "And not too short."

He laughed, then looked at me, held up the bottle, and glanced at my grandfather.

"God, no," Grandfather Prescott said, looking toward the kitchen. "Perish the thought."

I was disappointed. I had never tasted anything remotely alcoholic. Grandfather Prescott shook his head at me, and I hurried into the kitchen to help Grandmother Myra. She was banging things around, slamming pots a little harder, and clanking spoons and knives as if she wanted to take the kitchen apart. She turned sharply when I appeared, her hands on her small hips.

"I suppose she filled you with a lot of garbage and told you how wonderful her life is now, how she's on the Easy Street that she never stopped believing in," she said.

"No. I mean, she's hoping to be happy with Carlos, but she had one unhappy marriage already."

"Only one?" she asked with a wry smile. "You mean only one she admitted to having. I can't imagine marriage ever being happy for her. Or for the poor soul who blindly says 'I do.'"

She paused to catch her breath, her hand over her heart. Then she put her right hand on the counter to steady herself.

"Are you all right, Grandmother?"

"No." She paused and shook her head. "I knew this day would come. I dreaded it, if you want to know the truth. It was easier to pretend she was dead."

How hard, I thought. *Does she really hate her own daughter this much? Will she come to hate me equally?*

"That girl ruined her life. She could have had a decent life, even after . . . even then. Let this be a good lesson for you. Choose your friends wisely. If you lie down with dogs, you'll wake up with fleas," she said. She took a deep breath and returned to the food. "Let's get this meal over with."

She had made a pork loin roast with sweet potatoes and broccoli.

I quickly got to work chopping up the salad, and she checked on her homemade bread. The aromas were delicious. She never intended it, for sure, but this was a wonderful welcome-home meal.

"All right. Enough. It's probably the first wholesome meal they've had in days, maybe months. Tell them dinner is ready," she said.

All three were laughing when I returned to the living room. Grandfather Prescott's glass had been refilled. My mother's was nearly empty. They stopped and looked at me as if they had forgotten what we were waiting to do.

"Grandmother says dinner is ready. We should all go into the dining room."

Grandfather Prescott's face looked a little red from drinking the aperitif. Looking quickly at the bottle, I saw that more than half had been drunk.

"Get ready. This will be an experience," my mother told Carlos. "I'd have offered to help, but I'm sure my touch would have contaminated something."

They moved to the dining room, and I returned to the kitchen to help serve the salad first and bring in a jug of cold water. In silence, everyone gathered around the table. My mother and Carlos sat across from me.

My mother looked around and shook her head. "Believe it or not, Mom, I used to dream about this room and the meals I had in it."

"You weren't much of a help," Grandmother Myra said. "I'm sure you're not much of a cook now, either."

"Sure I am. I cook up reservations," she said, laughing. Carlos smiled. "Carlos can whip up a mean enchilada. I'll give you this. You were always a good cook, Mom. 'Slave to the kitchen, slave to the house, and slave to the man I love,'" she sang. Carlos laughed again. Grandfather Prescott risked a smile.

My grandmother looked disapprovingly at him, wiping the grin off his face as quickly and roughly as she used to wipe jelly off my lips. Everyone was quiet. She brought her hands together and lowered her head to say grace. I looked at Carlos and my mother. They didn't lower their heads at first, and then Carlos did, quickly. As soon as Grandmother Myra was done, she nodded at me, and I rose and began to serve everyone the salad, just the way I did when my grandparents had their friends, the Marxes, over for dinner.

"You could get a job at any restaurant," my mother said.

"Sure could," Carlos agreed.

"I would hope her ambitions will reach a lot higher than that," Grandmother Myra said.

"Got to start somewhere, Mom."

"Not in the devil's lap," she muttered.

I served myself some salad and then poured everyone a glass of water.

"The town doesn't look much different from the last time I saw it," my mother said.

"You must be blind," Grandmother Myra told her. "Many of the older classic buildings have been torn down and replaced, and many lie fallow."

"Like I told you earlier," Grandfather Prescott said, "it's become one of those second-home communities. People from New York gobble up the properties at ridiculous prices and use them for vacation homes."

"Love to have one of those houses on the lake," Carlos said. "We got just a short view of it coming here. How big is it?"

"Two miles from end to end, with some coves, of course."

"Who bought the Nelsons' house?" my mother asked. "The one closest to ours on the lake?"

"Don't know who they are," Grandfather Prescott said. "Some city people, I'm sure."

I looked down quickly. They were talking about Mason and Claudine's summerhouse.

"I remember one summer," my mother began. My grandmother cleared her throat loudly. "I was just going to say when we all took that boat ride with the Nelsons. Even you had a good time that day, Mom."

"That was a long time ago," Grandmother Myra said. "You were still . . ."

"Innocent and pure? Yes, I was. I enjoyed my high school life here," she told Carlos. "We were a small school, but we had great basketball teams and baseball teams. Great school parties, too."

"You'd think you enjoyed the school because you had good teachers."

"I know I did, Mom. They got me through well enough to get into SUNY Albany."

"A miracle if there ever was one," Grandmother Myra said, and nodded at me to continue serving the dinner she had prepared.

I rose and went into the kitchen to get the platter of pork. After I brought that out, I brought out the sweet potatoes and the broccoli.

"Does she clean the house and wash all the clothes, too?" my mother asked, looking at me.

"Hard work keeps her out of trouble."

"What trouble can she get in living locked up?"

"You should know," my grandmother retorted. "Curfews and rules were simply things to break."

"If you hold the baby bird too tightly in your hands, you'll kill it."

"Too loosely, and it will fly into a wall."

"I feel like I'm watching a ping-pong game," Carlos said, and Grandfather Prescott surprised us all by laughing.

He fell silent in the wake of Grandmother Myra's intense glare. Then he began passing the platter of sliced pork around. My mother was smiling. Suddenly, she laughed, looking as if the aperitif had finally gone to her head.

Grandmother Myra slammed her hand on the table, making the dishes and silverware jump. "I won't stand for frivolity at my dinner table. Food is a holy blessing. That's why we are thankful for it. There's no place at my dinner table for this sort of frivolity."

"No place anywhere in your home for any frivolity, Mom."

Grandmother Myra stiffened in her chair like someone who had been kicked at the base of her spine. She nodded, with her eyes narrowing, as she turned to my mother. "You're doing just what I predicted, setting a bad example for Elle. Look at you. You look like a clown in all that makeup and that ugly thing in your nose. You haven't grown up a day since you left. You poison the very air with your breath. Well, I won't permit you to bring any immorality back into this house. It still reeks of your former sins."

My mother stopped laughing. She looked at me and pushed her seat back.

"Hey," Carlos said.

"No, Carlos. This is not going to work out. We'll both get indigestion. I thought maybe, just maybe, the years had mellowed you, Mom, but if anything, they've made you even harder." She stood up and turned to me. "You would have been luckier if they had done what they had said they were going to do, given you up for adoption. At least then, you would have had half a chance at some sort of normal life."

"Normal? Call your life normal?" Grandmother Myra retorted.

"Anything is normal compared with this. Let's go, Carlos."

"But . . ."

"Let's go. I'm sorry, Dad. For a few moments, it was almost possible."

"I wish everyone would just calm down," Grandfather Prescott said. "If we calm down, we can get along and enjoy our first meal together in a very long time."

"Enjoy?" My mother laughed again and then looked serious. "You haven't changed, either, Dad. You're still looking the other way. You should have been there for me. You both should have been there for me."

"You should have been there for yourself,"

Grandmother Myra told her, her eyes strong, steady, and full of faith in her own beliefs. Not my mother, not anyone, would shake that out of her, I thought. She'd never doubt she was right. Was that good, or was that the arrogance she warned me to watch for in myself?

"Right. Well, I hope you don't ruin her the way you ruined me," my mother said, "but I don't see how that won't happen. If she has any sense, she'll run off now while she has a chance. That's what I did, and if ever I didn't regret it, it is now. At least I'm living in a world where sex isn't a disease, where you don't have to be ashamed of your feelings and treat your period like a stab in the groin."

For a moment, it felt as if the air had been sucked out of the house. The silence made my ears ring. It was like being in the eye of a storm.

That passed, and Grandmother Myra exploded. "Get out!" she shouted, standing and pointing at the front door. "I won't permit Elle to hear any more of this filth."

"She is my daughter, Mother. You can wash her until the skin falls off, and I'll still be part of her. You can't get rid of me that easily."

I felt as if my insides were burning. She was saying all the wrong things. If anything, after she left, Grandmother Myra would be even more vigilant and afraid that evil would show its face in mine.

Carlos looked terrified now. He rose quickly. "I'm sorry, Prescott," he told my grandfather.

My mother stood there defiantly. "You think of me

as the bad one, the evil one, but when I think of what you did to me, how you treated me when I came to you in great need, I know in my heart that Christ himself would wonder how you managed to use his name and put your foot in his church."

I thought Grandmother Myra would have a heart attack right then and there. She was so overwhelmed with fury she couldn't speak. Her mouth opened and closed. My mother turned and walked out of the dining room, with Carlos right behind her. I kept my head down. Grandfather Prescott looked as if he was gazing into a bright fire. We heard the door open and close.

After a moment, Grandmother Myra sat. She drank some water. "Finish eating," she told us. "It's a sin to waste good food."

My grandfather began eating like an obedient child. I pushed my food around, wondering how I was going to get any of it down my tightened throat. Somehow, in a wakelike silence, we managed to finish what was on our plates. When I saw no one was going to eat any more, I rose and began to clear the table.

"You shouldn't have encouraged them," Grandmother Myra told my grandfather. "Sitting there and drinking that . . . that whiskey."

"It was hard for a stranger to walk into all this, Myra. I tried to make it easier."

"You shouldn't have invited them in the first place. She thinks she can just walk in here after all these years, and everything will be forgiven?"

"She is our daughter."

"Not anymore. That ended when she . . . when all this happened and she refused to accept responsibility."

"She was raped," Grandfather Prescott said. I looked up quickly. This argument had never been conducted in my presence.

"I'm talking about afterward," Grandmother Myra said. "And you know how I felt about that . . . incident. She was bound to get herself into some trouble."

Grandfather Prescott shook his head and stood up.

"You'd better go lie down," my grandmother told him.

"I'm fine."

"Fine," she spat, and rose. "You're inebriated."

"I am not, thank you."

She ignored him and looked at me. "Finish up here," she ordered.

I hurried out with the dishes and silverware. While I washed and cleaned in the kitchen, the two of them continued their argument in the living room.

"She wasn't here five minutes, and look what sort of an influence she had on that child," I heard her say.

"She's fine," Grandfather Prescott said. "There was no influence."

I held my breath, anticipating the next comment from my grandmother being why they shouldn't send me to public school, but she didn't say it, and they both quieted down, my grandmother surely quietly fuming. I made sure the kitchen was spotless, along with the dining-room table, before stepping into the living room.

Grandmother Myra looked up at me sharply. "What did she tell you out there? I want to know exactly," she said.

"She told me how difficult things were for her when she left, how Uncle Brett had helped her find work." I thought carefully for a moment and then added, "She said she could never take me to live with her. She couldn't have the responsibility for a teenage girl."

"Amen to that," Grandmother Myra said. "I don't expect this new marriage of hers will last long anyway. I don't want to talk about her anymore. Go do your reading."

I looked at Grandfather Prescott. He was huddled in his chair, looking more like a whipped puppy. He glanced at me and then looked away like someone who knew there was little more he could do. I left them and went to my room, a room that had never looked darker and more dismal. Despite the bad argument at dinner and the way my grandmother talked about my mother, I couldn't help but envy her for her freedom, the places she had been, and the things she had seen. The contrast between where I was and where she was couldn't be any starker.

And yet this was not the mother I had fantasized about. In my dreams, she was softer and more loving, even to my grandmother. Time had healed all wounds. The mother I had wanted was a mother who wanted me now more than anything, not this person who had arrived and left. This woman was still little more than a teenager. She wouldn't have fled firing warnings back at me, warnings she thought I should consider. Where did she think I would run to anyway? Did she think life on the road, scrounging for some work to survive, would be my salvation? I didn't have Uncle Brett into whose arms I could throw myself. We hadn't even met. I would be more of a stranger to him than I was now to my mother.

It's stupid to dream and to live in these fantasies, I thought. I wouldn't permit myself to do it anymore. Yes, I'd learn everything I had to learn to succeed out there, but I wouldn't follow in my mother's footsteps. She didn't even remember the face of the young man who was my father, according to her. She had blundered into some trap and refused to acknowledge the results until she could do nothing about it, especially when she was back in the grip of my grandparents.

How did you learn to love a mother who wanted you to be disposed of and forgotten, either through abortion or through the anonymous world of orphans? I was just a blip on her radar screen. Now that she knew I existed, she had to look at me, and although for a few moments I had thought we could be friends, possibly even more, I realized that was even more of a fantasy than the ones I had preferred.

I fell asleep on a bed of disappointment. My grandparents argued late into the night. I heard them mumbling in the living room and then as they climbed the stairs to their bedroom. Their voices droned on as they reviewed what had happened. I was sure they both fell asleep thinking about the daughter they once had high hopes for, a little girl not yet stained by the temptations of the real world, not yet defiant, not yet so selfish that all she could do was service her own passions.

Maybe it was better to be like Grandmother Myra when it came to my mother. Maybe it was better to think she was gone forever, someone who had streaked in like a falling star and glittered just long enough to be noticed before she disappeared in the darkness forever. I welcomed sleep like the darkness that would drown out a glaring, painful light.

After I awoke and dressed, I went about the morning chores in silence, aware that my grandmother was watching me more closely to see if meeting my mother had changed me in some detrimental way. I asked her no questions and made no more comments about my mother. Neither she nor Grandfather Prescott mentioned her, either, but every time my grandmother began to speak to me, I held my breath, anticipating something that would mean my school enrollment was far from assured. She didn't mention it.

Late in the morning, I had gone out onto the back porch and tied my ribbon on the banister. As soon as lunch was finished and my grandmother was satisfied, I went for my art equipment and supplies. My grandparents told me they were going to do some grocery shopping, and Grandfather Prescott said he needed some things from the hardware store.

"Your grandfather thinks we should try that restaurant we took you to on your birthday," Grandmother Myra said, surprising me. "Somehow, in his wild imagination, he thinks doing that will cheer me up. We'll leave about five-thirty," she said. "You can wear one of the new dresses for school, if you like."

"I will. Thank you, Grandmother," I said. I smiled at my grandfather.

"Waste of time and money," she muttered.

They left the house before I did. The silence seemed heavier. It was as if my mother's visit, her presence in the house in which she had grown up, had changed the very air in it. Her voice and her laughter were still resonating, echoing in my ears. The sound of the phone ringing startled me. I looked at it for a moment. Probably the Marxes, I thought, and lifted the receiver.

"Hello, this is Elle," I said, as I was taught to say.

"You can come live with me," she said.

"What?"

"I feel terrible about leaving you there. I'm sorry I said that it wasn't possible. Carlos is willing to take you in, too. We'll manage. Whatever, your life will be better than what you're living there. Here's my address. Write it down." She repeated it slowly. "We're spending most of the year in Atlantic City, New Jersey. You don't have to go to school if you don't want to. We can find you some work in one of the hotels or restaurants."

She paused. I said nothing.

"I expected my mother to answer the phone, not you, and I didn't expect she would let you speak to me."

"They're out shopping," I said.

"Perfect. Pack your things, and get on a bus. I'll give you some credit-card numbers, and you can call ahead for your ticket. Call me on my cell phone and tell me the schedule. Here's the number." She dictated it twice. "We'll be there to pick you up."

"I can't do that."

"Sure you can. I did it, and I wasn't all that much older than you are."

"You were," I said. "I'm only fifteen."

"I felt sick leaving you there. It brought back all my ugly memories," she said in reply.

"I'm not ready to leave," I said. "I'm going to public school this fall."

"Don't be an idiot. Get out. I can see what she's doing to you. She's turned you into a house slave and probably convinced you that you're well on the way to hell. Hell is in that house, believe me."

"I can't," I said.

"I thought you had more grit in you. I thought you were more like me."

"I'm not," I said. I said it so fast. If I had thought first, I might not have said it so bluntly.

"I see. Well, you have my cell-phone number. Call me when you wake up. I have to go. I won't call you again," she warned. "I'm surprised I did, but as I said, I felt bad for you."

Do you? I thought. *Why didn't you feel bad for me the day I was born? A month later, a year? Why didn't you ever call to see what they really had done with me?*

I hated how hard and cruel Grandmother Myra could be sometimes. I hated the fear of evil she had embedded in my very soul, how she had made me doubt my own self-worth so many times, and what she had prevented me from enjoying, but I didn't think she was so terribly wrong about my mother now. I would fulfill the prophecy if I went off to be with this woman who had come bursting into my life and gone bursting out of it with lightning speed. Grandmother Myra wasn't wrong.

"Thank you," I said. "I appreciate your calling."

"Christ, you even sound like her," she said. "Good luck."

She hung up.

I held the receiver for almost a minute, rehearing every word of our conversation. Then I hung it up slowly. I was trembling, because I thought she might be right. I should be packing and running.

But then my thoughts shifted to my picture and the lake and Mason.

There were other ways to escape, I concluded. I gathered my things again and hurried out into the woods to follow my path, looking back occasionally as I went. I was more like someone fleeing than someone rushing toward someplace or someone she wanted to see.

My mother was right about one thing.

I wasn't living in the Garden of Eden.

But I'd be a fool not to realize that Satan had moved on to other gardens.

12

"I've got most of the afternoon," I said as Mason guided the rowboat to the shore. He wore a pair of white shorts and a light blue tank top, and he was barefoot. He got out of the boat to load my art equipment and supplies. "There's no dinner preparations. Tonight we're going to the restaurant where I first saw you."

"Oh, what's the occasion?"

I didn't want to get into my mother's unexpected visit.

"No occasion. My grandfather talked my grandmother into doing it."

He smiled and put his arm around my waist, kissed me softly on the lips, and lifted me comfortably into his arms. He didn't move.

"Claudine can put all the makeup in the world on and teach you how to use it, but it won't matter. You're a naturally beautiful girl, Elle. I can't get tired of saying it."

"I don't really want to put on a lot of makeup anyway," I said, recalling how made-up my mother was.

"Good." He kissed me again and set me softly in

the rowboat. "You've got to meet my parents. They know I came to get you."

He saw the look of concern on my face.

"Don't worry. They are cool parents."

It occurred to me as he started rowing back to the dock that I had never met any parents of anyone my age. What did "cool parents" mean? Understanding? Loving? Considerate? As wild as my mother? I didn't have to wait long to find out.

As we pulled up to the dock, Mason's father came walking quickly toward us. He was in bright red swimming trunks and a pair of black sandals. He looked as if he had been in the sun for months.

"Well, well, so this is the forest princess," he said, and Mason laughed. Mason's father reached down to help me out of the boat. As soon as I took his hand, he lifted me onto the dock, gazing into my face with a small smile on his. "I can see why you've captured Mason's heart so quickly. I'm Mason's father. You can call me Doug. Elle, is it?"

I nodded. I could barely speak. No grown man, not even my grandfather, ever had held me so closely. He released me and stepped back.

"What's with the easel?"

"Elle draws and paints, Dad. I told you."

"Right, right. You want to unload all that?"

"No. We're planning on going to our island soon, and she'll work there."

"Fine. So you're an artist, too," Doug Spenser said.

"I'm just learning."

"She's a natural," Mason told him.

"Best kind," his father said. "Mason says you live in that quaint house just south of us. With your grandparents?"

"Yes."

"Well, aren't they lucky? My parents and Mona's rarely see Mason and Claudine."

"That's not our fault, Dad."

His father laughed. What did Mason mean? His parents kept them from seeing their grandparents?

"C'mon," he said. "Before you get too involved, you have to meet Mona. She's giving herself a facial, so don't be frightened."

Mason took my hand, and we followed his father back toward the house. Claudine stepped out through the patio door. She was in a brief orange bikini and had her hair in curlers.

"Ahhhh!" Doug Spenser cried, holding up his arms in front of his face. "A creature from the lagoon."

"Very funny, Daddy boy," Claudine said. "Hi, Elle."

"Hi."

"We're having shrimp on the barbie for dinner if you can stay," Doug Spenser said. "My specialty."

"Your only specialty," Claudine told him.

"Her grandparents are taking her out to eat tonight," Mason told him.

"Ah. Well, maybe there'll be another chance for me to impress you with my culinary skills."

"What culinary skills?" Claudine said.

Doug Spenser pretended he was getting heart failure because of her remark. He put both hands on his chest and moaned. "What an unkind cut."

Then he walked up to Claudine and slapped her playfully on the rear.

"C'mon, Elle," he said. "Meet the woman who gave birth to these creatures."

He walked into the house.

I looked at Mason. He was smiling, and so was Claudine. The informality, the loose way they treated and spoke to each other, was shocking. I couldn't imagine ever talking like this with my grandparents. Doug Spenser was behaving more the way I imagined one of their high school friends behaved, not their father. Was that what Mason meant by "cool"?

He smiled. "We'll get all this over with and have another great afternoon at the island."

"Am I included?" Claudine asked.

"Does it snow in Norway?"

"You need to do something with your hair," she told me, ignoring him. "Would your grandmother permit you to have it done? Mom is a big deal at the local salon. She can get you in anytime."

I shook my head, hoping I didn't look as terrified as I felt at the very suggestion.

"We'll figure it out," Claudine told me, and we all went into the house.

Their mother was lying in a chaise longue in the center of the living room, her face covered in white cream, with two slices of cucumber over her eyes. She had her hair pinned up and was wearing a terry-cloth robe. It was a sight I had never seen, not even on television when I was permitted to watch.

"Someone here?" she asked.

"Just us mere mortals," Doug Spenser said. "And the forest princess."

Mona Spenser slowly lifted the slices of cucumber off her eyes and looked at me. She didn't speak for a moment. Then she put the slices back over her eyes.

"I hate youth," she said.

Doug Spenser laughed. "Don't worry. She doesn't mean anything personal by it, Elle. She saw some new wrinkles today when she looked in the mirror. It's upset her."

"Very funny," Mona Spenser said. "Men don't suffer with wrinkles. Everyone thinks that's distinguished." She took the slices off her eyes again. "Aren't you a pretty young thing," she said. "What grade are you in?"

"I will go into the eleventh grade this fall," I said.

"Don't be in a rush to get older. It's nowhere near what it's cracked up to be. Tweedledee and Tweedledum here can't wait to be twenty-one. Youth is truly wasted on the young."

"Nice one, Mom," Mason said.

"Please, spare us," Claudine said.

"Whatever," their mother replied. She smiled at me and put her cucumber slices on again. "It's very nice to meet you, Elle."

Doug Spenser put his finger to his lips and very quietly walked behind his wife. Then he leaned over and quickly drew an X through the cream on her forehead.

She sat up instantly, catching the slices of cucumber that popped off her eyes.

"You beast!" she cried, and threw the cucumber slices at him. He laughed.

"Children," Claudine said. "Ignore them. C'mon up to my room for a few minutes, Elle. I'll take out my curlers and brush out my hair."

"We'd like to get to the island, Claudine," Mason said. "I want to set her up."

"I bet," she replied. She seized my hand and pulled me along. I heard Doug Spenser's laugh.

We hurried up the stairs to Claudine's room, and she flopped onto the chair by her vanity mirror.

"I wish you knew some boys here," she said. "I haven't had any luck finding any worth a second look when we've gone to the mall or into the village. Didn't you ever think about that? You don't look like you matured overnight. I bet you've had your period since you were eleven or something."

"Not long after," I said.

"So?"

"I thought about it."

"And?"

"What could I do about it?"

"You never went into town on your own or spent any time at the mall?"

"No."

"Why not?" She thought a moment while I pondered how to answer. "Maybe it wasn't so much of a joke when I kidded you about living in a nunnery."

"My grandmother was very upset about my mother and tries hard to make sure I won't be like her," I offered as she worked on her hair.

"Tell me more about her, your mother, besides her

becoming pregnant and running off after you were born, I mean."

"I don't know a lot about her. My grandmother doesn't like to talk about her."

"She's the unmentionable. They say nothing about her? Really?"

"Not anything nice. They don't even have pictures of her displayed anymore."

"That's radical. She never called to see about you all these years, never came back once?"

I started to shake my head and stopped, my gaze dropping to the floor. She spun around on her chair.

"What? Tell me, for God's sake."

"You shouldn't use the name of God in vain," I told her.

"What?" She shook her head. "Forget that. Tell me what you're not telling me. I'm trying to be your best friend, Elle. Your only friend, apparently."

"My mother surprised us all yesterday. She showed up with a new husband."

"And how long was she away?"

"Since I was born."

"Christ!"

"You shouldn't . . ."

"What happened? Don't leave out a detail."

"Hey!" we heard Mason scream from the bottom of the stairway. "We're losing the best part of the afternoon."

"Hold that thought," Claudine said, fluffing her hair a little and then getting up quickly to grab a small bag. "We'll talk on the island."

I went downstairs with her. Doug Spenser was sprawled on the sofa, eating an apple and reading some typed pages that I imagined were a lawyer's brief. Mona Spenser was still in her chaise longue, a new pair of cucumber slices over her eyes.

"You looked better with the curlers on," Mason joked.

"You look better with a bag over your head."

"Children," Doug Spenser said, not shifting his eyes from his pages. "You have a guest. Pretend you're civilized, otherwise we'll get a reputation and be driven out of town by the chamber of commerce."

"Right, let's let you get to your art," Mason said.

Mona lifted the cucumber slices from her eyes and looked at us. "Don't do anything I wouldn't do."

Doug laughed. "That leaves them far too much."

She started to throw another slice at him, and he put up his hands. "We'll run out of cucumbers!" he cried.

Mason and Claudine laughed. It made me smile. Were my grandparents ever that playful with each other? Were they ever that young? In my mind, they were born old.

"See what I mean about them?" Mason said as we walked out to the dock. "Cool."

"Embarrassing," Claudine added. "Imagine bringing a boy home to meet them and have that sort of thing go on, and you'll appreciate what I have to go through."

"Usually, she doesn't bother bringing them home," Mason said.

"Why waste time sightseeing?" she told me. I had no idea what she meant, but Mason laughed.

"One thing about Claudine. She's turned foreplay into one play."

"Look who's talking. Mr. Wham Bam, Thank You, Ma'am."

"What?" I asked, and they laughed.

"Some guys," Claudine explained as we reached the end of the dock, "have only one thing in mind. When they satisfy that, they couldn't care less about you. That's the challenge."

"I'm not that kind," Mason said. "But I have met girls who were like that."

"You mean you've looked for girls who were like that."

"Will you stop?" he said, his voice a little testy. She winked at me, and we all got into the rowboat.

"You want to row?" Mason asked Claudine.

"No. I'm not in the mood."

"I'll row," I said. I never had. "You'll have to show me how, though."

"No problem." He patted the seat he was on and went back behind it on his knees.

I sat and took the oars.

"Don't dip them too deeply, and it won't be so hard," he told me, putting his hands over mine and pressing himself against my back. His lips were caressing my neck.

"It's all right to do it with Mason," Claudine advised, "but don't let any other boy get so close to you so quickly. Before you know it, they'll make you aware they have a pencil in their pocket."

"What?"

"An erection. I told you about that, and you know who's had one recently," she said. Then she laughed. "You look sunburned already."

"Don't pick on her," Mason warned.

"I'm not doing the picking."

"Can you shut up for a few minutes? Okay, dip and pull evenly when you're going straight out. When you want to turn left, pull only with the right oar, and vice versa for turning right, okay?"

I nodded and began to row. A few times, the oar came up out of the water, and Claudine screamed because she was splashed.

"Sorry."

"She's wearing a bathing suit," Mason said. "No 'sorry' necessary."

"I'll decide when and where I get wet, thank you," Claudine said. "I don't want to get my hair wet. I just washed and set it."

"I'm sorry," I said.

"It's all right," she told me. She reached into her bag and pulled out a bathing cap. As she put it on, she said, "What if we cut your hair a little bit each day? I can style it, and one day, you'll look great."

"She looks great now."

"My grandmother doesn't want me to cut my hair any shorter," I said.

"We could buy you a wig or inserts. What do you think, Mason?"

"If it's not broke, don't fix it. She's not broke," he said.

"What a bore he can be."

"Let me land us," Mason said as we drew closer to their little island.

I shifted back to my seat, and he rowed us onto the beach. He got out quickly and pulled the boat farther up on the sand.

"Hand it all to me, and I'll set you up wherever you want," he said.

Claudine simply rolled herself over the side of the boat and fell into the water, holding on to the boat to keep herself up. Then she reached over for her bag and walked to the place on the shore where we had last been.

"I left a blanket in the boat," she called to me as Mason began unloading my easel and my art supplies. I handed it to her.

I got out carefully and walked to shore. She spread out the blanket.

"Here good?" Mason asked, unfolding my easel. I looked out at the lake. It was the view I had drawn.

"Yes, thank you," I said. I began to set things up. Mason watched me, smiling. He looked at Claudine. She was putting on sunscreen. She threw it to him, and he offered it to me.

"For your face."

I nodded, but he opened the jar and began to smear it over my forehead, cheeks, and nose.

"You have a perfect little nose," he said. "And perfect lips."

"And perfect arms and legs and stomach and ass, not to mention boobs," Claudine added. She was lying back, her eyes closed.

"'O, beware, my lord, of jealousy; it is the green-eyed monster which doth mock the meat it feeds on,'" Mason told her.

"Ha, ha. I'm not jealous," she said. "I don't think I have to be jealous."

"Ah, the blush of modesty."

"Stop showing off," she said. "He thinks he's a big deal because he got a few As in English literature. Shakespeare."

"I read *Julius Caesar,*" I said.

"Whoop-dee-do."

"Hey. She's technically only in the tenth grade, Claudine. You aren't exactly a scholar yet."

"Neither are you."

He glared at her with a face of anger I hadn't seen. Was I causing them to have a real fight?

"I'm sorry," I said, because I didn't know what else to say.

They looked at me.

"It's not your fault," Mason said.

"Oh, please, you're oozing," Claudine said. I looked at her again. Why was she getting so upset with how nice he was being to me? She lay back again.

"You need a little water," Mason said, and he put some in the place for it on my tin of watercolors. I spread out my drawing of the lake on the easel. "I'll let you do some work," he told me, and went to lie down beside Claudine. He smeared some of the sunblock on his face, and they were both very quiet while I mixed colors and began to paint on my drawing.

After about five minutes, Claudine sat up, unfastened

the top of her bikini, and lay back again. I tried not to look. Mason glanced at her, then sat up and looked out at the lake. He caught my gaze.

"Women go topless all the time in France," he said. "When we were in southern France last year, my mother went topless."

I didn't say anything, but just the thought of being with your mother when she was topless shocked me.

"You're shocking her, Mason," Claudine said, seeing the look on my face. "I don't think Mason fully appreciates how cloistered you've been and still are."

I kept painting, but it felt as if bees were buzzing just behind my ears.

"Stop trying to make her out to be someone weird, Claudine."

"She is weird. She'll tell you that herself, won't you, Elle?"

I turned to look at her. She was still on her back, her eyes closed. "Weird?"

She opened her eyes. "How else would you describe someone who's lived like you have up to now? I was just joking about her being under lock and key before, Mason, but she'll tell you. That's exactly how she's been treated. We have a lot of work to do to prepare her for the real world. Your taking advantage of her is not going to help."

"I'm not taking advantage of her."

"Please. Every boy welcomes every opportunity to take advantage of you, Elle," she said. "Mason is very nice, but he's still the opposite sex."

"You make it sound like a war, Claudine."

"Well, isn't it? There are victories, and there are defeats, and usually, it's the females who suffer the defeats, because we get pregnant. If men could get pregnant, they wouldn't take advantage so easily and so quickly. Remember that, Elle."

"My God, you'll have her terrified of being in a classroom with boys."

"Don't use the name of the Lord in vain."

"What?"

She laughed. "I don't think Mason appreciates what you're going through, Elle. Let's enlighten him."

She sat up and put on her bikini top. I was getting so nervous now my hand was shaking too much to make even strokes with the paintbrush. I stopped and waited a moment.

"Elle's mother showed up yesterday after more than fifteen years," she revealed. "She's going to tell us about it, aren't you, Elle?"

I turned to them.

Mason looked frightened for me. "Really?" he asked.

"She decided to stop at the house while on her honeymoon," I began. "She just got remarried."

"So she was married before?" Claudine asked.

"She said so, but that marriage didn't last long."

"Well, tell us. What was it like meeting your mother for the first time?"

I was silent. I wasn't sure what to say to them. They both stared so hard at me, with so much expectation. The expressions on their faces were so similar that it was easy to see they were twins.

How much should I tell them? One part of me wanted to confide in them, welcomed their friendship, and longed for their sympathy, but another part of me felt that speaking at all about my mother and my grandparents was some sort of betrayal, and where there was betrayal, there was usually some form of sin. My biblical reading taught me that. There wasn't much that taught me trust in anything but God.

"How do you feel to meet a mother who deserted you right after you were born?" Claudine continued, trying to push back my resistance. "I can't imagine your feeling anything but anger."

"She didn't expect that I would be there," I began. "She was almost as surprised to see me as I was to see her."

"Why didn't she expect it?" Mason asked.

I looked out at the beautiful lake scene I had drawn and had hoped to paint today. Many times over the last twenty-four hours or so when I was feeling even more depressed than usual, I had envisioned my scene. The beauty brought relief. It made me smile and made me hopeful. There was a bright, colorful, and vibrant world out there, a world not very far away, a world I longed to be in.

"She thought my grandparents were giving me away as soon as possible."

"Why would they do that? Did they have any other grandchildren?" Mason asked.

"No. My mother is their only child."

"So?"

"Maybe they just thought it was too much to take

care of a baby and raise a child, Mason," Claudine
said. "At their age, they didn't expect to be doing that.
Right, Elle?"

I put down my brush. I was created in a world of
deceit. As soon as I could understand anything about
myself, I was taught that I was a child of darkness. If
anything, from the little time I had known Mason and
Claudine, I believed they were always being honest
with me. When I looked at the two of them now, still
of one face, I thought that maybe, despite all they knew
and had done, they were innocent in many ways, too.

Was the truth about me going to shock them so
much that this would be the last time we would spend
time together?

Would it especially change Mason's view of me so
radically that he would no longer be interested in me?

Would they bring my story home to their parents,
and would their parents then tell them not to spend
any more time with me?

It suddenly occurred to me that whenever we tell
the truth, we take risks, because the truth is something
you can't change. You can sculpt and shape lies so you
are safe. According to my grandmother, my mother
was like that.

"As soon as she opened her mouth to speak, I prepared myself for her new falsehood. If her first cry at
birth could be interpreted, it would have been her first
lie, I'm sure," she had told me. "You're thinking, how
could a baby lie, aren't you?" I didn't have to answer.
She saw that in my face. "The moment she touched
something she shouldn't and broke it, she shook her

head and said it wasn't her who broke it. It was already broken."

She'd nodded to herself.

"It wasn't her who broke it."

I remembered all those comments, and then I looked again at Mason and Claudine.

"No," I said. "That wasn't the reason they wanted to give me away quickly."

"What was it, then?" Claudine asked.

"My mother was raped," I said. "They believed and still believe that the evil in the man who did it was in me, too."

Neither spoke, so I added what my grandmother had made me believe since the day I could understand what she was saying.

"I'm one of Satan's children."

13

The stillness that followed was so deep and so heavy I could hear the slight breeze as it brushed across my ears. Neither Mason nor Claudine changed expression or moved. It was almost as if they were wearing identical masks or were captured in a photograph. I had to look away. I picked up my paintbrush and went back to the picture. A flock of ducks sounded as if they were complaining about us and continued to sail to another, deeper part of the lake.

"I'm sorry," Claudine said. "I mean, I'm sorry we made you tell it all."

"Yes," Mason quickly followed.

"I think it's terrible that your grandparents are taking it out on you. How can they possibly find any fault in you? Maybe we should say something to our father, tell him what's going on."

"No!" I cried, turning back to them. "Please. My grandparents have no idea I'm seeing you two."

"That would really bother them?" Claudine asked.

"I don't know. Yes. They would want to know all about you first, and because I didn't tell them, they would think it was a betrayal or some type of immoral act. Grandmother Myra is always very suspicious of everything I say or do."

"What exactly have they said to you, done to you?" Mason asked me.

I stopped painting again. "They haven't done anything to me. I mean, nothing other parents or grandparents who have to be parents do. They don't hit me anymore."

"Anymore? They hit you?" Claudine was practically on her feet.

"When I was little, I'd get a paddling sometimes."

"Paddling? You mean they hit you with a paddle?" Mason asked.

I nodded. "My grandfather's father's paddle. Didn't you ever get spanked?"

"No," Claudine said. "The worst ever done to us was they took away some privileges or toys. They yelled at us, of course."

"Still do sometimes," Mason said.

"But our parents don't believe in corporal punishment."

"Grandmother Myra used to say, 'Spare the rod and spoil the child,' all the time. She doesn't say that much anymore."

"What else have they done to you?" Mason asked. "Don't think about it. Just tell us," he added, sounding like a lawyer questioning a witness in court. I imagined he learned that from his father.

"Sent me to my room without dinner sometimes

or didn't let me have breakfast until I did a chore as punishment for something I had said or done."

"And kept you practically locked up in that house," Claudine said, nodding. "That's really why your grandparents homeschooled you, isn't it? They're ashamed of you. Mason, they're ashamed of her. They've made her feel terrible about herself. We have to tell Dad. This is so bizarre."

"Please don't do that," I said. "Please."

"You're frightening her, Claudine." He stood up and came to me to take my hand in his. "We won't do anything to make things worse for you. That's a promise. Right, Claudine?"

"Well, it makes me mad," Claudine said.

"Relax, will you? Just think about it. Suppose Dad did get the authorities involved, and they took her out of that house. Where would Elle end up?"

"Someplace better."

"You don't know that. It could be some disgusting foster home or even an orphanage. Do you hate your grandparents?" Mason asked.

"Hate them? No."

"See?"

"She doesn't know better."

"It's still the only family she has."

Claudine smirked, folded her arms under her breasts, and turned away to think for a few moments.

Mason caressed my arm and smiled. "I don't think anything's wrong with you. Don't worry about that."

Claudine turned back to us. "When you say they think the evil is in you, what exactly does that mean?"

"We all can do bad things. There's just more chance I will," I said, summarizing what Grandmother Myra believed.

"Do you think that's true about yourself?"

"I don't know. Maybe," I said.

"How can you think like that?"

"You know, most people, most women, want to abort the baby that results from a rape," Mason told her. "Maybe they don't see it as evil, but they see it as a detestable reminder of a horrible act."

Claudine looked at me, and in that look, I thought I saw a subtle change. "Your mother wanted that, didn't she? She wanted to have an abortion."

"Yes."

"So why didn't she have it?"

"She was at college. She covered up her pregnancy for a long time. She said she was in denial and then ashamed. By the time she came home to my grandparents, my grandmother told her it was too late. She told her they would give me away, and they kept her home until I was born. They wouldn't let her go out and embarrass them."

"You mean they locked her up?"

"Sorta, I guess. My grandmother tells it one way, and my mother tells it another."

"What changed their mind about not giving you away?"

"They realized it wasn't a baby's fault, Claudine.

She was still half their blood," Mason said. "Right?" he asked me.

I shook my head. "No. My grandmother especially believed and still believes that it's their responsibility to make sure I don't turn out evil or get someone else to do evil. The devil works through his own to destroy the holy souls of others."

"You believe this crap?" Claudine asked.

"That's all she's been taught," Mason told her. "What do you expect?"

"I don't care. How can you believe that?" she asked. She looked so angry.

"People do all over the country, Claudine. Remember reading *Paradise Lost*? Remember the fallen angel and how the devil ruined Eden?"

"That's it, exactly," I said. "My grandparents believe that, yes."

Mason looked at Claudine and lifted his arms. "See?"

"I don't care. They can't do what they are doing to her."

"Look at it from their point of view. They're letting her go to school now. They're behaving just like most grandparents or parents. So they spanked her or made her go to bed without dinner sometimes. Most parents still do things like that. It's not enough."

"Not enough. They kept her locked away, stifled all these years. No wonder she's still a child."

"Stop it. You're not a child, Elle. Don't listen to her."

"I don't know a lot of what I should," I admitted.

"Now I understand why," Claudine said. "She

reminds me of that girl who lasted half a year in our school, Millie Toby, remember?"

"She does not. Stop it."

"Who was she?" I asked.

"That was an entirely different situation, Elle. The girl had—"

"Mental problems. She behaved like a four-year-old sometimes, and she was twelve and already built like a twenty-year-old. She had something wrong with her, something they called precocious puberty. She was developed in the third grade. Some high school boys took advantage of her, all at once, when she was in seventh grade. It was a big scandal."

"That's not going to happen to you, Elle. You're not like that. It won't take you long to get the lay of the land."

"Wrong choice of words," Claudine said.

"Shut up."

"I think I have to speed up your education," Claudine continued, ignoring him.

"What do you mean, *you* have to speed it up?" he asked her.

"Okay, *we* have to speed it up," she corrected. "But you won't be any help unless you're completely honest with her, Mason."

"I'm always honest with her."

"No, I mean completely honest," she insisted. "As honest as we have been with each other."

He started to shake his head and stopped.

"Honest about what?" I asked.

"Look," Claudine said, "your grandmother has

probably done a very good job with your homeschooling. You won't have problems with your studies. Chances are you'll be a better student than most in
the public school because you have good study habits,
had to have them, but at least fifty percent of going to
school is social. I was kind of getting you into that, but
I had no idea about this other stuff. No wonder you
think 'sex' is a dirty word. I was teasing you half the
time, but I won't do that anymore."

"I never teased you," Mason said.

"Boys have their own way of teasing you," Claudine insisted. She paused and looked at me harder. "I'd
like to know something else."

"What?"

"These ideas your grandparents have about you,
about you being evil inside and such . . . you don't
really believe them, do you? I mean, about yourself?"

"I don't know."

She nodded. "She's brainwashed," she told Mason.
"Are you sure we shouldn't tell Dad?"

"She's not brainwashed. She's just a little confused."

"A little?"

"Okay, a lot, but it's still just confusion. She'll be
fine."

"How did this happen to your mother? Do you
know any of the details?"

"Why is that important?" Mason asked.

"There are rapes, and there are rapes."

"Huh?"

"Actually, my mother told me something like that.

She was drugged," I said. "She called it the famous rape drug. She was at a party when she was at college."

"See?" Claudine told him. "That goes on everywhere. If you're at a party, especially a party with many people you don't know, you don't let go of what you're drinking, and you don't take any drugs from anyone you don't know well."

"Don't take drugs at all," Mason said.

"Yes, Mr. Perfect," Claudine said, and sang, "'And he's oh, so good. And he's oh, so fine' . . ."

"Stop it, idiot."

She laughed and sat on the blanket. "Suddenly, I'm feeling a little sick," she said. "I never imagined anything like this."

"I'm sorry."

"It's not your fault. We're glad you told us the truth," Mason said. "Right, Claudine?"

"Yes, yes. I have to cool off." She got up to go into the lake.

We watched her dive in and start swimming.

Mason took my hand again. "What you told us doesn't make any difference to me," he said. "I mean about how I think of you." He leaned forward and kissed me. "Go on, work on your painting. I'll just sit here and watch you. I love watching you work."

He returned to sit on the blanket. I looked at Claudine. She was swimming laps hard, swimming like someone who had to beat the anger out of her body. I wished I knew how to swim as well. I'd probably be right beside her, I thought.

I returned to my picture, but it was harder to

concentrate on it. Every once in a while, I looked at Mason to see if the expression on his face had changed while he stared at me. Had he told me the truth? Did he still see me the way he had before I had revealed my mother's story and mine? He looked thoughtful but not disgusted. I smiled at him, and he smiled back.

Gradually, I felt myself get back into my picture. I thought of myself as an artist with magic powers. I would paint scenes in which I wanted to be, and as soon as the picture was completed, I could do just that: disappear into the canvas and enjoy the setting, the warm breeze, the sunlight, and feel I had truly escaped, even for a short time. Maybe I could even paint someone else in the picture with me, someone like Mason, and for as long as the picture lasted, we would be together, perfect, never visited by any disease, never in any danger, and never unhappy.

When Claudine came out of the water, she looked relieved. She took off her bathing cap and stood beside me to look at my picture.

"That's getting really good. You have a talent, Elle," she said. "Someone born with evil inside her couldn't do something as beautiful as that, especially without any formal instruction."

"Thank you," I said. That did make me feel better.

She kissed me on the cheek and then went to the blanket to get her towel. Mason got it for her quickly and handed it to her, seizing her hand at the same time to draw her closer to him.

"That was a nice thing to say," he told her, and he kissed her on the lips.

She shook her hair and playfully pushed him back onto the blanket. He yelled and tackled her, gently lowering her to the blanket before putting a handful of sand on her stomach. She screamed and threw some of it back at him. Then he turned away and came over to me.

"You want to have another swimming lesson?"

"I . . ."

"I have a bathing suit for you," Claudine said, surprising me. She dipped into her bag and brought out another bikini. "Mason will turn his back while you put it on, won't you, Mason?"

"Sure, but I'm not saying how many times."

"Very funny. Elle?" She held it up. "Go for it. One of these days, you might be able to swim out here all by yourself."

I looked at Mason. He put his hands over his eyes. I didn't want to refuse her offer and his, not now. I put down my paintbrush, walked over to Claudine, and began to change into the suit. It was going to be my first ever bathing suit. Every new day held out the promise of something new, something for the first time, I thought.

"Looks great on you," Claudine said. "Maybe even better than it did on me. But can't you take off that tree log of a cross?"

I looked at it. Did I dare? I nodded, and she helped unfasten it.

"Ten pounds off your chest," she said, bouncing it in her hand. She set it down. "Okay, Mason, you can turn around now."

"Wow," Mason said. "She's right. That bathing suit does look better on you."

"Shut up," Claudine said. "I can say those things, but you can't." She turned back to me. "Most of the girls you meet in school will tell you wonderful things about themselves, and when they give you compliments, you had better be a little skeptical. Doubly so about boys. Right, Mason?"

"Yes, yes. Can we go swimming now?" He reached for my hand, and I joined him.

We walked into the lake slowly. Another flock of ducks, this flock braver, landed a few hundred yards from us. When Mason and I were nearly up to our necks, he told me to lie forward again, and again he held me up while I kicked and dog-paddled. He told me to move my arms farther out and showed me how to cup my hands. We were at it for a good ten or fifteen minutes before I realized I was swimming completely on my own. He was still beside me, but he hadn't been holding me up.

Claudine yelled, "Congratulations!" from shore, and Mason clapped.

When I stopped, he told me to tread water and put his arms around me. We were like that for a while, before he kissed me again, and we moved closer to shore so we could stand and talk.

"What was your mother like when you finally met her? I mean, did you like her?"

"Yes and no," I said. "She seemed like she cared about me but then almost as quickly made it clear to me that she couldn't look after me. There was a big blow-up at dinner between her and my grandmother, and she and her new husband just left."

"So she's not someone you'd like to go live with if you could?"

"I don't know. I mean, I think she's having fun, but . . ."

"But what?"

"I don't think she's really that happy. She looked like she was still trying to find herself. With my problems, I don't think I'd be so welcomed. What I mean is, my grandmother is probably right about her."

"Wow." He bounced in the water and looked at me. "Things will get better for you when you go to college and get out on your own. I'm sure."

"I'll tell you a secret," I said.

"Another secret. Uh-oh."

"No," I said, smiling. "Nothing to do with my mother."

"What?"

"I always wanted to go to school, be with people my age, but now that's it going to happen . . ."

"You're afraid?"

"Yes."

"Don't be. Between Claudine and me, you'll be just fine."

He kissed me again. I looked at Claudine. She was staring at us, but she didn't look very happy. She looked angry again.

"Let's go back," I said. "I have to dry off and think about getting home."

"Right."

We waded in, and Claudine tossed her towel to me.

"My hair," I said. "My grandmother saw it was wet last time."

"We'll stop at the house before Mason rows you back, and you'll use my hair dryer if it's not dry enough when we leave."

"Thank you."

"Come sit next to me," she ordered, suddenly looking older. "Mason, you sit on the other side of her here. Go on."

"What's this?"

"Truth lessons," she said.

"Huh?" He sat.

"Mason, since the seventh grade, have you ever looked at a girl with interest and just wanted to be friends with her like you might be with another boy?"

"What? C'mon, Claudine."

"Answer truthfully, Mason," she said. "You saw their little boobs, and you thought about their bodies naked, and those were the girls you really tried to get close to, right? Even back then. Well?"

I looked from her to him.

"You told me stuff, Mason, stuff I didn't forget."

"You're making it sound too black-and-white," he complained.

"For now, we have to do that for Elle, Mason."

"She's right," he admitted. "The girls I was most interested in were the prettiest and the sexiest, and I wasn't looking just to do homework with them."

"Were you different from any other boy who

reached your level of maturity, Mason?" she asked. Now she was the one sounding like a lawyer.

"No."

"So first thing, Elle, as I have tried to tell you, is be suspicious. No boy just wants to borrow your pen or get the answer to number five on your math home-work."

"That's not always bad, Claudine. You're making it sound bad."

"It's not always bad when the boy you would like to be interested in you is the one. Just anticipate more than he will be, especially how you look," she added.

"And why don't you tell her how you get the boys you're interested in to be interested in you, Claudine."

"I will. First things first, Mason. Always beware of the boy who wants to give you something alcoholic to drink at a party or something else to, quote, make you feel good. Just tell him you already feel good."

"Oh, like you do that," Mason said.

"She has to be more careful, Mason. You know what we should do?"

"I can't imagine," he said.

"We should give her something, some X one after-noon, so she can see what it's like."

"C'mon, no."

"It's how I learned what to stay away from and what was all right," she told me. "Mason, do you want to tell her about the first girl you had sex with and why you weren't happy about it afterward?"

"No, I don't."

"Not fair. We're supposed to be honest with her."

He looked at me. "She's making it sound like I'm having sex constantly. It's not true."

"More than most in your class. You told me."

"Shut up."

"Boys like to brag about what they've done with you, Elle, and even if they haven't really done it, they'll say they have if you give them the opportunity. Whether you like it or not, you're very vulnerable, especially when other girls and other boys don't know much about you. Whoever makes up the first story will be believed. Isn't that right, Mason Spenser? Didn't you get even with Pamela Thornton that way?"

"She deserved it."

"Still, dirty pool," Claudine said. "And you've shown her a little about pool."

"The girl was making stuff up about me," he told me. "I just got even and got her to shut up, that's all."

"Wasn't that what happened with the other girl?" I asked. "The one who . . ."

"No, it wasn't that bad. This was just silly stuff," he said quickly.

I shook my head. "Going to school really sounds like walking through a minefield," I said. My grandfather liked to use that expression when he talked about doing something particularly difficult.

They both looked at me and then laughed.

"Exactly," Claudine said. "That's exactly what it is. Especially for someone who doesn't know anything about where to step and where not to."

"Great, you're frightening her again."

"Just trying to do what I said, speed up her real education."

"Yeah, well, why don't we get into some of your truths, Claudine? What happened when you went out with Seth Gates last May?"

"We're not ready for that story yet," she said.

"Oh, sure."

"I think I had better be getting on the way home," I said, seeing the time on Mason's watch and sensing that they might get into an argument.

Claudine felt my hair. "You might need my dryer. Let's see how it is after we pack up. You know what? Keep the bathing suit on. It's nearly dry. Put your clothes on over it."

"Really?"

"Sure. Later, you can look at yourself in the mirror and see why Mason is having heart failure."

"Will you shut—"

She laughed.

I smiled, but then I thought, how would I ever tell them that I wasn't permitted to look at myself in a full-length mirror? The only one was upstairs in my grandmother's closet.

"Please help me put my cross back on," I asked her.

Mason grabbed it first. "I'll do it."

"Talk about having to bear a cross," Claudine muttered.

She was right, of course. Someday I had to take it off and wear something more like what other people wore. Now that I thought about it and about some of what they had said, I felt a new emotion. It wasn't fear, either.

It was anger, anger that I had to live the way I was living, that I had to be so careful, and that I had to learn the things that girls much younger than me already knew. It wasn't fair. I wanted it to end.

Maybe I was feeling more like my mother.

14

By the time we reached their dock, I thought my hair was dry enough. I was cutting the time close anyway and couldn't afford to take the chance of staying longer. There was always the possibility that my grandparents had come home earlier than they had anticipated, and my grandmother had begun wondering why I had stayed out in the forest or near the lake so long, despite what my grandfather had told her about artists losing their sense of time. She could even have told him to go out looking for me by now. He could walk through the forest calling my name, panic, or go to the lake and see me with the twins. That was always a fear.

When we rowed up to the place on the shore where I had boarded the rowboat, Mason insisted on helping me carry my things back to the house or close to it, even though I told him I could do it fine. I tried to control my fear of walking into Grandfather Prescott searching for me so Mason wouldn't agree with Claudine and report how I lived to their father. I sensed, however, that he wanted to take the opportunity to talk to me without Claudine present, and the time we had spent in the rowboat traveling from the dock to shore wasn't enough.

He glanced back as if he thought Claudine could hear us or had followed us. I was pretty much convinced that neither of them wanted to speak ill of the other without the other present. From the stories they had already told me and the things they had suggested, I doubted there were many secrets between them.

"I know Claudine has good intentions and wants to help you," he began as we walked slowly along the forest path, "but she can be a little abrupt sometimes. She ought to prepare you before she tells you intimate stuff about us."

"Are all brothers and sisters as close as you two are, or is that just because you're twins?" I asked.

I was afraid it would sound silly to ask, but the truth was, I didn't know anyone around my age who had a brother or sister. All I knew about their relationships was what I saw on television or read in the books I had to read for my homeschooling exams.

"No, I'm sure not," he said. "And it's not only because we're twins. Of course, being twins has a lot to do with it. We shared so much from the day of our birth until now. We grew up playing with each other, sharing each other's toys, even more than just occasionally sleeping in the same bed together. Oh," he added when I looked at him askance. "Not because we were too poor back then to have separate bedrooms. We've always had that, but my parents have always been active professionals, my father the lawyer and my mother with her decorating business.

"From the first moments I can remember," he continued as we walked, "we had a nanny most of the day and often even at night. I should say nannies. My mother found fault with most of them and was always taking someone's recommendation and seeking a new one.

"What I'm trying to say is, Claudine and I are probably more dependent on each other than most brothers and sisters are, maybe even other sets of twins. We always seemed to be able to tell when one or the other was not feeling well before anyone else could tell, or when one or the other was sad. I think, even from the age of three or four, we were both terrified of losing each other and hated to be separated, even for a few hours. She always had to go along when my father took me for a haircut. We never seemed to go shopping for clothes and shoes without each other when we were very young. We comforted each other better than our nannies could, and we were always there for each other when one of us was frightened by a nightmare or anything."

"I think that's very nice," I said.

He smiled. "It was nice. It is nice. I'm her best friend, and she still is mine. Despite how she sounds now, teasing me, challenging me, she's always been overly protective when it comes to me. If she blamed me for anything, she kept it to herself until we were alone, and I always did the same if I blamed her. We've always defended each other in front of our parents and covered for each other so neither would get into trouble. Again, despite the way she sounded, we don't have what they call sibling rivalry. At least, I don't think we do."

"I've always wished I had a brother or a sister. I'm sure my life would have been easier if I had been one of a pair of twins."

"I bet. Had to be very lonely for you living in a house with elderly grandparents, especially yours. I'm surprised you're as normal as you are."

"Am I?"

"Believe me, you are. I know a lot of nutty girls."

"I don't feel like I'm normal."

"You just need more experiences, more contact with people your own age, that's all."

The house came into view, so I stopped. I breathed relief. Grandfather hadn't come looking for me. However, another half-dozen yards or so, and my grandparents could see us. The back door was shut, and the house looked quiet. I took my easel from him.

"I really wanted to walk you home because I wanted to tell you how sorry I feel about your first ever meeting with your mother. I could see in your face how much of a disappointment that was for you. You were probably hoping she had come by to take you off with her."

"I guess I was," I said. "I mean, I wasn't positive she didn't know about me. I had only what my grandparents told me, but even when I saw she hadn't known I was still here, I thought, hoped, that she would look at me and want to be with me or want me with her. I don't know about the legal rights or anything."

"A mother should have the most right to her child, but she did desert you. I'm sure she would have a difficult time gaining custody after all that, even though she's married now."

"Yes. She never threatened it. The truth is, she is still deserting me."

"I understand." He smiled. "For now, you can't think about it. You have a great time tonight," he said. "Try not to worry about entering public school and the stuff Claudine was describing. You're going to be fine. You're a natural." He kissed me softly. "I hope that ribbon will be out tomorrow. Weather report still looks good. Maybe we'll do something ourselves. Not with Claudine along."

"Won't she feel bad?"

He shrugged. "She might, but she'd understand. I'm not saying we'll ignore her the whole time or anything. Don't you want to spend some time with just me?"

I didn't hesitate because I had doubt. I hesitated because I didn't, and I was afraid to say it. He raised his eyebrows.

"Yes," I said quickly.

He stepped closer to me. For a moment, I thought that was all he would do. He was looking at me so intently, but then he kissed me again.

"I can't stand being this close to you without kissing you," he whispered. He had his hands on my shoulders. I wondered if he could feel the surge of heat that had risen from my stomach and into my breasts. His lips grazed my neck. I closed my eyes, and he kissed me again, harder, longer.

"Elle," he whispered. "Elle."

Never did my name sound so soft and lovely to me. I used to hate it, thinking I was given it for one purpose only, to defeat the darkness inside me, to urge God to welcome me and forgive me for sins I had yet to commit.

Was this the beginning of one of them?

I stepped back quickly. He took his hands off my shoulders but held them in the air.

"I really like you, Elle," he said. "A lot. Is that okay?"

I nodded, and the worry that had washed over his face quickly disappeared. He smiled.

"Tomorrow," he said, "and tomorrow and tomorrow." He laughed and then started back.

I just stood there watching him disappear into the woods until I heard some branches cracking, and my heart stopped and started. Had my grandfather come looking for me after all but gone in another direction first? Had he witnessed our good-bye? I looked slowly to my right.

Standing there so still that it was difficult at first to see her was the doe I had seen and drawn. I wondered if she was looking at me with the same sort of curiosity and admiration. Wasn't she at a disadvantage, not being full of fear at how close we were to each other? When big-game hunting season began here in Lake Hurley, deer that didn't have enough of an instinctive fear of humans were probably easy targets. They most certainly died with a look of surprise in their eyes.

I set my easel down and opened my pad to the drawing I had first made.

"Look, this is you," I said. She flicked her ears and then slowly walked deeper into the forest. I laughed. "I hope that wasn't criticism," I called after her. I smiled to myself and continued on to the house.

The moment I opened the back door and stepped in, my grandmother pounced. "I was just about to send your grandfather out looking for you."

"Why? I'm not late," I said, holding up my new watch.

"You're almost late. You should give yourself more time in case something delays you. I've told you that promptness is a very good indication of seriousness and dedication. I won't tolerate your being late for school once you begin. Your mother would get distracted easily by almost anything to avoid her responsibilities. Tardiness was her middle name."

"I'm not going to be like her, Grandmother. Not in any way," I said, with such determination that I even surprised myself.

I saw her eyes widen. "Well, I hope that's true."

"It's true," I said. "You can stop worrying about it." It was the first time I had ever told her to do anything, especially with that tone of voice.

Her eyes widened even more. "I'll be the best judge of what I should and shouldn't worry about," she replied. "Don't think you're in charge of yourself just yet, missy."

"Now what?" Grandfather Prescott asked, coming up behind her.

"We were just talking about her mother."

"I thought we agreed that Elle had the right attitude concerning Deborah. What did you say now, Elle?"

"All I said was that I wouldn't be like her," I told him.

"Well, that sounds good, Myra."

She nodded, still looking at me with those penetrating eyes. "Maybe she won't be like her, but that doesn't mean that she won't be like him."

I felt a cold chill at the back of my neck. Was it impossible for her ever to see any good in me, no matter what I did or said?

"Myra," my grandfather said softly. "She's given you no reason to—"

"Go get washed up and dressed to go out to this . . . this dinner," she said, turning away.

My grandfather watched her go and then flashed a smile at me before returning to the living room. I hurried to my room to put away the art supplies and then picked out one of the dresses they had bought me for school. I began to undress before realizing I was still wearing Claudine's bathing suit. Panic brought blood to my face. If she had been looking in at me and saw this on top of what I had just said, the roof would come down on my head.

Quickly, I went into the bathroom, carrying my clothing with me. As with all doors in this house, there was no lock on the bathroom door, so as fast as I could, I got out of the bikini and rolled it into a ball. I put it in the small trash can and covered it with some crumpled tissues just in case she walked in on me while I took a shower. It was then that I went into my biggest panic, however.

I had forgotten to consider what the sun could do. I was red everywhere except where the skimpy bathing suit had covered my body. If she walked in and looked at me, which was something she often did, I would have no way to explain it. I couldn't tell her I had taken off my clothes to lie in the sun in my bra and panties. Besides, she knew how big my panties were. They were gigantic compared with the bottoms of Claudine's bikini.

I had never showered and dried myself so quickly, my heart pounding the whole time. As soon as I could, I dressed. Luckily, Grandmother Myra had gone upstairs to fix her hair and put on a different dress. By the time she came down, I was out, and the bathing suit was hidden under my other undergarments in my dresser drawer. I actually felt exhausted, not only from the effort but also from the tension.

She came in to look at me. "You've had more sun than you should on your face, neck, and arms, young lady. You should have the sense to locate yourself in a shady area out there."

"I know, Grandmother. I forgot because I was so into my drawing and painting. I will be much more careful tomorrow."

"Um," she said. "I'm not sure it's good for you to spend so much time alone in the forest and by the lake. We couldn't help you if you needed help, if someone nasty suddenly appeared."

"Oh, there's no one in this area yet. It's just me and the deer and the birds and rabbits," I said. "I saw a fox, I think. It's truly awe-inspiring out there. You can feel more spiritual. I read that in one of the Bible stories you gave me."

"Hmm. Let me see what you've done," she said, nodding at my pad.

I opened it quickly to the lake scene. "I have much more to do before it's a finished picture, Grandmother."

She studied it. "That cloud you drew and painted . . ."

"Yes?"

"It looks almost like the face of Jesus," she said in a softer tone of voice, surprise in her face. "Did you do that deliberately?"

"No," I said.

She seemed to like that answer. She called for my grandfather.

"Now what?" he asked.

"Look at that picture she's painting. Tell me what you see," she said.

He drew closer to the picture. "It's a beautiful scene at the lake. I like the colors you're choosing, Elle. You going to put some birds in it?"

"Yes. I saw a wonderful flock of ducks today," I said.

"Well, it's a very good initial attempt at capturing nature," he said.

"That's not it," Grandmother Myra said impatiently. "Look at those clouds. One especially should remind you of something, Prescott Edwards."

He looked, glanced at me, and shook his head. "I'm not sure."

"Well, you should be sure. She's drawn the face of Jesus. Can't you see it?"

"Oh . . . yes, yes, I see what you mean. That's very clever of you, Elle."

"She said she didn't do it deliberately. It just came out of her."

"Really?" He studied the picture. "That's amazing."

"It's more than amazing. Don't you know what that means?"

"Oh, right," he said, and then asked, "What do you think it means, Myra?"

"Prescott Edwards, sometimes I think you're as dim as a dying lightbulb. Obviously, it means we've done a good job. There is grace in her now. I hope it continues."

Grandfather Prescott looked at me, truly surprised and full of admiration. "Well, yes, I see what you mean, Myra. And don't forget," he added, "she's done this after she met her mother."

"I won't forget that," Grandmother Myra said. "I won't forget any of it. Well, let's get started. I don't like eating late in these places. The food is probably warmed over too much."

My grandfather winked at me, and the three of us started out. I glanced back at my picture. If there was any resemblance to the pictures of Jesus we had on the walls, I couldn't see it, not even vaguely. I didn't think Grandfather Prescott really saw it, either. *I guess we all see what we want to see,* I thought, but I was grateful that was what she had seen.

Her vision of the cloud not only made her calmer, but it also made her surprisingly joyful. Her whole mood seemed to have undergone a facelift. When Grandfather Prescott talked about how often they used to go out to eat, she laughed. Whenever she laughed, it helped me feel more hopeful. Maybe with all the time that had passed and all that we'd been through, she was the one moving into the light and out of the darkness, not me.

"Your grandfather wasn't so keen on my cooking back in those days."

"Now, Myra . . ."

"Don't try to sugar-coat it, Prescott Edwards. You were too nice to be critical, or maybe too afraid."

"'Afraid' sounds more truthful," he said. She surprised me again by laughing.

"He knew I'd take a frying pan to him if he said something nasty after I had worked so hard."

"No question she would have, and nearly did a few times."

"Your taste was spoiled with all that eating out before we were married," she said. "A bachelor is another human species, missy. Don't you forget that."

"If she remembers all the things you've told her she has to remember, her head will explode."

"Never you mind. What I'm telling you is important to get along in this world," she said, turning to me. "Wisdom is different from book knowledge, and the only way to get wisdom is to listen to those who are older."

I nodded, and she stared at me so hard I thought

maybe I shouldn't have. Maybe she thought I was just agreeing with her to get along with her. She always used to suspect me of that. She surprised me again, however.

"I'm glad you had enough sense to keep your hair pinned up, Elle. As I told you, you have to be careful out in the sun, but I admit you have just enough now to look prettier. Maybe too pretty."

"Oh, you can't be too pretty," my grandfather told her.

"Don't tell me what you can and can't be. Lucifer was the prettiest angel in heaven."

"God made him that way."

"Yes, but for a reason," she replied. "Men don't sin so easily with ugly women, and women don't sin easily with ugly men. You keep that in mind, Elle."

"Another thing to store. There'll be no room for her schoolwork," Grandfather Prescott kidded.

"There'll be room," she said. "There'll be room."

We rode on. Maybe I was wrong to feel it so strongly, but it seemed that something was really changing, for the better. For the first time, I had the feeling that I was really and truly their granddaughter and not some child of the darkness who was born in their house and made to be the biggest burden of their lives, another test God had created. Very rarely during my growing up did I feel I was part of a family. Could that happen? Could my grandmother soften enough to express any love for me? If this mood she was in continued, that might happen, I thought.

It carried over into the restaurant. Grandmother

Myra didn't complain about the prices and the food as much, and when some old friends stopped by our table, friends they knew from when they had their mattress business, she was friendlier, even when someone referred to me with admiration.

Of course, by now, everyone in the community who knew us and knew I was their granddaughter knew at least vaguely what had happened to my mother. Through the years, I understood that some of their acquaintances admired them for the responsibility they undertook, but some did not. I often heard about them. According to my grandmother, there were many who said they could never do it, no matter what they were told about an obligation or a responsibility. The child of a rape had the mark of Cain on his or her face. Every good deed, every show of respect for prayer or God, was connived, a manipulation.

Whenever we did meet someone in the community, I searched his or her face to see which group he or she belonged to, the admirers or the condemners, those who saw me as a pretty young girl or those who saw me as the evil child, so evil they'd sleep with their bedroom doors locked.

"How big she's grown," Mrs. Frampton said. "Are you in college yet, dear?"

"No, ma'am. I'm going into eleventh grade," I said.

"They look so much older these days, don't they, Myra?"

"Yes. Don't know whether that's good or bad," she said. I expected her to state clearly that it wasn't an advantage to look older, as she always did, but she just smiled.

"Oh, I'm sure it's good for you to have a pretty young granddaughter."

"And why do you say that?" Grandmother Myra asked her.

Mrs. Frampton looked shocked at the questions. "Well . . . it's better than having a goose," she replied, and laughed. "Good to see you, Myra," she added, and left us.

"Town gossip," Grandmother Myra muttered. "Just looking to see how we were getting along."

"We're getting along just fine," Grandfather Prescott said.

Grandmother Myra watched Mrs. Frampton talking to some other women. They all looked our way.

"Busybodies," she said.

Later, when we were home and Grandmother Myra went up to her bathroom, Grandfather Prescott told me he was just as surprised as I was at my grandmother's approving our going out to dinner.

"I thought after Deborah, we'd have a hard time with her, but you made her feel very good about it, Elle. She and I talked about how well you handled it all. You said and did the right things. We're both proud of you. Truth is, this was a little bit of a celebration tonight."

I didn't think of it that way but didn't say so. I smiled. I didn't want to think of my disappointment with my mother as a reason to celebrate, but I knew what I had to do. Was I becoming as much of a conniver

as my mother, the conniver those who rejected me suspected I would become? When do you know you're
not doing the right thing for the right reasons? Couldn't
you lie to make someone happier and make life easier
for everyone, or was it always a sin?

In any case, this was one of the happiest times we had
had together. When my grandmother came down, she
told us that unlike last time, she didn't get a stomachache
from the food.

"We just caught them at the right time," she decided. "I'm sure the food isn't always as fresh. You
behaved very well, Elle."

"See why it's important now that she get out
more?" Grandfather Prescott said. "She's ready."

"I hope she's ready. I'm hoping you'll carry the
good things we've taught you into school when you
begin."

"I will, Grandmother. I've been thinking a lot
about it. I was wondering if maybe I shouldn't walk
there one day just so I can get a good idea of how long
it takes. I'd walk there and walk right back."

"That is a good idea, Myra."

"Um," she muttered. "Maybe we should all do
that."

"I think she should go herself. The girl's got to
know how to deal with traffic and such on her own.
You can't hold her hand all the time."

She thought. "Maybe."

"I could drive her back and forth tomorrow morning to show her the best route, and then either in the
afternoon or the next day, she can try it."

"I'd like that," I said. "I admit I'm nervous about it."

"Nonsense. There's nothing to be nervous about as long as you keep your mind on what you're doing. Okay," she said. "You show her the route in the morning. I'm going to go to bed. I'm feeling more tired than usual," she added, rising and suddenly looking her age.

"Are you all right, Grandmother?" I asked.

"I'll be fine," she said. "Just need a good night's rest. We all need that."

"I need to do some reading first," I said, rising, too.

"Okay, you two can desert me. I'm going to watch a little television. Elle, we'll go after breakfast."

"After cleanup," Grandmother Myra reminded him.

"After cleanup."

I left quickly, pleased with what I had gotten and afraid that if more was said, it would be retracted.

Before I went to sleep, I went out to get a glass of milk. Grandfather Prescott had already gone upstairs. Except for the kitchen, the house was dark and quiet. Just after I poured my glass of milk and turned off the lights, I gazed out the back window. The moon was not quite full, but it was so bright it lit up the forest. I wondered where the doe was and when she slept. Just as I was about to turn away, something caught my eye. It looked like a shadow had come to life just down to my left. When it moved into more moonlight, I realized it was Mason. What was he doing out there now? He paused, looked back at our house, and then disappeared into the woods.

He had been looking into our windows, I thought. *Why?*

I waited to see if he would reappear, but he was gone. Seeing him like that troubled me. What if Grandfather Prescott or my grandmother had caught him peering into our windows? I lay in bed thinking about it for a long time before finally falling asleep. For the first time in a long time, I overslept. I woke when I realized that Grandmother Myra was standing beside the bed looking down at me.

"You must have stayed up too late reading," she said. "I don't want you reading so much at night."

"Okay."

"Your grandfather is anxious to take you for that ride. I don't know why it's so important that it be done now. There's still more than six weeks before school begins."

I nodded but didn't move. I hoped she wouldn't remain in the room while I dressed. She'd see my sunburn for sure.

"Well, get your morning started," she said. "I want you to do some shopping for me, too, after your grandfather shows you the route to school. I have some of my old aches and pains this morning and need to rest."

"Okay, Grandmother."

"I'll make up a list."

I nodded. It probably was the dumbest thing for a girl my age to get excited about, but this was the first time I was ever going to do it.

"Your grandfather never pays attention to where things are in the supermarket, but I'm sure you'll find it all. You mind that you don't talk to any strangers," she added, and turned to leave.

Before she could turn around again, I scurried out of bed and quickly began to change into my clothes. Then I hurried into the bathroom to wash my face and hands and went to the kitchen to help her prepare breakfast. Grandfather Prescott was already sitting at the table. She was right. He was looking forward to taking me on the ride. It would be another first, the first time we were in the car without my grandmother. I never expected what that would mean, what I would learn.

15

"Your grandmother is worrying me a little these days," Grandfather Prescott said, once we drove out of the driveway and started for the school.

"What do you mean, Grandfather?"

"Oh, little things you might not notice. She's becoming more forgetful." He looked at me and lowered his head. "Just between us, I think that's why she wanted you to start doing the shopping. Anyway, watch the street so you know how to go. We're turning here. We'll go about a half mile and turn left. The school's not much farther once we do that," he said.

I looked out the window, mentally checking off the stores and places I'd like to stop by. Our town had a small park, too. It was on the left, and right now, there were mothers pushing strollers and talking to their friends. Children of all ages were following along or playing on the grass. In the center was a circular pond with a fountain shaped like a big fish, the water pouring out of its mouth sparkling in the sunlight raining out of a clear blue sky. Everyone seemed to have more energy, more excitement, and brighter smiles. I envisioned myself sitting there after school and just enjoying the rest of the day, seeing and talking to other people.

"She's a lot more tired lately, too," Grandfather Prescott said, almost as an afterthought. "I told her it was time for a checkup, but she's about the most stubborn woman on earth."

"I'll tell her, too," I said, not that I thought that would make an iota of difference.

"Here it is," Grandfather Prescott said, and pulled to the curb in front of the Lake Hurley public high school. He nodded at it. "It's the same as it was when your mother was attending. You'll probably have some of the same teachers."

The school was an old-fashioned redbrick building, with panel windows, a wide cement stairway to the double front doors, and a ball field visible on the right. It had a long front lawn, with old maple and hickory trees very neatly spaced. Two girls who looked about my age were sitting on the lawn and chatting. How I wished I had super hearing and could listen in.

"Not really much of a walk to get here," Grandfather Prescott said.

"No, it isn't."

"Well, let's hope this is the start of a happier time for you," he added, then looked in his side-view mirror and started away. He turned into a driveway, backed up, and took us to the supermarket.

"Got the list?" he asked after we parked.

"Right here," I said, holding it up.

"When your mother was a little girl, much younger than you are now," he told me as we started toward the store, "she would love to go along with me to pick up something here and there. She didn't like going for the regular weekly shopping. Even then, she didn't have much patience, especially when she was with your grandmother telling her to straighten up, not pick up dirty things, or stop staring at people."

He got us a cart, and we went right to filling the list. A few times, I lost him because he lingered over something. When I made a turn after the cereal aisle, I nearly bumped into Mason and Claudine's mother. She wore a white and pink tennis outfit with white tennis shoes and had her hair pinned back in a pony-tail. She wasn't heavily made-up, but her cheeks were rosy. Her wet, slightly orange lipstick looked very nice. In fact, despite what I was told about her mourning new wrinkles, I thought she looked very young.

My heart stopped and started when she turned my way.

Grandfather Prescott was still well behind me. He would surely want to know how I knew her. She did a double take. I could see that she recognized me, but she had forgotten either who I was or where she had seen me. We didn't talk to each other that much when I was at her house, and with her taking the slices of cucumber on and off her eyes, she probably didn't get a long enough visual gulp. She smiled.

How could I not be polite? I couldn't just ignore her or pretend I didn't know her.

"Hello, Mrs. Spenser," I said. She stared at me a

moment with a beautiful, soft smile on her face and then nodded.

"Oh, you're . . . the girl from the forest," she said, laughing. "I'm sorry, but I forgot your name."

"Elle," I said.

"Right. I don't know how I could forget it. Mason doesn't stop talking about you. I hope we'll see you soon. I've got to get done here. I don't normally dress like this, but I have a tennis lesson this afternoon," she added, and started away just as Grandfather Prescott came around the aisle to catch up.

"Sorry," he said, throwing a box of steel-cut oatmeal into the cart. "Sam Marx keeps telling me how much better this is for you."

I looked at Mrs. Spenser bending over the meat case and made a quick right turn down another aisle.

"We need some condiments," I told my grandfather, and I deliberately lingered over jars and boxes, reading ingredients. He stood just behind, smiling at me.

"You're as good a shopper as your grandmother," he said.

By the time we made the turn toward the meat counter, Mrs. Spenser was gone. I kept my fingers crossed when it was time for us to go to the checkout counter. I didn't see her anywhere and hoped she was gone. She was. She was out in the parking lot. I could see her putting her bags of groceries into the trunk of her car. Relieved, I no longer dallied but moved us along quickly.

She had driven away by the time we went to Grandfather Prescott's car. I breathed relief. My secret was still safe.

When we got home, we were both surprised to see that Grandmother Myra was not downstairs waiting for us. While I put away the groceries, Grandfather Prescott went upstairs to check on her and returned to tell me she was sleeping. He shook his head.

"Not like her to take a nap in the middle of the day," he said. "She'd be working on lunch."

"I'll make us a nice salad, Grandfather," I said.

He nodded, but I could see the worry deepening the lines in his face. I called him when everything was ready. He returned to the kitchen, and we sat at the kitchen table. I had remembered that he liked pieces of apple in his salad. He smiled when he saw it.

"This is as good as ever," he said. He kept looking toward the doorway and listening for Grandmother Myra's steps on the stairway. "She hasn't been the same since Deborah shocked us with her visit. She doesn't like to admit it, but that girl's desertion broke her heart, too."

"Wasn't there any way to keep her home?" I asked. Without Grandmother Myra watching and listening, I felt I could ask more questions.

"No. She never stopped being angry at us because we didn't . . ."

"Let her get an abortion."

He nodded. "If there was one thing that girl didn't want to ever have to do, it was give birth, go through all that. I have no doubt she's never gotten pregnant since." Then he thought a moment. "She didn't mention any other children to you, did she?"

"No."

"She was always too selfish really to care about anyone else. Don't ask me what we did to make her that way. We had high hopes for her. No matter what your grandmother tells you, you don't have a child like that and not find fault with yourself."

I said nothing.

He looked out the window and pointed to it with his fork. "Still quite a lot of beautiful day left for you, Elle. I'd come with you and stay with you for a while out there, but I'd better hang around and watch for her. Maybe I can get her to go to the doctor today."

"Okay, Grandfather," I said, and began to clear off the table and wash the dishes and silverware. He stood watching me for a moment and then quietly, slumped over a bit more than usual when he walked, left to go to the living room. I went for my art materials, quickly put on Claudine's bathing suit, and pulled my dress over it. Before I left, I looked in on him. He had his head back and his eyes closed. The house was so quiet. It had never seemed so quiet.

Without knowing why, I practically tiptoed out the back door. Moments after I entered the forest, I heard Mason say, "I thought you'd never come."

I jumped with surprise, and he laughed. "Have you been waiting here long?" I asked.

"Ever since my mother came home from shopping. Just before she left for a tennis lesson, she told me she had seen you and spoken to you. Do your grandparents know about Claudine and me now?"

"No," I said, looking back at the house. I wanted us to walk deeper into the forest. "I was just with my grandfather, and he didn't see me talking to your mother. She looked very pretty."

"Too bad. I was hoping that soon I'd be able to ask you out on a real date."

We walked on. He took the easel from me to carry it.

"You were at my house last night," I said, keeping my eyes forward and walking.

"Oh, you saw me? I wasn't playing Peeping Tom or anything. I was just curious about your grandparents." He stopped, and I stopped.

"What?"

"I was worried . . . about how they treat you. Claudine's been on my case, telling me we should do something, talk to my father. But don't worry," he quickly added. "I made sure she wouldn't do that. She knows how angry that would make me, and we don't risk angering each other that much."

He started walking again.

"I just wanted to make sure I wasn't making a mistake, that they didn't have you tied up and gagged or something. Claudine gives me nightmares. I guess all the bedrooms are upstairs?"

"Yes," I said. After what he had just said, I certainly didn't want to tell him where and what my room was.

"Anyway, Claudine went with my mother this afternoon, and my father is visiting with a local lawyer. They're talking about merging some of their business. We've got a good two, three hours to be by ourselves. To the island?"

"Okay," I said, "but I have to be careful about getting too sunburned. My grandmother noticed."

"I brought sunblock, but we'll pull the blanket back under the trees."

We reached the rowboat, and he began loading my things into it. Then he scooped me up and kissed me.

"If I can kiss you forever like this, I'll hold you forever," he said. He kissed me again.

"I believe you," I said. "I believe you."

He laughed and lowered me into the boat. Moments later, we were moving softly toward what was now a magical place for me, even though it was barely big enough to call any sort of island. He pulled the boat up on the small beach and again lifted me out so he could kiss me. After we unloaded everything, he found a shady spot and spread out the blanket. He set up my easel in the shade.

There was a slightly stronger breeze now. It wasn't too warm or too cold. It was delightful. I felt it caressing my body, playing with strands of my hair.

"Oh, I brought you this for when we go into the water," he said, and held up Claudine's bathing cap.

"Thank you."

"Just keep working on your painting. I'm fine watching you and relaxing." He lowered himself to the blanket. He put his arms behind his head, watched me, and dozed.

I wanted to draw the ducks that Grandfather Prescott had suggested. They weren't back yet, but the memory of them was strong enough for me to plan just where to place them. I did a half dozen and then began to paint them, concentrating hard so as not to ruin any other part of the painting. When I looked at Mason, he seemed asleep. I smiled, studying him now unobserved. He was very good-looking. If we were in the same school and I had to compete for his attention, would I win it as easily as I had won it now?

Quietly, I stopped painting and took off my dress. I put on Claudine's swimming cap and stuffed as much of my hair under it as I could. He opened one of his eyes, saw what I had done, and sat up quickly.

"Time for a swim break?"

I nodded, and he took off his shirt and shorts. He was already barefoot. He was wearing a different bathing suit, a smaller, tighter one. He saw that it drew my attention.

"Oh, this is my swim-team suit," he said. "When you swim in competition, you want as little resistance in the water as possible. I know guys who shave their legs."

"Really?"

He got to his feet and reached for my hand. When we walked into the water, he suddenly turned to me, embraced me, and tossed us both forward. I screamed, but he kept my face from going under.

"Best to do it quickly," he said, shaking the water off his hair and face. "Go on. Let's see you start swimming on your own. I'll be right close by."

Gingerly, I moved forward and began. I was surprised and excited at how well I was doing. Suddenly, I felt him seize my ankles and spread my legs a little as he moved in between and embraced me around my waist. I cried out and stood with my back to him. His hands moved up over my breasts as he brought his lips to the back of my neck and began kissing his way around, turning me as he did so. We kissed again.

"Being with you is like discovering another country," he said. "I feel like I'm just learning about it all myself. You're fresh and beautiful, and because of that, you're the most exciting girl I've ever known."

Listening to him, I suddenly wished Claudine were right beside us. One look at her face would tell me if I should believe him or not. But I realized I wasn't going to have Claudine beside me once the summer ended and she and Mason returned to New York and I began school. I'd have to find my own well of wisdom from which to draw the right responses, the right feelings, and drink what was needed to make the right decisions. Right now, that well was bone-dry.

Before I could say or do anything, Mason lifted me into his arms and slowly, his eyes never leaving mine, carried me out of the water and back to the blanket. He set me down gently. He went to his knees and then very slowly brought his lips to mine. This kiss was different. His tongue touched mine, and while he kissed me, he reached behind my shoulders and undid my top. Before I could utter a sound, his mouth moved down to my breasts. I closed my eyes and let my body relax, my head back.

"You're really very, very beautiful, Elle. I feel like I've discovered a precious jewel, a jewel I don't want anyone else to share, even see. You mustn't be afraid," he added, stroking the side of my face. "Claudine is right. You're so vulnerable. Some miserable bastard will try to take advantage of you. You have no experiences to draw on to protect yourself. I want you to understand how far to go, to know when you can't turn back. Okay?"

What he was saying was something I did think about often now. It was as if he had been to my grandparents' house many times at night and had pressed his ear to the walls and heard me thinking, worrying, and wondering what it would be like and if I would, as my grandmother so feared, turn out to be just like my mother.

I nodded.

He began kissing me again, only now moving over my breasts to my stomach. He put his hands under my buttocks and lifted me gently so he could bring his lips to the insides of my thighs, lifting me like someone cupping cool, fresh water and drinking. When his lips pressed between my legs, I gasped. He moved his mouth gently but firmly. I felt myself weakening even more. When he lowered me back to the blanket, his fingers went under the waist of my bathing suit and began to lower it slowly. My eyes were closed the whole time.

I could feel myself slipping, losing my grip on the side of a great chasm. My mother's face flashed before me, those childish, rebellious eyes. I could almost hear her whispering, "Good. Come with me. Follow me. I'm waiting. You're my daughter."

"No!" I cried, and seized Mason's wrists. He stopped. My bathing suit was down over my thighs. I opened my eyes.

He sat back, and to my surprise, he smiled. "Good," he said. "I wasn't going to go all the way, but I'm glad you stopped me. You understand what would come next. I'm pretty sure you don't take any birth-control pills, and I didn't show you that I was prepared."

The reality of what he was saying splashed cold water over me. I reached down to pull up my suit.

He smiled. "I'm glad you aren't as promiscuous as an innocent, inexperienced girl could be. Nevertheless," he added, widening his smile, "you don't know how I'm suffering right now."

"I think I can figure that out from the way I feel, too," I said.

He nodded, impressed. "This didn't just happen, Elle. I planned this. Actually, Claudine told me to do it and challenged me. Don't hate me for it. I was just showing you how easily someone could take advantage of you even if you're not willing."

Was he telling me the truth, or was he just saying this because I had stopped him?

"Another boy might have forced you. I could have pretended to stop but kept it up until your resistance weakened. Damn," he said, shaking his head. "Just listen to me. Tonight I'll beat my head against the wall remembering."

He turned over onto his back. I saw how excited he was. My body wasn't cooling down as quickly as I thought it might. I reached back to fasten the top of the bathing suit. I didn't know whether to thank him or be angry. Both feelings were grappling inside me.

"Claudine said I owed it not only to you but to all the girls I pushed too far or teased or ignored to go as far as I did, but stop if you didn't stop me."

He turned on his side to look at me.

"She's my conscience sometimes, just like I'm hers. You wouldn't think it from the way we talk to each other and tease each other, I know, but it's true." He paused and stared at me a moment. "Are you mad at me?"

"No," I said. "I guess I should be mad at myself for letting it go as far as I did."

"No. You can't blame yourself. I know this sounds conceited, but I'm not the easiest guy to reject. Hey, if you don't know yourself, feel comfortable in your own shoes, you'll fail in this world. My father taught me that."

"Conceit was what brought Lucifer to hell," I said.

"Excuse me?"

"Satan. He was an angel first, an angel jealous of God."

"Oh, right. You believe that stuff?"

"It's all I know," I said.

He nodded. "I'll call you in ten years after you've been out there and see if you still take it all literally. I've got to go into the water for a few minutes. Cool down, if you know what I mean."

He rose, smiled, and went back into the lake. I watched him dunk himself and swim. I didn't think my body was calm enough for me to return to my painting, but I went to it anyway. Whatever sexual explosions had taken place in me wanted me to put some suggestion of them in my scene. Grandmother Myra's interpretation of one of the clouds gave me an idea. I put in another, making the strokes carefully. It began to take the shape of a boy and a girl side by side. I did my best to disguise it. Then I stepped back to look at it. Satisfied, I put the brush down. Mason was floating on his back. As quietly as I could, I returned to the lake, and before he realized I was there, I splashed him. He cried out and then laughed and began splashing me. He pursued me as I stumbled along and finally caught me. He pretended he was going to dunk me, and then he kissed me.

He held me for a moment. Neither of us spoke, and then he said, "When you're ready, I want to be the one."

I didn't say anything, but I think he saw it in my eyes. *Yes, you'll be the one.*

After a few more minutes of swimming, we returned to the small beach and began to pack up. He had brought towels. I dried myself quickly and decided it would be all right to take off my suit and roll it up so I didn't have to worry about Grandmother Myra catching me wearing it. He didn't turn away, but he didn't say anything until I had my dress on.

"I am definitely going to beat my head against that wall tonight," he told me.

"Not too hard. I want to see you again."

"You will. Oh, you will," he swore.

We got everything into the rowboat and very quietly, neither of us saying anything, began to move away from the small and now magical little island.

When we reached my side of the shore, I asked him if he was going to tell Claudine everything. I had the sense that they really didn't keep any secrets from each other.

"Probably," he admitted. "Just to prove to her that you're not the foolish innocent she thinks you are and that I could restrain myself, too. She'll ask you for sure, and she'll know if you were lying, so no problem."

"Okay."

"Be prepared, however, to get a Claudine lecture and a dozen lessons on how to handle men. Admittedly, she knows of what she speaks. If she was a fighter pilot, she would have dozens of kills represented on her fuselage. Claudine has quite a fuselage."

"Didn't she ever have one boyfriend for a while?"

"When it comes to boys and sex, Claudine has ADD. You know what that is?"

"I'm not sure."

"Attention deficit disorder. She loses interest, because she's always thinking there's someone better around the corner. When I tell her she's probably thinking of me, she usually throws whatever's available at me. Once that was nearly a dozen eggs."

As before, Mason wanted to walk me as close to my house as he could. While we walked, he told me more about his own romances, his ambitions, and why and how he and Claudine had become so independent and dependent on each other.

"I suppose," he said when we were very close to the end of the walk, "just like you, we were deserted in some important ways, but we also had ways to compensate. We love our parents, but we've never fooled each other when it comes to what we can and can't expect from them. Hey, that's just the way it is. 'Live with it,' Claudine always says."

"I guess I really would have benefited from a brother or sister."

We paused. We could see the house now. It looked as quiet as ever. Grandmother Myra was not out on the back porch waiting for me. After my afternoon, it really looked more like a prison.

"I hope we can figure out some way soon to let me visit and take you out," Mason said. "Maybe I can be just walking by with Claudine or something."

"I don't know. I'll think about it. I've got to go slowly with them, or my grandmother will put an end to my going to public school, Mason."

"Okay. I won't give up. I'll be watching for that ribbon," he added, then kissed me quickly and started away.

I knew he was getting frustrated with meeting me secretly all the time. I wondered how much longer it would last. Both depressed and excited by the afternoon, I headed for the house.

The first thing that struck me after I entered was the same silence. I went into the living room, saw that no one was there, and put my things away as quietly as I could, assuming that they were both taking naps now. I hid the bathing suit and then sat on my bed thinking. It was getting to the time when Grandmother Myra would begin working on dinner and having me do things.

I rose and went to the stairway to listen. There were no sounds coming from upstairs. Quietly, I walked up the stairs and went to their bedroom. Surprisingly, the door was open. I peered in and saw no one there. Confused now, I hurried back down the stairs and looked in the garage. Grandfather Prescott's car was not there. They had gone somewhere.

I wandered back to the kitchen and stood wondering if I should start preparing a salad. Wherever they had gone, when they returned, Grandmother Myra would be very happy I had. I started for the refrigerator and stopped. I didn't know how I had missed it. I had walked through the kitchen, but there it was.

A note.

It read, "Taking your grandmother to the hospital in an ambulance. I'll call when I know more. Grandpa."

16

The thing that struck me most was his using the word "Grandpa" instead of "Grandfather." Never in my life did I call him Grandpa or Papa. Grandmother Myra always made a point of calling him "your grandfather." I especially never called her "Grandma." The formality seemed very important to both of them.

Not now.

I stood staring at the note as if the words might change, like words on a television screen. Very rarely was either of my grandparents sick. Oh, they had their colds and aches, but never once did either of them spend any time at a hospital. Consequently, it was likewise very rare for me to be home alone and not to anticipate hearing or seeing Grandmother Myra at any time. During my early years, she would hover over me or surprise me as if she believed she was stopping an evil thought or action from occurring.

The silence around me suddenly made me aware of sounds usually floating beneath the surface in the house. It wasn't only the familiar creaks in the wooden structure that were heard at night. It was the ticking of clocks, a small drip in one of the kitchen-sink faucets, and the tapping of tiny birds as they strutted on the porch floor just outside the back window. I heard the swish of automobiles passing by on the road, but most of all, I heard the trembling of my heart. I could almost feel it cringing under my breast, folding over itself because of the blanket of fear that had fallen over me.

I wasn't sure what frightened me most.

Was I afraid my grandmother would die or afraid she wouldn't?

Was I frightened by the possibility that if she died, my grandfather would claim that he couldn't be responsible for me any longer, that it was too much for an elderly man to raise a teenage girl and perhaps it was better if some social agency took control and placed me in a foster home? Or perhaps even worse, send me to live with my mother, something I once dreamed of doing and now feared?

I turned slowly to look through the house, to study every shadow, listen to every creak, so I could distinguish the ordinary from something new. Was Satan himself there with me? Grandmother Myra claimed that death came into the world when Adam and Eve committed original sin. I imagined it to be like a great dark cloud that swirled over us all, everywhere, and when it sensed an opening, it pounced. Was something seriously wrong with Grandmother Myra? Had death taken a firm grip on this house? Could I smell it, feel it, or see it?

Throughout my childhood, Grandmother Myra

had molded so many different terrifying creatures, children of Satan and sin, for me to visualize. She had me watching for them constantly. She designed them, the seven deadly sins and their offspring, grotesque imps, spidery dark shadows, just waiting to embrace me and make me one of their own. She would categorize something I had done, pointing her finger of accusation at me.

"That's lust."

"That's sloth."

"That's wrath."

I was on constant alert all my waking hours. Just think a bad thought, just weaken once to the temptation of cheating and lying, and one of them would seize me. If they didn't do it right away, she told me, they would come at night when I was asleep and helpless. They would crawl into my bed beside me, and slowly, like a paper towel absorbing something spilled, my body would absorb them.

And when I woke in the morning, I wouldn't even know it had happened, she said. But she would know. She would be able to take one look at me and see immediately that one of Satan's own was inhabiting not only my body but my very soul. During those early years, I would look anxiously at her to see what she saw in me. She kept the warnings warm and frequent.

"And once they get a grip on your soul, only God's deific forgiveness could rescue you from the fires below."

I walked out of the kitchen and sat on the sofa,

thinking. Shouldn't I start preparing dinner? If they returned from the hospital, Grandfather Prescott would probably be hungry, even if Grandmother Myra wasn't. Both of them would be very impressed that I had done what had to be done and not waited for instructions.

But as the minutes passed, contrary to what I anticipated in myself, I didn't continue to worry about Grandmother Myra's condition or what would become of me if the worst happened. I couldn't stop it. What came over me was not continued and increased fear but a warm excitement. I closed my eyes and actually moaned, recalling the passion between Mason and me on that tiny beach. Those images and feelings swept everything else aside.

Once again, I felt the electric moist warmth of his lips on my neck, my breasts, and my stomach. I replayed his hands gently widening my legs and his fingers moving under the bottom of the bathing suit, inching it down. It excited me more to remember it all in my grandparents' living room, on the sofa. It was more than simply sex. It was defiance, and that defiance heightened the passion, quickened my breath, unfolded my fearful heart so it could beat to a different rhythm, a rhythm that began between my legs and thumped up my body until I couldn't restrain the cry of pleasure that reverberated under my breasts and made my body tremble and tremble until I could feel it explode.

The relief that followed was welcomed, but it was as if I had been lowered back into my body, into the house, and into all the rules and restrictions that had kept me caged for so long. I looked around fearfully, expecting to see some distorted, slimy creature smiling licentiously and joyfully at me.

"You're one of us now," it would say. "Welcome to your destiny."

But there was nothing there, nothing in any shadow, and nothing hovering in any corner. There was only that silence. Passion between two people wasn't the doorway to hell after all, I thought. It was something wonderful, something that made us feel alive. Yes, it opened doors but not the doorways to death and damnation. God didn't do this to us to test us and then punish us. He did it so we could enjoy the full blessing of the gift of life. Yes, you could misuse it. Yes, you could ruin your life the way my mother had, but it didn't have to be that way, to cause that dreadful destiny. This didn't confirm any prophecy. I was strong enough when I had to be. *I will be the master of my own fate, the captain of my own soul.*

It was truly a liberation. I laughed in defiance and stood up slowly but confidently. There was nothing there to fear; there never was. This was simply the home of people who had become afraid and who had tried to impose that fear on me. Why couldn't they understand that by doing all this, they had permitted my mother, my self-centered, rebellious mother, to win, to control their lives, and almost to control mine, too?

Still riding on that stallion of defiance and new confidence, I practically galloped up the stairway. I had wanted to do this for a long, long time. I went into their bedroom and began to search drawers, not taking great care to cover up that I had done so. That was part of my new defiance.

I found it under Grandmother Myra's Bible, the key to my mother's bedroom, the forbidden room. I hurried out and went to the doorway eagerly, but when I faced it, I hesitated. Had I overestimated the strength of my defiance? Could I do this? Wasn't I still afraid? Suddenly, for me, that door was more than a door; it was a barrier that for all my life had separated me from myself. What had my grandmother shut away from herself? What did she fear that I would see, and why?

My fingers trembled as I inserted the key into the lock. For a few moments, that was all I did. Then I turned it, heard it click open, and reached for the door handle after taking a deep breath.

The afternoon sun set on the side of the house. It was low but still very strong, so that it leaked in around the closed curtains enough for everything in the room to be seen. I was anticipating a room completely stripped down, only a mattress on the bed and nothing on the walls or on the dresser. I didn't expect the light switch to illuminate the room through two bedside lamps with pretty pink shades, each with a cute ceramic girl in a pink and white dress and funny red shoes and a purplish table with an orange-striped cat sitting on it.

The queen-size four-poster bed was in antique white. The canopy had scrolls that matched the scrolls on the headboard and footboard, with flowery tops. The side tables matched. Each had one drawer and two open shelves with what looked like fresh tissues popping out of tissue boxes, stacks of children's picture books, and, on the right-side table, a wooden jewelry box. The floors of the room were a polished light maple, with an antique white fluffy area rug that was so spotless that it looked brand new.

On the left was a desk that matched the bedroom set. There was a scrolled desk chair with a pink soft cushion. To my surprise, there was a computer on the desk. It was not very old-looking, either. I had seen some pictures of earlier computers. They were large and bulky, but this one was slim.

Because the room was so immaculate, I was hesitant to enter, but I finally took the first step, moving like someone navigating over jagged rocks that jutted out of a raging current. As I became more courageous, I touched things, looked at and fingered the toys, petted the doll with almost human hair on the bed, noting how lifelike it seemed with its soft blue eyes and simulated wet lips. I examined some of the games and then opened the closet door, expecting an empty space, but I saw instead racks full of dresses and skirts and blouses. On the right were two shelves of shoes, many obviously bought to match outfits.

Anyone who looked at this room would swear someone was still living in it. I was stunned and confused. My attention went to the pictures displayed on the dresser and the two side tables. They were framed photographs of my mother when she was nine or ten,

with my grandparents. Everyone looked happy, buoy-
ant, and, most of all, loving.

I turned around and around, repeatedly looking
at everything. It was as though time had not stopped
in this room. It was still the way it had been when my
mother was a little girl, yes, but it did give the sense
of being a living shrine to hope and happiness. In this
room, there were no heavy religious icons and no
framed biblical sayings. The room was an island in a
house filled with religious warnings, threats of damnation, and reminders of our spiritual weaknesses.

As I stood there, a realization took form in my
mind. This room wasn't simply my mother's old room.
It was Grandmother Myra's dream, her respite, a ca-
thedral, the place she came not to pray but to hope. She
wanted to return to this moment, to begin again, and
to prevent the darkness from coming into their lives. It
was where she admitted to herself that she was warm
and loving once, when she was optimistic and trusting.

Whenever she wasn't in it, absorbed by all that was
there, she saw it as sinful. She probably asked God
for forgiveness after every time she visited the room.
There was a child, however, whom she loved and
cherished in this room, a child she dreamed of having
again. In her mind, that was some sort of defiance,
too. Maybe she sat in there alone and asked herself a
thousand times, "What did I do wrong? Was all this
too hedonistic? Did I give my child too much love,
instilling the conceit and arrogance and thus the tragic
flaw in her? Did I turn her into a creature of comforts
and luxury and make her weak and selfish?"

Was this a question most parents asked themselves? "Are we giving our child too much? Are we
teaching him or her the wrong things? Are we failing
to instill a respect for others and values in our child?
It brings so much pleasure to us and to our child to
give him or her things and see the joy in his or her
face." How did you know when you'd gone over the
top? How did you hold back when so many other
parents were bestowing so much on their children? If
you didn't give your child just as much, would your
child resent you, perhaps resent everything and turn
mean and self-centered?

Yes, it was in this room where Grandmother Myra
could whip herself, could cry, could pray for forgiveness, and could remember when she was a different
person, someone who saw more to love and take pleasure in than who she was now, fearful of every laugh,
distrusting of every warm feeling, and condemning of
every small promise.

I thought I was going to discover more hate in the
room. I even imagined I would see things deliberately
broken, dolls smashed, maybe even a mattress slashed
in rage. I certainly anticipated religious icons and
framed sayings covering the walls. I wanted the room
to reinforce all the anger I had toward my grandmother. I wanted everything confirmed, but instead, I
felt tears come into my eyes.

I stood there feeling sorry for her, imagining the
pain she had endured, the nights she had spent crying, and the great disappointment she felt in herself
and in my mother. This was where she bore her cross

and carried herself to her own Golgotha to be crucified and someday, somehow, resurrected, if only in a
dream.

Slowly, I left the room, the way you would leave
a sacred place, silent, respectful, and in awe of God's
power. I closed the door softly and locked it again.
After I put the key back under Grandmother Myra's
Bible, I descended and went to the kitchen to work on
dinner preparations.

A little more than an hour later, after I had set the
table and breaded some chicken cutlets, Grandfather
Prescott came home. He looked peaked, tired, and
much older. I quickly looked to see if Grandmother
Myra was with him, perhaps just behind him, but he
was alone.

"She's had a stroke," he said. "She's lost the power
of speech and movement on her right side."

I didn't know what to say. I was crying, maybe for
him more than for her, or maybe for myself.

"We'll see how she is tomorrow."

"Can I go with you to the hospital, Grandpa?"

He nodded.

"I have dinner prepared, Grand . . . Grandpa," I
said.

He smiled. "I told her you would," he said. "I'll
just go wash up."

I returned to the kitchen.

When we sat down to eat, he described what had
happened. "I saw she was awake, but she wasn't moving, and then she started making this horrible noise.
She was trying to speak. From the way she was trying

to move, I could tell that she was suffering some paralysis. I called the paramedics immediately, and after they loaded her into the ambulance, I followed in my car."

"I'm sorry I wasn't here, Grandpa."

"Yes. I looked out the back window twice before rushing out, but there just wasn't time for me to go looking for you, so I wrote the note."

He ate some more and then paused.

"Maybe I should go back tonight."

"You can't exhaust yourself now, Grandpa. You'll know more in the morning."

He nodded. "This will be the first night I'm not with your grandmother in more than forty years," he said.

After dinner, he went to the living room to watch television, but when I looked at him, he seemed dazed. I couldn't help but be surprised. So many times, I had looked at both of them and wondered if there had ever been any real affection between them. Did they love each other or just become dependent on each other? Was it easy to look at other couples and know the difference? Did they know the difference? Did you really fall in love with someone or just become very comfortable with him or her? Maybe if love itself wasn't such a mystery, there wouldn't be so many mistakes.

I sat on the sofa where Grandmother Myra usually sat and watched some television with Grandfather Prescott. For a while, I didn't think he even noticed I was there. Then, suddenly, he turned to me and said, "If you don't like this, change the channel."

Suddenly, even though I was being given new privileges and powers, I decided I really wasn't interested.

"I think I'd rather go work on my picture, Grandpa. It's coming along."

He nodded. "Bring it out here," he said. "There isn't enough good light in that room."

"Okay."

I brought everything out to the living room, something Grandmother Myra would certainly forbid, and began working on some details in the picture. He watched me for a while and then began dozing off. When he opened his eyes again, I stopped painting.

"Maybe we should just go to sleep. I know you want to get started early in the morning, Grandpa."

"Yes, yes. Very wise," he said, and rose. He came over to the easel and looked at my picture. "This is remarkable," he said. "To think you've done this without any formal training."

"I've been reading the book you gave me."

"Still remarkable," he said, and then he did something he rarely did. He leaned toward me and kissed me on the cheek. "See you in the morning," he said, and started for the stairway.

I watched him go up and then I started to put my things away. I heard a distinct tap on the living-room window. At first, I thought perhaps the wind had started up and blown some dust, but when I heard it again, I focused and saw Mason silhouetted in the starlight. I glanced quickly at the stairway. Grandfather Prescott was upstairs and in his room. I gestured toward the back of the house and went out the back door. Dressed in a white T-shirt and white shorts, he was at the foot of the short stairway.

"What are you doing here?" I whispered.

"My mother and Claudine said they saw an ambulance in your driveway when they came home this afternoon. I wanted to come over earlier, but I was afraid of getting you into trouble. When I saw you were only with your grandfather, I concluded something had happened to your grandmother. I waited for him to go upstairs."

"How long were you there?"

He looked at his watch. "Close to an hour. What's happening?"

"My grandmother had a stroke."

"Oh. Too bad, I think."

"It is too bad, Mason. I once told you I didn't hate them."

"Right. Sorry. Well, what do they think will happen?"

"We don't know yet. We'll go over in the morning."

"Who's worse, your grandmother or your grandfather?"

"What do you mean?"

"If I should drop by and only he knows, would that be bad?"

"I don't know. There's too much going on right now. Let's wait," I said.

"Well, I just wanted you to know I'm here for you. So is Claudine. Whatever we can do to help you, we'll do. Just ask."

"Thank you."

"Do you have to go right back in, or can we talk some more?"

"I should go in," I said.

He stood in the dark looking up at me. I could feel his disappointment. Maybe I was feeling my own, but there was something more, some other vibration in the air between us.

"You don't go upstairs to sleep, do you?" he asked.

"What?"

"I've . . . I've been at the window more than I admitted," he confessed. "I saw your grandparents go up to bed, and then you went somewhere downstairs, but I don't see any windows other than in the kitchen, the living room, and the dining room. There's a window in a bathroom."

"You shouldn't have been such a spy, Mason. It's not nice."

"I know, but I really like you, Elle. I just wanted to know more about you, about what was happening. I'm sorry."

"I sleep in a room downstairs, yes," I said.

"Without any windows?"

"It has an air vent."

"But this house surely has another bedroom upstairs."

"I can't talk about it right now. It's just too much!" I cried. "You shouldn't have spied on me. Go home. I'll see you when I can," I said, snapping at him, and turned around quickly to go into the house.

After I closed the door behind myself, I stood there fighting to catch my breath. Contradictory feelings were twisting and knotting around each other inside me. Was I upset at Mason for taking such liberties and observing us like that, or was I upset at his discovering how I had been living? Was I embarrassed or angry? Did I want to drive him away or welcome his sympathy and comfort? I wanted to hurt him, but almost immediately, I regretted even having the feeling.

He hadn't come to be a Peeping Tom. He had seen me naked. Surely he wasn't like that. He was concerned about me. I shouldn't have treated him that way. My regret brought tears to my eyes. I spun around and opened the back door again, hoping he was still there, perhaps standing stunned but hoping I would be upset with myself.

"Mason?" I called, and waited for him to appear. He didn't. There was only the darkness, the starlight silhouetting the trees, and the far-off sound of a car horn. All the birds were asleep. Even the owls were silent. I felt as if I had driven away all of nature.

After a few more moments, I backed up and closed the door again. It wasn't going to be easy falling asleep tonight, I thought. I returned to the living room, gathered up my painting, the easel, and the supplies, and brought it all back to my room, my dreadful room. I hated the very sight of it.

"It's all your fault," I told the baby Jesus, and then I felt stupid for doing that.

Exhausted, I prepared for bed and crawled into my corner of the darkness. Even so, I lay there with my eyes open for a long time. I had never felt secure about my future. If anything, I felt like someone or

something just drifting without any purpose or direction. I did well with my homeschooling but always
wondered what it was for. Even my interest in art
seemed futile. Who would see anything I did?

Then, as suddenly to me as a curtain being pulled
open, the future began to reveal itself. I would go to
school. I would have a boyfriend. I would get better at
art. I would find a purpose. I would know my name.

Was that curtain still opened?

17

Grandfather Prescott was up early in the morning, earlier than I was. I leaped out of bed when I heard him moving around in the kitchen. I was glad of that. Part of what had kept me tossing and turning all night was my fear that something would now happen to him, that when he had gone upstairs the night before so tired and depressed, he would also have a stroke or maybe just die in his sleep. When I came out, he did look very tired.

"Why did you get up so early, Grandpa?" I asked when I entered the kitchen.

"Doctors make their rounds early in the hospital," he said. "I want to get there right after they examine her."

"You want me to make some oatmeal? You can't just have toast and coffee."

"It's enough for now. Make yourself what you want," he said.

I poured myself some orange juice and had a little cold cereal, eating quickly to keep up with him. I was afraid he would tell me to stay home, but he looked as if he wanted me along. We were out of the house and on our way less than fifteen minutes later.

On the way to the hospital, I was tempted to tell him, to confess, that I had gone in the forbidden bedroom and had seen how heartbroken Grandmother Myra was about my mother, how much she had wanted to cling to a happier time. I was torn between assuring him that I didn't hate her as much as I suspected he believed I did and keeping quiet about my mother's room so as not to admit to violating one of Grandmother Myra's sacred commands. I decided for now to say nothing.

When we arrived at the hospital, we went to the intensive-care unit because Grandmother Myra was still there. Grandpa Prescott went in to speak with the doctors while I waited in the small lobby just outside. There was only one other person there, an elderly lady who looked very frightened. She had been crying softly to herself when I sat across from her. I thought she didn't even know I was there, but she suddenly turned and asked, "Who is here for you?"

"My grandmother," I said. "She had a stroke."

She nodded. "I'm waiting for my son. My husband had a heart attack this morning. They let me ride with him in the ambulance."

"I hope he gets better," I said.

"Thank you. We've been married fifty-two years. He always says he wants to be the first to go, but when you're married more than fifty years, you should go together. My son says that's silly talk."

I just smiled at her and wondered what enabled

some couples to stay together so long. Whatever it was, my mother lacked it. Maybe golden-anniversary couples were a thing of the past. Maybe the only commitment anyone made today was to himself or herself. They should probably add *until I get bored* to the vow *to have and to hold,* I thought.

The woman turned away, but when Grandpa Prescott came out, she stopped dabbing at her eyes and turned back to listen.

"She's not improved," he said. "The doctors want to continue to evaluate her condition before they'll tell me any more."

"I'm sorry for your trouble," the elderly lady said. Grandpa looked at her as if he hadn't seen her and nodded.

"Can you talk to her?" I asked.

"Yes," he said, "but she's so angry about what happened to her that she won't look at me."

"Should I try to speak to her, too?"

He thought a moment. I knew he was wondering if my presence would make her even angrier. When you're married as long as my grandparents were, you probably could anticipate what your wife or husband is feeling and thinking. You almost could go through the entire day without speaking.

"Okay," he said. "Maybe that will work. Maybe hearing your voice will get her to stop pouting and cooperate with the doctors and nurses."

"It's good to be angry. It keeps you alive," the elderly lady said. We both looked at her.

"Or it eats you up alive," Grandpa replied. He

nodded at me, and I got up and followed him into the ICU. We passed other patients, two of whom were elderly men, both hooked up to monitors and breathing through oxygen leads. I wondered which was the woman's husband. At the very end of the row, we walked around a curtain to see Grandmother Myra lying there, doing just what Grandpa Prescott had said, staring up at the ceiling as if she was staring down God.

Her face was thinner. Her mouth was twisted, and her eyes were bulging. They looked more like two small egg yolks. I didn't touch her hand. I stepped up closer, first waiting to see if she realized I was there. I looked at Grandpa Prescott. He nodded, and I started to speak.

"I'm sorry you're ill, Grandmother," I began. "I hope you get better soon. I'll take care of the house until you get better and come home. Don't worry about Grandpa," I added.

When I said "Grandpa," she turned and looked at me. It was impossible for me to tell what she was thinking. Her face appeared to have lost its ability to show any new emotions. It was frozen in a distorted visage, locked by her inner rage as much as by the condition caused by the stroke. Her eyes were inflamed with the same fury she had been directing toward the ceiling. It was as if she blamed everyone and everything, even the doctors, whom she had often accused of making up illnesses to make money.

"She made a good dinner for us last night, Myra,"

Grandpa Prescott told her. "She's learned a lot from you. She's a good girl."

Grandmother Myra opened her mouth to speak and, after making a little effort and some difficult-to-understand sounds, closed it and turned away.

"I'll stay close to the house and take care of things," I added.

She shook her head.

One of the nurses came up beside us. "I think it's better if you let her rest for now," she said.

Grandmother Myra made another distorted sound.

My grandfather patted her hand and then leaned over to kiss her cheek. "We'll return to see you late this afternoon, Myra. We'll both pray for you."

She shook her head and closed her eyes. Grandpa Prescott tapped me on the shoulder, and we walked out of the ICU. In the lobby, the elderly lady was talking to her son. He looked as if he had been yelling at her. She held her hands over her eyes, maybe hoping that when she opened them, she'd be home and all this was just a bad dream.

"Your grandmother is just very angry right now," Grandpa Prescott told me as we walked to the elevator. "I know she thinks God deserted her. Or she thinks she's made some sort of mistake with you, and now she's being punished for it. That's the way she thinks. Don't blame yourself for anything," he concluded before I could say anything.

We got into the elevator, and except for relating to me what the doctor had told him they would do before they even considered therapy, he said very little.

"I didn't get much sleep last night," he said as soon as we entered the house. "I'm going to take a little nap. Don't worry about my lunch or anything. Just enjoy the day, Elle. I know what," he added with a smile. "After we visit her late this afternoon, we'll go to another restaurant for dinner. It's a little depressing right now eating in our house, so don't worry about making anything."

"Okay, Grandpa."

I watched him start up the stairs. "Grandpa?"

He paused.

"Do you want to call my mother to tell her? Because if you do, she gave me a phone number."

He shook his head. "It won't matter to either of them, I'm afraid," he said, and continued up the stairs.

I didn't want to just run into the woods and wait for Mason or Claudine to see me on the shore. I felt I needed to be alone for a while and think, so instead, I walked out the front door and followed the route my mother and I had taken that day.

Was Grandpa Prescott right? Wouldn't it make any difference to either my mother or my grandmother if my mother was told about what had happened? Was it really my mother's surprise appearance that drove Grandmother Myra into her stroke? If that was true, she was still hurting both her parents, and me, for that matter. It was as though all the things she had done to disappoint them echoed for years and years.

So much anger had swirled around this house for so long, I thought, when I looked back at it. It was an unhealthy garden that grew only dark, ugly weeds.

I could almost see a tornado-like cloud of rage circling the roof. If people who had most of what was necessary to love each other ended up hating each other, what hope was there for love in this world? What bond could possibly be stronger than the bond between a child and her parents? Whom could two adults love more than their only child? What adult out there could care for my mother as much as her own father and mother? How could she trust anyone? In the end, all three of them had their hearts torn. Defiance hadn't brought my mother real happiness, and refusing to forgive her for it hadn't brought my grandparents any real satisfaction or contentment. None of them was any better off.

I had read enough and seen enough to know that children grew up with a sense of security and optimism when they saw and felt how much their parents loved them. If their parents loved each other dearly, then they could believe they would find someone to love just as dearly. Your family was either heaven or hell. You either believed there were angels, or you believed there was only darkness, selfishness, and hate. In the end, you were what you believed you were.

Was my mother as bad as my grandmother came to believe she was? Was she a victim, or did she victimize them with her poor behavior and promiscuity? Would anything have made any difference, or did God just pass by some houses and families and not touch them with his grace? Was Grandmother Myra so angry in that hospital because she realized she had been praying to closed divine ears, or was she angry at herself for somehow bringing all this to their family doorstep? I feared I would never know the answers to any of these questions. They were the kinds of questions you took with you to the grave.

I knew I was too young and too inexperienced to fathom what was out there in the world. Soon I would make my own discoveries and turn out either more like my mother or like someone in between her and my grandmother. Maybe I would turn out to be something new but not necessarily something better. I was both afraid and excited about the day I would walk out the door and start my own journey.

I didn't realize how far I had walked right now until I heard Mason yell, "Hey!" I looked up to see him leaning out of the driver's side of their BMW convertible. I had reached the turnoff in the road that led to their summerhouse. Claudine was in the passenger's seat. Both looked surprised but happy at the sight of me. I was just as surprised to see them and didn't move. He pulled over to the side of the street, and both of them got out of the car.

"Were you coming to see us?" Claudine asked after she hurried over.

"No. I just went for a walk. I didn't realize where I was until you shouted."

"What's going on? How is your grandmother?" Mason asked.

"I was there this morning with my grandfather. She still can't talk. No change at all from yesterday," I said. "She's still in the intensive-care unit. Her face looks all twisted."

"Oh," Claudine said. "Tough."

"She can't move the right side of her body."

"You mean she can only move the wrong side?" Claudine quipped.

"Shut up," Mason told her. "You're not funny. How's your grandfather?"

"He's tired, upset. I feel bad for him."

"Sure. Anything we can do for you?"

"No."

"If she dies, you'll still be able to live with him, won't you?" Claudine asked.

I looked at her sharply. That question haunted me. "Yes, I guess so," I said.

"Maybe she won't die, Claudine. People have strokes and live," Mason told her.

"Yeah, but they can be paralyzed or something for the rest of their lives. You'll really become a slave in that house," she told me, "not only taking care of it but taking care of her. They'll turn you into a nurse's assistant or something, emptying bedpans."

"You're a great help, Claudine. Can't you see she's very upset? Why tell her that stuff now?"

"Sorry," Claudine said. "I'm just thinking of you. I never met your grandmother, but from what you've told us about her, I have a hard time feeling sorry for her."

Now that my grandmother was very ill, I felt guilty for revealing all that I had. The betrayal seemed that much greater. "I told you that I didn't hate her."

"But look how mean she's been to you."

"She's the way she is because she believes she did something wrong, brought up my mother wrong."

"If it's the way they're bringing you up, it's wrong," Claudine insisted. Mason gave her another dirty look. "Well, isn't it? You don't assume someone, your own grandchild, is definitely going to be bad and keep her from living a normal life, Mason. She didn't cause her mother's rape. We both decided that. Don't pretend something different now that Elle is standing in front of us."

"I'm not." He looked at me. "She's just very sad right now, and it's better if we don't make her any sadder."

"My grandfather thinks this happened because my mother just popped in on us after all these years. It was too much of a shock."

"Too much of a shock to see your own daughter?" Claudine asked.

"It was quite a shock to me," I admitted. "They fought. It was very unpleasant. My grandmother was blue with rage that day."

They were both quiet a moment.

"We're just going downtown to pick up my mother's dry cleaning and have some lunch. Could you come with us?" Mason asked.

I actually considered it. Grandpa Prescott had just gone up for his nap. If he came down and I wasn't there, he would assume I had gone to the lake. He did tell me to enjoy the day and not worry about anything. Was it terrible for me to do this, especially now?

"Oh, c'mon," Claudine said. "You're not exactly running off or anything."

"We'll bring you right back after we have some lunch."

"I probably should make my grandfather his lunch."

"Isn't he capable of making himself a sandwich or something?" Claudine asked. "You're going to go to school soon. He'll have to make his own lunches then."

"She's right," Mason said. "C'mon," he urged, tugging me toward the car.

He opened the door and pulled back his seat for me to get in.

"You can sit in front," Claudine said. "I'll get in the back. You never rode in a convertible, did you?"

I shook my head and stared at the passenger seat. I would never dare think of doing something like this, but how I wanted to do it. Claudine got into the back.

"Let's go. Stop thinking about it," she told me. "You're going to have much bigger and more important new decisions to make very soon."

I took a step toward it.

Mason went around and opened the passenger-side door. "Your chariot awaits, m'lady," he said.

I glanced back toward our house and then hurried around and got into the car. I felt as if I had just gotten into a spaceship. Mason smiled, got in, and started the engine again.

"Turn up the music," Claudine ordered. "It's harder to hear back here."

He did so and then pulled away, Claudine screaming with delight. The warm breeze filled me with new
energy and life. I felt Claudine's fingers on my hair
and sat forward. She undid my ribbon, and my hair
fell softly.

"Rock and roll!" she cried. "Get loose. Let go.
You're with the Spenser twins."

"I'm starving all of a sudden. We'll get some lunch
first," Mason told us. "And then stop for the dry
cleaning."

I sat back. How quickly my mood had changed. It
was as if the world was opening up as we sped along
and reached the village. With every new mile away
from my house, I felt freer, but the freer I felt, the
guiltier I felt. A voice inside me told me I should be
home with my grandfather, but another, louder voice
said, "You should live, too."

Mason drove to a restaurant called Burger City. It
was round, with a replica of a hamburger on the roof.
There was so much, even in this small town, that I had
yet to see. When Mason pulled into the parking lot,
Claudine didn't wait for me to open the door and pull
back my seat. She climbed out. Then she opened my
door and hooked her left arm with my right. Mason
did the same on my other side, and the three of us
marched toward the front of the restaurant, with them
singing, "We're off to see the Wizard . . ."

When we entered, the hostess led us to a ruby
leather booth. I looked around and saw other teenagers laughing and eating. It looked like a different
world, a world where no one thought about anything

sad or any work there was to do. Only fun was permitted. As I watched them poke and playfully taunt
each other, I realized more of what Mason and Claudine were trying to tell me. I had been kept out of my
childhood, my youth, and my sweet teenage years.
I was made to be older than I should be, and now I
longed to go back.

The waitress brought the menus.

"Have a City Burger with all the trimmings and a
malt," Claudine suggested. "Go for it."

"Really?"

"That's what I'm having," Mason said. "Claudine?"

"I prefer the chicken salad myself, but in your
honor, I'll do the same."

We handed the waitress the menus, and Claudine
began to plan all sorts of trips and adventures for us.

"We have only weeks left to the summer," she said.
"We've got to get as much in as we can, especially now
that you'll be free."

"I won't be that free," I said.

"Sure you will. Your grandmother won't be out of
the hospital until after the summer, at least, I bet."

"But there'll be extra work for me to do, work she
would do."

"You can do that and still have some fun."

"Don't feel guilty about it," Mason said quickly.
"You don't want to just appear on the school's front
steps without getting out and about a little first.
Maybe you'll meet some of the other students in your
class. We'll make an effort to talk to them, won't we,
Claudine?"

"Absolutely. We'll squeeze years into these three weeks," Claudine pledged.

Their excitement was boosting my own. Could I really do all this?

Three girls about my age started out of the restaurant, walking past our booth.

Mason held out his hand. "Excuse me, girls," he said. They paused. "Are you all students at Lake Hurley High?"

"Yes. I'm a junior, and these two are going into their senior year."

"My sister and I go to school in New York City, but our good friend here is going to attend Lake Hurley this fall. She's going into the junior class, too."

"Oh. Hi," the girl said. "I'm Denise. This is Marjorie and Cissy."

Mason turned to me, indicating that I should speak up.

"I'm Elle," I said.

"You on the cheerleading team at the school you were in?" Denise asked.

"No, I . . ."

"She wasn't, but she wants to be," Mason said quickly. "We were just talking about that. My sister is on the cheerleading squad at our school in New York."

I looked at Claudine. She had never mentioned anything like that.

"I showed her some of our cheers, and she picked up on them immediately. She could be terrific," Claudine added.

"Good. Come out for it," Denise said. "Cissy's cheerleading captain."

"Where are you living?" Cissy asked.

"Berne Road," I said.

"It's not on the way for any of us."

"I'm fine. I'm going to walk."

"Until you get someone to pick you up every day," Denise said, smiling. "Until then, we'll look out for her," she told Mason.

"I'd appreciate your looking out for her, period," Mason said.

"Why not?" Denise said. "See you soon, Elle," she added, and the three walked off.

"That's how easy it's going to be for you, Elle. You'll see," Mason told me.

We were served our burgers and malts. While we ate, Claudine rattled off all sorts of advice. Some girls would be friendly, and some would be jealous, especially if the boy they liked was interested more in me. Some girls would be competitive in sports and cheerleading, and some would be competitive in grades, too.

"A new girl is interesting, but it doesn't take long for you to know who is sincere and who is not."

"How do you know?"

"I'll tell you how I know. I figure out who thinks like I do and go from there. If I'm insincere with someone or about something, good chance they'll be, too."

"You'll get it. It's not rocket science," Mason said. "Just don't get so interested in anyone's boyfriend too quickly," he added, and Claudine laughed.

"He's already planning on making weekend trips to see you," she told me.

"Really?"

"I was hoping to tell you that myself, but someone can't keep her mouth shut."

"Look who's talking," Claudine said, and she rattled off one example after another of him saying too much to their parents.

They went at it like that for a few minutes more, and then they laughed, and we finished our lunch. I had never enjoyed one as much and told them so.

Claudine sat back as Mason paid the bill. She was staring at me differently suddenly.

"What?" I asked.

"I just hate how you've been taught to think about yourself as someone evil just because of what happened to your mother. That's so stupid." She leaned forward. "What exactly did she tell you about it?"

"I told you what I learned. She didn't tell me that much."

"She didn't want to talk about it, Claudine. Why make a big deal of it now?" Mason asked.

"What exactly did she tell you about your father?"

"She didn't tell me anything, really. His father owned a bar, and they used to drink there, and she and her girlfriends got to know him and some of his friends. They liked them more than they liked the college boys, and he took advantage of her."

She sat back, disappointed.

"That was all she told me, Claudine. That and his

name. She said she didn't even remember what he looked like."

She practically leaped over the table. "She told you his name?"

"Yes."

"Do you remember it?"

"Yes. Sean Barrett."

She looked thoughtful.

"What are you plotting, Claudine?" Mason asked.

"Albany's only about two hours from here, isn't it?"

"So?" he asked.

"Our parents are leaving tomorrow. They won't be back until next weekend."

"So?"

"So why don't we take a ride to Albany?"

"And do what, exactly?"

"See if her father is still living there. I can get on my computer and look up the bar and see if he's running it or something."

"Why do you want to do that?" Mason asked her. "What good will it do?"

"She should see what her father is like, don't you think?"

"He hasn't been her father her entire life."

"But he is!" Claudine insisted. She turned to me. "Aren't you in the least curious about him?"

Mason waited for me to reply. I thought about it. I was disappointed at my mother's response when I had asked her about him.

"Maybe he's a real creep," Mason said when I said nothing.

"Maybe he's the mayor," Claudine countered.

"That's ridiculous, Claudine. The man raped her mother."

"Date-raped or whatever. It's going on every day, and some of the boys doing it are now congressmen."

"Stop it," Mason said, but weakly.

"What do you think, Elle?" Claudine asked. "If you could see him, would you want to?"

"I suppose," I said.

"See?" she told Mason. "It's only natural."

"You don't even know if he's still there. You're getting her hopes up for nothing."

"Maybe. I'll let you know later," she told me.

Mason looked very upset for me. I was trembling inside.

"Let's go get the dry cleaning," he said.

We left the restaurant and drove over to the dry cleaner's. While he went inside to get the clothing, Claudine continued to talk about a trip to Albany.

"Chances are he never knew you were born," she said. "Did your mother say one way or another?"

"I didn't get to ask her that. She didn't want to talk about it, really."

"That's what always happens. The girl feels ashamed, and the guy gets away with it. Your grandparents should have called the police or something."

Knowing what they had done to keep my mother's pregnancy a secret for as long as they could, I smiled at the very thought of that.

"Well, they should have! What kind of parents would let their daughter be so abused and not do anything more about it? They blamed her, too, and also blamed you. It was easier to do that," she said, taking on all the anger and indignation I should be showing.

I stopped smiling.

"Call me twenty minutes after we drop you off," she said. "By then, I should know if I can locate him. There are Web sites that will help me find him. Will you call?"

Mason came out of the dry-cleaning shop.

"Well, will you?"

"Yes," I said. "I will."

18

Mason put the clothing in the trunk and got into the car. He looked at the two of us, shook his head, and started the engine.

Claudine leaned forward. "Don't make her feel bad for wanting to know about her father, Mason."

"I'm not. If that's what she wants, I said we'll help her."

"Good," she said, and sat back.

It was a different ride home. I was too deep in thought to appreciate the music and the open-air ride. The wild excitement I had felt earlier dissipated like smoke in the breeze. When we drew close to my house, I was a little nervous. I didn't want Grandpa Prescott to see me with them, not yet. Mason looked at me and understood. He drove a little farther down the road before stopping.

"I don't see why having some friends is a crime," Claudine said.

"I'll tell him about you soon," I promised. "Right now is not a good time."

"Call me as soon as you can," she said, and I got out of the car.

"Thank you for lunch. It was great fun."

"That's just the start," Claudine said.

"Let us know how things are with your grandmother, too," Mason said.

"Yeah, we're on pins and needles about it," Claudine said, getting out of the rear and into the front
seat.

I watched them drive off and returned to the
house. It was as quiet as it had been when I had left.
I looked in the kitchen first and saw that nothing had
been disturbed. Grandpa Prescott had not made himself any lunch, and I remembered he hardly had eaten
anything for breakfast. Softly, I went up the stairs
and listened at his door. I heard nothing. Now worried, I knocked gently. He didn't respond. I waited a
little longer, knocked harder, and called, "Grandpa?"
When he still didn't respond, I opened the door
and peeked in. He was in bed, lying on his back, his
mouth open.

Terror shot through me.

"Grandpa?" I cried from the doorway. He didn't
move. "Grandpa!" I shouted, and stepped in. His
body shuddered, and he opened his eyes.

"Wha . . . what?" he said, and sat up.

I breathed relief. "I'm sorry I woke you, but
you've been sleeping so long. You haven't eaten anything. I was worried," I said.

"Oh. What time is it?" He looked at the clock.
"Oh. Okay. I'll come down. It's all right," he said,
wiping his cheeks vigorously. He looked at me and
smiled. "I'm fine, Elle."

"I'll make you a ham and cheese sandwich, toasted," I said. I knew that was one of his favorites.

"Okay. Thanks." I thought he still looked a little dazed. I was sorry I had woken him. "Give me ten minutes or so. I'll wash up and wake up proper," he said.

I left and went down to make his sandwich. I knew he liked coffee at lunch. Grandmother Myra usually simply heated what was left over from breakfast, but I also knew he loved having a fresh cup. While I was preparing it, the phone rang. I stood staring at it. We had so few calls. When it rang again, I thought Grandpa Prescott must be in the shower, otherwise he would have answered. After the third ring, I picked up the receiver. My hand was trembling as I brought the receiver to my ear. Was it the hospital or Grandmother Myra's doctor calling?

"Hello, the Edwards residence," I said.

"Elle," I heard. "It's Claudine. Can you talk?"

"Yes," I said. I didn't remember giving her or Mason our telephone number, and I was sure we weren't in the phone book. My grandparents didn't want any solicitations over the phone. "How did you get this number?"

"I paid two dollars and ninety-five cents. This was easy, as was finding the man I'm sure is your father."

Those words took the breath out of me the way a punch in my stomach might.

"Hello? Did you hear what I said?"

"Yes. How?"

"Tracked him through that bar, Barrett's on Greene Street. It's still there. It's probably some sort of landmark by now. He's listed as the owner of record. I checked him out, Elle. He's the right age. I even found his home address. Our parents are leaving tomorrow. Maybe we can go up there the following day."

I heard Grandpa coming down the stairs.

"I have to get off the phone," I said quickly. "We'll talk later."

"Gotcha," she said. She sounded so excited it was as if she had found her own father.

I hung up quietly.

Grandpa Prescott turned toward the kitchen. I fixed his sandwich and put it in the toaster oven just as he entered.

"Did I hear the phone ring?" he asked.

"Yes," I said.

"It wasn't the hospital, was it?" he asked quickly.

"No, Grandpa. It was someone calling the wrong number," I told him.

"Oh. Good. I mean, good that it wasn't the hospital."

"It will be just a few minutes for your sandwich. I made some coffee. It should be ready any minute."

"Oh, fresh coffee. Good. You've stepped right into your grandmother's shoes smoothly, Elle. She would have done just what you did, come upstairs to tell me I'd been sleeping too long."

"I didn't mean to frighten you."

"No, no. It's fine. I'm actually pretty hungry."

"Just sit, Grandpa. I'll get everything," I told him.

When the coffee was ready, I poured his cup and cut his sandwich in half and then into quarters, which was the way Grandmother Myra always prepared it for him. After I served him, I sat watching him eat.

"I pity those your grandmother's and my age who have no one but themselves," he told me, and started eating.

My whole body was trembling. Should I have told Claudine it was all right for her to find my father? What if he wasn't my father? What if my mother had made him up or didn't know who my father was?

"This is good, Elle."

"What do you think is going to happen with Grandmother Myra, Grandpa?"

He shook his head. "We won't know for a while. For now, we'll do the best we can," he said. He looked at the clock. "We'll head back to the hospital in half an hour, and afterward, we'll go out to dinner as I promised."

"Okay, Grandpa," I said, and began to clean up. I could feel his eyes on me.

"We had no reason to be afraid you'd turn out bad, Elle. I'm sorry," he said. "Watching you, I don't see any resemblances, bad resemblances, between you and your mother. By your age, she was more than a handful for us."

It seemed funny to thank someone for saying you were completely different from your own mother, but that was what I did.

Before we left, I went into my room to change into one of my new dresses and brush my hair. Grandpa hadn't said a word about how I was wearing it since I had come back from lunch with Mason and Claudine. Grandmother Myra was always after me to keep it pinned. When I stepped out, he smiled.

"You are much prettier than your mother was at your age, Elle, and I don't see that as a bad thing, not at all."

"Thank you, Grandpa."

"Well, we'd better go. As your grandmother would say, procrastination doesn't change what's waiting for you."

This time, when we arrived at the ICU, Grandmother Myra's doctor was in the lobby, talking to the relatives of another patient. He signaled to us that we should wait. He was a young man with wavy golden-brown hair. When he started toward us, we both rose.

"Mr. Edwards," he began, and looked at me.

"This is our granddaughter, Dr. Rosen," Grandpa Prescott told him.

He smiled. "Very pretty young lady," Dr. Rosen said. He lost his smile immediately when he turned back to my grandfather. "As I told you earlier, Mr. Edwards, your wife has suffered an ischemic stroke." He looked at me. "Blood was blocked from her brain by a blood clot. She suffered from a condition known as atrial fibrillation, an abnormal heartbeat, which was responsible for the clot. Brain cells in the left hemisphere of her brain were destroyed, and that area controls the right side of the body and speech ability. We'll continue to evaluate her for a few days, and then, if she stabilizes some, we'll move her to a room where she will still get intensive care and start therapy."

"Will she get better?" I asked.

"It's difficult to predict precisely how much of what she's lost she'll regain. The important thing is to make her comfortable, prevent any more damage, and get her spirits up. I know that's going to be hard," he added quickly. "Right now, she's pretty angry."

"We know," Grandpa Prescott said.

"Well, visit, spend time with her, keep talking to her. I'll let you know when we're moving her."

He smiled at me again and walked away.

"We're in for the long haul," Grandpa Prescott muttered.

I followed him into the ICU. One of the nurses brought a chair for him. I stood beside him as he talked to Grandmother Myra, telling her how I had made him his lunch, cleaned up the kitchen, and been a great support. She looked at me with less anger this time, I thought. Her face seemed to tremble. Grandpa Prescott clung to her good hand and spoke softly, telling her that she was going to get stronger and better. She shook her head, but this time, she didn't even attempt to speak. After another ten minutes, the nurse thought we should let her rest.

I promised her I would look after Grandpa Prescott. When she looked at me this time, I thought I saw a keener look of suspicion in her eyes. It was almost as if she knew what Mason, Claudine, and I were planning to do. There were many times when I believed she had the power to read my thoughts, even when I wasn't close by.

Grandpa Prescott was very subdued after we left the hospital. I tried to buoy his spirits by reminding him that when the doctor said it was impossible to predict how much recovery she would experience, he was also saying that she could recover a great deal.

"I know now what it is about you that's so different from your mother, Elle," Grandpa Prescott said as we drove to the restaurant he wanted us to try. "She was always dark and pessimistic, always predicting the worst for all of us, especially herself. Despite everything, you never lost the sunshine in your face."

It was then that I felt like crying. I sucked back my tears, because I didn't want him to be any more despondent than he already was. On the way to the restaurant, we passed Burger City, and I smiled to myself. My life was going to change now, I thought. It would be better, and not just because Grandmother Myra wasn't ruling over us anymore. I was really going to enter the world. So much of what other girls and boys my age were experiencing and doing would be brand-new and exciting for me. They wouldn't understand, I'm sure, but that was what it would be, and I had no intention of hiding my joy so that I could cover up what sort of life I had led. If I had gotten anything from Claudine, it was a stronger sense of self-confidence, even defiance.

Grandpa Prescott took us to a small Italian restaurant called Dante's Inferno. He told me he had wanted to go there for a long time, but Grandmother Myra told him the food would be too spicy for him. She said that was why it was called "Inferno."

"She meant well," he added. "She was only looking out for my welfare. You can't hate people whose intention is to help you."

The restaurant had small booths and was a lot darker than Chipper's, but I thought it had more atmosphere. The aromas of garlic, tomatoes, and cheese permeated the air. Grandmother Myra would have liked this place, actually, I thought. Now she'd probably never see it.

"I don't hate her, Grandpa," I said.

"Good. You're my strength now, Elle. I have faith in you," he said.

We ordered and enjoyed our dinner. He was far more forthcoming about his younger years and told me stories about him and his brother, Brett, that I had never heard. It was always difficult for me to imagine either of my grandparents younger, but his anecdotes about school pranks and the things he and his brother had done brought laughter and smiles to both of us.

It was terrible to think that as a result of my grandmother suffering a stroke, my grandfather and I would become closer and more loving. I didn't want to be happy that she was sick, but it wasn't easy not to when I considered how things were a short time ago, how they were now, and how they were surely to be. It felt sinful, and I knew I would pray and ask God to forgive me for having these thoughts. I hoped he could see what was in my heart instead. It wasn't easy ignoring all the fire and brimstone I had heard. The God Grandmother Myra worshipped was just as capable of anger as he was of love. He could lay down punishments on your head as easily as he could lay down blessings.

That night and the following morning, I worked harder than ever in the house. I told Grandpa Prescott to go to the hospital without me, because I wanted to keep up the schedule Grandmother Myra had created. I was going to work over the living room, polish furniture, vacuum, and air things out the way she liked. I would also do the windows. And then I would plan our dinner.

"She'll be happy to hear about all this," he told me. "It's the best way to show her how much you care."

I smiled, but deep inside, I knew that I was working harder not to please my grandmother but to perform penance for the bad thoughts I had and the pleasure I was taking in how her illness opened up my life.

Later that morning, the phone rang three times. The first time, it was Grandpa Prescott telling me he was having his lunch in the hospital. The second call was Claudine.

"My parents just left," she told me. "What time do you think you can get away tomorrow?"

"I don't know if I should do this, Claudine."

"Of course you should. You have a right to do this. Mason is really for it now, too."

"Maybe I should ask my grandfather first," I said.

"Are you crazy? I thought you were afraid to tell him about us."

"I am, but maybe not as much now. I think he'd understand my having friends."

"Yeah, whatever, but he'd surely tell you not to do it, that it was only going to cause more trouble. Look, this is something you owe to yourself, Elle. Stop worrying about everyone else for a change. Get a little selfish. It's how you survive out there. You'll see. Better you start thinking this way now. If we leave at ten, we can be there just after twelve, you can be back before dinner, and no one has to know anything. How's that?"

"I don't know," I said. "It scares me."

"There's no reason to be afraid. Mason and I will be right beside you the whole time. Don't think about it any more. We'll be at your house at ten."

Before I could say anything more, she hung up. Five minutes later, the phone rang again. This time, it was Mason.

"I heard the way she was talking to you, Elle. I want this to be something you really want to do."

"I don't know what to do."

"Do you want to see him? Do you want to learn about him? Do you want to talk to him? Did you ever want to do this?"

"I've thought about it, even dreamed about it, yes."

"So?"

"Okay," I said. "I'll go."

"I can come over to see you," he said. "We can talk about it some more."

"I don't know when my grandfather is coming back, Mason. He's having a hard time. If something happened, I wouldn't be able to go tomorrow."

"All right. Call me whenever you want," he said. "Regardless, we'll be there at ten."

"Okay," I said.

After the call, I had to sit for a while. My legs felt weak. I thought I was being courageous and adventurous meeting them at the lake, but now, going to Albany and confronting my father? Did I have the courage for that? Grandpa Prescott really seemed to like me, even love me, so much more now. Wasn't I risking all that?

Claudine had told me to be a little selfish. Was she right? Was that what I needed to survive? Was I too soft, too innocent and trusting, to succeed?

I began a debate with myself.

Why do you want to see the man who raped your mother? Will this help you answer the question, "Who am I?"

Yes, it might. Didn't all children look at their parents and search for resemblances, not just physical ones but mental and emotional ones? Didn't that help them understand their own identities, guide them when they made their choices, and strengthen them when they had to face challenges? Didn't I feel like half a person?

Until now, I had accepted my grandparents', especially my grandmother's, view of me. Whenever I looked in the mirror, I believed I saw the same face hiding potential evil that she saw. She had molded and shaped me as if I was a chunk of clay, but suddenly, now there was a heartbeat in that clay and a mind that had other thoughts, other questions.

Maybe it was like what Dr. Rosen said had happened to Grandmother Myra, only it had happened to me. Blood had been blocked from my brain, and in that blood was my true self, my true nature, and my true soul.

Going with Mason and Claudine to see my father was my therapy. It was my road back, not to who I was in the past but to who I was now.

I would have to be a little deceitful about tomorrow, I thought, but I had to do it. Strengthened with this new resolve, I went back to my work, and when Grandpa Prescott returned, I listened to his description of how Grandmother Myra was and what the doctor had decided.

"She's going to be moved tomorrow," he said. "I want to be there early. I'll probably be there most of the day. It's better if you come after she's been set up. Besides, the weather looks good. You should be outside. Don't spend the day working on the house anymore. It's fine, Elle. Go back to your art, and finish that picture."

"Okay, Grandpa, but I will get something prepared for dinner before I do."

"That's fine. We're going to get through this together," he said. "I'm sure of it."

He did look more cheerful and hopeful. I watched television with him after dinner and then went to bed when he did. I said my prayers to the picture of the baby Jesus, and I asked him to forgive me for any sins I had committed and sins I might commit.

As Grandpa Prescott once told me after my grandmother had ordered me to say my prayers that way, "A little insurance doesn't hurt."

Nevertheless, I took trepidation and great concern to bed with me. It wasn't an easy sleep when it came, either. I had all sorts of terrible dreams. In one of them, Grandmother Myra rose from her hospital bed and made her way back to the house to face me after I had returned with Mason and Claudine from Albany. She was as twisted as she looked in the hospital, and she lifted her bad arm along with her good one, but both of her hands were on fire, all of her fingers like candlewicks. I thought I must have screamed in my sleep and woke in the darkness, trembling.

Slowly, I looked down the hallway to see if she was there the way she often was, spying on me, watching me, waiting to see if Satan would visit my bedside.

Maybe, I thought, he had, and that was why I had those dreams.

I didn't fall back to sleep easily. In fact, I think I did just before it was time to get up, but I didn't want to be lying in bed when Grandpa Prescott came down. Everything had to seem as normal as ever, especially today, I thought, and rose quickly.

He seemed to be in good spirits and ate a bigger breakfast than usual. He began talking about Grandmother Myra in a more positive light.

"When she comes home," he said, "we'll need to make some changes. I met someone at the hospital whose husband had a stroke, and she told me about this mechanical chair that takes someone in your grandmother's condition up and down the stairway. I'm going to look into that.

"Soon you'll be busy with your schooling. Obviously, she couldn't continue homeschooling you, even if she had changed her mind and thought that better. So I'm getting information about some private-duty nursing at home, at least for the first few months.

"Even after she's home, I'll have to take her to therapy back at the hospital almost daily. I was thinking about finally trading in the old jalopy for one of those vehicles that has more comfortable seats and a place for a wheelchair. So I might be home later than I ordinarily would today," he continued. "If you get hungry and want to eat earlier . . ."

"Oh, no, that's fine, Grandpa."

He nodded. "Lots to do. Lots to think about. But don't worry yourself about any of this. I have it under control. Just go about your day."

"I will," I said. I was glad he wasn't asking me anything about how I intended to spend it. I could see his mind was elsewhere.

When he rose, he paused to hug me and tell me again how proud he was of me.

"She's calmed down a lot," he said as I walked him to the door. "She doesn't have to speak for me to know what she's thinking or what she wants to know. I told her all you've been doing, and I can see that it pleases her."

He hugged me again and left. Everything he had

said and done made me think again about taking the ride with Mason and Claudine. If, for some reason, I didn't get back in time, he'd be very upset, heartbroken. Once again, I questioned whether I should do it. As I cleaned up the kitchen, I was tempted to call them and tell them not to come. I even lifted the receiver once, but I put it back.

"I've got to do this," I told myself. "I've got to."

Just before ten, I went outside and waited. My heart was pounding. When I saw their car approaching, this time with the top up, I started down the short stairway, but it was as if I had thick glue on the bottoms of my shoes. They pulled up and waited.

"Who had the stroke, you or your grandmother?" Claudine joked.

"I have to get home early enough to set out his dinner," I said.

"No problem," Mason told me. "This car can move when it has to."

"Stop worrying. Let's make a fun day of it," Claudine said when I still didn't move toward the passenger's side.

Fun? I thought. This didn't feel like fun. Was that how she saw it?

Mason read my thoughts. "What Claudine means is that this won't all be full of tension for you. We'll find a nice place for lunch, and you'll see a little of a city you've never seen. We've not been up there in years. Luckily, I have a GPS, so we'll have no trouble finding our way around. C'mon, Elle. Let's get moving so we can get it all done and be back when you want."

I hurried around the car and got in. Claudine had left the front seat for me again.

"We're off," Mason said, and sped away from my house.

I glanced back only once, took a deep breath, and sat back. I was either crossing a great divide or creating an even bigger one between myself and the only family I had.

19

Needless to say, this was the longest ride I had ever taken and the farthest I had ever been from home. I knew both of them were trying to calm me down by talking about everything under the sun except my seeing and maybe talking to my father.

Did you really call men who raped women fathers? I wondered. Shouldn't *father* mean more than just procreating?

"Tell me about your father," I said. "I mean, he seems very nice and lots of fun, but what's he really like?"

What I really wanted to know was what a father was like. What should anyone expect of his or her father? Surely, they were different from grandfathers.

They were both silent a moment, each waiting to see who would begin.

Mason started. "Dad's dedicated to his profession. He brings a lot of work home, but somehow he always finds time for us. I've never felt afraid of asking or telling him things."

"Some things," Claudine corrected.

Mason shrugged. "We're not any more secretive in our house than other families."

"You want to put your hand on a Bible?" she challenged.

He glanced at me and looked ahead. "Claudine and I are certainly no angels. Sure, there are things we've kept to ourselves, but if we ever got into trouble, he was always there for us, right?"

"Usually, it was too late for anything else by then," she said. "He's all right. We love him, and he's always bragging about us. He's done a lot more with us than our mother, especially on vacations. We would never have learned how to water ski, ice skate . . ."

"Play pool," Mason added.

They both laughed and then started talking about their mother whenever she joined these activities.

"Who else had to have her hair done before she went skiing in Aspen?" Claudine said. "The simple answer, Elle, is we love our parents, accept their faults, and don't blame them for anything. At least, I don't."

"There's nothing magical between you and them, then?"

"Magical? What do you mean?" Mason asked.

"I read this novel about a mother who lost her little boy during the Second World War. It was part of suggested reading for my homeschooling. At the end of the war, she went from one camp to another where lost children were being housed. It was some time afterward, but magically, she was drawn to him."

Neither spoke for a moment.

"It made me cry," I said.

"Don't expect any magic now," Claudine said. "He'd probably walk right by you on the street. Nothing unusual might happen even if you stopped him to ask a question."

I nodded. We rode in silence, and then they started talking about the music again. A little more than an hour later, Mason took the exit the GPS told him to take, and we were entering the city. I couldn't help being fidgety and nervous.

Claudine put her hand on my shoulder. "Just relax. We'll be right beside you the whole time."

I nodded and gaped at the traffic, the people, the buildings, just the excitement that came from so much activity. I couldn't imagine how anyone could find his way home over so many streets and corners. It was a world of strangers, people who walked past each other, concerned only with getting to where they were going and avoiding bumping into anyone on the way. Unless they were walking in groups or couples, they didn't speak to those they passed by or faced on the sidewalk. Horns sounded, music poured out of other cars, people shouted, all of it making me turn this way and that. I'm sure I looked like someone who had just been released from prison after having gone in before cars or electricity was invented.

Claudine leaned forward to look out at everything with me. "This whole city is like one neighborhood in New York," she said.

"I can't imagine," I said.

"One day soon, you'll come see us in the city," Mason said.

"Really?"

"We have a beautiful guest room in our Manhattan apartment," Claudine said. "We'll take you to shows on Broadway, to Central Park, to the Village, SoHo, even to the top of the Empire State Building and the Statue of Liberty, if you want."

Could I really do all that? Surely I was feeling like a newborn chick as the shell began to crack and fall away. All sorts of new possibilities loomed out there. Things I wouldn't even dare to dream were suddenly realities. The day would come when I could go anywhere I wanted and do whatever I wanted.

When we stopped at a traffic light, Mason looked at me. "You doing all right?"

"Yes," I said.

"We're almost to Greene Street." He nodded at the map on the GPS.

"This oughta be something else," Claudine said. I turned to look at her. Her face was full of excitement.

"You're something else," Mason told her.

"I hope so," she said.

I wanted to laugh with them, but my heart was beating too hard and fast. I just wanted to be able to keep myself from passing out and be able to walk when I had to.

"Here we go," Mason said, turning onto Greene Street. "Watch the numbers, Claudine."

"I see it," she said. "Look for a place to park."

Right ahead of us was a sign on a brick building that simply read, "Barrett's."

Mason had to drive by it to find a place to park. I

saw a sign on the door that said, "Restaurant and Bar." Two men in jeans and T-shirts were entering. After we parked, Mason leaped out and came around to my side of the car quickly. When he opened the door, I took a deep breath and stepped out with him holding my right arm. I think I wobbled.

He reached in to release the seat and let Claudine get out. The three of us stood there for a moment looking at the bar.

"What's the plan?" Mason asked Claudine.

It didn't occur to me until that moment that we didn't have one.

"I think we go in, ask to speak with him, and hit him right between the eyes with the number one fact."

"What's that?" I asked.

"You," she said, and hooked her left arm onto my right. "C'mon. This is like making a parachute jump out of a plane. If you think about it too hard or too long, you won't do it. Just do it," she urged, tugging me a little forward.

We walked down the sidewalk to the front of Barrett's.

"'Onward Christian soldiers,'" Claudine sang, and opened the door for me.

I looked at Mason, who nodded, and then I entered the bar. They came up beside me. The three of us stood looking around.

On our left was a bar almost the length of the room. It was built out of dark mahogany and had a brass-plated foot rail. The top looked recently redone. There were at least twenty bar stools, all made of the same wood as the bar itself. Right now, there were about a dozen men sitting, having beers and drinks, snacking on peanuts and chips, and talking. Two bartenders were dressed in very neat white shirts and bar aprons. Behind them running the length of the bar were large panels of mirrors framed in the same mahogany. Below that were shelves and racks of bottles in all sizes. At the center, separating the mirror panels, was a table with a computer register. At both ends of the bar were six different beer taps.

None of the four television sets mounted above the mirrors was on. The ceiling looked as if it was the original, with all sorts of intricate molding. The only modern part was where some air-conditioning vents were installed. The wood floor seemed to be the original floor, too. There were tables and chairs across from the bar and at least a quarter of the bar's length more toward the rear of the restaurant. All of the tables had tablecloths and centerpieces with fake flowers. Along the walls were many photographs, some of people who looked like celebrities from sports and entertainment, along with pictures of men who looked like politicians.

Everyone at the bar gradually turned to look at us. A hostess in light blue slacks and a white blouse came toward us quickly.

"Lunch for three?" she asked. She looked like someone barreling down on her sixties, although she could easily have been in her late forties. She wore her hair cut stylishly at her shoulders, but the light brown color seemed to emphasize her wrinkles and take away from her hazel eyes.

"No, we're here to see Mr. Barrett, Mr. Sean Barrett," Claudine said.

She took a step back and tightened her smile. "Is he expecting you?" she asked.

"No, this is a delightful surprise," Claudine added. "Where would Mr. Barrett be?"

"He's in his office. I'll show you the way," she said, now full of curiosity.

"What a great place," Mason said as we started through it.

"It's been here a long time," she said, her smile warmer.

"Have you been here long?" Claudine asked.

"Twenty years. I started when Scan's father was running it. This way," she said, nodding at a door in the rear. She opened it for us. "His office is the second door on the right."

"Thank you," Claudine said.

The hostess saw she had two couples entering the restaurant, nodded, and headed back toward them. We walked down the short hallway. The door to the office was closed, but we could hear someone speaking. It sounded as if he was on the telephone.

"I'll get it started," Claudine said.

"Like we didn't know that," Mason told her, and smiled at me, but I could see a little nervousness now in his eyes and the way his lips quivered.

Claudine knocked on the door.

We heard the man stop talking. "What's up?" he shouted.

Claudine opened the door.

What would anyone feel like looking at her father for the first time? The first thing I wondered about was whether I looked at all like him. He was a good-looking man with my color auburn hair neatly cut at a good length and a well-groomed goatee. But the other feature that told me this man could very well be my father was his eyes. They were the same shade of blue as mine, but they also had those tiny black dots swimming in them.

He didn't get up, but I thought he was close to six feet tall. He looked as if he did some bodybuilding, because his shoulders were wide, and his arms, sprouting out of his strawberry-red short-sleeved shirt, were roped with muscle. He told whomever he was speaking to that he would get back to them and slowly hung up the receiver before leaning back in his black leather desk chair. He wore no watch but had a gold bracelet on his left wrist.

"Who are you?" he asked us.

"My name is Claudine Spenser. This is my brother, Mason, and this is Elle Edwards. You knew her mother, Debbie Edwards."

He stared a moment and then sat forward, resting his forearms on the desk. "Debbie Edwards?" He started to shake his head.

"She was a student at SUNY Albany. She and her girlfriends used to hang out here. You knew her fifteen years ago. Elle is fifteen," she added.

He raised his eyebrows. "Debbie Edwards," he said, and looked more at me.

"Yes. Is it all coming back to you, Mr. Barrett?" Claudine asked.

"What exactly do you mean?" he asked.

"You're looking at your daughter, Mr. Barrett," Claudine said.

His face took on a crimson shade rapidly. "What?"

"About fifteen years ago, you put something in Debbie Edwards's drink and had your way with her."

"What is this?"

"We thought it was time you met your daughter," Claudine replied, not skipping a beat or backing down an inch.

He looked at me again. "First of all, that's a bullshit story," he told Claudine. He started to rise.

"It's not difficult today to prove paternity," Mason said, sounding like a lawyer. "You know blood tests will confirm it."

He thought a moment and sat again. "I never put anything in anyone's drink. I was never that desperate. Look, miss," he began, turning to me, "I don't know what you've been told, but . . ."

"Her mother told her you drugged her, raped her, and left her. She was too ashamed to reveal it, even after she realized she was pregnant with your baby. She kept it a secret until it was very late, and when she finally went home to get help from her parents, they forced her to have the baby, Elle," Mason recited.

"She's been living a hellish life ever since," Claudine added.

I looked at her. I knew my life was difficult, but "hellish" seemed too much.

She was on a roll and didn't want to stop. "Her mother deserted her soon after she was born, hating

her parents for forcing her to give birth, so her grandparents raised your daughter. They're religious, in-
sanely religious. They treated her like an evil child
because she was born out of a rape."

He shook his head. "Look," he said more calmly.
"I was a hell-raiser when I was younger. I'm not going
to deny it. I went out with a lot of college girls in those
days."

"You mean you might have more illegitimate children?" Claudine said.

He opened and closed his mouth.

"We're concerned only with Elle," Mason said.
"We thought, she thought, it was time to meet you and
let you know she existed."

"You can see the resemblances between you,"
Claudine added, now sounding more reasonable.
"Why deny it?"

He just stared at me for a moment.

"We're not here to blackmail you or anything,"
Mason said.

Claudine gave him a dirty look. Maybe she
thought that was something we should do. It wasn't
what I wanted to do.

"I never drugged your mother so I could have sex
with her," my father told me. He looked very sincere
now. "I remember her well. She was quite a flirt. We
had a thing . . ."

"A thing?" Claudine said.

"A little affair. I don't think I went with her more
than a few weeks, maybe a month. She told me she was
on the pill. Suddenly, one day, she stopped coming

or answering my phone calls, so I gave up on her and honestly never thought much about her until you walked in here."

"Well, now you can," Claudine said. "Think about her, but more about your daughter."

"Why didn't anyone contact me?" He looked at me for an answer this time.

"My grandparents were very ashamed," I said. "I hadn't seen my mother for fifteen years. She stopped by just recently and told me about you."

"Not very much," Claudine added.

"I don't know what to say. Maybe if I had known . . ."

"You would have paid for an abortion?" Claudine fired at him.

"I wasn't in love with Debbie Edwards. I don't know what I would have done. She made the decision herself."

"No, Elle's grandparents made the decision. Her mother ran off, and Elle was the only one who ended up doing any suffering at all," Claudine summed up.

"Look," my father started to say.

Suddenly, the office door burst open, and two little girls, one who looked nine or ten and the other six or seven, came charging in. Both were wearing cute pink and white blouses and shorts. They had the same shade of hair as my father and me, their hair cut neatly at shoulder length. A tall, beautiful, light-brown-haired woman with soft green eyes followed them. She wore a Kelly-green blouse and a pair of dark blue slacks that hugged her shapely hips and long legs. When she looked at us, she smiled, a small dimple flashing in her left cheek. She was stunning.

My father held out his arms, and both girls ran to give him a hug.

This, I thought, was the man my mother and my grandmother had characterized as an evil, violent rapist?

"Oh, I'm sorry we're interrupting," the woman said. She waited obviously for some sort of introduction.

My father looked incapable of speaking.

"We're the children of parents who attended SUNY Albany and used to hang out at Barrett's," Claudine said. "I'm Claudine Spenser. This is my twin brother, Mason, and this is Elle Edwards. We're up here looking at colleges, and we promised our parents we would stop by to say hello to Mr. Barrett if we had the chance."

"Oh, that's so nice. I'm Colleen Barrett," she said, offering us her hand. "That's Annie and Suzanne. Annie's the older. Say hello, girls."

They both turned to us, still lying against my father for security, and said, "Hello."

"We're just off to the club for the afternoon. I wanted to remind you to bring those extra steaks home later, Sean," she told him, and turned to us. "If you're all staying, you're certainly invited. We're having a barbecue tonight with a few friends. Oh, isn't Kenny Taylor a graduate of SUNY Albany, Sean?"

"Much later," he said, "than their parents."

"Oh. Well . . ."

"We'd love to stay. Thank you for your invitation," Claudine said. I looked at her sharply. "But we're on our way home and just stopped by for a quick hello."

"Oh. Okay. Well, if you attend SUNY or another one of the nearby schools, stop in again. Come on, girls," she said, holding out her hands. Her daughters kissed my father and then joined her. "Have a safe trip home," she said. "Where is home?"

"Lake Hurley," Mason replied quickly.

"Lovely. I think we were there, what, five years ago, Sean?"

I looked at him. He was there? Close to me?

"Yeah, about," he said.

She smiled at us and left. When she closed the door behind her, it felt as if she had taken all the air out of the office with her for a moment.

"Thanks for that," my father said.

"We told you we weren't here to make any demands on you," Mason said. "We simply thought you should meet."

He nodded, looking at me. "Have you guys had any lunch yet?"

"No," Claudine said.

"Why don't we all just go have lunch here?"

Mason and Claudine looked at me.

"That's okay," I said.

"Good."

My father rose. Mason opened the office door. Claudine gave me a smile of satisfaction and followed him.

My father stepped up beside me. "You look a lot like your mother," he said. "I don't know what she's like now, but she was a very pretty girl."

"She's still pretty," I said.

I walked out, and the four of us entered the restaurant. My father directed us to a table and then got three menus and returned.

"My favorite thing we serve for lunch is the Chinese chicken salad," he told us, "but order whatever you want. We do have great hamburgers, and there's a turkey burger on the menu."

"Yeah, I like that," Mason said.

When the waitress came over, both Claudine and I ordered the Chinese chicken salad, Mason ordered the turkey burger, and we all ordered lemonades.

"It's freshly made," my father said. "I made some changes in the restaurant when I took over from my father. I got religion."

We all looked up at him.

He smiled. "By that, I mean I started eating healthier, exercising. When you get married, have children, you realize pretty quickly that you have a responsibility not only to them but to yourself to be healthy for them. I don't go around preaching about it," he added, holding his hand up.

Mason laughed. "I'm on the swim team," he said. "I usually watch my diet."

"My grandparents don't like frozen foods, anything ready-made," I said. "We eat fresh mostly, too."

He nodded.

"Her grandmother just had a stroke," Claudine said.

"Oh? How bad?"

"Bad," Mason said.

No one spoke for a moment.

"My grandfather's fine," I said. "We'll be fine."

"What grade are you in?" he asked, and I began to tell him my short life story. He was surprised to hear that I would just be starting public school. I described Grandmother Myra's homeschooling me. I did most of the talking, with Mason only interrupting to tell him about my artistic talents.

"I can't draw a straight line. You've got to be inheriting that from your mother's side," my father said.

As we ate and I described in more detail what my life had been like, he grew more and more despondent.

"I do remember now that your mother was unhappy with her parents. She was quite a rebellious girl. In those days, for guys like me, that was pretty exciting."

"She never told you she was pregnant, then?" Mason wanted him to reiterate.

"Never did. As I told you in the office, she was just gone from my life one day. Maybe she knew we weren't going to be a steady thing much longer." He thought a moment. "I could find a way to get you some money," he told me.

"No. I don't want you to do that," I said. I wasn't about to tell him that this visit was a secret, that if he began to send me money or called or even wrote, it would make things even more difficult at home for me.

"Maybe she'll end up going to one of the colleges around here," Claudine suggested.

"Yeah, that could be. There's about ten schools," he said. "Of course, if that happens . . ."

"I'm not going to bust in on your family," I told him.

Mason looked at his watch and then pointed to it.

"We've got to go," I said. "I have to be home when my grandfather returns from the hospital today."

"Sure."

We all rose.

"I'll walk you guys out," he said.

Everyone, every customer and employee, was watching us leave. I wondered just how he was going to explain it. Claudine had given him a good way. She was pretty smart when it came to thinking fast. But then again, I thought, remembering the stories she had told me, she had a lot of experience creating excuses.

"I'm sorry I didn't know about you," my father told me when we all stepped out of the restaurant. Mason and Claudine took a few steps away from us. "You're a beautiful girl, Elle, and you seem pretty bright to me. I'm sure you'll be all right. If you do get into serious trouble, call me. I'll find a way to help you."

"Thank you," I said.

I didn't expect it, especially out front in view of customers gaping at us through the windows and customers coming and going, but he embraced me, kissed me on the cheek, and walked back into the restaurant.

"I think this isn't going to really hit him until later," Claudine said when I caught up with them.

I was silent until we were all in the car and Mason turned to me. "Are you sorry you did this?"

"No," I said. I turned to Claudine. "Thank you. You were great in there. You both were."

"Hey, we're the Three Musketeers," she said, and then tapped Mason on the shoulder. "Home, James, pronto," she said.

He laughed, started the engine, and turned on the radio.

I sat back and took a deep breath.

Claudine hadn't been completely accurate back there, I thought.

My father wasn't the only one who was going to feel all of this more deeply later.

20

"I like him," Claudine said as we left the city. "I think he's telling the truth."

"I agree," Mason said. He turned to me. "Your mother was a complicated woman."

"Still is, right, Elle?"

"Yes."

"The important thing is, you have no reason to blame yourself for anything or think any less of yourself. Don't let anyone put you down," Claudine said. "Understand?"

"Yes," I said.

I did understand. I think I understood a great deal more than they possibly could. One day, I would confront my mother with it, too. I was convinced now that she didn't get pregnant by accident. She wanted to get pregnant. She wanted to hurt my grandparents deeply and thought I was the way. She was betting on my grandmother and grandfather being so wounded that they would want to quickly erase any evidence, but she underestimated Grandmother Myra's moral and religious strength. Maybe Grandmother Myra was always talking about my mother when she said my father was the evil one. Maybe she never believed the story my mother gave her. Maybe she imposed all that on me intending not to have me inherit my father's sinful ways as much as my mother's.

The long silences in the car on the return trip came from all three of us being in deep thought, me reviewing my whole life and them probably thinking about what it would be like for them if they were in my shoes. I knew Mason wanted the ride to be shorter. He was going pretty fast and came very close to getting a speeding ticket. At nearly the last moment, he saw a highway patrolman about half a mile ahead and dropped his speed.

"Lucky you," Claudine told him as we drove on past the patrolman. "You'd have a lot of explaining to do."

"I'd just blame it on you," he told her, and they got into one of their back-and-forth arguments, looking as if they might really get angry at each other until one of them said something funny and they both laughed at themselves.

It lightened things up for me, but when we drew closer to Lake Hurley, my mind went back to worrying about my grandfather and what would be coming next in our lives. This time, Mason stopped right in front of my house. It was nearly five, but I remembered Grandpa Prescott telling me he was going shopping for a new car after he had left the hospital.

I just sat there a moment. None of us spoke.

"Thank you," I finally said.

"I think it's time you told your grandfather about us," Mason said.

I nodded. "I will."

"Are you going to tell him about this trip?" Claudine asked.

"Not right away, but someday."

"Call us as soon as we can see you again," Mason said.

I nodded and got out.

Claudine got into the front seat. She reached for my hand. "That took guts," she said. "Remember, don't sell yourself short."

"I won't."

I watched them drive off and turned to go into the house. Just as I reached the front steps, the door opened, and Grandpa Prescott stood there looking out at me. I froze.

"I came home early," he began, "because I wanted you to come along with me when I looked at new cars."

He looked in the direction Mason and Claudine had gone.

"Who were they?"

"They're our neighbors who live closest to us on the lake. I met them when I went into the woods and down to the lake to draw and paint. I'm sorry I never told you about them, but I thought Grandmother Myra would be angry and stop me from going into the woods and to the lake."

"She might have," he said. He stepped back. "Come on in, Elle."

I walked into the house. He walked ahead of me into the living room, and I followed. After he sat, I sat on the sofa.

"I'm sorry, Grandpa," I said.

"I told your grandmother many times that I thought you should have friends your own age. She always said there would be time enough for all that. What are they like?"

"They're twins. They go to a private school in New York City. I met their parents, too. Their father's a lawyer, and their mother has a decorating business."

"So when you went out to paint, you were really spending the day with them?"

"I painted, too, but they have a rowboat."

He nodded. "Maybe for now, we don't say anything about it to your grandmother," he said. "Where did you go with them today?"

At first, I thought I would make something up, be as fast on my feet as Claudine had taught me, but then I thought, my days of lying and sneaking around were over. Maybe my mother went in the direction she had gone because she was never honest with her parents. In the end, the punishment you suffer is greater once all the lies and deception are revealed.

"When my mother was here and we took that walk . . ."

"Yes?"

"She told me who my father was. She didn't remember all that much about him, or else she lied and said she didn't remember."

"I vote for she lied," he said.

"Anyway, I couldn't help being curious, wanting to know more about him, about what had happened."

"What did you do? Where did you go?"

"Claudine, that's the girl's name, went on her computer and found him. He's still in Albany running what was his father's bar and restaurant."

"You went to Albany?"

"Yes."

For a moment, I thought he smiled, but I think it was more of a look of astonishment. "And?"

"We found him and spoke with him. He's married with two children, girls. He denied raping my mother, but he admitted to being with her. He said she never told him she was pregnant. She just stopped seeing him."

"And you believe him?"

"Yes, I do, Grandpa."

He nodded. "I never believed your mother's story. I don't think your grandmother really believed it, either, but it was easier to accept it and go on. They were both trying to hurt each other in the end, your mother coming home pregnant and your grandmother refusing to give her an easy out. Your mother ran away for that reason as much as any."

"You really knew all this?"

"In my heart, I did, but I would have lost both of them, and maybe you to boot, if I had told what I really thought about it all."

"I'm sorry if I disappointed you, Grandpa."

"You didn't, Elle. I was always afraid your grandmother had beat the grit out of you. It was why I was reluctant to push for you to go to public school and be with other kids your age. I was afraid you'd be mincemeat for the bullies, but I think you're going to do more than just hold your own now." He took a deep breath. "I think I'm a little hungry."

"Oh, I prepared your favorite meat loaf this morning. I just need to get started on it and the vegetables and salad."

"Sounds perfect," he said.

"How is Grandmother Myra?"

"No change, but at least she's cooperating with the therapy. Knowing her, she'll make some progress. You can come with me tomorrow, and afterward, we will look for that new car."

"Okay, Grandpa." I rose to prepare our dinner.

"And bring your friends around one day," he said.

"I will."

At dinner, I went into more detail about our trip to Albany. He told me about some times he had been there on business. I couldn't remember a more relaxed dinner. It was truly as if we were finally getting to know each other, or I was finally getting to know him.

That evening, he had a phone call that surprised him. It was from his brother, Brett. Apparently, Grandpa had decided in the end to call my mother to tell her about Grandmother Myra. She didn't say she was going to come right up to see her, but she told her uncle. They had a long conversation, and when it ended, I saw how pleased Grandpa was.

"He says he'll be coming up as soon as he can get away. About time you met him. Myra won't be happy about it, but she's not happy about anything right now."

"Will my mother ever return?"

"She says she'll try. She has her own demons to battle. We can't worry about it right now, Elle."

I loved how he included me in everything he said and everything he planned for the future. It was as if I had truly become part of the family. It was beginning to happen before Grandmother Myra's stroke, but now it was on a fast track. We would share decisions, share happy moments, and share disappointments, but that was what a real family did. The secrets that lived so comfortably in the dark corners of our house slipped out through the open windows that invited more and more sunshine.

One morning, Grandpa Prescott sat back at breakfast in deep thought.

"What is it, Grandpa?" I asked.

"I want you out of that room today, Elle," he said. "You go upstairs and fix your mother's old room the way you want it, and move all your things to the closets. Get rid of whatever you want."

"You know how she kept it?"

"I know, but that's over. It should have been over a long time ago. I'm sorry about that."

"I don't want to get rid of everything, Grandpa."

"The choices are yours to make," he said. "I'll help you move your things, if you like."

"No, I can do it. I know where the key is," I confessed.

"I had a feeling you did. That's fine. I want all of

the ghosts out of this house." He leaned back and shouted, "You hear that, you ghosts? You're out of here by high noon or else!"

Right after breakfast, I went to work. I opened all the curtains, packed up some of the clothing I couldn't use, and moved whatever I had into the drawers and closet. While I was working on the room, Grandpa Prescott was downstairs putting the door on the room I had lived in all my life. He didn't take the religious pictures and icons off the walls, but I told him I didn't mind bringing the baby Jesus picture up to my new room.

"It's been with me too long," I said. "I'll still say my prayers."

"Of course you will. That's fine."

He was happy to close the room downstairs otherwise. It seemed so strange to me to see the door closed. It was like seeing the past cut out of my life. We didn't tell Grandmother Myra about it. Grandpa thought it would be better if she learned that when she came home. He believed she would in the near future. He did what he had planned and looked into a mechanical chair for the stairway. It was kept on order and would be installed as soon as her release was imminent.

I spoke with Mason and Claudine a few times, and one day, Grandpa let me invite them over to have dinner with us. I had told them how close my grandfather and I had become and how he had not been angry about what I had done. Claudine was nicer to him than I was anticipating because of that. They were both very talkative, and Grandpa Prescott seemed genuinely interested in learning about their lives in New York and what their parents' summerhouse was like. He talked about the good times he'd had on the lake. The conversation was so pleasant that it was like having a party.

I held my breath when Mason let it slip out that he had been teaching me how to swim. I expected at least a dark look of shock, but Grandpa only nodded and said it was always a worry of his that I hadn't learned how to swim. He laughed when they invited him to go in the rowboat.

Right about this time, I took an evaluation exam at the high school and did what they called exceedingly well. I was given a packet of papers describing requirements and my class schedule. These were days of excitement. At the end of that week, Uncle Brett arrived. He was as handsome as my mother had said, his face capturing all of Grandpa's good features but with a little darker complexion, and he was a little taller. He made a big deal over me and brought me a beautiful gold bracelet and matching earrings.

At first, he and Grandpa Prescott sat and talked about their early days, teasing each other about the things they had done. Then Uncle Brett gave us a brief history of his life after he had left home, describing the places he had been and the famous singers and musicians he had worked with. Despite the way he talked about his romantic and exciting life, he admitted that he missed having his own family.

When he spoke about my mother, he spoke sadly, apologizing for his failure to help her become more stable and mature.

"I did what I could for her, Prescott," he said. "I was doing what I could for you just as much as for her. I hope you believe that."

"Sure do," Grandpa said. "It is what it is. We can only pray something will open her eyes one day. Maybe a good angel will take her on. Angels like challenges, too," he added, making light of it.

When it came time to visit my grandmother, Uncle Brett hesitated. "Maybe it would better if I didn't come along, Prescott," he said.

"No, no. At first, she'll think you're gloating, but let her see that family is stronger."

Uncle Brett smiled at me. "You're having a good influence on him, Elle. Guess I have to find time to hang around with you more, too."

He talked about my visiting him in Vegas one day.

"You can come to one of the big shows. I think I'll be there a while. Feels good to stay in one place for a change," he said. "I don't guarantee your mother will be there," he added.

When we visited Grandmother Myra together, she had the initial reaction that Grandpa Prescott had predicted. She took one look at Uncle Brett and, by now able to dramatically change her expression, mumbled something that sounded like, "I'm sure you're glad."

Uncle Brett laughed at her and surprised us all by lecturing her about getting herself better and up and at it again. "This is the wrong time to get sick and dependent," he told her. "You've got a granddaughter to help get on her way to some good schooling and a good career. She's a bright young lady. And Prescott could never take care of himself."

I could see the surprise in her face. She seemed at the end to be buoyed by our visit. Her therapist told us she was making good progress. He thought she would need a wheelchair for sure, but the possibility of getting up out of it and using a walker was, in his opinion, quite real.

Afterward, all three of us feeling better about everything, we went to a wonderful dinner at the most expensive restaurant in Lake Hurley, Très Mystique, where I had my first lobster fra diavolo and, thanks to Uncle Brett, a glass of expensive red wine. He paid for our dinner, but both Grandpa Prescott and I laughed at the thought of Grandmother Myra seeing the prices. I had chocolate soufflé for dessert.

"She's spoiled now," Uncle Brett told Grandpa Prescott. "You can't take 'em back to the farm once they've seen Paris."

"Then she'll have to marry someone rich," Grandpa said.

"What other choice is there?" Uncle Brett joked.

He stayed late into the following day and left promising to come back the first chance he got but only if Grandpa would agree to let me come to Vegas on one of my school vacations. He agreed.

The final weeks of summer seemed to have twelve hours per day and not twenty-four. I spent as much time as I could with Mason and Claudine and did have dinner at their house when their parents were up for what was their final weekend of the summer.

Afterward, Mason and I went off alone. Claudine understood.

We rowed out to the little island and sat on the sand under the evening stars. I could already feel the air getting cooler. The coming fall was sending out feelers to find out where and how it would bring in the northern winds and begin to work on changing the colors of the leaves. The ducks and geese were already planning on leaving. One thing about the lake was that it revealed the onset of seasons faster than the land. The water was cooler, and even the color seemed to take on a subtle change.

When I told Mason that, he said, "Of course you would see that. You have an artist's eyes now."

Did I? I wondered. I hadn't gotten back to my painting for some time.

We lay back, and I cuddled in his arms. He kissed my hair and my forehead and worked his lips over my nose to my lips. I wanted to do more, and so did he, but we didn't. There was something precious about the moment that was more important. We could feel it solidifying into a wonderful lifelong memory.

"Wherever we go and whomever we're with twenty years from now, we'll always remember this night, Elle," he said. "You've missed a lot of your childhood and youth, but you'll make up for it."

"How can you be so sure?"

"You have the hunger for it. Both Claudine and I agree about that."

"Maybe I do."

"After we're gone, for a while, at least, feel free

to use the rowboat. Just walk up to the house. It'll be tied to the dock. We come up to winterize the house in November."

"Nothing will be the same without you, Mason."

"It won't be the same, but it will be something, Elle. This whole thing was your first real art studio, don't forget."

I laughed and thought maybe he was right.

"I'm not saying good-bye tonight," he told me when it was time to row back. "We're leaving tomorrow, but I'll be up the first weekend I can. Let's just say *à bientôt* like the French do."

I nodded but didn't say anything. I was afraid of crying.

Claudine came out onto the dock as we approached. She wanted to assure me that she would be coming up with Mason whenever she could, too.

"After all, you're going to need your social tutor and romance advisor," she said.

"She'll be too involved with someone to do that," Mason assured me, and they went at it for a few minutes, before breaking into a laugh and this time, maybe for my benefit, a hug.

Mason decided to row me back to the shore by the woods just like the first times. He wanted to carry me over the rocks and then walk through the woods back to the house with me.

"It's the way I always think of you," he said.

Claudine hugged and kissed me and went back to the house.

We rowed to the shore, and he carried me, kissing

me just like he used to. On our way back through the woods, we heard something nearby, and there, in the moonlight, was my doe. She stood there watching us.

"About time you came by to say hello," Mason told her.

I laughed, and her ears went up. She nodded and trotted on through the darkness to disappear to wherever deer went to be safe and content.

At the back steps, we paused.

"Thank you, Mason," I said. "You helped open the world to me."

"Maybe I did, but you opened it up a lot for me, too. I'm not letting you get away so fast. I know I'll be competing with a lot of guys soon."

"As I will with a lot of girls."

"The next girl I kiss will have your eyes and your hair whether she does or not," he said. "And the girl after that, and after that."

"Then kiss me now so you won't forget."

He did.

It was as if everything around us stopped to watch, especially the stars. I walked up the stairs to the back door.

"Keep a ribbon on the railing," he whispered.

"Always," I said.

He turned and walked into the shadows, disappearing like a dream to find its place where it could be safe and content.

Epilogue

It was a good six weeks before Grandmother Myra was released from the hospital. Just before that, Grandpa Prescott had the mechanical chair installed on the stairs. She had gotten to where she could stand and had begun to take steps. The hope was that she would be able to use the walker in perhaps six more weeks.

Grandpa had decided that it would be better if he told her before she left the hospital that he had moved me into my mother's room. I was with him when he told her. She looked at me, but she didn't have as bad a reaction to it as both of us had been anticipating. She just nodded, and he went on to talk about other small changes he had made in the house. Then he told her about the new car he had bought. It was an SUV with plenty of room for a folded wheelchair.

She didn't look displeased when she saw it. She watched me carefully fold up her wheelchair and get it into the rear of the vehicle, while Grandpa and the nurse helped her into the rear seat. The nurse strapped her in, and then Grandpa and I got in, and we drove home. He talked most of the way, telling her about

some people who had called. He didn't think she was
ready to greet visitors yet but promised he would let
them know when she thought she was ready.

Arrangements had been made for a private-duty
nurse to be at the house most of the day. Her therapy
at home would occur five days a week in the afternoon.
When we arrived at the house, I went around and unfolded the wheelchair. Then Grandpa and I got her into
it, and he wheeled her while I went ahead to open the
door. A wooden track had been built and attached to
the stairway so she could easily be wheeled in and out.

Inside, Grandpa proudly showed her the mechanical chair. He even went up and down in it himself to
demonstrate. I thought she was smiling, but it was still
hard to interpret her expressions. The private-duty
nurse was there to help get her situated once she was
brought to her bedroom. I went into the kitchen and
prepared lunch for her and brought it up. Grandpa
Prescott took his lunch with her. I sat and had lunch
with the nurse. It was decided that Grandmother
Myra would get the day off from any therapy, assuming the trip from the hospital would be tiring enough.
She didn't seem all that tired to me. She was interested
in everything Grandpa told her about the house and
my preparations for beginning school.

We both thought the transition had gone well.
When she expressed something she didn't like now,
she would make a very harsh, long, guttural sound.
Because it was so disturbing, that alone made us both
move quickly to please her. Her nurse took her vitals,
and then she slept until it was time for dinner. Again, I

brought the tray up to her. She looked over everything carefully and seemed to be pleased, even impressed. Grandpa Prescott praised everything, of course.

After dinner, the nurse washed and brushed her hair and got her ready for the night before leaving us. Grandpa Prescott stayed with her until she fell asleep and came down to watch some television before going to bed himself. I was with him for a while, and then I went upstairs, expecting only to go to my room to sleep, but I looked in on her and saw that she was sitting up, her eyes wide open. With her good hand, she beckoned to me. I listened for Grandpa Prescott and then entered the bedroom. She patted the bed, and I walked over and sat.

It was always going to be difficult to understand her, I thought, but she had made enough progress for me to figure out some of her words, especially when they were short sentences. I listened hard. I believed she asked, "What have you done?"

I knew she wasn't talking about the house or my moving into the bedroom. I knew that Grandpa Prescott had told her about Mason and Claudine and how much he liked them. I was present when he told her some of it, but he told me that he had told her I had gone to their house for dinner. He said she was fine with it now. I wondered if he was mistaken.

"You mean making friends with our neighbors?"

She shook her head and repeated her question, but I did pick up the added words, "With them."

All sorts of possibilities ran through my mind. I knew Grandpa Prescott wouldn't want to tell her about my trip to Albany, but she seemed to know something more. It was always my belief that she could read thoughts and sense things going on. Perhaps it was my imagination, my fears, or perhaps she knew me better than I thought.

I shook my head again, and she closed her eyes and almost clearly managed the word "Albany."

I stared with disbelief. Grandpa surely had lied to me. He had told her.

"Grandpa told you?"

She shook her head.

This was something she had obviously been waiting impatiently to know. I nodded and then began. I told her first about my mother revealing my father's name and then how Claudine, Mason, and I had located him and confronted him. She listened intently, not wanting to miss a word. When I told her what I believed, she nodded.

The information seemed not so much to please her as to bring her some closure, to answer the same questions I had, perhaps. She closed her eyes, and then, when she opened them, I thought she had managed a good, full smile. She took my hand and held it.

We sat there like that for a while, neither of us trying to speak. Then she closed her eyes again and lowered her head to the pillow. I fixed her blanket and said good night. She moved her lips but didn't open her eyes.

She wouldn't be with us much longer, I thought. Whatever journey she had begun was coming to an end. She surely had many regrets, but when I left her that night, I thought she had found some comfort, some satisfaction. I was confident that her mind was full of her own memories, recalling her own youth, her parents, her difficulties, maybe the hope her marriage promised and my mother's birth seemed to bring. All those disappointments dwindled until they were so tiny they couldn't be resurrected.

The following day, while she had her therapy, I went for a walk and turned into the driveway to Mason and Claudine's summerhouse. I went out back to the dock and untied the rowboat. I rowed smoothly and comfortably to our small island, took off my shoes and socks, rolled up my jeans, and pulled the boat onto the shore the way Mason always did.

Then I just sat there looking out at the lake, watching the boats and hearing the shouts and laughter. In many ways, I was born on this island. I felt myself move into my womanhood and my independence. For most of my life, I had felt I was unwanted. I was someone's mistake. I had no reason to be here, but surely no one who could enjoy and understand the beauty in the world could possibly be unwanted.

We were needed.

We were needed because we understood how to bring happiness and how to bring love back to those who needed happiness and love.

I would return to my painting, to many more paintings, and through them, I would continue the long journey to discover who I was and who I was meant to be.

Pocket Books
proudly presents

Bittersweet Dreams

V.C. Andrews®

Available November 2014 from Pocket Books

Turn the page for a preview of
Bittersweet Dreams . . .

Prologue

Beverly Royal School System
18 Crown Jewel Road
Beverly Hills, California

Dear Mr. and Mrs. Cummings:

As you know, the school has been conducting IQ tests to better address the needs and placement of our students. We always suspected that we were going to get extraordinary results when Mayfair was tested, but no one fully understood or anticipated just how extraordinary these results would be.

To put it into perspective, this is a general scale by which most educational institutions judge these results.

IQ scores of 115 to 129 indicate a bright student who should do well with his or her educational pursuits.

We consider those with scores of 130 to 144 moderately gifted and those with 145 to 159

*highly gifted. Anyone with scores between 160
and 179 is recognized as exceptionally gifted.*

*Rare are those whose scores reach 180. We
consider such an individual profoundly gifted.
To put it into even better perspective for you,
statistically, these students are one in a million;
so, for example, in the state of California, with
a population of approximately 36 million,
there are only eleven others who belong in this
classification with Mayfair.*

*Needless to say, we're all very excited about
this, and I would like to invite you in to discuss
Mayfair's future, what to anticipate, and what
to do to ensure her needs are fully addressed.*

*Sincerely yours,
Gloria Fishman, Psychologist*

1

"For what you did, you belong in a juvenile home, maybe a mental clinic, but certainly not a new school where you'll undoubtedly be coddled and further spoiled, an even more expensive private high school than Beverly Royal," my father's new wife, Julie, muttered bitterly.

Even though they had been married for years, I didn't want to use the word *stepmother*, because it implied that she filled some motherly role in my life.

Her lips trembled as anger radiated through her face, tightening her cheeks. If she knew how much older it made her look, she would contain her rage. I did scare her once by telling her that grimacing too much hastened the coming of wrinkles.

It was the morning of what I thought would be my banishment from whatever family life I once could have claimed, something that had become a distant memory even before all this. I knew that few, least of all Julie, would think that mattered much to me. They saw me as someone who lived entirely within herself, like some creature who moved about in an impenetrable bubble, emerging only when it was absolutely necessary to say anything to anyone or do anything with anyone. But family did matter to me. It always did, and it always would.

I didn't have to go on the Internet and look it up to know that a family wasn't just something that brought you comfort and security. It provided some warmth in an otherwise cold and often harsh and cruel world. It gave you hope, especially when events or actions of others weighed you down with depression and defeat. All the rainbows in our lives originated with something from our families.

In fact, all I was thinking about this morning was my mother, the softness in her face, the love in her eyes, and the gentleness in her touch whenever she had wanted to soothe me, comfort me, or encourage me, and how my father glowed whenever we were with him. How I longed for that warmth to be in my life again. Yes, family mattered.

True friends mattered, too, even though I had few, if any, up to now. Just because I was good at making it seem as if I was indifferent and uncaring about relationships didn't mean I actually was. Students in the schools I had attended thought I was weird because of what I could do and what I had done, most of it so far above and beyond them that they didn't even want to think about it. I didn't need to give them any more reasons to avoid me, especially adding something like being a social misfit, which in the minds of most teenagers was akin to a fatal infectious disease.

I knew most avoided me because they believed I was too arrogant to care about anyone else but myself. I mean, who could warm up to someone who seemed to need no one else? From what they saw, I didn't even require teachers when it came to learning and passing exams. I was a phenomenon, an educational force unto myself.

Maybe I didn't need a doctor or a dentist or a parent, either. I already knew as much as, if not more than, all of them put together. It wasn't much of a leap to think I didn't need friends. I'm sure most wondered what they could possibly offer someone like me anyway. Besides, being around me surely made them feel somewhat inferior. They were afraid they would say something incorrect, and who likes to worry about that, especially when you're with friends? I would have to confess that I didn't do all that much to get them to think or feel otherwise. Perhaps it really was arrogance, or maybe I simply didn't know how to do it. I didn't know how to smile and be warm just for the sake of a friendship. One thing I couldn't get myself to do was be a phony. I was too bogged down in truth and reality.

Julie moved farther into my room, inching forward carefully, poised to retreat instantly, like someone approaching a wild animal, even though the wild animal was in a cage. Thinking that was where I was made sense. If anyone should feel trapped and in a cage right now, it was me.

In fact, the more I thought about it, the more I realized that wasn't much of an exaggeration. That was what I felt I was, and not just because of what I had done and what was happening today. I've always felt this way. Deep down inside, despite my superior intellect, I sensed that people, especially educators and parents of other students, believed I was like some new kind of beast that needed to be kept apart from the rest of humanity, a mistake in evolution or the final result of it, and because of that, I was chained to something I'd rather not be, especially at this moment: myself.

As she drew closer, the sunshine streaming through my bedroom windows highlighted every feature of her face. I wished it hadn't. I was sorry I had opened the fuchsia curtains, but I had needed to bring some light in to wash away the shadows gripping my heart. I had no desire to look into Julie's hateful, jealous, dull hazel eyes. Sometimes they followed me into dreams, those envious, vicious orbs floating on a black cloud, invading my sleep like two big insects that had found an opening in my ordinarily well-locked and guarded brain.

I lifted my shoulders and stiffened my neck as if in anticipation of being struck. My abrupt action stopped her, and she retreated a few steps. She fumbled with her cowardice. She never, ever wanted to look as if she didn't have the upper hand in this house, especially when it came to confronting me. However, she never seemed to get the satisfaction she sought—at least, not until now, when I was most vulnerable, practically defenseless, but with no one to blame for that but myself.

"I don't care how smart people say you are. You never fooled me with your complicated excuses and fabrications concerning things you have done and said. Right from the beginning, I could see right through you as if you were made of clear glass," she said, more like bragging, to give the impression that she had some special insight that neither my teachers, my counselors, nor even my father had. She was always trying to get my father to believe that, to believe he couldn't be as objective about me as she could and thus was blinded to my serious faults.

To emphasize the point, she narrowed her eyes to make herself look more intelligent, inquisitive, and perceptive. I nearly laughed at her effort, because she was so obvious whenever she did that and whenever she spoke with a little nasality and used multisyllabic words like a fabrication instead of a lie. She was the queen of euphemisms anyway, always trying to impress my father with what a lady she was, never without a perfumed handkerchief, the scent of her cologne whirling about her, her head held high and her posture regal. She loved giving off that aristocratic air, practically tiptoeing over the floors and carpets as if she floated on a private cloud.

I think Julie had long ago convinced herself that somewhere in her background and lineage there really was royal blood. She believed she was born with class and had inherited elegance and stature. Heaven forbid she heard any profanity out of my mouth or her daughter's. Didn't we know it was unladylike, made us look cheap and unsophisticated? She would go into hyperventilation and have to sit quickly, especially if it happened in front of my father, who would rush to her side to apologize for me, because he knew I wouldn't. He couldn't see that small smile of satisfaction sitting on her lips, but I could.

Why were men so easy to fool or so willing to tolerate phoniness just to sail on smooth water? What wouldn't they compromise to keep the pathways to their beds unobstructed? Were women really the superior sex? Was sex, in fact, a big disadvantage for men?

Ironically, I had been thinking about writing a paper on that topic. Women seemed more able to avoid sex, hold off longer than men, and certainly use it as a weapon when necessary or a device to get what they wanted. I read a theory that developed the idea that women craved sex with nearly the same intensity as men only when they were ovulating, while men craved it continually.

"I always knew you were very capable of being mean, evil, and selfish," she ranted. "Your intelligence doesn't make you any sort of angel. In fact, in your case especially, it's just the opposite. You're sly and conniving. We already know how effective you are at manipulating people, especially someone younger than you. You're just better at these evil ways than most people."

She waited for my reaction, but I just continued to stare at her as if she were some sort of curious form of life. It was getting to her, despite her claims of invulnerability.

"You don't intimidate me with that 'I'm better than you' look. It hasn't happened to you yet, in my opinion, despite what others might think, but someday you'll get your just desserts," she concluded.

I finally had something to say. "I can tell from the way you're saying that expression that you are spelling it wrong in your mind," I said.

"What? What the hell are you talking about now? What expression?"

"'Just deserts.' *Desert* in the sense you mean is actually spelled with one *s*, not two. You're using that expression to mean I'll get my proper punishment."

She continued to glare at me but now with her

mouth fallen slightly open, her salmon-pink tongue looking like a dead fish.

I straightened up, and I'm sure it looked to her as if I was in front of a classroom, my classroom. I was a good inch and a half taller than she was, a little broader in the shoulders, but with just as small a waist, long legs, and just as ample and firm a bosom. Despite the fact that we had no facial resemblances or similar hair color, I was always afraid that someone who didn't know us might make the wrong conclusion that we were actually related.

"*Dessert* with two *s*'s is most always that course in the meal that gets people excited and happy. And getting what you deserve might also mean you're finally receiving the accolades and rewards you've earned. That's certainly nothing to fear. But the expression does come from a book called *Warning Faire Women*. The exact quote in question is 'Upon a pillory—that the world may see, a just desert for such impiety.' It's spelled with one *s*, coming from *deserts* in the sense of things deserved. Understand?"

"Understand? That's how you treat what I say even after all you've done? Do you think I'm one of your dumb high-school classmates? Why, you pedantic little bitch," she said, spitting the words out through clenched teeth. "I bet you think you're so superior to the rest of us because of that computer you have for a brain and those bureaucratic school administrators who fawn over you as if you were the next Albert Einstein. They're just as much a cause of all this as you are, by encouraging you to think of yourself as . . . as someone who doesn't need to go to the bathroom or something."

I didn't change expression, even though I was laughing at her on the inside. My father wasn't home. He had an errand to do before we left, so he didn't hear her say all this, not that I thought he would have done much to reprimand her for saying any of it anyway at this point. I recalled the expression on his face yesterday when he didn't think I saw him looking at me. It was soaked in disappointment. Vividly recalling that look, I thought he might even agree with her now, every nasty and mean word. I imagined him nodding and putting his hand on her shoulder, not mine, to bring her comfort and whisper something to make her feel better and show her how concerned he was for her welfare. "Don't get yourself too upset," he might tell her. "It doesn't do anyone any good for you to get sick, especially now, in the middle of all this."

"I don't mean to be condescending," I said, with just the quiet, matter-of-fact tone that irritated her. "You use the expression so often, Julie, that I thought you might want to know about it. I know how important it is for you not to look like a fool in front of your friends. Not that any of your so-called friends would know the difference anyway. If you surround yourself with mediocrity, you become mediocre," I added. "You probably think you stand out, but believe me, they pull you down, not that you had all that far to fall."

Her eyes widened, and her face reddened, with cheeks that looked like fully matured red apples. She balled her fists and readied her vocal cords for screaming. I loved the way I was getting inside her and tying her already twisted little heart into tighter knots. For me, it was sweet revenge, and for the moment, that took my mind off the pool of trouble in which I was swimming, maybe drowning.

"It's not unlike another favorite expression of yours," I continued. I felt as if I were on a roll, like a contestant on *Jeopardy!* "'The icing on the cake.' I notice you're always using it for negative remarks like 'His wife's suing him for divorce is the icing on the cake.' It really is used more for positive comments. Think about it. Who doesn't like licking the icing on a cake?"

She continued to glare at me, as if hoping her fiery eyes would make me explode and drop into a pool of dust at her feet. She could do that so easily to her daughter.

"Is that what you do? You analyze all my expressions?" she asked, amazed. "You judge my every word and do a critique behind my back?"

I shrugged and turned away. "Believe me, it's not brain surgery," I said, hiding my smile.

"What else have you criticized about me? Well? Let me have the whole bag of ugliness you're so capable of filling and flinging in my direction before you leave us. We already know some of the distortions and lies about me that you spread, and don't think I was ever unaware of what you had told your father about me. You never understood how important I've become to him and how much we trust each other now. Well? Go on. What else? What other things have you told my daughter? You might as well get it all out before you leave."

I acted as if I didn't hear her anymore. I knew that was one of the things she hated the most. A woman like Julie can't tolerate being made to feel as if nothing she said or did mattered. She can't stand being ignored. Her ego would stamp its feet, pull its hair, and scream.

The truth was that most of the time, I really didn't listen to the things she said, even if I gave her the satisfaction of pretending I was listening. I didn't only do it to her. I could shut people out as quickly as I could shut off a light, especially someone like her. I didn't go into a trance. There was no faraway look in my eyes that would reveal that I was gone. It was almost impossible to know when I was listening and when I was not. Sometimes I imagined that I had two sets of ears and two brains. You know, like an extra hard drive in the computer that she thought was my brain? My mind had a zoom lens. I could just focus on some interesting thing and cut out the distraction.

But this morning, unfortunately, I did hear her every mean-spirited word. To be truthful, I welcomed her verbal whipping, even though she was certainly no one to accuse anyone else of being mean and selfish and had no right to assume the role of judge and jury. If there ever was someone who should be restrained by being without sin before casting the first stone, it was my father's wife, Julie. It was lucky she didn't have a twin. She would have smothered him or her in her mother's womb just to be sure she would get all of her parents' attention.

But despite what she thought, I wasn't feeling particularly superior this morning. She was at me like this because she knew I was down and incapable of defending myself very much. That was usually when someone like her would pounce. I call them coyote cowards. They're parasites that will only swoop down on the small, wounded, or handicapped. Otherwise, they hover in the shadows, feeding their green faces of envy with hopes for your failures, waiting for you to become crippled and weaker, but too frightened to challenge or compete when you weren't.

"I don't know how you will live with yourself," she continued. "If I were inside you, I'd scratch and kick my way out."

I turned and glared at her. Despite what she claimed, I knew I could frighten her with a look like the one I had now. I had practiced it facing a mirror. It was a look I often employed at school. My eyes were like darts. I had the face of someone capable of sending curses out like e-mails.

Fear began to overtake her in small ways. She embraced herself quickly, swallowed hard, and took another step back.

"At last, we agree about something," I said. "If you were inside me, I'd rip you out. You know, like a bloody cesarean section?"

I held up my hands as though they had just been in a mother's womb and were dripping with blood down my arms.

She gasped, turned quickly, and marched out, holding her head high. She was always worried about what she looked like, even when she was alone and wouldn't see anyone else. However, frustrating and defeating her didn't give me as much satisfaction as she thought it had. I had long ago given up on baiting her and making her look foolish in front of my father, hoping it would open his eyes. I certainly had nothing to gain from it today. It was far too late, too late for many things. I was soaked in regrets.

I stood by the window in my bedroom, looked

out toward the Pacific Ocean, and thought it should be gray and rainy today, at least. That would fit my mood, everyone's mood. I didn't pay much attention to the weather. Maybe that was because we lived in Southern California and took beautiful days for granted, or maybe it was because I spent most of my time inside, my face in a book or at a computer screen. I wasn't one of those people who stopped to smell the roses. We actually had beds of them out front, along with other flowers. If I stopped, it wouldn't be to enjoy the scent and beauty of anything but, instead, to examine the flowers, looking for some microscopic, genetic change. I couldn't help it. As my teachers were fond of saying, which was probably true, it was part of my DNA.

Moments after Julie had stopped bitching and left, I heard someone behind me and thought she might have returned to say something else that was even nastier, something that had crawled into her clogged brain, a brain I imagined infested with little spiders weaving selfish, hateful webs of thought. This time, I would face her down more vehemently, not with calm sarcasm, and I wasn't going to stop with just *bitch*, the one profane word she permitted herself to use, at least in my and her daughter's presence, but with what she hated—cold, dirty language. When I spit back at her, she would rush to cover her ears as if my words would stain her very soul.

However, when I turned, I saw it was my thirteen-year-old stepsister, Allison. That surprised me. I was sure her mother had told her to stay away from me, especially this morning. She probably told her I had done her enough damage, and maybe, like Typhoid

Mary, I would contaminate her further. "Stay in your room, and keep the door locked until she's gone," she surely had said. She was unaware of the short but honest and sweet conversation Allison and I had had the night before. Her mother was on her this morning, however. She wanted nothing to happen to change anything now.

Allison did look very nervous sneaking in here, but, like last night, she looked very sad, too, sad for both of us. She stood there staring at me.

"What is it, Allison? I thought we said our good-byes last night."

"I know, but I remembered something. My father gave me this the last time I saw him," she said, holding up a silver pen. "He said it was a special pen, the ones the astronauts used in space. You could write upside down or sideways with it, everything. I wanted to give it to you to use." She stepped forward to hand it to me.

"You want to give it to me? Why? Do you think I'll be upside down or sideways?"

"No," she said, smiling. "It's just a very special pen."

I looked at it. On the surface, it didn't look like anything terribly unusual, but I did make out the word *NASA*.

"Please take it," she said, waving it. She looked as if she would cry if I didn't.

"Your father gave it to you? Are you sure you want to give it to me?"

"Yes."

"Why?"

"The words you'll write with it will be better than the words I'll write."

The way she said the obvious truth, with no self-deprecation or self-pity, made me laugh. In some ways, Allison was already head and shoulders above her mother.

I took the pen.

"Okay. Thanks. Who knows, maybe I will hang from my feet in my closet when I do my homework up there. Some people think I'm a vampire."

She smiled. "No, you're not. No one thinks that. You're too pretty to be a vampire."

"Pretty?" I glanced at myself in the mirror. I didn't feel especially pretty today. I thought my face was pale, my eyes dull and dim, and my hair unkempt. If anything, I looked more like some homeless girl wondering what in the world had happened that she should find herself so lost and alone.

"That's a nice color on you, too, turquoise. Remember? I made my mother buy me the same blouse, but it didn't look as good on me as it does on you."

"It will," I said. "You're going to have a nice figure, Allison." As hard as it was for me to say it, I added, "As nice as your mother's." What was true was true. Julie was physically attractive. If she could only be kept under glass like some wax figure, I thought, and not bother or hurt anyone else.

Allison smiled again. "Okay, see you when you come home for the holidays." She started to turn to leave.

"We don't get holidays," I said.

"Really?"

"I don't know. Things are very different there. I'll let you know."

"Will you? Really? I mean, let me know and not my mother first?"

"She'll know, even though the moment I leave, she'll have a moat built."

"A what?"

"Forget it. Like I said last night, I'll send you an e-mail or text you."

"I know you said it, but will you really?"

"You sure you want me to do it, Allison? You know you'll have to keep it secret from you-know-whom."

"I'm sure. Please, send me e-mails. My mother doesn't know how to use a computer."

I stared at her with a hard look to emphasize it. She knew why.

"I'll keep this secret. I swear," she said in a deep whisper, with her hand over her heart, and then turned and went to the door, checking first to be sure her mother didn't know she had come in to see me. She looked back, smiled, and then hurried away.

I put the pen into my bag.

My father's wife was in her glory, my father was in a deep depression, and my stepsister was terrified of breathing the same air I breathed.

How would I go about explaining all of this to anyone if I had trouble explaining how it all happened to myself? I thought I should write it down so I could study it all exactly the way I would study a math problem or a science theory—pause, step back, and analyze. Maybe if I did a full, intelligent, and objective review, I would have an easier time living with myself, not that it was ever easy to be who I was or who I was going to be.

Was I cursed at birth or blessed?

I suppose the best way to answer such a question is

to ask yourself how many people you know your age or a little younger or older who would want to trade places with you, would want to have your talents and intelligence, or envied you for your good looks enough to accept all the baggage that came along with it.

Right now, in my case, despite my accolades and awards, people like that would be harder to find than the famous needle in a haystack.

But the thing was that despite it all, I didn't even want to look. I didn't want to be validated, complimented, or even respected in any way.

I looked in the mirror again. Allison was right. This was a nice color for me.

I wondered.

Would anyone where I was going notice and, if they did, even care?

I must have wanted someone to care. I did want to have friends, and I did hope that there was some boy out there about my age who would find me attractive.

Otherwise, why would I have taken so long to choose my clothes, the way a prisoner on death row might contemplate his last meal?